POSSESSION POINT

DETECTIVE ROBERT LUI
BOOK 5

GLENN BURWELL

Published by arrangement with Somewhat Grumpy Press Inc. Halifax, Nova Scotia, Canada. SomewhatGrumpyPress.com The Somewhat Grumpy Press name and Pallas' cat logo are registered trademarks.

ISBN 978-1-998555-13-0 (paperback)

ISBN 978-1- 998555-14-7 (eBook)

October 2025 v3

POSSESSION POINT

A string of construction accidents plague Vancouver. Deaths have occurred. Robert Lui doesn't do accidents, but as he finds out more, tentacles reach out, and not friendly ones.

People kept saying 'Change is a good thing'. If he'd heard that crap on a podcast, he'd be asking for a refund plus damages. Robert Lui had his doubts, but made a couple of changes, one professional and one personal, to make life safer for him and those closest to him. These and other thoughts tumble around his mind as he heads to Surrey. What could be more continental than sitting down on a Saturday afternoon for coffee and a pleasant chat with a man tasked to murder him?

Fifth book in the Detective Robert Lui series.

If someone is so nice as to offer you a decently paying
desk job, take it.

A few clunks emanated from the front of the car, followed by a sharp ping, as though the Silver Streak was trying to make a case for being donated to aid an organ fundraiser. Sounded to Robert as though something had finagled its way loose and escaped, but he couldn't spot anything on the tarmac with a brief look in his rearview mirror.

Sophie looked over at her father. "Doesn't sound good, Dad." Sophie and Robert were on the road, sun glinting off the windshields ahead of them, irritating Robert, even with his sunglasses on. The mid-week day was warmer than it should be for May. They were heading north over the Knight Street bridge in the midst of an endless line of vehicles, returning from a shopping expedition in Richmond to help outfit Sophie for university in the fall. Robert was clueless about the noise. Engine? Some other vital part, like steering? The car seemed to be continuing in a straight line, no further sounds for now, as though it had issued its warning and expected to be heeded in the very near future. He shifted uneasily in his seat, darts rising from his lower back.

He glanced over at his daughter. "Nothing to worry about."

"Right."

"Sandra's cooking tonight."

She smiled back. "What?"

"Not sure, something from the ocean, I think."

"I really like her. She's almost like a big sister. Too bad I'm leaving for school soon." Sophie was silent, then grinned like a mischievous imp. "Are you sure she's not too young for you, Dad?"

"As if. Despite all my wounds, I feel rejuvenated just having her here with us." He could hear his cell ringing in his shirt pocket. A call. It could wait. Probably his latest employer, BC Coastal Insurance. Sitting at home on suspension, waiting for a verdict to be rendered by the Vancouver Police Department over his last escapade proved to be overly boring. Robert had finally called Dan Prudence in BC Coastal Insurance's claims department to see if he could be of some use again on a part-time basis. There was tuition coming due for Sophie, not to mention the myriad other expenses associated with her move to Calgary to attend their university's planning school. The VPD didn't know he was doing this, and probably wouldn't have countenanced the double dipping by their best detective as he was still being paid by them to stay away from the office.

Sophie's phoned blipped. A text, Robert supposed. She looked down, then shrieked, startling Robert. He looked over at her again. "Yes?"

"Rose got accepted, Dad!" The sun couldn't match the glee appearing on Sophie's face.

"Sounds like trouble in Calgary. Instead of trying for residence, maybe you two should look for a place together, what do you think?"

Sophie nodded thoughtfully. "Can you drop me there, Dad?"

"I guess. Would you like me to take all your things into our house for you as well after I get home?"

Sophie rolled her eyes. "That would be nice. Thanks, Dad." Robert shook his head ever so slightly, but he was happy to hear that Sophie wouldn't be braving a new city alone. Knight Street was the usual traffic mess. Diesel fumes from semis heading to Vancouver's port, amped up by the afternoon heat, wafted into the car. He took a left as soon as he could to shift over to Fraser Street, a more sedate route north.

"Make sure you are back for dinner." He turned off Fraser, delivering Sophie to Rose's home before driving the few blocks to his family's townhouse on Inverness Street.

Samuel Brown shifted in his bed, bored to death of being sick. He had lost interest in the book lying by his hand, one of the few books in the house that he hadn't fully read. Rereading the first few pages had jogged his memory as to why he hadn't read any further. He'd need to ask his mom to get some more in.

Sam was a reader, and he also loved dinosaurs. One of

his favourites was the big beast, Tyrannosaurus Rex. He liked it so much that he had given himself the nickname 'Rex'. So far, only his mother had gone along with this fantasy. His father still called him by his given name, unfortunately.

Rex was fatigued, although he hadn't really done anything after eating breakfast. He was continually tired, the aftereffects of that darn virus that had swept through the population, but only lately had picked ten-year-old Rex out of a crowd to infect. His mom said he'd get better, but this pep speech was wearing thin three weeks on.

He sighed, shifted his covers aside, got out of bed, and shuffled over to the window where his binoculars rested on the desk. The family was renting a modest home in East Vancouver, just two blocks south of 41st Avenue. Rex had been following the construction progress of a building not far from his house. It was fascinating to him, watching it get higher and higher. He thought it might be something he'd like to do when he got older — build towers.

There hadn't been much to see at first, other than the crane swinging around relentlessly, but after the building had appeared over the roof of the house across the lane, it seemed to switch into high gear, adding a new floor each and every week. The best part came when the crane flew the metal and plywood pieces up a level to prepare for all the work needed for the next floor before the concrete slab was poured. It looked dangerous as the crane swung the large sections of panels with their associated support framing out of the floor they had been on, then pulling them up, finally coming to rest on the newly set concrete of the floor above. He sat down, picked up his binoculars and studied the top of the tower.

High near the top of the building under construction that Bobby was studying, a labourer was performing the menial yet important task of affixing safety railings to the edge of the recently poured floor slab. The forms used to support the concrete for the floor above had just been removed and flown up a level by the crane, being placed for the twentieth-floor slab work. There were only two workers on this floor, the eighteenth. The remainder of the crew were up two levels, starting all the work needed in preparation for the next concrete pour.

The labourer installing the railings, Jackson Wong, couldn't reach the next section he was to complete. His safety tether was tied off at the central elevator core and would need to be moved to the next tie-off point farther along before he could continue. He waved at the only other labourer on the floor, pointing to the tie-off anchor. The other man, Ollie, was a total loser. This was Jackson's kindest assessment of his work partner. Ollie was tall and powerfully built but suffered from a smallish head that emulated a bullet. Greasy brown thatches of hair hung down over a protruding brow. His eyes were set so close together that from a distance he could have been mistaken for a cyclops.

Ollie had been waiting for this moment, anticipating the amount of beer he'd be drinking just as soon as work was over, and his bank balance had received the promised boost. He went over to the concrete wall and detached the safety line, looked around to make sure there was no one else on the floor, then turned and walked directly back to Jackson.

"Hey, you didn't tie the line off, you fucking moron."

Ollie looked down at the line in his hand but didn't stop his approach. He crowded up to Jackson, smiled, then pushed him off the slab edge, barely remembering to let go of the free end. As he heard the scream flutter up from below, he turned and realized that now he'd have to fix the remaining safety rails into place. Shit, he should have waited until Jackson had almost finished. The screaming had ended, but now Ollie was cursing Jackson for the unfinished work. He could hear some yells from below, so he went over to the slab edge to see what the commotion was about. He assumed that Jackson had landed somewhere. It was stupid of him to try fixing edge rails into place without his harness securely attached to an anchor. This is the kind of thing that happens when you ignore the safety rules. Ollie shrugged. Horns were blaring. Perhaps work was over for the day.

***

Sam couldn't believe what he had just seen. "Mom!" he yelled, as he kept his binoculars trained on the eighteenth floor.

"Be there in a minute, Rex."

CHAPTER
TWO

After parking off the lane at his townhome, Robert checked the phone message before leaving the car. It was Thomas Harrow, his boss at the VPD, requesting a meeting tomorrow morning. Hmm, maybe a result finally? His suspension had entered the twilight zone as far as he was concerned. It had gone on too long. As he was about to open the car door, a message pinged. He looked down, and read the message from Dan.

> Another one filed today. This is becoming a real problem. Can you come in?

> Yes, tomorrow pm? Two?

> Sure.

Looked like tomorrow was going to be interesting, career-wise. He carefully got out, straightened up and went to the car's rear, his back at rest for now. He opened the trunk and tried to grab as many boxes and bags as he could. Pain shot around his ribcage. He stopped and took a few breaths, then dropped a couple of bags back into the trunk. His ribs were only now feeling somewhat healthier after the abuse they had suffered the previous autumn, but the aches were a constant reminder. The doctors hadn't found anything wrong with his back, but the pain said differently. He went to the door and rapped his head gently on the glass a couple of times to get Sandra's attention, his hands full. She looked up, finally laid her knife on the cutting board, and came over to let him in.

She studied the bags of items hanging off his arms. "I didn't think men shopped."

"Ha. They don't, but some are gallant enough to schlep things. This is Sophie's stuff for school."

"Gallant?" Sandra cocked her head before laughing and grabbing Robert's neck for a long kiss. The packages slid to the floor as Robert wrapped his arms around Sandra. She was wearing tight-fitting black jeans and a simple indigo tee.

"Robin home?" He whispered, as he got lost in her eyes once again.

"Mmm, yes."

Robert reluctantly relaxed his hold. "Better get back to that knife thing then. Whatcha making?"

"A scallop risotto. With a radicchio side salad. Approve?"

"I approve of everything about you, Sandra. And no, I don't feel at all threatened that you have taken over my kitchen." Everything on the counter was in order, the onion perfectly diced, all the surfaces clean. Totally unlike the mess that accompanied his cooking.

"Right. My kitchen." She chuckled, "How'd it go out there today?"

"Shopping? Fine. Got a message from Thomas though. Going in tomorrow."

"You going to do it?"

"I'll see what he says, but probably. Then I'm going to see Dan Prudence downtown. More trouble, I think."

Sandra nodded, then continued her prep work. She hid it well, but she was thrilled to finally be with Robert. She had a large case of 'head over heels' love for him. That he had probably saved her life the previous fall was no small addition to the equation. She was also thankful to finally be back in Vancouver. A bad relationship had precipitated her escape from Surrey up to BC's northern coast, to work at a fishing lodge, a couple of years earlier. Even several years hadn't dulled the feeling of betrayal. So, she was careful. That her father had thought the boy ideal son-in-law material hadn't helped in the least. Her mother was more understanding, but Sandra also knew her mother missed her terribly since the move up-country.

Robert poured a half-glass of wine and went over to the family area where he flipped on the early local news and slid onto the couch to watch. The announcer rolled through the usual litany of minor assaults and a complaint from an east side business association. Then Robert's attention sharpened.

Another construction accident, this time on the east side of Vancouver. As usual, details were sketchy, but it seemed as though someone had fallen from a great height and died. Robert grimaced, imagining the man's brief terror. This was the sort of incident that had caused Robert to be re-hired by BC Coastal Insurance a month earlier. Due to the lack of hard facts, the story petered out, but not before some riveting footage of yellow police tape being placed along a street.

The weather segment started. Robert often complained about the lack of hard facts while watching the news, but at least it was a starting point. He'd usually get the details at work, things the public would never know about.

At the dinner table, the conversation was monopolized by Sophie and Rose, who had followed Sophie home. They talked about their upcoming university year even though it was only the end of May and they had yet to graduate from high school. Robert hadn't seen Sophie this animated in months.

While everyone made short work of the dinner, Robert savoured his risotto slowly, enjoying it immensely. Robin looked more relaxed to Robert. He knew about Robin's two-year crush on Rose. It seemed that Robin had finally realized that it was time to move on, especially with Rose now heading to Calgary to enter the pharmacy program at the University of Calgary, one possible route to eventually apply for medicine.

"Think I'm going to look for a job," Sandra said, after she had eaten the last of her salad.

"What?" Robert was startled. This hadn't come up prior to dinner.

"Yeah. It's time I did something productive."

"But …."

"Yes?"

"Nothing. Sounds good, Sandra." Sandra had returned to Vancouver from Arnott Bay at the end of March, moved in with Robert, and was probably itching to do something in the culinary end of things. "Just don't agree to anything too wacky, okay?" Robert knew exactly what kind of hours chefs were asked to put in.

"Don't worry. I'll be firm."

And Robert knew she would be. Sandra had a tough streak inside that was not to be messed with, as he had learned the previous autumn.

Next morning, after Robert had finished a breakfast of toast and some strawberries found in the fridge's rear, he went up to his room. He pulled out his shoulder holster and started a search for his service weapon when he remembered — his gun and badge were at the station, surrendered the previous November. Well, one of his guns at any rate. He still owned two weapons. He wasn't one of those officers who hated guns. On the contrary, particularly after one had recently saved his life. He went over to Sandra, who was still lounging in bed and, bending over, kissed her slowly.

"Good luck, Robert." She whispered as she reached up to stroke the side of his neck. Robert almost broke but steadied himself. Need to head to Cambie Street, yes. He nodded, straightened up and went downstairs, out the back to his car. He started it, fearing some warning noise, but it seemed to be at peace today, so far.

He pulled out and headed west to the station on Cambie, where he hadn't been seen since the previous November except for two gruelling days of interviews. The questioners had made a determined attempt to trip up his version of events. And they had waited a couple of months before starting the inquisition, time he used to organize his version of affairs, and also probably to forget a few select items. He could only pray that the other participants came up with something similar to back him up.

He pulled into the underground parking area and used one of the guest stalls on offer. He felt apprehensive about what might unfold but got out and walked slowly up the stairs onto his old floor. He vainly looked for Ranit, the last gatekeeper for Thomas Harrow when he had been there. After he explained who he was, her replacement stood up and went over to Thomas's door. Robert eyed the bullpen area, spotting Detective Vito Cotoni, Finn Black missing.

"Thomas will see you now, Robert." No smile. Ranit's replacement didn't seem impressed to see Robert in the office. Perhaps someone had been telling tales.

Robert moved past her, no greeting on offer. He still harboured resentment at how things had unfolded in the office the previous fall, even if he had been the cause of most of the problems.

"Thomas!"

"Hello, Robert. Great to see you. You can close the door."

Robert obeyed, shook hands, then sat down across from Thomas, waiting for whatever was to come. Thomas seemed tense, not smiling. Robert had only seen him like this when cases weren't going well. Did this mean a continuing suspension?

"How have you been?"

"Fine, Thomas. Body is healing, sort of. Slightly antsy at how long this has taken, though. What happened to Ranit out there?"

"She transferred to the PR section."

Robert looked puzzled. "More money?"

"Probably. Her choice. Perhaps it was too busy here for her."

"Don't you have to have, what's that word? Rhymes with sympathy … empathy, that's it, when you are dealing with the public?"

"Suppose."

"I don't think she has any," Robert concluded.

Thomas shrugged. "Back to your suspension. These things always take time. There has been some discussion around here about you from the upper level."

I bet, thought Robert.

"They have reached a resolution of sorts finally. You may return, but on desk duties."

"What the fuck does that mean, Thomas?" He knew exactly what it meant, he just wanted to force Thomas to say it aloud. He realized he had more than a few faults as he went about his business, but he also knew he was Thomas's best detective by a mile. And he got results, maybe not fully inside the ever-thickening rulebook, but results, nevertheless.

"It means you won't be interacting with the public, or suspects. Amongst other things, there is some apprehension about your new girlfriend and her relation to known gang members."

This was not unexpected. "Former gang members would be more accurate. They are dead, Thomas. Remember? Only one was really a gangster, anyway. The other guy was just a whacko. And I don't appreciate the apparent lack of trust exhibited here."

"Still, it wasn't my call, you should know. I pushed for you back on full duties."

"Yeah, I get it." He paused here, knowing the size of the step he was about to take. "I've come to my own decision, Thomas. Resigning. Effective immediately." He stood. "I'd give you my gun and badge but think you already have them somewhere. I've enjoyed our time together, Thomas, you should know that, but I don't think I'm a good fit here anymore. I've thought about this long and hard, but there it is."

Thomas seemed hurt, stunned, and at a complete loss as to how this had gone sideways. He remained silent, staring up at Robert.

Robert continued. "Thanks Thomas, you were a great boss. Think I'll go up the street once more, for old times." He left the room quietly and, looking over at Vito, signed the coffee ask. Vito nodded, rose, and the pair walked over to the stairs.

They remained silent until they hit the street. "How are you, Vito?"

"Good, Robert. Keeping busy. How've you been? We've missed you, at least Finn and I have."

"Fine. Just let Thomas know I'm not returning, though. I'm done here."

"Really? Wow. Thought you'd be back for certain." Vito slowed and stared sideways at Robert as they headed up to Cafe Paulo. "You sure about this?"

"He offered me desk duties. Don't think that's my strong point somehow. I spent months thinking about it, and Thomas's offer just cemented the decision."

"How are you feeling? You have a hint of bitter about you."

"I suppose I would have preferred a different outcome, but it's done now."

"Well, I must say that I'm not happy about this."

They entered the cafe. The owner, Gilberto, looked over and roared a greeting, "Roberto! Long time no see." Robert smiled as he went over to try to make up for an absence of several months. He then had a few words with Carmelita, the barista, before ordering a couple of Americanos. He joined Vito at the rear of the cafe, his favoured window seat having lost its gloss after the events of the previous fall.

"How strong do you think Thomas pushed to get me back?"

Vito shrugged.

"I suppose he has his own career to think about. He's not about to threaten quitting over me."

"I'd say some in the office are going to miss you, but you haven't been around for months. I know Finn and I will. What are you going to do?" Vito asked.

"Remember that insurance company I did some sleuthing for on the Greenside case? I'm back doing a few things for them. We'll see where it takes me." Carmelita signalled, so he rose and fetched the coffees. "What's on your plate these days?" he asked after returning.

"Not much of interest. A construction company asked us to look into a subcontractor, something about injuries on a site." He shrugged. "Sounds like some petty dispute, I think. Not sure why we're getting involved. Seems more like a WorkSafeBC thing. I suspect someone high up is pulling a few levers. By the way, I heard that cousin of Tony's got hired."

"Sergio? That was quick. They must be desperate for officers. You'll need to watch out for him, now I'm no longer there to do it."

Vito nodded. "I need to find out where he's situated, first. Probably on a highway somewhere giving out complimentary tickets to scofflaws or something similar."

"Well, maybe we'll run into each other. Your construction case might be similar to what I've been tasked with." The two then started reminiscing about past work.

"How is Finn?"

"Doing well. Aren't sure exactly what cases he's working on these days, but nothing of interest, that's certain."

They finished their coffees slowly. Eventually Vito stood. "Got to get back. Come visit at least, Robert." Robert nodded as Vito turned and went out the door.

CHAPTER
THREE

Robert hung around for a while after Vito left, eventually ordering a tuna panino and a second coffee, talking with Gilberto and informing him of his change in employment. He considered what he had just done — basically kissed off his career at the Vancouver Police Department. Who was sitting in his shabby office now? At least it wasn't that ungrateful cretin, Rod Fister, who had had the manners to leave the VPD of his own accord. Robert still couldn't believe that he had saved Rod's life the previous October. Where was the thank-you card? Maybe he should have let him swing for a moment or two in the noose before ending Mr. Dhillon's run of success.

Was he having second thoughts already? Too late. Even if he wished to change his mind and return, he was certain Thomas would suggest trying another police force. Robert's reasoning was simple enough. He had had enough of the inquiries, the suspensions, not to mention being added to the lawsuit brought forward by one of the suspects from the previous fall's events. And this didn't even factor in the personal danger he had gone through, coming close to losing his life on two occasions, never mind the threats to his immediate family. Looking down at his splayed fingers, he could also add the physical trauma he had suffered. All in the aid of law and order for the City of Vancouver.

He idly watched the sidewalk action, what little there was, then, shaking his head, switched to food — dinner. He took an idea out of the depths of history for this, but he needed to let Sandra know. The kitchen on Inverness was getting competitive indeed.

He took out his cell. "Sandra, I'm going to do the Hack tonight, if you haven't come up with an idea yet."

"No, sounds good, I guess. What's the Hack?"

"It's Chinese by way of Australia. I'll pick up a few items after meeting Dan and explain the meal at home. I did it, by the way. I'm out of the VPD."

"Wow. Good for you … I think. You okay?"

"I guess. It's pretty much the only thing I've done, or been somewhat good at, so there is going to be a little regret."

"What are you going to do for money?"

"Oh, shit, forgot about that." Robert burst out with a small laugh. "Those insurance people pay far better than the VPD, so I should be fine, I hope." He sounded more confident than he felt but wasn't going to let Sandra know about his apprehensions. He was heading into the unknown, career-wise. Checking his watch, he realized he had some time to kill before his meeting downtown. He ambled out of the cafe's door and headed south to check out the newer retail offerings on Cambie Street, the weather warm and agreeable for a stroll.

Just before two, Robert arrived on the twelfth floor of BC Coastal Insurance's building on West Hastings and asked for Dan. The million-dollar view of the North Shore mountains hadn't dropped in value one cent since his last visit over a year earlier.

Dan floated into the lobby, his black-framed glasses still making him look bookish. He was wearing a different suit from the previous time Robert attended, but miles better than anything Robert owned. His dark hair was longer, starting to run riot around the ears, the overall effect not so buttoned down. His face looked healthy, its skin almost glowing. Was it the job or the job's money that radiated the apparent serenity? Perhaps Robert really had chosen the wrong line of work.

"Robert, how are you?" He shook his hand, then led Robert into a smaller conference room with the same view north, closing the door.

"I am well, Dan. Recovered from last fall, mostly."

"Yes. I remember the news clips. You don't lead a dull life, do you?" They both sat, across from each other.

"Well, it may have just gotten a trifle calmer. I resigned from the VPD this morning."

Dan didn't reply immediately, obviously considering what he had just been told. "So, you are available for more work then?"

"I would say so."

"Sounds good, but we need to get a few things clarified. No gang connections, and no killing people. Doesn't fit with our image. We are a somewhat conservative outfit, as you may have guessed."

"Didn't know you had a research arm."

"Common knowledge. News reports from last fall."

"Don't know if I'd be relying on the news for facts these days. Some dead people. They got that part correct, but that's about it. I have no gang connections, and any shooting last fall was self-defence. If I hadn't fired my weapon, I probably wouldn't be here to help you out," Robert responded. "However, I understand your concerns."

"Okay, to business. We've just been named in another lawsuit. Construction accident on another project we supplied funding to. I use the word 'accident' judiciously. We really don't know what is happening on these sites, but past statistics indicate it's something awfully strange. People are dying. I'd like you to find out what's going on. Our legal team needs more than good intentions and hard work if we are going to be able to defend ourselves successfully. We need some behind the scenes intelligence about these incidents, not to mention the people involved."

"I assume you have some of the basic facts; who got injured or killed, and how, things like that?"

"Yes, it's in this file."

"Any chance of an office or closet here? I may want to come downtown once in a while, use your photocopier, talk to the statistician, steal some pens. You know, office stuff."

Dan smiled. "We keep closets for supplies. I don't know what you are used to at the Police Department, but we can do you an office, with a view. I'll have your compensation document modified and sent to you." They shook hands, then Dan gave Robert the file with the particulars on the four lawsuits in which BC Coastal was named.

"These are the accidents that we are named in, including the one I told you about yesterday. It's first on the list. We also know of at least two other lawsuits where we were not involved. Our last one on the list was solved in an agreed filing, didn't go to court. The other two are pending trial. Our donation for the first one was one hundred thousand."

"Jeez, that sounds like a lot of money. The same legal firm has brought all the suits forward?"

"Oddly, yes. Skyler, McDouguld, and Moon. Vancouver outfit, construction litigation is their putative expertise. But these cases are personal injury and civil in nature. Not sure about their experience there, or why all the complainants are using them. Definitely something needing looking into."

"Who is behind the suits?"

"The families, supposedly."

"That firm name's a mouthful. Why do legal people seem to travel in threes?"

"Not sure, so they can surround you?"

"Sounds about right. Thanks for the paperwork. I'll wrap my head around this and get back to you when I have questions."

"While you are at it, also think about joining us full time. I believe you may be useful here."

Robert nodded and grabbed the proffered files, taking his leave. He'd been stupid to regret leaving the Vancouver Police. This work was going to be so much safer. Tedious? Maybe, but his thoughts were on home life these days. And he recalled more than a few tedious days sprinkled in amongst the dangerous action that had been his previous work life.

Once he had escaped downtown, he headed southeast, stopping at a grocery store to provision up for dinner. When he arrived home, the place was empty. He assumed Sandra was out looking at job opportunities. He did some prep work in the kitchen, then put the ingredients back into the fridge in readiness for some wok action once hungry people showed up. He cleaned up the counter and washed the knives. Sandra was certainly keeping him on his toes.

He looked over at his wall of cookbooks in the family area. As he scanned the rows, he lingered on a title: *Italian Country Cooking*. He remembered his vow to find an *Osso Buco* recipe to make in memory of Tony. It was the least he could do to honour him. The events leading to his partner's death the previous fall were still fresh to Robert — Tony's body lying on the park's grass, carelessly left by his killer, the violence horrific. The ache started again, his ribs complaining.

He grabbed the file Dan had given him, sat down at the dining room table, and started leafing through the contents. The dollars being asked for in the suits astounded Robert, but maybe this was normal, he didn't know. Some gruesome photos accompanied the descriptions of the supposed accidents. Victim names were all Chinese, which he found odd. He wasn't aware that the Chinese had taken up construction locally. Other ethnic groups, yes, just not Chinese. All four were common site labourers, the bottom of the ladder in the construction site pecking order. Three had died on their jobsites while the fourth languished unconscious in a hospital for a few days before passing away. Names of the victims were included, but no addresses or contact info. Once he had this, he'd do some visiting to any relatives in town to flesh out that side of the story. He'd also check out the firm launching these suits. Last thing would be the construction sites, developers, and the contractors involved. They were also named in the lawsuits, so maybe they'd be doing their own research? He wasn't sure what he was supposed to be looking for, but it didn't seem overly complicated or dangerous.

First through the door was his son, Robin. "Hey Pops, what's for dinner?"

"Doing the Hack tonight. Could you pull the rice maker out?"

"Sure. Guess what."

Robert looked back at his son and shrugged his shoulders. "A hint?"

"Got a job lined up for the summer through my welding course."

"Wow, I guess. You're only sixteen though."

"Old enough. I'm keen. Wouldn't mind having some money."

"What kind of job?"

"Labourer on a construction site. My teacher has a connection with a contractor."

"Jeez, Robin, I don't know. My new job is looking into some recent accidents on construction sites. People died — labourers."

"My teacher mentioned something about that, but said this contractor is really good. No accidents. The name is Fairweather Construction."

"Think I'll have a little chat with your teacher first. I don't want you ending up as a statistic, okay?"

"I guess." Robin looked disappointed. The front door opened, and laughter was heard from the hall. Both Sophie and Sandra crowded through into the kitchen, giggling about something.

"What's funny?" Robert asked.

"Nothing you need to know about," Sandra answered. "I just landed a job. Caterer over on Main Street. Crazy Eats."

"Really? Why do catering companies have such bad names?"

"Don't know, maybe their minds are on food, not anything else. Or they're trying to be overly clever?"

Robert shook his head. Sophie and Robin left the room, heading upstairs. "When do you start?"

"A couple of days. They seem desperate. I set the terms, so don't worry. Not working Christmas, things like that."

"That's great. Congratulations, Sandra."

"So, what is this Hack thing you've been advertising?"

"It's a chicken stir-fry courtesy of an Australian chef and cookbook producer of Chinese heritage. Some television goof made the mistake of showing a bunch of her television episodes in a row one day. Each show was a half-hour, and after the third or fourth one, I realized she was using the same five god-damned condiments in every dish she made. She'd just say them in a different order and add them at different times. From that day forward, she was the Hack to me." Then he delivered the judgment. "But the dish is great, nevertheless. Believe me, I wouldn't do it if it wasn't. Stand back, I've got some wok magic to perform."

Sandra laughed as she went to the fridge and grabbed an unopened bottle of Chardonnay. "Don't want the chef getting thirsty, do we?"

"Good thinking, Sandra. Can you also pull out the *gai lan*? We need something green."

She retrieved the vegetables, then went over to the sofa, sat, and proceeded to watch Robert pare the greens, readying them for blanching. "This isn't bad at all, watching someone else cook for a change."

"Exactly what I was thinking when you were preparing yesterday's dinner," Robert answered.

"I talked with my mother today. It's time I went out to Surrey for a visit."

"Do you drive?"

"I used to, so yes."

"Maybe you could use the Silver Streak."

She nodded at the offer.

As he looked across at Sandra, he came to a conclusion. He was going to ask for her hand. If she would have him, that is. He hadn't felt this way about anyone since Susan, years ago, and he wasn't about to let

Sandra slip away. All he had to do was plan the proposal, and hope. And, as usual when he dealt with the fairer sex, he had no idea of the Pandora's box he would open.

His thoughts slipped back to Susan, who had become everything in his life. Before meeting Susan, his trail to finding a career had seemed destined to be an attempt to match his father's talent as a renowned Cantonese chef. As if that were likely. Robert wouldn't have been the detective he was without Susan's prodding and support.

He met Susan at a weekend running club. 'Club' was being overly generous. He didn't know what attracted these people to each other. He wasn't really looking to meet more runners, running generally being a solitary pastime. The exception being if they were of the fairer sex, then interest rose. A neighbour had told him about the group, so he gave it a try, not expecting much.

He showed up one Sunday spring morning at Trout Lake on Vancouver's east side. It was just past seven, a time when most sane people were in bed, communing with their pillow. About fifteen people were standing around, waiting for stragglers to arrive. The lake was dead placid, a mirror reflecting the still grey sky. Nothing moved. Robert greeted his neighbour, but after eyeing the crowd, didn't know anyone else. Some looked fit, some not so much. Most sported way too much clothing for the temperature, much of it shiny new. Belts and harnesses holding water bottles, snacks, and energy capsules adorned at least three quarters of the people present, as though they were embarking on a trek through the Sahara.

"Thought we were just doing a 10 K, Bert," Robert commented, sizing up all the equipment.

"Many here are terrified of getting thirsty," Bert responded.

Robert shook his head. He was wearing shorts, a tee, and good runners. He spotted a woman who was similarly under-equipped. She looked his way while he was appraising her. Neither looked away. Long auburn hair gathered in a ponytail framed a strong face, all angles. Eyes reminiscent of his mother's. She looked fit, her legs seemed Olympic-style fit.

"Do you know that woman?" he asked Bert. "Introduce us?"

Bert did as he was asked. They ended up running together, staying well clear of the others. Susan ran easily, but Robert matched her.

"How long have you been doing this?" Robert asked.

"With these people?" Susan responded. "Not long, and not much longer either."

"They seem more interested in their clothes and accessories," Robert noted, as they were leaving the pack behind.

"Reminds me of all those cyclists one sees these days looking like they're in the Tour de Something, except less money is involved, I suppose."

"And what does Susan do to get by in Vancouver?" It was a trifle nosy to ask this of someone he had only met a few minutes earlier.

"Planner with the City of Vancouver, just started. How about yourself?"

"Training to be a chef, in a Cantonese kitchen. Not going well, frankly."

"Unusual."

"My dad is a chef — top-notch, actually. I'm getting hints that I'm not measuring up, so I've been thinking about something else. My tastes run to more than just Cantonese, anyway."

Susan turned her head and smiled, no change in her stride. "It's good to be flexible."

"That's what my dad said, oddly. I think I'm going to apply to the Justice Institute for courses, then the VPD, if they'll have me."

She didn't respond immediately, obviously digesting this bit of information. "Would you like to do this again? Without the circus?"

"I think that would be an excellent idea," Robert responded. He was attracted to her but quickly doubted if anything would come of it after learning how educated she was, and what she did for a living. The only person he knew with those kind of smarts was his mother, the university professor. She had told him time and again that success was down to hard work and discipline, not intelligence. He was pretty certain being smart wouldn't hurt any though.

Susan and Robert ran again and were married six months later, two children following promptly. Twelve years on, Susan was diagnosed with pancreatic cancer, the kind with a less than optimistic prognosis. The doctors weren't wrong. Susan lasted a mere five months, leaving Robert, Sophie, and Robin hopelessly heartbroken, searching for answers.

After dinner was over and the smoke from the wok had finally dissipated, the range fan being no match for Chinese cooking, Robert readied to clean up. Sandra gently reminded him of the golden rule: Those who don't cook do the cleaning.

He smiled gratefully. "This version wasn't my best. Haven't done it in a while — rusty. What did you think?"

"Your analysis was bang on. That is one good dish, despite your lack of edge. I am suitably impressed. Tried any other of her recipes?"

"No. Maybe I should check her book out."

"Does Sophie know how to cook?"

"Yes. Both kids can cook — we made sure of that — but it's the cleaning part that they have some trouble with. Some recipe tune-ups might be in order if Sophie and Rose are to survive a winter in Calgary."

"I could do that with her this summer, give her a few tips," Sandra said.

"Pretty sure she'd like that, Sandra. She seems to be a big fan of you."

Sandra smiled as she loaded the dishwasher.

Robert grabbed his laptop and sent a message to Dan reminding him to provide the missing information on the victims. As it was Friday evening, he wouldn't expect anything before Monday. Then he relaxed, grabbing a glass of wine and watched as Sandra efficiently dealt with what little mess there was.

CHAPTER
FOUR

Monday, Robert started trawling through the internet in search of anything he could find about the legal company giving Dan such a hard time. While he waited for the needed contact information about the victims, Sandra had gone out, taking her knives to get them sharpened in anticipation of her upcoming employment. His children were at school, leaving the townhouse empty and quiet.

Skyler, McDouguld, and Moon had been around for at least twenty years, but there wasn't much to be learned about the partners. He tried to think of any interactions he had had with lawyers, but he realized he mostly tried to stay away from them as a general rule. He went through his many contacts added over years of detective work, but again, couldn't think of any obvious sources. Perhaps his reporter friend, Bernard Lily at the CBC might be of help. God knows, he had supplied more than a few stories to him the previous fall when cops were being murdered. Time to call in a chit or two.

He went the direct route, calling him. "Bernard. Do you remember this voice?"

"Robert, correct? Wow. How are you? Last thing I heard was you being suspended for not getting out of a psychopath's area of expertise quickly enough."

"Yes, Bernard. How are you?"

"Local crime news is a mite slow these days, probably due to one Robert Lui being out of action. Other than that, I've moved house, and I'm still learning things at the CBC."

"Sounds good. Don't know if I'll be able to help you with news stories anymore. I've recently left the VPD and I'm now working for BC Coastal Insurance. Pretty boring stuff, I'm both thinking and hoping."

"That's not the Robert I know." There was silence. Robert guessed that Bernard's brain was going to engage any second. He waited.

"So why have you called?" Bernard finally asked.

"Wonder if you can help me out. I'm investigating some construction accidents and could use some info on the legal team suing the company employing me. Well, they are suing a bunch of entities, my new company just happens to be on the list. Name is Skyler, McDouguld, and Moon. Development and construction law is what they are reputed to be good at, but these lawsuits are personal injury and civil in nature, so somewhat outside their area of expertise. Any information would be much appreciated."

"I'll see what I can find out. Do you know why I'm doing this?"

"Cause you're an ace bloodhound reporter aiming for a news award of some sort?"

"No. Because I owe you, and I'm guessing I just might get a juicy story out of this, based on past experience."

"You're smart, Bernard. You might be right on the second item, but I'm hoping not."

"Oh, I would bet big money on being right." Bernard's voice quivered. Robert could sense excitement building, over what? Nothing much, he hoped.

"There is something else, Robert. You heard about that worker falling off a tower last week?"

"Yes."

"One of our camera techs has an interesting story. His son claims to have seen it happen."

"How so?"

"They live south of the tower, and the son is home ill. He watches the construction progress daily. Thing is, the son, whose name is Sam, says the guy was pushed off the tower."

"They called the police yet?"

"I don't know. The guy is not sure what to do."

"Well, I wouldn't blame him. Who knows what is behind this? But I think he should call the police and at least report it." Robert lapsed into silence as he re-considered options. "I could have a word with one of the detectives, without naming anyone if he prefers to go that route."

"I guess. I'll let the guy know."

"Thanks, Bernard. Has he told anyone else this story?"

"I don't know."

"Tell him not to. I know the guy is worried for his son,

and no one would blame him. I am also impressed that you haven't spilled the beans on the local news yet. Are you maturing? Talk soon." He ended the call, then wondered if this was the kind of thing driving the lawsuits he was to look into.

His stomach told him to make breakfast, so he complied. While sipping coffee after eating, he heard his computer signal something. He checked and found some of the requested information sent by his employer. Three of the labourers had Vancouver addresses. The last one had lived in Richmond, the airport city immediately south of Vancouver. A couple of phone numbers were missing. That was fine by Robert. A face-to-face meeting always generated more information. He realized some discretion would be needed if he succeeded in getting anyone to open up. The families would surely have been warned by their lawyers against talking with someone representing the opposition.

He looked up the addresses. Two were close to each other in Strathcona, the area just to the southeast of the epicentre for the poor and troubled in Vancouver. Chinatown also lay close by and in earlier times a good portion of Strathcona had been home to Chinese immigrants. The third Vancouver address related to the concluded lawsuit and was farther east, past Commercial Drive. Well, he supposed a labourer wasn't going to be living it up on the west side, was he? Robert went out to his car, got in, and started it. After a few groans, the engine caught but didn't sound terribly healthy. Good enough, he hoped. Definitely time to look for a newer car, but it would be another expense not needed at the moment.

He started out, threading his way north, finally stopping on Campbell Avenue in front of a tired looking three-storey apartment block. There were several other residential buildings in the immediate area with exterior corridors, appearing markedly different from the building he was in front of, so he re-checked the address. Seemed as though some architectural genius had figured that outside corridors were the thing of the future, ignoring that it rained half the year, temperatures slightly above freezing. Maybe they felt making people suffer a little more before entering their home would generate gratitude once inside. Robert was certain it would probably generate something more along the lines of swearing.

He got out and went up to the lobby door, expecting an entry phone at least, but no, the door wasn't even closed properly. The front of the building was covered in graffiti, none of which was comprehensible. Siding, glass, concrete, it didn't seem to matter to the 'artists' what they sprayed on. It was as though the residents or the building owner had given up.

He let himself into a dark lobby smelling vaguely of a fish fry. The single light sconce couldn't repel the gloom. He checked the address again and made for the stairs, much preferable to an elevator. Robert always felt trapped in an elevator, so he avoided them when he had a choice. He walked up and onto the third floor. The carpet was greasy brown, light dim, some of the fluorescent bulbs out, walls heavily scuffed. He came to the door marked

307, paused, then knocked. He couldn't hear anything from within.

After a full minute, the door opened a few inches, security chain engaged. Robert was looking at a young Chinese woman, thirtyish? He started his spiel in Cantonese about possible insurance money for Jason but only managed to get a few words out. Something flashed in her eyes. He felt she understood what he had said, but when she responded, it was in Mandarin. Shit. Robert had no idea what she was saying, but it wasn't lengthy. Then the door slammed shut. He stood there, undecided, then realized he'd need a translator if he was to make any inroads with this lady. The address represented the most recent suit brought, so things might still be very raw for the young woman, but he really had no idea of her relationship to the victim. He reluctantly left the way he had come, looking down at his list of victims as he walked to his car. He'd try the next closest one.

After driving only a couple of blocks west, he checked the address again and got out of the car. He walked a half-block up to a three-storey house adorned with tired grey siding, its maroon paint blistered and peeling. A couple of metres above the sidewalk, a porch was attached to the front, sort of, one end succumbing to gravity. All the homes on the street had seen better days, about fifty years ago. He realized the address for Andy Ho was probably a basement suite, accessible from the side or rear.

He walked past the tilted porch down a cracked concrete path between the house and its neighbour. He gingerly squeezed past a couple of filthy garbage cans. Something with a tail skittered away under a broken piece of trim board. Probably one of the many Norwegian rats calling Vancouver home. He came to a blank metal door down a couple of steps. The number screwed to the stucco beside the door matched. No doorbell. He rapped on the door. It squeaked as it slowly moved inwards. It hadn't even been properly closed. Stale air leaked out past his head.

"Hello?" Nothing. He pulled some latex gloves out of his jacket, entered the darkness and yelled again. Silence. He was standing in a small living area. He flipped on a light switch next to the door, and a bare bulb hanging from the ceiling came to life. One small window looked back onto the path he had just been standing on, admitting little light. He stepped over pieces of mail on the floor. A worn jade green sofa sat behind a badly chipped coffee table made out of pressed board of some kind. Stained rings adorned its surface. A faded red table with one chair gave testament to the loneliness of this man's life. A couple of books lay prone on the upper shelf of a bookcase, where a mottled ivory Buddha sat in place of pride on the centre shelf, testament to the gods that were supposedly looking after Andy's life but had recently come up short.

As he studied the basic shrine, his thoughts drifted to his own confused religious upbringing. His mother had insisted on some basic Christian education by sending him to Sunday school for three years after they had emigrated back to Canada from Hong Kong. His father's religious beliefs seemed more in line with what he was looking at; family gods, offerings at temple, and observance of the standard Chinese holidays when family and food dominated all. However, none of it looked to have been any benefit to Andy Ho in the end.

The kitchen was a dark alcove off the living space. He looked in but didn't enter. Rancid noodles sat in a bowl. A jumble of soiled cutlery and plates covered the counter and half-filled the sink. He left the fridge alone. He turned around and made for the small bedroom containing only the basics. A single bed with a rumpled cover lay across from a closet, which was wide open. He was looking at shirts and pants hung in relative order. Three pairs of worn shoes sat on the floor under the clothes, nothing remarkable. Robert turned to open the chest of drawers, all the drawers, but again, nothing of interest was found, just underwear, t-shirts and a couple of sweaters. No papers, no money, no passport, nothing.

Something bothered Robert besides the lack of papers, but he couldn't pinpoint what it was. He stood for a while, thinking, but no illumination came. The picture was of a man only eking out a subsistence, not really living. It was time to leave. He bent over and picked up the mail, thumbing through it. A hydro bill sat among a wad of flyers. Nothing of note, so he dropped everything onto the table.

He gently closed the suite door, then a branch breaking made him look to the rear of the house. A wispy man in a black satin top and pants was walking away from him. His hair was in a long queue under a short tasseled black cap. The man turned and looked directly at Robert, as if he had heard the door close. He seemed middle-aged. Perhaps he was one of the 'old fellas' — the bachelors or married men who had emigrated to Gold

Mountain in hopes of sending money back to their families in Canton.

Robert heard another noise behind him. He turned and was looking up at a thin elderly Chinese lady, wearing an ivory dress printed with blue flowers, grey hair cut to a stylish bob. She leaned out over the adjacent home's porch railing, grinning down at him. Robert didn't know why. He glanced back to the lane, but nothing remained of the Chinese apparition. He had encountered other spirits from the past, but none had ever acknowledged his presence before. This was new territory, alarming territory.

He tried Cantonese on the lady, asking if she knew Andy Ho.

She nodded. "Andy, nice man, lived alone. No visitors."

Robert wondered how much spying she did to know Andy had no guests.

"Did you hear he had an accident?"

"Yes. Very bad."

"Did he have any family?"

"Not here. Maybe Hong Kong."

"But you don't know for sure?"

It was as if he had insulted the woman, which, given her busybody tendencies, probably wasn't far off the truth. Her smile vanished as she shrugged.

"Andy own a car?"

"He biked places he needed to go."

Robert stood, flummoxed. "So, no visitors at all?"

She shook her head. "No, except for two men who came three days ago. *Gweilos.*"

Robert considered this. "Uniforms?"

She shook her head.

"They stay long?"

"Twenty minutes. I didn't like the look of them."

Pretty precise. He smiled up at her, thanked the woman, and returned to the street, his chest aching again. Two white men. What were they doing there?

He considered the labourer's home he had just left. It was more than depressing. What was any different about this man's life from some of the early Chinese immigrants to Vancouver? Not much, would be a good answer. The first Chinese had shown up in Saltwater City in the 1860s, looking for a new life. In the beginning, they came up from San Francisco, then directly from Canton, some via Victoria. Many more followed in episodic waves, following tales of possible gold at first. Some ended up helping to build a railroad connecting British Columbia to the rest of Canada, some dying for their efforts. They were not afraid of the menial and sometimes dangerous tasks that few white people would stoop to, but that didn't stop the never-ending prejudice and efforts to send the Chinese back where they came from or prevent them from coming in the first place. And here seemed something similar, death from performing a dangerous job, over one hundred and sixty years later. And seemingly, no one to mourn the loss of a life, just someone trying to collect money for a death.

Robert headed back home. If the next two addresses didn't yield anything more than the first two, he'd need to re-evaluate his tactics. He thought about the accident reports Dan had given him. They were sketchy at best. He assumed WorkSafeBC, the entity tasked with workplace safety and accident investigations in the province, would have more detailed information on each incident. How to get at it was the question. Dan had suggested that dire accidents such as these only came along once in a long while. He entered his kitchen and put some water on.

Then he called Dan. "Hi, it's Robert. These accident essays are flimsy. Any chance of getting more information? I mean, in a lawsuit, isn't the defence supposed to have access to all relevant facts?"

"Usually, yes. We have already asked those lawyers, but they told us this was all they had."

"I don't like it." Robert was just venting, but Dan had to agree with him.

"I'll try again. Let you know."

"I visited two of the victims' addresses today. First one wouldn't open the door, lady spoke Mandarin, undecipherable to me. Second one lived alone, apparently no family or friends in Vancouver. So how did a lawsuit get filed for him? Our lawyer friends, SM & M, sound very aggressive. I'll go visit the other two tomorrow." He paused. "Do you have anyone good computer-wise at your office?"

"We have a decent IT guy, if that's what you mean."

"It's not. Let me think. I'll be in touch." He hung up and made coffee.

The next morning, Robert headed down to Richmond, his car behaving for now. Perhaps the Silver Streak favoured flat terrain, which was all of Richmond. The city covered a large chunk of the western Fraser River delta. After driving through the mess of No. 3 Road traffic, he turned east, ending up on Cooney Crescent. It wasn't but a few blocks from the supposed centre of Richmond but seemed to be in an area of drastic change, like much of Greater Vancouver.

Some large new buildings were being erected, seemingly in someone's backyard, while the few single-family homes remaining looked to be on life support, awaiting a developer's offer. Pickup trucks sat half on crabgrass and weeds, half on concrete, as if their drivers couldn't bother negotiating a driveway. Garbage on lawns was the decorating theme for some of the homes. A few toys lay scattered, no children evident. Open ditches lining the roadway were the storm sewer option, no sidewalks.

He re-checked the address. It was a house, but again,

probably a secondary suite at grade. Robert knew Richmond didn't have basements, the water table eager to enter any rooms built too low into the ground.

He stopped the car and stared at the home, a nicotine-stained Vancouver Special, the locally famous stuccoed model that in two floors got the maximum floor space allowed onto a thirty-three-foot-wide lot. He got out, looked around, but the area was silent. Again, he was walking between two houses, but with slightly more space this time. It was the suburbs after all. No rats, but he was sure they were around, keeping a low profile.

He knocked on a patterned side door and waited. The door opened slowly. A youngish woman dressed in blue jeans and a sunflower gold top stood waiting for Robert's pitch, her face expressionless. Tortoiseshell eyeglasses framed dark brown eyes, black hair corralled by a scrunchie into a loose ponytail.

"Is this the home of Sherman Li?" He started in English.

"Yes. Who are you?"

"Robert Lui. I work for an insurance company that is connected to the construction project where Sherman had his very unfortunate accident." All true so far. The woman seemed confused. English maybe wasn't her first language. He tried Cantonese. "Are you related to Sherman?"

Her face softened slightly. "He was my brother."

"I am very sorry for your loss."

She acknowledged this by looking down. She was silent, then asked, "What do you want?"

"I'd like to talk to you about Sherman, what he was like, how long he had been working. Things like that." It wasn't very compelling, Robert knew, but he was loathe to lie to someone who had just suffered such a loss.

"They told us not to talk to anyone."

"Who told you?"

"Lawyers."

"I just want to know about Sherman, the man and brother, nothing sinister." Robert could sense the indecision. "It's okay. I know you are grieving. I'll let you be." He turned and was about to leave, when she relented.

"Would you like to come in?"

Robert looked back, nodded gratefully and entered. At least the rooms were larger than the hovel in Strathcona he had visited yesterday. They were in a living area. The protective family god was sitting, flanked by candles on an old teak credenza against a white wall, again, not doing its job.

"My name is Alice. Would you like some tea?"

"Please." Robert was pointed to the long beige couch, while Alice went into the kitchen to put water on. The furniture wasn't top-notch, but at least this home was clean. Alice's touch, he was sure. Most men tended to the porcine end of the housekeeping spectrum, left to their own devices.

After almost ten minutes, Alice reappeared with a small metal tray holding two steaming porcelain cups. She offered a cup to Robert, then sat down very close to him. "What do you wish to know about Sherman?" She sipped at her cup, not taking her eyes off Robert for a second.

Robert was pretty certain that brother and sister were relative newcomers to Richmond. "How long had he been working at the construction job?"

"Less than a year. We had just arrived after the offer of a job for Sherman."

"Who offered him a job?"

"The company. Bamboo something or other."

"And this was here?"

"The offer came to us in Hong Kong. It was arranged by an immigration lawyer."

This sounded bizarre. Since when were local construction companies going offshore for basic site-grunt talent? "And you came with him?"

"Yes, and my older brother, Denton. Sherman did not want to come alone."

"Any other relatives here?"

"No."

"Is Denton around?"

"No. He's out fishing."

This was getting weirder. "Does Denton work for Bamboo as well?"

"No, he didn't want to. He does some fishing out of Steveston with someone he met."

Robert sipped his tea. It was good, near the high end of quality, he realized. He was playing for time, unsure if he'd ever get to talk with Alice again. "Did Sherman make any trips back to Hong Kong?"

"Yes, two."

"Do you know why?"

"Not really. I assumed he was visiting our parents, but they said they hadn't seen him."

"Was he happy in his work?"

"No. It was the worst. It is also very boring here. I

wanted to return to Hong Kong, but Sherman said we couldn't yet."

"Why not?"

"He wouldn't say."

Robert tried a different tack. "Are you aware of the circumstances around Sherman's accident?" He had the brief report from his employer that told of Sherman being crushed by a load of gravel from a height on the pit floor of an excavation. Not much detail. And not much left of Sherman either.

"He was hit by something. It fell on him. They said it was an accident and that they were truly sorry."

It sounded as though Alice knew even less about her brother's death than Robert. He remained silent, assessing options. "Something doesn't sound right. Would it be possible to talk again, in the future?"

"Maybe. Who do you work for?"

He couldn't avoid answering this one even as he was loathe to. "BC Coastal Insurance." He could only pray she wouldn't spill the beans to the lawyers. If he asked her not to, she would most likely sense something wrong, and give him up to SM & M.

"How did you find your lawyers here?"

"I didn't. They called me."

"I'll leave now. Again, my condolences, Alice." He stood up. Alice rose also, uncertain. Robert smiled. He knew he had a good smile even if the circumstances didn't warrant one. As he returned to his car, he wondered what the hell was going on. This assignment had suddenly veered into the twilight zone. He decided to leave the last victim for now.

Next morning, he made a call. "Vito? It's Robert."

"Nice to hear from you. This social?"

"No, business. Know that construction accident last week? Guy diving off a tower? Well, it may not have been an accident. Witness says there was some pushing going on."

"Why haven't we heard about this? Who saw it?"

"It's a kid, so that's why. Frankly, I don't blame the father one bit. It sounds like he hasn't called it in so far. I don't know any names yet, but maybe I can do some poking around, unofficially of course. I'll let you know what I come up with."

"How did you come about this?"

"A source who works with the father. That's all I'll say for now until I see if he'll talk with me."

Vito was silent, then said, "This will have a bearing on the site investigation. I'll look into it myself. We may need to meet at some point."

"Talk soon, Vito."

CHAPTER
SIX

Just after seven, Friday morning, Ben Skyler walked through the front door of his legal firm. The lights were on, so some eager beaver must already have their nose buried in research or case preparation. The sun had been up for almost two hours, but traffic on the downtown Vancouver streets was still muted. He went to his office, dropped his briefcase, then turned and made for the smaller conference room. As usual, he was first to the senior partner's meeting held every week. He looked for a coaster, gave up, and set his cup of coffee down on the maple conference table and stood, staring at the office building across the street, which exhibited almost no activity.

The firm of thirty-five was smallish in the legal world, so premises looking at the North Shore mountains were left for others with more money to spend on rent. Ben was fond of the office space despite the lack of a view. It reflected his taste in modern layout and finishes. He knew

Ross pretty much hated the look, whining for a rather more traditional appearance featuring darkly stained oak. If he had been so concerned, Ben figured he should have paid attention when the plans were being drawn up, and decisions made. God knows, he had plenty of opportunity. Ben came from Vancouver money and had founded the firm, bringing on the two other partners one by one as he grew the business.

He heard movement behind him. He turned and nodded at Candice Moon as she entered, then they both sat, no words, waiting for the third partner, Ross McDouguld. Candice was dressed in her usual no-nonsense jade green pantsuit with an ivory blouse, which nicely complemented her long flaxen hair with its precisely cut ends.

After ten minutes, the glass door finally opened again and a dishevelled man entered, dark hair sticking up in a few different directions, with what looked like two days' growth on his cheeks. Ross was short, bordering on plump, but still solid, for a little while longer, anyway. A pale-yellow stain adorned the lapel of his powder-blue suit coat, as if he was a sloppy emissary of a Swedish furnishings company coming straight from dinner. Which wouldn't be the first time. Ross had a habit of burning both ends of the candle. He collapsed in a heap at the head of the table.

"You guys been to Bayonne's yet?"

"What the hell is Bayonne's?" Ben spoke sharply, seemingly irritated. Candice remained silent.

"New steak place on Alberni. Some chefs from Jersey

started it. Outstanding. They have those Italian mushroomy things."

Ben was certain Ross was drunk. "You mean truffles?"

"That's the one." Ross stared at Ben. "How are the site suits going?"

Ben had heard this cute phrase a few too many times. "Wilson seems to have a handle on things. Why are we doing this anyway? Not exactly our area, is it?"

"What makes the world go round, Ben? Money. Even a moron can understand that. Tell him to find out when the cases will get court time. Big paydays in the offing based on how the first one turned out."

Had Ross bought a new yacht or something? Lately, he seemed to be chasing money relentlessly.

"I'm not a fan of what you are doing."

"Why?"

"Operating out of our field of expertise, that's why. Trouble will follow, I don't care how much easy money you make doing this."

Ross shrugged. "Someone is asking questions about us in Victoria." The change in tone, abrupt.

"What kind of questions?" Ben puzzled as to why Ross would be concerned.

"The kind I don't want answered. I'm gonna find out who is behind this." Ross glared at Ben.

Ben wondered what was generating the paranoia but didn't pursue the matter further. The meeting devolved to more mundane matters. After twenty minutes, one final topic was raised.

"We need to finish planning for the summer party," Candice stated. "You still want to do it at the winery?"

"Like, totally," Ross responded, slurring his words. Ben couldn't figure out where this teenage language came from. It wasn't as if Ross had any kids, that he knew about anyway.

"Then we should use a caterer in Oliver," Candice responded.

"No. Use Crazy Eats. They can figure it out."

"Really? Are you kidding?"

"No, do it. The caterers around Oliver are useless."

Candice looked down at the table, declining for now to get into a fight over a trivial matter.

Ben had heard about the connection between Ross and the owner of the catering company, but it still seemed ludicrous to be using a Vancouver company to work an event in the wine country of the Okanagan, four hundred kilometres away.

Meeting over, Ben followed Ross to his office, wanting to find out who in Victoria had told Ross about the enquiries. If he had to guess, one of their targets in the various lawsuits recently filed was snooping around, perhaps gathering intelligence. It was what he would do.

On Inverness Street the same day, Robert came to a decision about his lack of computer abilities. He texted Rory's cell and left a message.

> Interested in doing some freelance work
> on the side? Robert.

Rory was one of the cyber-officers doing time deep in

the bowels of the Cambie Station, where Robert had spent several years with the Vancouver Police Department. Robert speculated that Rory'd be only too happy to be doing something different and probably more challenging by now.

While he waited, his thoughts devolved to some household issues, such as his less than stellar car, and his promise to talk with Robin's shop teacher. He went with the educational item, less expensive than thinking about a car.

He rang the school. "Hi, it's Robert Lui. I have a couple of kids attending your school. I'd like to talk with the welding instructor if I may."

"Pertaining to what?" The gatekeeper, wary.

"He has my son, Robin, lined up for a summer job, and I'd like to discuss it with him."

"I'll take your number, and he will get back to you, okay?"

"Sure." More waiting. He went over to the window looking out onto his tomato patch. Things looked promising. Many flowers adorned the plants, hints of fruit to come. He had only managed to fit ten plants into the small piece of dirt, but if he could pay attention to them, gold would be the payoff starting mid-July, or rather, red and gold. His phone dinged. He went back to the counter and looked down. Rory had responded.

> Interested in doing some freelance work on the side? Robert.

> Very interested.

Can you meet? Apollo Cafe on Main later
this pm?

Yes, five?

See you then.

Robert felt a tinge of guilt asking Rory to help him. He had basically shanghaied him the previous fall into the final episode dealing with a cop killer. He had taken Rory with him to a hostage rescue situation he probably had very little training about. Of one thing, he was sure. Rory was no dummy, and his talents were being wasted on the job the VPD had him doing. And that he had responded indicated he didn't fear what Robert might get him involved with this time.

Sandra had started her employment with the caterer and had left for Main Street and points unknown, leaving Robert alone in the townhouse. He could go for a run. Some redress was in order, his fitness recently fading from lack of attention. He changed into his shorts and left, thankful that, due to the lack of danger, he no longer needed to strap on his ankle holster. He laughed. Wearing a Beretta while running in the summer would probably net him a visit by a black and white unit and possible unpleasantness. He had barely managed to hang onto the gun after the fallout from the previous fall's investigation, eventually being advised to license it, which he ignored.

After returning, he managed some research on the other construction company building projects where accidents had happened. He already knew that Bamboo

Construction was shonky due to its past connection to an infamous Surrey criminal gang, so he looked at Taipan Construction. He did a net search, which turned up the usual bullshit about how great the company was. He looked at a few of their finished tower projects, then thought it was time to put the pressure on Bernard again, to find out who was behind the company, directors, owners, etc. This time, he e-mailed Bernard with the questions. While he waited for his five o'clock meeting to draw closer, he considered the construction company's name, unusual for Vancouver. A very wealthy Hong Kong businessman had secured the entire Expo lands around False Creek for a massive redevelopment after the world's fair was over in 1986, and Robert knew names were important. It was a time when immigration from Hong Kong to Vancouver was at one of its episodic heights. English was generally the go-to when naming a project or a local company, lest the locals fear that they were being taken over by foreigners. This meant Taipan Construction was a bit of an outlier. Perception was everything — facts, less so.

It was almost five, so he went out to his car. When he tried to start it, the engine moaned twice then quit, no further noises at all. Shit. He remembered that he had purchased a membership in the province's auto club, so he'd give them a call to see if they had any words of encouragement, however not now. He'd need to quickly walk over to the Apollo.

He entered the cafe, spotting Rory at a table near the rear wall. He didn't recognize any of the help behind the counter, but then, it was the graveyard shift for coffee shops.

"Hey Rory, sorry for the lateness. My car died, so I had to hoof it over here."

"Hi Robert. You live close by then?"

"Sort of, Inverness Street."

"I was surprised to get your message. I didn't know you had left the force."

Robert would have been shocked if Rory had known. The VPD wasn't any different from most institutions and companies. Information, particularly of the bad kind, was seldom shared, and Rory's location in the basement probably made things worse. "Seemed like the right thing to do. I almost died twice on that last case, and after the suspension they were going to put me on desk duties. I declined." He paused. "Coffee?"

"Small one will be fine. Work week's over."

Robert stood and went to the bar and ordered, then returned with a question. "Your last name?"

"Hillier."

"Thanks. Guess we really didn't have time to get acquainted last fall. I think that is about to change."

"So, what are you doing and how can I help?"

"Good questions. Working for an insurance company now, doing some investigating. Not sure exactly how you will help, but the rabbit hole I am going down will need your skills. Of this, I have no doubt."

"Rabbit hole?"

"I'm looking at some construction site accidents. Labourers died and lawsuits have been filed. I've only been looking at things a couple of days and already something doesn't smell right. I assume you have a setup at home you can work from?"

"Yes. Can we discuss payment terms?"

"No idea. Let me know what you need, and I will expense it. I'll tell my employer I've got someone working for me, but that's it." Robert smiled. "And I promise I won't drag you along if I need to do dangerous things."

Rory looked hurt. "Last fall wasn't so bad. Pretty exciting, to be honest."

"That's because it turned out okay in the end. It could easily have gone wrong several different ways."

"I guess."

"Texting you okay?"

"Yes."

"Outstanding. I'll call you Jimmy, Jimmy Olsen. I'll be Clark, Clark Kent. Just to confuse anyone nosing around."

Rory smiled and finished his coffee. "I sense life is about to get interesting."

Robert nodded but remained silent.

Robert made his way back to the townhouse. Only his son was in, so he searched through the freezer for something, finally locating a container of meatballs at the bottom he had put together a month earlier. There was no sign of Sandra or Sophie. "Looks like it's just us guys tonight. If you can find some pasta, I'll get this stuff heated up." Robin looked happy as he opened the pantry. Robert checked his landline, but there were no messages. He supposed that Robins' shop teacher had more than one parent chasing him, so patience would be required.

***

It wasn't until late Sunday afternoon that Robert received a call from Bernard. "Robert?"

"Yes, how is Bernard?"

"Not sure. I've been warned off. The questions about the law firm? Not well received, apparently. I haven't been attacked this time, but the threat was there. I'm not sure that doing any research for you is very healthy. Know what I mean?"

Robert was silent, thinking back to when Bernard had had his arm smashed due to unwelcome questions.

"You there?"

"Thinking, Bernard. Who did you have asking the questions? I'm assuming it wasn't you directly."

"My government contact in Victoria. I've used him before."

"And?"

"He didn't know the guy talking to him, only that he wasn't pleasant, kind of thug-like and large. The contact let the guy know that it was the CBC doing the asking. Didn't give up my name, however. At least, that's what he told me."

"I'm thinking that you can stop. I'll go about this in another way. Thanks, Bernard." He stayed on the line, knowing Bernard would now be stressed at possibly being left out of the coming action and stories.

"But ...."

"Worried, Bernard?"

"Yes."

"Taipan Construction. Try them per my email. Let me know. I'll be in contact." Robert hung up.

He considered dinner. Sandra was working an afternoon fundraiser at a hotel downtown, not due home until much later. He polled his children for ideas. They voted for burgers, and the weather was very burger friendly, so it looked like a grilling night. He fortunately had the ingredients in the freezer, so all that was needed was to assemble the fixings. He included everything he could find in the fridge, from bacon, cheese, and pickles, to lettuce, mushrooms, and a tomato. There was barely room for the burger patty in the bun after all the extras were added. They disappeared quickly.

Sandra came in the front door after being dropped off by a taxi, after eight. "Hey Robert, I'm exhausted." She dropped her bag and made for the couch. "Turns out that I am the senior person in this outfit. I'm spending half my time showing the others what to do and how to do it." She grimaced. "Not exactly what I thought I was signing on for, but it's okay. The staff are nice, just green, neon green."

"Drink?"

"Read my mind. Wine if there is any open, thanks." After Robert slipped her a glass, she continued, "Speaking of wine, it looks like I'm going to be heading up a little expedition to the interior, wine country."

"What for?"

"We are catering at a winery just north of Oliver in

mid-June. Annual summer party for a Vancouver law firm, SM & M or something."

"Say again?"

"We're doing a summer shindig."

Robert cut her off. "No, I mean the firm's name, what is it?"

"Skyler, M and M something, not sure. I wasn't listening to that part."

"I think that's the firm I am trying to get information about. They are behind the lawsuits that BC Coastal Insurance has been named in."

"So, you are interested, correct?"

"I would say so."

"Good, because I was going to ask if you wanted to come to Oliver with me." She smiled.

"That is a one hundred percent yes. Have you ever been to the Okanagan?"

"No."

"Neither have I, oddly. What is the winery's name?"

"Possession Point, I believe."

"Really? That name is something out of Hong Kong's past, from when the British staked a claim to the island in the eighteen hundreds. Odd name for a winery in Oliver."

"You spent time in Hong Kong, correct?"

"As a kid, yes." Robert started to think. "Do you require any additional help out there?"

"You mean as part of the team?"

"Exactly."

"Hmm. I know you clean up well. How about being one of the servers?"

"I believe I could do that flawlessly."

"It is a distinct possibility. I've already heard some pushback from a couple of staff about going all that way. I'll let you know this week. Of course, if you do a good job, you may be able to get on permanent." Sandra smiled.

Robert grinned back. "Good pay?"

"Not really."

He shook his head. "Thanks for the offer."

Monday morning, Robert called the auto club. They promised someone would show up inside an hour, which was good. Taking a bus over to the fourth victim's residence would be harrowing. He assumed the technician would get his car going. He had only heard good things about the people tasked with bringing cars back to life, but perhaps he was being overly optimistic. Sandra was home, taking her time getting out of bed. He was nursing a third cup of coffee when his front doorbell rang.

Robert answered the door and sent the young man around to the lane, where he met him, pointing out the wayward vehicle. He handed over his keys and went back inside, not really wanting to hear about the finer points of automobile wizardry. He was studying his laptop, a half-hour later, when he heard a rap on the rear door. He opened it, waiting for the judgment.

The man studied Robert. "When was the last time you

had this serviced, mate?" He could have just disembarked off a boat from Yorkshire.

"Don't remember."

"Sounds about right. There seems to be a couple of things wrong here. I won't be getting this going for you today. You have a shop we can tow this to?"

"Not really. I'll have to do some looking," Robert responded.

"No worries, let us know and we'll arrange the towing for you. Cheerio, mate." With that, he handed a sheet of paper to Robert and got back into his service truck. He slowly drove away, leaving Robert standing in the lane, cursing silently to himself as he studied the diagnosis given to him. He returned inside, thought, 'Screw the bus', called a taxi, then yelled a goodbye up to Sandra.

Twenty minutes later, Robert found himself in front of a short four-storey apartment block on Pender Street, east of Commercial Drive, at the address of the labourer whose lawsuit had been settled before going to court. The area looked slightly more orderly in comparison to Strathcona, but light-years from the money of the West Side. The victim's name was Li Hong Lam. Robert assumed whoever answered the door, if anyone, would be less guarded given that the suit had concluded, with money in their pockets. He buzzed the number and waited.

"Hello, who is this?"

Robert went right to Cantonese. "Robert Lui, representing an insurance company to do with Hong Lam's accident."

"What do you want?"

"I'd just like to talk with you about the case, if possible. Are you related to Hong Lam?" Robert sensed this was bordering on another strikeout.

"I am his father." Silence ensued. Robert was about to give up when the man relented. "You may come in. It is suite 205." The door hummed. Robert quickly grabbed it, hardly believing his luck. Perhaps the man sensed more money might be on offer. He walked in, ignored the elevator and headed to one of the exit stairs.

After knocking on the suite door, he waited. He could hear thumps and a mild curse just before the door opened. A thin man stood in the doorway, mid-fifties, wearing an older dress shirt that had once been white, with worn grey slacks. His shirtsleeves were rolled up. Various items were strewn across the floor behind him.

"Please come in. Sorry for the mess. I am packing up my son's things." He extended his hand. "My name is Alvin."

"Robert Lui. Please accept my condolences to you on your loss."

"Thank you. What is it you wish to know?"

"Where are you going?"

"I am returning to Hong Kong. There is nothing here for me. Hong Lam lived for eighteen months in this apartment before his accident. I do not like it here. There is a bad feeling to this place."

"Perhaps because of your loss." Robert wasn't used to hearing dislike spoken of his city.

Alvin shrugged.

"I only have a few questions. Could we sit?"

"I am sorry, of course. Come in." He led to way to a

small wooden dining table with two robin's egg blue plastic chairs.

Tea or coffee wasn't offered, so Robert started in. "I understand that your lawsuit was settled before going to court."

"Yes."

"Dare I ask how much you were able to end up with?" It was very nosy to be asking this, but Robert felt he had nothing to lose by trying.

"Just under two hundred thousand dollars, Canadian. A lot of money for our family."

Robert's eyes widened. "But the settlement was for eight hundred thousand, wasn't it?"

"Yes. Lawyers told us this was normal fee for their work. They said they would charge us nothing if they were unsuccessful."

Robert's eyes widened. He literally had to bite his tongue to prevent giving his opinion about the lawyer's fee. He wasn't even sure if it was legal.

"Did you get any outside advice before you signed the agreement?"

"No. The lawyer in Hong Kong handled it."

"Is this how the law firm was hired here? Through Hong Kong?"

"Yes. They called me. They also handled immigration issues for Hong Lam to come to Vancouver."

Robert was silent, thinking about what a godsend it was having an all-in-one legal firm, so tidy. "Were you given any more information as to how your son had his accident?"

Alvin shrugged again. "Nothing." He stared at Robert. "What are you doing here again?"

"The insurance company I work for was one of the entities that added money to the settlement fee, and they wish to know that everything was above board."

"Above board?"

"That your son's accident was really an accident and not something else."

"What do you mean?"

"I am not certain yet, which is why I am asking questions. You are not the only one who has suffered a loss through construction activities recently."

Alvin remained silent but looked puzzled.

"Did Hong Lam visit you in Hong Kong while he was working here?"

"I know he came back twice, because he called me, but I didn't see him. He said he was too busy."

"That sounds odd. Was it?"

"Yes. I thought so. He said it would soon be all over, and then he would be back home and spend time with us."

"What would be over?"

"I don't know."

"Do you have the name of the legal firm in Hong Kong that was so helpful?"

"I believe it was something like Mc something, a British name."

"McDouguld?"

"Could be."

Wow, a double godsend. What luck to have a Hong Kong firm possibly related to a Vancouver firm! Robert couldn't immediately think of anything else to ask, so he asked for Alvin's contact information. He wrote his down as well on a small pad of paper Alvin produced, no cards to give out as yet.

"He had such hopes for coming to Gold Mountain." The weariness in Alvin's eyes spoke of a grief yet to be worked through. "But it wasn't to be."

"Moving to a new country is never easy, even with all the promises. Thanks very much for talking with me, Alvin. Safe travels with your return to Hong Kong. I must tell you that something doesn't sound right about this whole affair. I may be in contact again sooner than you might think." Robert rose, left the apartment, and grabbed his phone out of his shirt pocket to order a cab back to Inverness Street.

As he entered his townhouse, something came to him. The picture of Alvin packing finally triggered a question. The first basement suite he visited, Andy Ho's, had no suitcase of any kind. The suite was missing many things, but one would think that a traveller to Vancouver would need a bag of sorts. He was pretty sure it wouldn't have been buried with Andy, so what happened to it? He needed another talk with the nosy neighbour. But what he really needed was a car that worked, or this whole enterprise would quickly become very painful. He also wanted to talk with the woman in Richmond, Alice, to see whether her family was the recipient of the same fabulous fee deal that Alvin had. Maybe talk to her about suitcases.

Robert rummaged through his fridge for something to make lunch out of, eventually finding some smoked ham, a half-eaten block of sharp cheddar, and lettuce. Adding some condiments, he fashioned a sandwich, and as he sat at the table eating, he realized he should find out if the CBC tech whose son had seen something was up for a conversation.

He finished up and made a call. "Bernard, it's Robert. Is your camera tech around today? Would he talk to me?"

"I saw him earlier, so I'll get back to you, okay?"

"Roger." As he ended the call, his landline rang. It was the shop teacher from his son's school. After some back and forth, the teacher mollified Robert's concerns about Robin's upcoming employment, somewhat.

Robert had a thought before ending the call, "My car has been certified as dead by the auto club. You wouldn't know of a repair place that I could send it to, do you?"

"There's a place on Frances Street, Ricky's, that I can vouch for. They're straight shooters, and I think they work on any type of car."

"Thanks for the tip." He hung up and thought back to the previous fall when a dead policeman had been discovered in a body shop on Frances. Also, not exactly the land of high-end vehicles, but then, the Silver Streak was extremely short on pedigree. He had decided that for now, fixing his car had to be cheaper than getting a newer one, didn't it?

He called Ricky's, warning them of impending incoming, then dialled up the auto club to get the towing done. He felt good, like he was accomplishing things, even if they weren't directly related to his case.

He was drinking another cup of coffee, after his car had been picked up, when his cell rang.

"Robert? It's Bernard, the tech will talk with you. His name is Jay Brown. Can you come by this afternoon? He hasn't notified the police as yet."

"I'll be over shortly."

He grumbled to himself as he reached for his cell to call another cab. Perhaps he had been taking his car for granted, a mistake apparently. He went out his front door and as he waited, he texted 'Jimmy Olsen' about looking into the law firm with the all-encompassing skillset, SM & M. He added something about taking care while doing it if he valued his safety.

Twenty minutes later, he got out of his taxi on Hamilton Street in the downtown core, searching for the entry into the CBC fortress across from the main library. The building was less forbidding now, after an enlightened renovation, but he still had problems finding the front door. Once inside, he naturally didn't get very far, having to wait for Bernard to come fetch him. The plump security guard standing just inside the door appraised Robert. Robert returned the stare, not blinking. The guard looked away after a moment.

Bernard came and took him for a few twists and turns, finally entering a small boardroom. The sole occupant stood up. Jay Brown, Robert assumed. Worried eyes stared out from behind 'granny' glasses, his portly body clad in jeans and a lavender checked shirt.

"Fill him in?"

"About you?" Bernard asked.

Robert nodded as he sat. "You have a tale to tell, I understand."

"I can trust you?"

"To do what? Look, I have my own kids." He did not want to be thought of as some kind of saviour.

Jay looked less than impressed by the short speech but started, "My son, Sam, says he saw a man push that unfortunate worker off a tower last week. Sam's sick at home, trying to overcome that virus thing, so he hasn't been to school and told anyone else, to my knowledge."

"Keep it that way for now. May I talk with him?"

"I guess."

"How old?"

"Ten."

"I'm not with the police anymore. I know two detectives at the VPD that I'd trust with my life, but that's as far as it goes. If you went there and told your story, they'd promise your son would be protected and no one would need to know who he was. Then they'd tell you your son could testify anonymously if there was a court case and there'd be no danger to him. Not sure that's totally correct. You've done the correct thing, so far as your family goes." He didn't have the heart to explain to Jay that he had screwed that up when he told Bernard about the incident. But life sometimes presented those unpleasant choices when the correct course of action was murky at best.

Jay's eyes started to water slightly but he didn't reply. Bernard remained motionless.

"So, when can we do this?" Robert asked.

"I want to be present. How about tomorrow evening at our home?"

"Okay. Address?"

On the way out, Robert raised his brows at Bernard. "Be in touch."

He needed to talk with Vito. He left a text and made his way home. He had just walked into his home when the cell rang.

"Robert?"

"Vito. The diving incident. Do you have any photos of people from the site, preferably from the floor in question? I am going to talk with the kid tomorrow."

"I'll see what I can find. I believe there was only one other person on that floor."

"Guess that'd be the pusher then."

"Likely, if that's what really happened." Vito hung up, and Robert then realized it'd come down to an adult's word against a kid's.

After the call, Robert ruminated on all the sticks he had in the fire, deciding one more wouldn't hurt. He texted Rory again, asking him to also look into Possession Point Winery. That done, it was dinner ideas time. He didn't feel particularly inventive this evening, so he hauled a couple bags of frozen tortellini from the freezer and looked for something green in the vegetable drawer, eventually finding an English cucumber in reasonable shape hiding at the bottom. Sandra was due in after six, and the kids were home looking hungry, so he set to work. A quick check on the sage out back confirmed his idea of butter, garlic and sage for a simple pasta sauce. Sage took a while to get going every summer, but fresh shoots had started, helped along by the warm weather.

As dinner wound down, Robert looked Robin in the eyes. "We're going to take a site visit next week. I talked with your shop teacher, but I want to check this contractor out for myself."

Robin's eyes widened as hope crept back for his summer job idea. "Sounds good, Pops." Sandra nodded in approval.

The next day, Robert remained carless, so he went for a run, thinking about his upcoming talk with Jay's son. Ten years old, he'd need to tone it back a bit. He also could use information on the victim before the interview. Was he another Chinese labourer? If this kept up, construction in Vancouver was going to nose into the lead as the most dangerous job in the world. The weather was holding as he loped along, but white stripes in the southeast sky heralded doom, or maybe just rain.

When he returned home, he showered, then called Ricky's on the off chance that his car might be ready. The phone guy yelled at someone, then returned, "You can pick it up after three today."

"Fantastic. What's the damage?"

After Robert was read the itemized list of work and parts, he almost choked at the total.

"But you've only had the car for a little over a day!"

"It was very sick, meester Robert."

The newer car idea suddenly sounded much better,

but too late, and there was no point in arguing about the price now. "Okay, I'll come by then." He hung up, not without a curse or two afterwards. Ricky might be a straight shooter, but apparently warning someone before performing the work wasn't in his operating manual.

Robert put this out of his mind and made a cup of coffee to help him reflect on reasons for construction labourers' unexpected run of bad luck. If they were being murdered, something desperate must be at work. After all, these incidents were very public.

His cell rang. "Vito here, think we could meet this afternoon? I have some photos, and I'd like to hear your thoughts on all this. Paulo's?"

"After four. I need to pick up my car from the hospital first." Robert responded.

"Nothing terminal, I hope."

"We'll see. You might have to pay for the coffees though."

"As bad as that then." Vito ended the call.

After Robert reluctantly paid his invoice inside the car shop, he was led out to the Silver Streak. It was sitting in the back lane close to a giant dumpster, as though another solution had been contemplated for it. He got in, adjusted the seat and tried the engine. It started immediately, no groaning, and he had to admit, sounded like a sewing machine, pretty sweet. At least it took the edge off the size of the bill. He reckoned Ricky could now take a nice vacation pretty much wherever he fancied.

He shook his head, shifted into drive and headed over to Cambie Street, admiring the engine's smoothness the entire way. The sky had darkened, wind whipping pieces of paper and coffee cups around on the streets as spots of water landed on his front windshield. Because he no longer rated a stall at the VPD headquarters, he scrounged around for a street spot and paid, something he hated to do on principle. He longed for the days when street parking was mostly free, and it wasn't the only thing he missed about the 'good old days'.

Robert walked into Cafe Paulo and yelled his greeting to Gilberto, who looked up in surprise. "You're back, Roberto! I knew it. Just a matter of time."

Robert beamed. "Only visiting, Gilberto, I'm afraid, but good to see you."

Gilberto nodded his head in Vito's direction, who was sitting at the back, watching the interaction. "Vito's waiting."

"Roberto," Vito said. "You really are a minor celebrity here, I'll say that for you, even after the time away."

"Just minor?"

Vito smiled and pointed to the counter where Carmelita had placed two Americanos. It seemed that Robert was now expected to be the gofer. Things changed, he supposed.

He returned with the steaming mugs. "How is Vito?"

"Good, but these construction things are starting to take on a life." He reached into his sport jacket and pulled out some three by five photos. Robert leafed through them. The last one appeared to be a representative of the Cro-Magnon family with a narrow head.

"Thought this line of evolution died out a good while back."

Vito smiled. "Guess not. This is the guy who was working on the floor with Jackson Wong. I've given you a few others to show the kid. Don't lead him, of course."

"So, the diver was Chinese then?"

"Yup. New to Canada. From Hong Kong."

"Maybe you should post someone at the airport and get these guys to do an about-turn when they clear customs. Warn them that life may be short in Gold Mountain."

"Gold Mountain?"

"Chinese name for this relatively new city/country we live in." They each took a small sip from their mugs.

"Wanna know what I think?" Robert asked.

Vito nodded, so Robert started in. "Drugs."

Vito looked at him thoughtfully. "Adds up, I suppose."

"As stupid as it sounds, it makes sense to me. I've found out that a couple of the deceased labourers made trips back to Hong Kong without explanation. Family there didn't know what they were doing, no contact. What else would they be up to? Don't think they're bringing back dim sum, there's plenty of that here already."

Vito didn't say anything.

"Maybe you could check with Donovan," Robert said, suggesting contact with the drug squad.

"Those assholes? I generally avoid them. If drugs are coming in that way, wouldn't be surprising to find some in their lockers or homes, ready for resale. But I also heard there were a couple of sharp increases in product recently, with no real explanation."

"If it's our labourers, wouldn't the airport sniffers find the stuff?"

"You'd think."

"I'll see if I can find out dates for a couple of their trips. Maybe we can match something up." Robert suggested. He drank some coffee, staring vacantly at the remaining customers. "Do those dogs sniff every last bag?"

"No idea."

"I need to do some re-visiting to the victim's families. I'll keep you posted, Vito."

Vito sipped at his mug. "So, how are you and Sandra?"

"Best thing that's happened to me in a long time."

"Any gang relatives come over for a visit or dinner?"

"Fuck off." He smiled. "I am visiting the kid tonight. Ten years old. We'll see what he's made of, but I don't really want to put him in the VPD's clutches. At least until we know more."

Vito nodded in agreement, checking the action on the street outside.

"How is Thomas?" Robert asked.

"Good. Leaves us alone mostly. I think he misses you."

Robert laughed. "That is touching." Then, "Really?"

"He would never say it, but that's what I think."

"I should get going. I'll be in touch about tonight. Always good to see you, Vito." The wind had died down. A steady patter of rain was bouncing off the sidewalk — Vancouver's natural state. Robert stepped out of the cafe, blinking at the raindrops, then headed for his refurbished ride.

Robert nosed into his carport and, putting the gear in neutral, revved the engine a couple of times, then cut the power. He smiled to himself. He walked into the kitchen, where Sandra was doing something culinary. "Car back?" She asked.

"Hundred and ten percent, and it should be for what I paid."

She moved over and kissed him slowly, languidly. He wrapped his arms around her, holding tightly. He was so happy that he made a tactical error.

He had his head buried in her hair, inhaling her scent. "Would you, Sandra Kour, consider marrying a man such as myself?" She pulled back a bit, eyes wide. For a second Robert was mortified that he had done what he had done, sure of being rejected, then her face lit up as she said, "Wait 'til I tell my mom."

As they kissed, holding each other tightly as they circled the kitchen, Robert's brain restarted, and he realized how complicated the whole affair could become. He hadn't thought this through, that was obvious. His intended had a family, and the family had a gang connection, a fairly famous one at that. A vision of Sandra walking down the aisle under crossed rifles came to him, gang members on one side of the aisle, police officers on the other. He was also unsure if he deserved this kind of joy. Then he realized that he had no ring. Oops.

A while back, an acquaintance of his on the force had buggered off to a Vegas chapel with his betrothed to tie the knot, officiated by Elvis. At the time, Robert considered it a trifle flaky to be celebrating something important that way. It didn't sound so bad now. Maybe he could convince Sandra that eloping would be ultra-romantic. As he contemplated how to do this, he watched as Sandra texted her mother on her cell. Looked like the elopement train was already speeding out of the station, without any passengers aboard.

"Sandra, that really wasn't how I intended to do this."

She looked up and grinned. "I suspected as much. It doesn't matter to me. I am so happy!"

"We should do a meal out somewhere to celebrate this."

"Where, Robert? Where do they cook better than us?"

"Nowhere? At least not many places, I'd guess. Okay, let's think about it at least. And I'll start a search for a ring. What are you doing here?" He spied potatoes sitting next to eggs on the chopping board.

Sandra stepped back and gestured with her palms up at the counter. "*Salade Niçoise*. It is almost summer after all."

"*Tres bien*."

"Wine?"

"No, you go ahead. I have to go out after dinner to talk to a child about something he saw. Maybe when I get back."

After dinner concluded and Robert had filled the dishwasher, he took his leave. "I may do some driving around on my way back, try to get my money's worth out of the day."

Sandra shook her head gently, still smiling at what had

transpired before they had eaten. "I won't wait up then. But I also won't be asleep, Robert."

Robert rolled up to Jay Brown's house on the north side of East 43rd Avenue. Beyond it rose a concrete tower topped by the standard construction crane. The tower in question. He walked slowly up painted concrete steps to the front door of an older but well-maintained home clad in stone dash stucco with taupe-coloured trim boards. Grass edges trimmed perfectly. It looked utterly like every other home on the block, built in the sixties — one storey with a basement half out of the ground.

He knocked, and the door opened quickly, startling him. A middle-aged woman dressed in dark slacks and a tangerine blouse stood there, alone. Her head sported a dark beehive hairdo that came straight out of the fifties. Robert figured she had spent a good half-can of workable fixative on the affair. The only thing missing was a pair of those wacky catseye glasses. And she had obviously been standing in the entry hall, waiting for his arrival.

"Please come in. I am Juanita, Rex's mother." She smiled uncertainly, her eyes heavily made up.

"Happy to meet you." He stepped into the entry hall. "Rex?"

"Samuel likes to be called Rex, after his favourite dinosaur. He is our only child," she added, just so he knew the stakes.

Nothing like a little added pressure, Robert thought. "Where can we talk?"

"Please have a seat in the living room and I'll go get him." Robert followed her pointing finger and saw Jay already sitting in the corner by a fireplace, shifting nervously in his chair. He was wearing a checked shirt similar to yesterday's. Today, going with orange. Maybe he had purchased a pallet-load of them from the local big-box store. Robert nodded at Jay and sat.

A moment later, Samuel walked in, followed closely by Juanita. He wore glasses and had a mask over his mouth but, unlike his father, was quite thin. He studied Robert intently before sitting next to him on the sofa.

"How are you, Rex? Pleased to finally meet you. My name is Robert."

Sam beamed at having his name recognized. Robert glanced over at Jay. He didn't seem quite as happy.

"I hear you have a bit of a story to tell." Robert opened.

Sam squirmed a bit, unsure how to start, Robert assumed. "I don't have much to tell you. This guy pushed the other guy off the tower. I saw him do it."

Robert nodded. "That is what I heard. Where were you when you saw this? Outside?"

"Nope. In my room. I've been sick, so I watch the building from my bedroom. It is interesting to see it go up."

"Sounds like you might want to do something in construction when you get older, am I right?"

Sam nodded vigorously. "I've been thinking about it."

"Could you show me where you watch from? If your parents don't mind, that is." Robert looked over at Jay, then

Juanita. They both gave their assent, apparently satisfied with how the conversation was going. Robert rose and followed Sam into his bedroom. He pointed to his desk against the window. Robert went over, picked up the binoculars sitting amongst a menagerie of plastic dinosaurs and looked out at the tower. He raised them to inspect the top, which was lit up by the setting sun. After adjusting them, everything was in sharp focus. If Jackson Wong had gone off the south side, then little Sam indeed had a front-row seat. Robert stood there a moment but couldn't think of anything further to ask at the moment. "Thanks, Rex. You've been helpful. I'm just going to have a word with your parents before I go." Sam remained in his room, picking up a book.

Robert returned to the living area, sitting back down on the sofa. "Your son seems to have taken this event in and handled it okay. What do you think? Some people might suffer through a few nightmares over seeing something like that, particularly a child."

Jay stared at Juanita. She spoke. "Well, it seems so. I agree. So far anyway."

"That's good for Sam. Until we see what is really going on here, keeping quiet is paramount, I believe."

There was silence while the parents digested this. "What are you going to do?" Jay finally asked.

"Not sure yet. Possibly nothing. It is going to be Sam's word against an adult's as to what happened. The police may get this guy to crack, but if not, then a decent lawyer would probably run roughshod over your son, even with a judge trying to rein it in." He paused. "But on the other hand, if he goes back to school, he'll likely eventually tell someone even if he's told not to. It's just nature. Does he have his own cell phone?"

"No, not yet," Jay answered.

Robert realized he had forgotten about the photos. "Can I show Samuel some pictures to see if he can identify the guy in question?"

Jay shrugged. He called his son back into the room.

"Rex, these are some pictures of construction site people. I'd like to see if you can pick out the guy who did the pushing."

Sam looked at the pictures Robert laid out on the coffee table in a row, but didn't hesitate, picking out the Cro-Magnon labourer. "Yup, that's him. He's kind of ugly."

"Rex, you shouldn't say things like that." Juanita looked embarrassed.

Robert stood up, his chest aching. He gathered the photos, placing them back into his jacket. "I'll be in touch at some point through Bernard. Thanks, Jay, Juanita. Again, nice to meet you, Rex."

Robert left and got back into his newly refurbished car, thought about a short drive around town to savour its performance, but instead headed home and a rendezvous with his intended and a whisky. The car could wait.

That same evening, Bernard Lily drove towards his home in Burnaby after getting off work at eight but continued past his building to a local park where he was to meet someone. He had just been able to scrape enough together to buy the one-bedroom apartment in a lowbrow building located in a good neighbourhood. It was a financial stretch, but his job at the CBC looked as secure as anything could be these days, which wasn't very.

A woman had called him at work earlier in the day, furtive, voice low as though she was being listened to. She had a tale to tell, on background, of course, like ninety percent of the stories these days. The number she called from was blocked to Bernard. He couldn't not find out what this was about, so he acquiesced.

He saw the park ahead, slowed and rolled to a stop on the verge. The place was deserted. He looked across and someone who appeared to be behind the baseball backstop. A darkening forest lay close behind the steel mesh. He got out of his car and stood in place, undecided. Could this be another ambush? He shook his head. Time to act like the professional he was striving to become.

The grass was squishy as he made his slow way across the diamond. It wasn't doing his best loafers any favours. As he rounded the chain-link fencing, he could see that this woman appeared to be on the large size. It didn't fit the voice. The person had their back to him. He closed the gap and the person turned. It was a man wearing a dark hoodie. His lower face was covered by a blue mask, one of those virus masks. An aluminum baseball bat dangled loosely from his right hand. Bernard felt ill. He knew what was coming. He looked around for help. There was no one in sight. Should he run?

"You've been asking questions in Victoria. Who for?"

"How did you get my name?"

The man raised the bat, came closer and tapped Bernard's left arm.

"I'm doing the asking. If you can't tell me, I'll re-arrange some of your limbs, no charge."

Bernard stupidly tried to be brave. "I am a reporter for the CBC. It's what we do, ask questions."

The bat came at him so quickly, he didn't have time to move. He heard a crack as his left forearm was slammed into his hip. He yelled, then sucked in a breath. The pain was bad, then it got worse. The man swung the bat into his thigh. Bernard went down, bouncing off the backstop, whimpering.

"Excuse me? I can't hear what you're saying." He swung back and hit Bernard again on the upper arm, another crack. Bernard groaned, realizing he was going to be killed. "Robert. Robert Lui. That is who I am asking for." The words came out in a gasp, spittle drooling down the side of his cheek onto the gravel. He should have tried to run while the chance was there.

"Wasn't so hard after all, was it?" The man finally turned and walked away, leaving Bernard shaking on the ground. He turned his head, watching his assailant stroll nonchalantly back across the baseball diamond. His breathing calmed slightly as he realized two good facts. One, he wasn't dead, and two, he was correct about his assessment of Robert. There was obviously a story here. One perhaps he no longer wanted to pursue. He groaned as he tried to stand up. Then he reached for his cell with his good arm.

CHAPTER
NINE

Robert woke up the next morning and, reaching over, cupped one of Sandra's breasts, teasing the nipple, gently coaxing her from sleep. The bedside clock indicated that his children should be well away to school, leaving the adults to do whatever they found pleasurable, which was a lot. An hour later, Robert reluctantly remembered that his work to-do list was full and that maybe he should get on it. He was finishing up showering when he heard his cell ringing from the bedroom.

Sandra looked over at the night table and answered, "Hi, Robert is busy, can I take a message?"

"It's Bernard. In the hospital again, Burnaby General. Could you ask Robert to call?" His voice was low.

"What happened?"

"I'd prefer to talk to Robert directly."

"I'll tell him."

As Robert came out of the ensuite, naked, Sandra smiled, then delivered the news. "Your Bernard friend called. He's in Burnaby General."

Robert's skin on his neck tightened, not from the cold. "What's he doing there?"

"Sounded like he's a patient. You'd better call him."

Craps, craps, craps. This wasn't good. He got dressed in a hurry, went downstairs and called Bernard using his landline. "It's Robert. What happened?"

"Two for two, Robert. Got beaten again. And I had to give up your name, or I likely wouldn't be talking to you right now."

"Where?"

"A baseball diamond in a Burnaby park. The guy only had a bat, no glove. I had neither."

"Jeez, Bernard, I had no idea this would be dangerous. But then, I think I've said this to you before, haven't I?"

"Well, guess I was correct. There is a story here, isn't there?"

"Seems so. When do you get out of there?"

"Today, I think. My left arm this time, broken upper and lower bones. Hit my thigh as well, but only deep bruising. Good thing there are drugs. Would you mind doing me a favour?"

Robert could hardly refuse. "Anything."

"My car is still at the park. Could you come get me so I can pick it up? I can still drive, sort of, I hope." He didn't sound totally certain to Robert, but Bernard was young — he could do it. Plus, Bernard was now a veteran as far as this type of treatment went. Robert was sure he'd manage.

"Call me when you are being discharged."

Time for a call to his boss, but first coffee, so he could cogently organize his thoughts. But even before this, he texted 'Jimmy Olsen' telling him again to exercise maximum caution in his work. He'd explain soonest.

He yelled to the upper floor. "Sandra. Want coffee?" A muffled yes came back, so he proceeded to make extra. As he waited for his toast, he realized that this all seemed to be about money. Perhaps a lot of money. There were the lawsuits with the highly imbalanced fees favouring a certain downtown law firm. And there was possible drug running, with again, more money involved. And violence, maybe murder after what Rex had said. His thoughts ran to his old job and what the VPD were making of all this, if anything. If it was murder, why? Was someone cleaning up?

The aroma of toast and coffee drew Sandra into the kitchen. She came over and hugged Robert. "Do we have to go anywhere today?"

"Good question. Maybe, maybe not. Bernard got attacked last evening, a few broken bones. I feel responsible, so I'll be getting him from the hospital at some point, but really, other than that ...." Then he added, "And I've got to call my boss, fill him in on all the bad stuff happening. But that can be later, Sandra. You didn't make the bed, did you, after you got up?"

"No, Robert, and it's still warm."

"Excellent. You don't need to go in?"

"No."

"Then we should work 'from bed' today." Robert hugged Sandra tightly, then both sat as they drank coffee rather quickly, gazing at each other across the table. It was all they could do to finish their toast. They ran upstairs like teenagers, shedding their recently donned clothing as they went, Robert's problems forgotten for the moment.

Much later, Robert felt weakened but rose and showered again. Was this how Rome fell? People making love all day long while the mobs howled? He hadn't heard from Bernard, so he called his employer after dressing for the second time this day.

"Dan speaking."

"It's Robert. I have much to tell you." After he had finished the rather lengthy monologue, there was silence. Robert waited.

"I can't believe this. We are being chased by shonky lawyers?"

"Maybe. And there could be murder in the air. Which would make their legal claims extremely suspect."

"Evidence. That's what we need. What are Vancouver's finest doing about all this?"

"They seem slow. I've given them a few clues, but I'll find out and maybe do more hinting for them. Then there's the violence. I thought when I came to work for you, I had left all that behind, Dan." It was almost an accusation. But then, the previous time he had done things for Dan's company, bad karma had attached itself like a virus. He wasn't going to ask for danger pay, but it sure felt owed.

"I think, in the interim we may not be part of any more deals out of court."

"Wise move. I have some people to see again. More

questions. And oh yeah, I've found a computer person. I'll use him as a consultant, so to speak."

"Do I want to know about this person?"

"You do not. Just pay the invoices, please."

There was silence, then, "Be careful, Robert."

Robert couldn't have said it any better. Care would be needed, as someone now knew his name. A hint of worry nagged at him, but he was also hungry. The morning had given him a raging appetite. Sandra came into the kitchen just as he hung up. She looked famished as well.

"Eggs?" Robert asked.

"Omelettes?"

"I'll do them." Robert pulled the items from the fridge, then went outside to cut some chives from the patio herb collection. He briefly fretted, knowing some chefs judged a person's culinary skills by how well they made an omelette, and this was his first time doing it for Sandra. Well, he could only do his best, and hope approval followed.

His cell rang. Bernard, for sure. He answered.

"Clark Kent?"

"Yes, Jimmy?"

"We should meet. End of day, same place?"

"See you there."

Half an hour later, they finished eating. "Not bad, for an ex-cop. Too bad you broke it in half getting it onto the plate. D minus for presentation."

Robert shook his head. "Taste?"

"A."

"I try." Robert gathered the dishes, then his cell rang.

"Robert?" The voice quivered.

"Meds wearing off, Bernard?"

"Maybe. I'm being released."

"Be right over. Half an hour or so. Gotta figure out where you are first." Robert checked his computer, located the hospital, then looked over at Sandra. "You drive, right?"

"I think I already told you I do."

"Come on. You can help. We're rescuing Bernard and his car for him, and I really doubt if he could keep it in a straight line today."

After the pickup, the car retrieval and before Bernard got out of the car, Robert asked what he had told the authorities when they had shown up the previous day.

Bernard grimaced. "I told them I had hit a dinger and was rounding third, heading for home when I tripped and broke my arm."

"They buy it?"

"Not for a second. Said no one wears loafers when they play baseball. I have to admit, they got me right there, but I didn't elaborate. That there were no other people or equipment anywhere near the diamond didn't help my story. They had a few more snarky comments but didn't ask anything further."

"Cops show up? Or just the medics."

"Ambulance only." Just before he turned away, "Robert, I don't want anymore of your 'this is what career memories are made of' crap. Now both of my arms ache. I'm done with your questions, understand? Completely."

"Heat of the moment, Bernard. Get some rest, you've

earned it." Robert was expecting this type of reaction. He watched as Bernard entered his lobby, then he headed home with Sandra. "I need to meet my new consultant at the Apollo. I'm going to walk over. You seemed to drive fine today. Didn't hit anything. That's always good."

They drove into the carport. "Like a bicycle, I suppose, you don't forget. Think I could borrow the car for my Surrey trip?" Sandra asked.

"Right now?"

She nodded. "I should go while my skills are still razor sharp, don't you think?"

"I guess. Be careful, please."

"See you in a while. I'll dream up something for dinner when I return."

Robert headed west, not in a hurry this time. He hoped Rory had something interesting. He needed something, anything, to help explain what was going on. When Robert entered the cafe, Rory had yet to arrive, so he ordered an Americano and sat at the rear, back against the wall, waiting. He watched a young couple enter, both dressed in ripped black items, hair streaks of white and black. Robert couldn't discern if it was the going style or a lack of money. As he studied them, a large man followed them in, dusty work clothes, large boots, tan overalls and a ripped denim shirt. His eyes strayed across the cafe, lingering a second too long on Robert. Robert tensed. Bernard's baseball incident was having an effect. The man looked back at the barista, who had asked him something.

Then Robert's order was called out. He went to the counter, keeping his eye on the worker the entire time. As he picked up his cup, Rory entered, nodding at him.

"What'll you have, Rory?"

"Same as you." Order completed, they returned to Robert's table. The worker left the cafe with his coffee.

Rory studied Robert's face. "What's with all the warnings?"

"Minor violence on a consultant working for me."

"That's a new term."

"Just a broken arm, not killed or anything like that. Well, a couple of fractures, actually. I had a journalist asking questions about our law firm before I got you involved. Didn't seem to turn out well in the end."

"Oh."

"And now someone knows it's me doing the asking."

"Double oh."

Robert took a sip from his cup as Rory's order was called out. He fetched his cup, returned and sat down, facing Robert. "Didn't they teach you not to sit with your back to a door?" Robert asked.

"Well, maybe. Are you serious?"

"I would be practising extreme care going forward if I were you. So, what have you found out?"

Rory shifted his chair around, so he was sideways to the entry. "I tried to enter the computer system at SM & M and found something odd. It is protected as well as the U.S. Mint."

"And how would Rory know what the U.S. Mint is protected like?"

Rory shrugged.

"Were you a tourist there?"

Rory remained silent.

"So, you couldn't get in?"

"I didn't say that." Rory smiled. "I found that the three partners are owners. About what you'd expect. Ben Skyler seems to be the founding partner. The shares aren't equal, Ben's being larger. There is a fourth partner financially, an equity partner, if you will, a company based in Mauritius, which seems odd to me. I can get into their financial records or case files if you wish. I'm not sure what you are looking for. It's just very unusual for their system to be that well protected."

Robert sipped his coffee, staring into the middle distance at nothing. "Yes, check out the case files and financials, please. The winery?"

"One owner, again, a company based in Mauritius. Different company. I haven't gotten any further yet, but typically these things are shells within shells within shells, yada yada, like those Russian doll sets. And when you get to the end, the owner is someone's mother-in-law who doesn't drink — wouldn't know a Chardonnay from a Chihuahua and has no clue what Mauritius or Oliver is. The winery sits northwest of Oliver on a mountainside bench, not far from the town."

"Mauritius? Where's that?"

"No one knows, not even the Mauritians."

"I'm going to Oliver next month, see what I can see. The law firm is hosting a party there at which Sandra will be catering."

Rory wasn't finished. "I looked at some nearby wineries for fun and found an oddity. A winery called

Enchanting Grape is right next door. Stupid name if ever I heard one, so I looked into it. Chinese owner, mainland. Might be Communist Party affiliated, I'll find out. Whoever it is has owned the winery for several years, pumped a shitload of money into it."

"Possession Point came along after then?"

"Yup, at least the winery was purchased and the name added after Enchanting Grape had got going."

"Must irritate the Communist guy no end. Why not just shove a pointed stick in his eye? Maybe it's a party official moving money out of the country."

Rory nodded. "Probably."

"Rory, promise me you'll be careful. They are not to know you've been snooping around. It's for all our good. I could use info on the construction death cases. The fees they 'negotiated' are terribly one-sided. The victim's families are basically being screwed out of a lot of money if the suits are successful."

"Can you give me some names?"

"I'll send you the list. I'm going to re-question one or two of the victim's relatives. See what light I can bring to bear." As Rory rose to leave, Robert had a final question. "McDouguld. Can you find out if there is a law firm in Hong Kong? They may be working with SM & M or even be related somehow."

Rory nodded, then headed out, his head now on a swivel.

TEN

The following day saw Robert driving down to Strathcona for another word with Andy Ho's neighbour. The day was bright, tree leaves' shadows etched perfectly on the sidewalk. He had to park his car a street away, nothing closer available. He meandered back and gingerly walked up her porch steps. The front yard was barren save for a couple of flowerpots full of weeds. Grass had given up. He rapped on the door, waiting for Mrs. Busybody to answer. The street was empty of people, but not of cars. There were very few spots available on the street, and all were for locals according to the signs. After a moment, he heard movement and the door opened. It was the same woman, this time wearing old jeans and a mauve polka-dot blouse. She smiled again at Robert, as though he was a favourite relative dropping by for a visit. An upper tooth was missing in action. The vacant tooth look didn't mesh well with the stylish bob.

"You are looking great." Robert tried some buttering up before the questions.

"Thank you." The smile broadened.

"May I ask a couple of more things about your departed neighbour, Andy?"

She remained silent, which Robert took to be an assent.

"Did Andy have a storage place he used, not in his home?"

"There is a shed out back of the house. He might have used it. I don't know."

"The *gweilos* who visited several days ago, did they take anything away with them?"

"Yes. A suitcase. Large with hard sides. Who knows what was inside it? Nothing else."

"You said Andy had a bike. Where did he keep it?"

"In the shed? I don't know."

"Has the place been rented again?"

"Who would go into it? A dead person lived there. It will be hard to rent now."

"Perhaps a *gweilo*?

"Yes, they can be kind of stupid."

Robert declined to explain that he was half *gweilo*. "Did he make any trips back to Hong Kong?"

"Yes. He told me he had after he returned once."

"Do you remember when this was?"

"He returned February 14."

Robert wondered again if Andy knew his life was under constant supervision.

"Anything else you can remember about Andy?"

The lady shrugged. It seemed that the vein had finally run dry, so he thanked her and left.

"Come again anytime!" She was still smiling at the

back of the handsome man who thought to brighten her day.

He headed carefully down the path beside Andy's house, looking for the shed. He rounded the rear corner and there it was, rotting plywood walls with a canted roof covered in bright moss. The door was partially ajar. He opened it wider, squeak missing. A single bike sat against one wall, basic, no fenders or lights, a bit of dirt on the frame and probably the cheapest model on offer. Some rusting gardening tools lay against the rear wall, but nothing else of note, not even a rat. Robert gave up and returned to his car. Pretty much a waste of time, except for the suitcase revelation and the date of his trip.

Robert sat in his car, thinking, and what he was thinking was that he wasn't getting anywhere. He put the car in gear and headed south to Richmond, his sole remaining possibility for enlightenment. Forty minutes later, he was parking on Alice's crescent. Nothing seemed to have changed in the area other than the weather, which was beautiful enough to lift Robert's spirits. As he approached the side door to Sherman's suite, it opened, and Alice stepped out wearing a printed dress. Discs of lemons on an ivory background made her seem like a fruit retailer. She stopped immediately when she saw who was visiting.

"Robert, correct?" She asked.

He nodded. "Are you heading out? I can come another time. I just have a couple more questions, if I might?"

Alice looked at Robert, obviously gauging whether she really needed to do what she had planned, then relented. She smiled at Robert. "Please come in." She turned, re-opened the door, and ushered Robert inside. Before Robert could say anything, she asked, "Tea?" as she pointed to the couch.

"Thanks." He sat down and waited. With a swish, she left for the kitchen. There didn't appear to be any sign of her other brother. Was his name Denton? He should be taking notes, even if it was no longer a requirement of his job. While he waited, he sensed that Alice's initial wariness from his first visit seemed to have evaporated. Ten minutes later, she entered the living room with the same two cups as before. Robert tried the tea. It was the same high-quality blend. He nodded approvingly.

"What do you wish to know?" Alice asked, as she sat down only inches from him.

"Is your brother around?"

"No. Travelling back home."

"Do you know why?"

"No. He wouldn't say." She continued looking at Robert, unblinking.

"Could I ask you questions about your lawyers?"

She hesitated but relented. "Okay, I guess."

"When Sherman was getting his paperwork in order for coming to Vancouver, did he have lawyers handling it?"

"A lawyer contacted Sherman, asking him if he was interested in working in Vancouver. He said yes. It looked to be a way to immigrate over here. Our family is not wealthy, but we heard there were riches to be made in Gold Mountain."

"What was the firm's name?"

"McDouguld Law, I believe."

"How did you and your other brother get to come?"

"Sherman asked us and then insisted on including us when we said yes. They did not object."

Robert wasn't sure what else he could glean from this. "And when Sherman had his accident, you were contacted here by a local firm?"

"Yes, their name is Skyler, McDouguld and Moon. They offered to help me get my due compensation for Sherman's accident, with no charge if they weren't successful."

"Did they say they were related to the firm in Hong Kong?"

"They did not mention it."

"What percentage of the fee would you get if they are successful?"

"Twenty-five. They said this was normal."

Robert couldn't hold it in any further. "It is not close to being normal. The maximum the lawyers should be entitled to is forty percent. Your money should be a minimum of sixty percent, not twenty-five." Robert paused. "Who is your contract with, if I may ask?" Maybe the contract was with the Hong Kong firm. Perhaps they had different ideas of what a fair fee was.

"I'm not sure. Would you like a biscuit?"

Robert looked down at his tea, distracted by the change in subject. "Yes, please." Alice rose to get the cookies. She didn't seem perturbed in the least by Robert's news. When she returned, she offered Robert a cookie. Then she sat again, very close to him. "You are not entirely Cantonese, are you?" She glanced quickly at his left hand, which was bereft of a wedding ring.

He smiled in return. "No, my mother is from here. I spent some years in Hong Kong growing up."

"Would you like more tea?"

"Thanks, yes. It is very good." He took a stab. "Jade Dragon?"

"I am impressed. You know your teas."

"Actually, more of a coffee man." Robert tried to steer things back from what seemed to be turning into a social visit. "Sherman must have had a suitcase to travel with, no?"

"Of course."

"Is it here?"

"I think Denton took it for his trip."

"It would be helpful if you could tell me the dates when Sherman returned from Hong Kong, if you remember, that is."

"I would have to check. Is there a number you could be reached at?" Alice grinned.

Robert had a strong feeling that Alice's mind was on more than her brother, or money. "Here is my card. You can contact me anytime." He handed her one of his newly printed insurance cards, the first time he had given one out after finally receiving them from a delivery van. He felt like a businessman, somehow different from when he was police. He figured it was time to leave. "I'll be in contact, Alice."

"Please do, Robert. I will get that information to you." She stood up as Robert made for the door, anxious to escape whatever web Alice might be constructing for him.

However, he couldn't avoid brushing by her body as he left. She made sure of that.

He headed for home. Something to eat first, then a call to Vito. As he drove, he realized that Alice's obvious interest in him might be used. It wasn't something he liked doing, but ....

After a lame lunch of curly noodles at home, he called Vito. "It's Robert."

"And?"

"Talked with the kid. He definitely saw the guy pushing the other one off the tower. Front-row seat. Positive ID on the mug shot, the ugly one. Don't know where it leaves us though. Maybe you guys can use your highly persuasive powers to get a confession? Without the kid, of course."

"We'll put our best man on it."

"That's what I was afraid of. We should keep the kid as a last resort. This whole thing stinks."

"Are you certain you left the VPD? Cause it doesn't quite sound like it."

"Talk soon, Vito."

After hanging up, Robert realized that tomorrow, Friday, he was slated to meet on a construction site about Robin's summer job. It would be good to get some distance from his case, even if only for a day.

***

The evening meal was pizza, ordered in. Robert was happy to see Sandra had no objections to this laziness. They sat in the family room after dinner, talking softly about Sophie and Robin, who had absconded upstairs. Robert relaxed, the events of the last couple of days fading. Even his chest felt better, the aching receding for now. Robert poured a couple of whiskies, Sandra partaking as well today.

"Time to spill the beans, Sandra."

A puzzled look appeared.

"Need to know a bit about your family if I'm going to be joining it, don't I?"

"Yes, we should do a dinner with them. My mother's name is Amrit and my dad is Lal. They live in Surrey. And I'm their only child."

"You were born in Canada?"

"Yes, shortly after my parents emigrated from the Punjab."

"And the relation to Andy?"

"Sort of, my father and Andy's mother are brother and sister. So, he was a cousin to me, I suppose, if I ever thought about it, which I didn't."

Robert thought this through. "Did your aunt marry Manny's father?"

"Not sure. I don't think so, anyway. My mother would know, but I haven't asked. I was trying to get away from all that."

"And are there any other cousins around who might have been partial to Andy?"

"There are a couple, but no one who kept close to Andy. He was one of a kind, as you know."

"That is one way to describe him. What about relatives close to Manny?"

"I don't know about any connections, and I don't want

to know." After some more quiet discussion, they turned in.

Sandra was desperately saying something to Robert. He couldn't make it out, but she seemed to be terrified. He strained to reach his hand out to her, but she was slipping away from him. Her hair was flying in several directions, her eyes round and enormous as though Robert was her last chance ….

A whump. What was that? Robert opened his eyes. He knew he had been dreaming. Was it part of that? He looked around the bedroom. Nothing. The window was open, cool air wafting in. Sandra was beside him but hadn't stirred. What was that light coming through the blinds? It wasn't morning yet, was it? He looked over at the alarm clock. Green numbers said 2:35 am. He got up, went over to the window, pried the blinds apart and looked outside.

"My car! Holy shit! My car's on fire!" Flames were dancing from under the Silver Streak, growing as he watched, beginning to reach for the carport roof above.

"Get up! Everyone up!" He yelled as he went for his cell, dialled 911 and called it in. Sandra sat up groggily while he went to shake his children from their sleep.

"Put some clothes on. We have a fire out back. Quick!"

Thirty minutes later, water ran everywhere in the lane as the last smoke tendrils were finally extinguished. Robert stood staring at his beloved car, steam rising from the hood, destroyed. The underside of the carport was charred, but the whole affair was still standing. A patrol car had pulled up as the firefighters started rolling up hoses and returning equipment to their truck. Two officers got out, skin a doughy colour. Several neighbours stood around in their finest sleepwear watching the action while trying to avoid the remains of the water coursing down the centre of the laneway.

"Lucky man. Could have lost the whole building," offered one of the officers who came up to Robert. He didn't know either of them, but he guessed that their whole VPD life had been spent in a patrol car. "Spontaneous combustion?" asked the same officer.

"Really? You guys know your stuff, I'll say that," Robert answered.

The other officer was on his knees looking under the car. He eventually stood up, adjusted his belt, and looked at Robert. "Incendiary device, from the looks of it."

"Incendiary device?"

"Bomb to you." Both officers knew they were talking to an ex-detective. Disdain hung in the air like the dissipating smoke.

"Thanks, I didn't know what that word meant." Robert knew nothing else would transpire, so headed back into his townhouse. Sandra, Robin, and Sophie had been standing at the rear window watching the action once it became apparent that the firefighters had things under control. Robert felt lucky that his windows hadn't been blasted out by the hose spray. He also thought it fortunate that the press hadn't appeared.

"You guys want anything to eat or drink?" His kids didn't reply, seemingly stupefied.

"Wasn't I supposed to start my driving course next month?" Robin finally asked.

"They don't do it in the client's cars anyway. You can still start, we just need to figure out what our next ride might be." Robin didn't respond, still groggy. He turned and, with Sophie in tow, they retreated upstairs.

"Well, I'm having a drink, want anything, Sandra?"

"Sure, a small one, thanks."

He poured a couple of shots, and they sat, staring at each other. "It was a bomb, Sandra. I forgot to mention that part of hanging around me might be dangerous. You may decline my wedding offer if you so choose. I won't be offended."

"No. You won't get off that easy." She moved closer to Robert. "What's going on?"

"I am not sure. And I just spent a bucketload of money fixing that car up." He shook his head. "I suppose it could be a warning, like Bernard."

"Is there something safer you could do, Robert?"

"I don't know what that would be." He sipped the Japanese whisky, feeling the relaxing effect take hold.

"Are we in danger, Robert?"

"I fear so, Sandra. I'll have to figure out how to handle this. Tomorrow." They finished and went back to bed, searching for sleep that didn't come until dawn.

R inging woke Robert. He pried both eyes open and looked over at the clock. Half past eight. He never slept in this late. He reached over, grabbing his cell from the bedside table, almost dropped it, then managed to sit upright.

"Robert? Thomas here."

"Kind of thought you might call."

"We'd like to pick up your car if we may. Examinations, etc."

"Sure, and you may keep it. Doesn't look as though it will be wandering the streets of Vancouver anymore. The tires melted, Thomas."

"Care to come by for a few words?"

"Sure. Guess I'll cab it."

"I'll send someone over. In an hour?"

"Fine. See you soon."

An hour later, Robert was in a ghost car driven by Finn Black. Hints of cigarette smoke mixed with plain old body odour were the tasting notes for this vehicle. "How has Finn been lately?" he asked, as he lowered the window.

"Good, Robert. Busy but a bit bored, unlike your life."

"You should be happy. I really don't need this shit anymore. I'm planning on marrying Sandra. Don't expect she is impressed by the things happening to me."

"Congratulations. Well done!"

"Yes. Her family might be a complicating factor, but I'm happy."

"So, what's going on? Vito said he's been in contact with you."

"Yes. Construction accidents with a large side of weirdness added. I think it's partly about drugs. You didn't see the rear of my house, but my car got firebombed last night."

"Jeez, what's going on?"

"I must be ruffling feathers somewhere."

"You've always been an expert ruffler, Robert." Finn laughed.

Robert entered Thomas's office, gently closing the door behind him.

"So soon you're back. Seems like we just had a conversation, then you up and left."

"Hello to you too, Thomas." He sat in the offered guest chair, a familiar spot. "Has Vito filled you in?"

"About what he's been up to, yes, but your

contributions? Not totally. And now you seem to be a target once again."

"Once again, and I'm not even with the VPD anymore. I'm developing a complex, Thomas."

"We don't want that. Who are you with now?"

"BC Coastal Insurance. Same outfit as before. Investigating, principally some construction accident lawsuits that they have been named in. I am poking around and finding strange things. It hasn't taken long for violence to come along. I had a journalist asking some questions for me. He got his arm broken the other evening at a Burnaby baseball diamond. Now my car magically blows up at night after I spent a boatload on fixing it."

"Didn't know they played baseball in Burnaby. And perhaps you should talk to your mechanic about the car. Is he certified?"

"The mechanic? No idea, but the cop last night said it was an incendiary device."

"Impressive for a patrol officer."

"That's what I thought. You giving them extra training or something?"

"No idea. So, what exactly are you up to?"

"Checking out the legal firm behind the lawsuits, which seems to have provoked the beating. Skyler, McDouguld and Moon. I've also been talking to some of the victims' family members where possible, and found the victims made a few trips back to Hong Kong for no identifiable reason. They all seem to have hailed from there. I'm thinking this may be about moving drugs. Someone has set up a pipeline using poor buggers from

Hong Kong. I also found that the most recent construction accident wasn't an accident at all."

"Vito mentioned something about that."

"It seems that the fees for a successful lawsuit are terribly one-sided, not in the client's favour. Not sure this is a crime, but maybe the firm needs a severe scolding from the law society, who knows."

"I am sure they can police themselves." Thomas's eyes rolled as he said this. "It's the accident I am interested in. The man falling off the tower?"

"Pushed off, said a young boy. Positive ID on the pusher."

"Why is it that you know this, but no one here does?"

Robert shrugged. "Well, I could have been here to help and lead things, but ...." He waited, then, "I've been keeping Vito abreast of what I've been doing."

"Who is the kid?"

"I don't remember, Thomas. And I think it should stay that way until I or you have a better grip on what's going on here. Don't really want to jeopardize the life of a child, do we?"

Thomas didn't answer, obviously mulling lines of enquiry without a star witness. They sat like this for a couple of minutes, then Thomas broke the silence. "Do you have any cameras on your home?"

"Yes. I thought it prudent after Siggy tried that visit without an invite last year. I'll forward what I have to Vito."

"Have you thought about the possibility of someone from one of your past cases coming after you?"

"I'll admit, no." He thought about his most recent

case, a miffed suspect who had likely coached murder a couple of times. "Seems a bit beyond Mary's capabilities, don't you think?"

"Perhaps she's made some new friends."

"There's something to contemplate."

"Please stay in contact with Vito. What are your plans moving forward?"

"I'll get some dates to Vito on when these labourers returned from their trips. Perhaps we can match something with sudden increases in street product. And there is someone overseas right now. I'd like to catch his return somehow." Before Thomas could object, he added, "Lives in Richmond, so RCMP. I'll keep them informed, and yourselves of course." He added the last so Thomas wouldn't squirm too much. He rose, left Thomas's office, didn't see anyone else he knew on the floor, so he went up the street to visit Paulo's. There wasn't any offer of a return ride to his home, so he started thinking about what kind of car he'd want to drive around town in.

***

Robert entered Paulo's and waved at Gilberto. He walked up to the counter's edge and beckoned him over.

Gilberto smiled as he came closer, resting his hands on the marble. "What's up, Roberto?"

"You have a car?"

"*Sí.*"

"What kind, if you don't mind?"

"An Oldsmobile Cutlass, a coupe. Blue. It is a great car!" he said proudly. "Why do you ask?"

"I need a newer car suddenly. Mine blew up last night. I don't know what to get."

"Sadly, I do not believe they make Oldsmobiles anymore."

"Why not?"

"Who knows how those car companies think. It is a mystery. You will need to find something else. I am not selling mine." As though Gilberto was in possession of the last Oldsmobile on earth.

"Fine. I'll think further. A latte, please." He paid and went to the cafe rear to wait. It seemed that the visit to Fairweather Construction would need to wait. He texted his son that they'd do it after they had a car again. Instead of thinking about cars, he worried about his family's safety. He looked up. Gilberto had ferried his coffee over to him.

"Thank you, Gilberto. You are too kind."

Gilberto nodded then returned to his command post.

He sipped his coffee, mulling over the idea of putting his kids with his parents again until he knew what was happening. Maybe the bomb was a warning, and that was it. Perhaps he could relax a bit. He was thinking hopefully, not rationally, he knew this. Time to call his dad, anyway. He wanted to know if Ethan knew of a McDouguld Law while he was cooking for gang members as well as the police in Hong Kong long ago.

Robert finished up, waved a goodbye to Gilberto and headed up to Broadway to catch one of the double-long joys of transportation in Vancouver. He had given enough money to the taxi industry recently.

During his bus ride east, a thought came to him while

he looked out the windows. He'd call up Ricky to see if he knew of any cars available. It wasn't a bad way of looking for a car — sure beat getting the schmoozefest from a salesperson at a dealership. With those people, it was only a question of how you were being screwed, not if.

Once home, he rang Ricky's. "May I talk to the proprietor?"

There was silence on the other end. Robert realized his word choice might have been overwhelming.

"What?"

"Is Ricky there?"

"Jus a second." After a minute, Robert heard a couple of thumps, then, "Ricky speaking."

"It's Robert Lui. I just had my car in there for a badly needed service. Thing is, it's blown up and ...." He had to stop. Ricky was making strange noises.

"Not your fault, Ricky." He added quickly. "Some people don't like me, I think. Anyway, do you know of anyone wanting to sell a car? I'm suddenly on the market."

Ricky calmed down, now that the opportunity to make more money was laid at his feet. "Let me think and get back to you, okay?"

"Nothing too recent. I'd like to pretend that I'm smarter than my car, even if I know it's probably not true. CD player too." Robert gave him his number and hung up, then sadly realized some of his precious car music could be melted plastic by now.

He rang his father.

"Dad, it's Robert. How are you? How's Mom?"

"Nice to hear from you, son." The carefully hidden

accusation attached — 'why don't we hear from you more often?' "We're both fine. Trying to get outside with the warm weather."

"I have a question about the old days, Dad." The silence was deafening. Robert knew how much Ethan hated the old days, for the very reason Robert was calling about.

He plowed ahead anyway, "McDouguld Law. Ever run across them in Hong Kong?"

It only took his father two seconds to scan his memory. "Oh yes. I understand they helped some of the Triad people on occasion, amongst other things. Why?"

"It's complicated. I also have a few things to tell you and Mom. Would you like to come over for dinner soon? This Sunday, regular time?"

"Sounds nice, Robert. You aren't in trouble again, are you?" Ethen was no fool.

"No, just a few things have happened lately that you should know about — all good." He knew the lie was thin, but there was much catching up needed for his parents.

"Okay, Robert. See you Sunday. We'll look forward to it."

Robert hung up and scrounged around the fridge looking for something to eat. He took a look out the window at the rear garden for anything to work with and almost choked. His entire tomato patch was blown to smithereens. A couple of the herb pots were on their side, flattened into two dimensions by the fire hoses, dark fingers of soil drying on the pavers. He hadn't noticed these details the night of the excitement. The carport was empty, just blackened tarmac. Bits of solidified rubber lay where his tires used to be, all that remained of the Silver Streak. Someone had hung up yellow police tape around the carport posts; he had no idea why. He shook his head, turned, and proceeded to make coffee. He felt ill.

Two hours later, the phone rang. Maybe Ricky?

"Thomas here, Robert. Got some preliminary info back on your car. Sounds like amateur hour, for what that's worth. First, the explosive wasn't enough to kill. A rudimentary bomb. Second, there was a timer involved. The boys aren't certain yet, but it seems it might have been supposed to go off twelve hours later, while you were driving. Probably an AM/PM thing, which can be challenging for some. Perhaps not the brightest and best were sent after you, but maybe that's all they have. I know good help is hard to find. Not sure about an intent to kill, but definitely a stern warning."

"No clues from my cameras, I suppose?"

"Not really. Two hooded figures, average size, etc. We're checking some local traffic cameras, might get lucky on a vehicle."

"Before half two. That's when the car went whump. Where is my car, by the way? I'd like to check if a few things might have survived inside."

"I believe it's close by. I'll let you know. What exactly have you been up to that warrants such attention?"

"Not much. As I told you, the lawyers I've been checking out is the only thing of note. But this type of action is not what you'd expect from a professional law firm, unless times are a-changing. Are they changing, Thomas?"

"Wouldn't think so. We'll let you know if any camera info pans out. Keep in touch. I'd tell you to also stay alert, but I'm guessing you have that part figured already." The line went dead.

Robert wanted to make Sunday dinner special. Fortunately, Sandra did not need to work, so it was all hands on deck for the prep work. Prior to starting, he beckoned both his children and led them outside for a walk around the block. It was time to tell them what he planned.

"I did something important a couple of days ago. It will affect our lives in a big way, and I hope you agree with it." The three walked along the sidewalk, Robin on one side, Sophie on the other. They both looked sideways at him, curious as to what he was going to tell them.

He finally exploded. "I asked Sandra to marry me!"

Sophie tittered as she grabbed her father's arm. "I was kind of guessing this'd happen. I love it." She hugged Robert as she looked over at Robin, who seemed surprised.

"What?" Robin said.

Robert wasn't shocked by his children's reactions. A

daughter expecting something and a son seemingly oblivious.

Then Robin recovered. "Wow, Pops. That's great. I like her a lot." He slapped Robert on his back, grinning as he did so.

"I'll be telling your grandparents tonight over dinner. I thought it was about time I told you. Give it some thought, and if you have any reservations about all this, let me know. Let's get back. We have some prep to do," Robert said, as he turned around. They hadn't even covered fifty metres from home.

"I'm nervous, Robert," Sandra finally admitted. She had been making minor mistakes as she did the prep, something Robert hadn't seen before.

"Only natural, I suppose, but my parents are very nice." Neglecting to mention how intelligent they were. He had only told them about Sandra in passing. They didn't even know she had moved in with him. Wasn't that what made life interesting, surprises?

"Set the table? Knives and forks today — best stuff," Robert asked Robin.

Robin had spotted the rice maker on the counter. "Not chopsticks?"

"Change in plans. You can stow the rice maker, going with spuds instead." He went to the sideboard and pulled out their finest bowls and plates. Wine and water glasses followed. Then the linen napkins came out. Sophie went over to help Robin with the arranging of the plates, glasses, and cutlery.

A half-hour later, the front doorbell rang. Sandra straightened up from cleaning the counter, wiping her hands, looking over at Robert. She took off her apron.

"Showtime," he said. He had spruced up the back terrace as best he could and got rid of the yellow tape, but the charred carport ceiling and lack of car were going to require some nifty explaining.

The door opened. "Mom, Dad, great to see you." They hugged, even Ethan joining in, then Robert led them into the family area where the grandchildren reunited with Mary and Ethan.

"Mom, Dad, this is Sandra." Sandra stepped forward and they shook hands. Mary looked past Sandra and winked at Robert.

"So nice to meet you. Robert tells us you cook as well?" Mary asked.

"I do. I'm also working for a caterer over on Main Street, keeping busy."

"And how's the police work going, Robert? Catching bad people as usual?" Mary switched to her son.

"Well, I've been meaning to let you both know, I've left the force. For good this time."

Mary looked taken aback, while Ethan had a hint of a smile on his lips. He had never been a fan of Robert's chosen profession, mostly stemming from his time spent in Hong Kong.

"My suspension was over, but they wanted me inside the office. I told them no. I'm back working for that insurance company again — better work, more money, and maybe safer."

Ethan looked out the rear window and spotted the exterior charring. "What happened there, Robert?" He moved closer to the window, staring at the carport.

Robert thought it best to be economical with the facts. "Had my car serviced. It exploded the other night. We were lucky, fire people got here quickly." Mary's eyebrows raised at this revelation.

"Where did you take it?" Ethan asked.

"A place up near Hastings. First time."

"And the last time, I assume. You'll need a car."

"Yup, got someone on the lookout for me. We'll see how that goes." His parents then heard Sophie's news about Rose joining her in Calgary in September.

"Sounds exciting, Sophie. So, what are we dining on tonight?" Mary asked.

"Grilled steelhead, pea tips with garlic, and roasted potatoes." Sandra answered. "Drinks?"

After everyone had their drink of choice and were seated in the family area, Robert let loose with his announcement. "Mom, Dad? This will be a big surprise for you, but Sandra has agreed to marry me. We're going to do the deed at some point in the near future but haven't got to the planning stage as yet. I realize you've only just met her, but …" here he stuttered, "we love each other very much." He finished with trepidation, waiting for the verdict.

His mother rose and came over to Robert, hugging him so tightly he almost lost his breath. He grunted in pain.

"I'm so happy for you," she whispered in his ear.

Ethan stood up as well, smiling. "Got any bubbly? I noticed flutes sitting over there." Nothing escaped Ethan's attention.

"We have a Taittinger waiting expectantly."

"Release it, son. This is great news!" Ethan's reserve had fled, replaced by an exuberance not seen in years by Robert. Robin got the cork out without getting hit in the eye and poured successfully, not losing any in the process. Toasts were proposed, and all six had smiles as the champagne quickly disappeared.

Robert thought it as good a time as any to strike. "Dad, could you help me out on the terrace? Need to get the grill ready."

Ethan quickly realized what was happening as he assented. Robert had pulled many variations of this trick to get Ethan alone so questions could be asked. They both went out the rear door, and Robert pulled the grill forward to load up the charcoal.

"What do you want to know about this legal firm, Robert?" Ethan asked.

"McDouguld Law, correct?"

"Yes."

"Was it a large firm?"

"No. It seemed to be run by one person, a Travis McDouguld, I believe. He had a few helpers, I would guess."

"I wonder if he is related to the McDouguld here."

"He had a son, I know. Apparently, a bit on the dim side. Similar age as you, I think."

"Well, I don't know if being dim is an impediment to becoming a professional in any discipline. And how did you know about them, Dad?"

"Just peripherally. I'd hear all kinds of things as I cooked for those assholes. Travis was the go-to when the triads had legal problems, which was pretty much always. He seemed to be very good at managing situations. I assume he was well rewarded, but really, I had no idea."

"Do you know if the gangs had any other lawyers working for them?"

"No idea, but McDouguld was the only name that came up in their dinner conversations."

"Any idea what happened to the son?"

"No."

Robert finished stuffing some paper under the charcoal chimney and, after loading it up, signalled a return inside. "Thanks, Dad. It helps a bit."

Ethan wasn't done. "He had a name, or a title if you wish. They called him 'The Mandarin'. And there were rumours he liked the horses."

"That sounds like a way to get into debt."

"I'm sure it is. I've heard it's only the insiders that make the money; the rest lose, usually quite a bit if they are hooked."

Robert didn't ask anything further. They went inside, where the potatoes had been put into the oven and wine poured.

Once the fish came off, the dinner plated, and everyone seated, conversation returned to Sandra.

"How did you two meet? I'd like to hear the story." Mary asked as she started eating. Both Robin and Sophie leaned forward slightly, their food forgotten for the moment. They knew the outline of how it happened but not any details.

Sandra started. "I was working up the coast at a lodge across the water from Bella Kind on Raven Island. Mostly sport fishing people visit, at least in the good weather. Robert showed up one day last October to stay a couple of nights. I knew immediately." What she knew didn't need elaboration.

"Really?" Robert asked.

"Yes, really."

"You were pretty good at hiding it, I'll say that."

Sandra smiled as she looked over at Mary. Mary returned the smile. Robert shook his head at the machinations of the female mind.

"He acted all cool and aloof, as if he was really on a case or something and needed to work."

"Hey, I was." This came out a bit louder than intended. Sophie giggled. Both kids were listening intently, arms on the table.

"Then he was going to leave, but fate had other plans. I assume you heard about his bad flight. He showed up again at the lodge that afternoon, dripping wet, no reservation. Luckily, I was able to fit him in. The gods were being generous with this man."

"The place was empty!"

"It only seemed that way. And the rest is history."

"But …." Robert came to a stop as he slowly realized that free choice was just a clever illusion propagated by philosophers with nothing better to do, especially for the male of the species. "You don't know how to use a drill, do you?"

"I could probably manage, why?"

"Just curious."

Robert's parents had puzzled looks. Sandra continued. "But I was eventually forced to visit Vancouver. Robert was apparently too scared to get onto a float plane again or even visit Bella Kind on a real plane. He sent one of his partners up a few weeks later instead."

"I was in charge of a murder case, which you became part of, if you will remember."

"I recall something, but it all worked out in the end." Sandra finished triumphantly. Robert smiled thinly at his parents as the word 'bamboozled' flitted through his mind. His kids were grinning at him.

"Would anyone like dessert?" Sandra asked. She had put together some sweet pastries that afternoon, baking being another of her talents. As Robert and his children were clearing the dishes and dirty cutlery in readiness for the last course, Robert's cell rang. It was sitting in the family room. He glanced over, thought about ignoring it, then relented.

He picked up. "Hi Robert." It was Alice. "My brother is returning to Richmond this coming Wednesday. If you want to meet him, you should come by. And I have some other dates on Sherman's trips for you as well." She paused.

Robert waited, but after a long moment it became

obvious that she wanted him down in Richmond again and wasn't going to give him any information until then. He sighed. "Okay. What time?"

"Anytime after noon hour."

"See you then, Alice."

THIRTEEN

B y Tuesday, Robert still hadn't heard a thing from Ricky, so he rang. "Any luck on a car for me yet? It's Robert Lui."

"Today could be your lucky day. I was just about to call you. A gentleman was in this morning, wants to sell his Volvo. An S-40 in excellent condition. Interested?"

"A Volvo, hmm." He had only ever driven Japanese cars. A change might be just fine. "Okay, I'll come by."

"Tomorrow. Sometime after noon? Oh yes, I forgot to say, it is a standard transmission. Can you drive such a car?"

"A standard? Sure, see you then." He hadn't driven stick in years but looked forward to it. He hoped the car really was in good shape, and that he wasn't being taken in.

Robert tried talking with WorkSafeBC about the accidents in his file, but they were very unaccommodating, citing the legal issues at play. He unfortunately didn't have any contacts on the inside, so after a quick lunch of noodles, he added a task for Rory, texting him.

> Check WorkSafeBC files for the labourer's
> accidents if you are able to. Thanks.

He really had no idea how good Rory was, or if he was successfully covering his tracks. He could only hope for now. There was no further word from Vito as to whether they had questioned the labourer from the pushing incident. He didn't have a car, so dealing with his missing herb plants would also need to wait. He went for a run.

Next day, he lounged around at home until noon, then cabbed it over to Ricky's, hoping against hope that his car problems would soon be a thing of the past. He walked inside and stood waiting while the assistant went to collect Ricky. A stack of new tires sat next to the service counter, off-gassing a luxuriant rubber odour. Some mysterious auto parts hung off the back wall. Robert had no idea what their function was. Ricky finally came out of a door, clad in a stained lab coat as though he had been conducting experiments behind a curtain, the salesman's smile in place.

"Welcome, Robert. The car is out back. It's a 2012, last year for the model, so possibly a collector's item." The sales spiel already starting. "What happened to the car we fixed for you?"

"Blew up. A bomb, apparently."

"What do you do for a living, if I may ask?"

"Insurance industry."

"Hmm, sounds dangerous. I thought insurance was one of the more boring businesses."

"Shows how much you know," Robert responded, then he followed Ricky to the lane where the Volvo sat. Dark blue, and clean. Robert circled it. A couple of dings, but otherwise it looked decent. Tires, newish. No cracks in the glass.

"The guy wants seven thousand."

"For a twelve-year-old car?"

"Low mileage. Less than eighty k. One owner."

"You've checked it over?"

"Yup."

"Service records?"

"I'll ask him."

"Take it for a spin?"

Robert had no idea what the 'yup' encompassed. He also wondered what the owner really wanted for the car. Ricky dropped the fob into Robert's open palm. He got in, adjusted the seat and mirrors, then fired it up. It took Robert all of ten seconds to get reacquainted with a standard as he pulled away down the lane. It had the kind of pep and response that you just didn't get out of an automatic. He turned at the street and slowed, stopping at the roadside, then pulled a jewel case from his jacket, sliding the CD into the player. It worked just fine. He was sold. He returned to Ricky's.

"Would he take sixty-five hundred?" Robert knew he was a terrible negotiator.

"I'll ask. He's in my office."

Ten minutes later, Robert was the owner of a new car, sort of. It was new to him, anyway. Ricky got on his phone and called an insurance agent. Forty-five minutes later, everything taken care of, Robert was mobile again. He headed south, to Richmond and a date with Alice, and hopefully, Denton.

He loved the car immediately, dropping a gear once in a while to make the engine scream a bit. He should have got one of these years ago. It was quicker than the Silver Streak, but then, that was a very low bar. Pulling up in front of Alice's house, he let the engine idle, listening to it before cutting the power. He was satisfied, intensely happy to be mobile again. One never knew how important a car was to your life until it was missing. He scanned the street, looking for signs of life, but the area was still deserted.

Robert walked up to Alice's door and knocked, anticipating finally meeting Denton. The door opened. Alice didn't look happy. She motioned him in, pointing at the couch. She sat beside him.

"I haven't heard from Denton. His plane landed, I know that. He should have been here by now."

Robert didn't know what to say, but Alice definitely seemed worried. "He has a cell, I assume."

"Yes. No answer. I got one text, that he had landed, that was it."

"Is there any other place he might go to before coming here?"

"I don't know. Maybe the boat?"

"Why would he go there?"

She shrugged.

"Where would the boat be?"

"Steveston. That is all I know."

"Do you know the boat's name?"

"Something like pickled herring, no, wait," Her brow furled as she tried to remember. "It is *Herring Juice*, I believe. I remember thinking it was such an odd name."

"You have the dates for Sherman's trips to Hong Kong?"

"Yes." She looked down at a sheet of paper sitting on the table. "November 4th of last year, and March 23rd of this year. Those dates are when he returned."

"Thanks. Maybe I'll take a trip down to Steveston, see if I can find Denton."

"May I come with you?"

"No, I work better by myself. I have your cell number. I'll call you when I find him."

"Thank you. I'm going out to get some food for a welcome-home dinner."

He let himself out, got back in his car and aimed south. He didn't know much about the fishing port, only that it was large. He headed for the one area he knew — Columbia yards at the eastern edge of Steveston, where he had rescued his son a couple of years earlier.

He drove up Trites Road and straight into the yard, eventually coming to a stop in front of a large, corrugated metal building. He shivered slightly as the kidnapping memories came back. He had successfully rescued his son from the grips of a triad gang in this very shipyard but had also come close to losing his life in the process.

A cafe was advertised, so he headed inside. The place was small, only twenty seats at most. Two patrons were eating something at a small table against the wall, maybe fish tacos? He went up to the till manned by a pimply-faced teenager, bright eyes, unkempt blond hair.

"*Herring Juice*. Heard of the boat? I'm looking for it."

"Lester. Do you know the *Herring Juice*?" This aimed at one of the diners.

"Nope. Might try the yard by the cannery."

Robert looked back at the cashier. "The cannery?"

"Go back up to Moncton and head west till you can't. That's the Cannery. Heritage site. Yard is in behind it."

Robert thanked him and left. He retraced his route, found Moncton and turned west. It didn't take long for him to be gliding slowly through small-town history. A nice two-storey brick building on the south side harkened back to an era when Steveston was sending canned salmon all over the world. He had to be careful not to run anyone over. Pedestrians definitely had the run of the streets. Coffee seemed important here. Every block boasted a shop of sorts. Maybe this was his kind of place. It had a pleasant small-town feel missing from most of the Lower Mainland communities. Of course, old town Langley had the same vibe, and he had almost lost his life close by to it.

He parked at the street's end next to a two-storey hotel with a lot of miles on it. Ahead sat a large metal building sporting a Canadian flag and several federal signs, including its name, Gulf of Georgia Cannery. It seemed to be some kind of heritage site, just as the kid had indicated. As he walked up to it, he couldn't see any shipyard behind the large building. He tried skirting the cannery by heading west and entered a yard at the first open gate. Trucks, fishing gear, crab traps, and sheds littered the area. Beyond this, south, he could see row after row of fishing vessels. This wasn't going to be easy. Most of the buildings were clad in siding painted off-white. Dull trims the colour of dried blood surrounded every opening on buildings on one side of the alley. Pale blue trim was used on the buildings to the west. He couldn't figure a reason for the difference, perhaps they had different functions?

He buttonholed the first guy he came to. "Do you know of a boat called *Herring Juice*?"

The man with weathered face and hands started to laugh. "Didn't know Ukrainians were fishing around here. No, I haven't heard of such a boat." He went over to another worker, asking him. The worker pointed north, saying something Robert couldn't hear.

"What did you say?"

The worker looked Robert up and down, perhaps assessing his ensemble, or his intelligence. "North slough, beyond the park. Know which way's north, do you?"

"I'll do my best to figure it out, thanks." Robert turned and found his way back to his car. Park? What park? He negotiated a three-point turn in front of the old hotel then went north until he found a cross street and headed west again. The road ended at a park. It had to be the one.

As he drove up the entry lane into it, a pickup truck, leaving, headed past him in a great hurry. Two men seemed to be arguing with each other in the cab, then it was gone. Robert travelled a little further and parked. He looked northwest at a line of low trees before finally spotting the corner of a structure about one hundred metres away, barely visible between the vegetation.

Most of the park itself was flat out bald. Scrub trees bent by wind and low shrubbery defined some paths, otherwise, it was devoid of anything you'd associate with a normal park. Wind was ripping across the point. A solitary man jigged a long-tailed kite up and down. Only grey water could be seen beyond the land on three sides. The Salish Sea, Robert supposed.

He walked north. After he skirted more trees, he walked up a wide road to what appeared to be a long boat shed outfitted with the same colour scheme he had seen at the yard. It indicated more boats somewhere in the vicinity.

He made for what he hoped was the access point to the shed. He walked up to a gate set in a chain-link fence topped with rusty barbed wire. He tried to remember when he last had a tetanus shot and was about to do an about-face when he noticed the lock to the gate had been smashed off and was lying on the asphalt. He pushed the gate open.

No one was around. Inside the fence, he moved from the building corner to the south side deck, testing each large white door as he passed by it. At the west end of the building, a red wooden ramp descended to the single dock stretching away to the slough's western end. Maybe twenty boats were lined up along it. The slough was narrow, one-way traffic only. He made his way slowly along the wood dock, avoiding the holes and the warped decking. Then he saw it.

Herring Juice 2 was a grey rusting scow with a smallish cabin. He stepped across the hull's edge onto its deck and knocked on the door. It opened slowly. A distinct smell wafted out, a smell Robert was unfortunately familiar with, burning flesh. The hairs on his neck prickled as he realized he was un-armed.

He took another look around before stepping into the cabin. He almost retched. A man was sitting in the captain's chair, taped to the arms. An electric charcoal lighter was sticking out of his mouth, still on. The man was mercifully dead. Robert kicked the cord out of the socket.

The victim's face was covered in burns, cigarettes he supposed. Two bullet holes in the forehead had provided a release. The man was Chinese. He assumed he had found Denton, then realized that the truck racing by him probably contained the killers. He pulled out his cell as he stepped back onto the dock. He took a deep breath as he punched in the number. Was he really in the insurance business? He gazed north at the coastal mountain ranges rising beyond UBC's headland.

"Alice?"

"Yes?"

"It's Robert. Where are you?"

"At the store, buying food."

"Stay there. Don't go home. I'll come get you."

"Why?"

"Your life is in danger. Whatever you do, don't go home."

He got her location, then dialled the RCMP. As he waited, he turned and looked west across the strait at what he assumed was Vancouver Island in the distance. It was all very flat in this world. Dead flat.

"Troy? Robert Lui. I'm out Steveston way, at a slough,

north of the Garry Point Park. It's a bad one, Troy. *Herring Juice 2* is the boat. I need to go pick up a girl whose life is in danger. I didn't touch anything in the boat."

"But —." He left Troy hanging and started running for his Volvo. Twenty minutes later, he pulled into a parking lot adjacent to one of the many open-air malls littering No. 3 Road. Alice was standing on the curb, a shopping bag at her feet, with a puzzled look. He drove up and got her in.

"What is going on?" Alice asked.

Robert gripped the steering wheel tightly, his knuckles turning white. "I think your brother is dead, I'm afraid, Alice. I'm sorry." He turned to her.

She obviously couldn't comprehend what Robert had said. "You must be mistaken. He just arrived back from home today." She started to squirm, her hands twisting the cloth of her blouse.

He didn't want to give her any hope that it wasn't Denton, as he wasn't certain it was her brother. Only Alice could confirm it, and he didn't really want her seeing him like he was found. He put the car in gear and headed to the city's central community centre, where they could be alone in the middle of crowds.

"And why can't I go back to my place?"

"This wasn't an accident, Alice. It was murder. And I think they might come after you." He didn't want to add anything for the moment.

CHAPTER
FOURTEEN

They sat in the Volvo, facing a running track. Alice sniffled as she grappled with Robert's news.

Robert called Troy as he got out. He leaned back against the hood of his car after parking in the middle of the lot serving an ice rink, pool, library and assorted other Richmond community facilities. He watched people circling the adjacent running track.

"What's going on here, Robert?"

"Seen the body?"

"Yes. You were correct. This is disgusting."

"Seems pretty obvious that someone was either after information or something of value. My bet is on the latter. I think this guy was a courier. Drugs. He just arrived from Hong Kong today, and he didn't stop at his sister's to say hello before going out to the boat. He wasn't a professional at this. I think he was roped into it somehow. Have the boys found anything yet? Look for a suitcase."

"No. They've searched the boat."

"How about the shed? Or other boats?"

"We'll be thorough."

"I'll leave you to it, then. I may have been passed by the killers as I drove into the park. Maybe they got the case in the end, I don't know. There were two of them, arguing in the front seat. A dark green Chevy pickup, not old. I didn't get the plates, but the colour was unusual, evergreen-like. I don't know what street cameras cover this part of town, but … and if you haven't heard, I'm no longer with the VPD. I resigned. Been working for an insurance company. This, unfortunately, seems to be part of my case." Robert paused. "Think you could you have an officer meet us back at Alice's place? I'm betting they made a beeline to her home if they didn't find what they were after at the boat. That is why she is with me. I thought she was in extreme danger."

Troy responded, "Alice is the guy's sister? Someone will meet you there in twenty minutes or less. Address?"

Robert thanked Troy and got back into his car, feeling like he was in no-man's-land without the backing of a police force. One thing was certain; he was going to start carrying a firearm again. He got Alice out of the car, and they walked a few slow laps of the track on the outside lane, avoiding others, talking quietly, then headed back to her home. A squad car was waiting in front of the house. Robert introduced himself and led them towards the door, which had been left ajar. He looked in. Alice could see past his shoulder, and she wailed. Robert walked in to a mess. So, they probably hadn't recovered Denton's suitcase. The constable pulled her gun and, with the barrel pointing skywards, entered cautiously.

Robert said, "They're long gone. Probably pissed at

finding nothing." The constable looked back at Robert, puzzled as to who he was. She started taking some notes and snapped a few pictures to document the destruction.

"Might be some prints here of value," Robert suggested. "They were angry and may have made a few mistakes in the process."

"Who are you again?"

"Robert. Ex VPD. Check with Troy."

"It'd be a good idea to stay in a hotel for a couple of days, Alice," Robert added.

Alice looked back at him. "I am too frightened, Robert."

Robert knew she was, but he also knew what she was trying to do — make him take her with him. That wasn't happening. He asked the constable, "Any money available to help her out on a short-term basis?"

"Maybe. I'll check with Troy."

"Please do, as a favour to Robert. Do you know of any inexpensive places that are okay?"

The constable named a couple of hotels nearby, so Robert had Alice collect some things, including her papers, and headed out. Richmond, being an airport city, wasn't short on modest accommodation. As they neared the hotel, Alice made a declaration: "I'm going home to Hong Kong. There is no longer anything here for me. And if my life is in danger …." She trailed off.

"How large was Denton's suitcase?"

"One of the larger ones."

Pretty hard to stow something like that in an airport locker. Robert wondered where it was. He parked and walked in with Alice to the front desk.

"Four nights — one person, this person." He pointed to Alice, then prepaid with his card. The girl took Alice's information. He'd see later if Troy would reimburse him.

"I'd arrange that travel as soon as you can. But please let me know how I can reach you when you get home. I'm afraid the RCMP will want you to identify your brother before you go, and they'll want your fingerprints to exclude them when they go through your apartment. I'll let them know what your plans are." He genuinely felt sorry for her.

She stared at him, turmoil still wild in her eyes. "Thank you, Robert."

"If you need to return to your place, call the police first. They will escort you. I'll try to arrange it. They owe me a few things." He turned and left Alice standing by the desk. When he got back in his car, he called Troy again.

"Find anything yet?"

"Nothing useful. Maybe it's somewhere else. Perhaps he didn't even return from Hong Kong with anything."

"Those sadists thought differently." Robert then related Alice's plan to leave.

"We need her to ID the body to see if it's her brother."

"I told her. Try to arrange it soonest. She needs to get out of here. I'll text her number to you. And if she wants to go back to her place to get things, please escort her." He told Troy where he had placed her in the interim. "I'm heading back to Vancouver to do some considering. Talk to you when I talk to you."

As Robert drove back north, he wondered how Denton's location had been pinpointed so quickly. Perhaps he had been followed from the airport. He couldn't come up with any other explanation. But then, they would have been able to retrieve whatever Denton was bringing back from Hong Kong. It didn't seem as though they had been able to, though. He shook his head. Perhaps it was more of the 'B Team' in action.

Home, he immediately went to his cabinet and chose a Japanese whisky, pouring three fingers. He had parked the Volvo in front of his townhouse, figuring it'd be slightly safer there than in his carport. He called his landlord, explaining a few things, asking for some repairs to be done, trusting the insurance was fully paid up. He left out a few details. No need for other people to get unduly concerned.

It was late afternoon. The kids were somewhere else, and Sandra had yet to arrive home. He fretted, worried for those closest to him. He rose and walked up to his bedroom, opening the top drawer of the bureau where he kept his guns. He pulled out the Tomcat with its holster from under a pile of socks along with a box of cartridges, leaving the larger gun for now. He loaded it and returned to the main floor, retrieving his glass, leaving the gun in its holster on the coffee table.

He called Vito. There was no answer, so he left a message. He texted Sandra, asking where she was. Then he did the same with his kids. Normally, his whisky had a relaxing effect. The opposite was happening. Jitters were setting in. The more he drank, the worse it became. Why did he leave the Vancouver Police again? Pride? Stupidity?

His cell blipped. Sandra. She was finishing up at a golf club in Richmond and would be home inside the hour. He relaxed slightly, still awaiting his kids' response. He didn't call his parents, figuring they were too removed from what he was doing. But he'd been wrong before. His phone burped. Sophie was close.

Who were these people? The lawsuits, he understood. Why was a legal firm possibly running drugs and using killers? His phone rang. Robin?

"Vito here. Got your message. You're not the police anymore, Robert."

"Thanks for the reminder. You can talk with Troy in Richmond about the boat thing. I have some dates for you to check. Maybe we could meet tomorrow. Paulo's? I'd like to hear your take on this."

"Yes. Nine?"

"Okay. Any luck on my car fire?"

"Possibly. A couple of cars and a truck leaving the area."

"Green Chevy pickup?"

"How did you know?

"Wild guess. Plates?"

"We're on it, now we have a clue."

"So, you are clueless without my guidance? Haven't missed a beat since I left, have you."

"Not so. Efficiency on case wind-ups has doubled since then. There's also talk of Paulo's needing to close."

"Don't even joke about shit like that."

"Pretty chirpy for an ex-employee."

"See you tomorrow." Robert ended the call.

First Sophie, then Robin entered the townhouse. They

came into the family area, immediately noticing the gun on the table.

"What is going on, Dad?"

"I feel some danger, so I'm getting prepared. I'd like you both to keep your eyes wide open as you move about. I'm going to say the same to Sandra."

Both children nodded, eyes a little larger, but this was not new territory for them.

"On a lighter note, got a new car today. Newer, anyway. Blue Volvo. It's out front. Let's go. I'll demonstrate."

CHAPTER
FIFTEEN

The next morning, Robert worried while he waited for Vito at Paulo's, tapping the table as his coffee was constructed. When he went to the bar to retrieve it, Vito walked in, face grim.

"Same as Robert, please." Order placed, they sat together at the rear.

Vito started. "Truck was a dead end. Stolen. Found in an alley off Commercial last night. Techies are giving it the once-over. You never know."

"I asked the Horsemen to look for prints at Alice's. It had been turned over. You should check with them about the boat. Any prints should match." Robert said.

"I hear it was ugly."

"Disgusting, Vito. That's a better word. Judging by how I found Denton, at some point they no longer cared what he had to say." He sipped his coffee. Vito's order was called out, and he went to get it.

"Did you question that labourer?" Robert asked, when he returned.

"Waste of time. Clammed up after I brought up the pushing allegation. Says Jackson was careless, dangerous job, etc. I didn't bring up that someone had seen him do it. No reason we could hold him at this point."

"That's disheartening. Don't suppose you got prints off of him, did you?"

"We are not totally useless without you, Robert. I gave him a glass of Coke after he requested it. We have the glass, his prints, and we can always get him back in. Not a terribly bright guy. We did a check but no form on him to date."

Robert nodded. "I'm now worried for my family."

"Yeah, a bomb would do that to a person."

"Any feedback on how it was constructed, what was used? Thomas mentioned the illiterate were involved."

"Working on that. We should have something soon. Whether it's of any use is another question."

They both drank their coffees, watching patrons come and go, then Robert noticed someone familiar walk by the window.

"What's Donovan doing on Cambie? Looking for needles on the sidewalk? Is this how he finds dealers or kingpins?"

Vito declined to answer, studying his coffee.

"Did you talk to Donovan?" Robert asked.

"No."

"Looked into this law firm?"

"Well … not a huge amount of support on that from the upper levels."

"I seem to recall not caring too much what the senior people thought as we went about our business."

"You were a bit of a maverick."

"Not going soft on me, are you?"

"Don't worry, Robert, we'll check them out. Not sure what we'll be able to find though."

"I get it. I'm doing my own research."

"What does that mean?"

"I have my own team, Vito. A bit ad hoc, I'll admit, and not exactly going full bore, due to some injuries, but we're making out as best we can."

"No rules to follow, I assume?"

"Exactly. The freedom is exhilarating." Robert was openly boasting now, ignoring his recent regret at leaving the force. Even as he said it, he had second thoughts.

"Sounds good, Robert. Just don't get in our way, okay?"

"Understood. But please remember who is giving you some hints." He pointed at his chest, eyebrows raised. He slid a piece of paper across the table. "The dates when Sherman returned from Hong Kong. Also, the date when Andy Ho returned. I believe Denton must have had a suitcase with him on returning from Hong Kong, but no one's found anything yet."

Vito nodded. "Thanks. I need to get back. I'll check this. Stay in touch." He finished his coffee, rose and left.

It wasn't more than two minutes later that Donovan entered Cafe Paulo, eyes scanning the customers until they rested on Robert. He came over and sat down across from Robert, uninvited. Thinning white hair drooped over a skinny, pale, malevolent face. Donovan was one step removed from being an albino. His restless fingers drummed on the tabletop as he waited for Robert to say something, then gave in.

"What are you doing here?" Donovan started.

"Drinking coffee. Trying to enjoy the neighbourhood. Which was working, before you came in. Thanks for asking." Robert looked past Donovan, trying to ignore his presence.

"Why are you talking to Vito?"

Robert leaned back as he gauged how far he could go with Donovan. "I'm getting married again and need a best man."

"Bullshit."

Robert shrugged, sipping at his coffee.

"Getting married? To that gangster bitch? That makes sense if you need to move some drugs, I suppose. I heard you were getting your fingers dirty recently."

Robert felt the cords in his neck tighten. It took all his willpower not to grip the edges of the table, which would have only egged Donovan on.

"You should know better than to get mixed up in things you know nothing about. You were useless as a detective and undoubtedly are useless at whatever it is you think you're doing now. I'm surprised they kept you on staff as long as they did."

Robert forced himself to look past Donovan again. "Unseasonably hot these past few days."

"Fuck around all you want, Robert. Let the adults handle things, before you get hurt."

Robert finally stared at Donovan but remained silent. He could actually feel his blood pressure rising several points. Donovan finally relented, the baiting not working.

He stood and left the cafe. Robert wondered what the visit was about. Robert moved his head in a circle to loosen his neck muscles. Perhaps the drug squad knew something about the construction labourers, but he doubted it. This seemed too sophisticated for them to figure out. They were probably sniffing around, trying to find out what others knew. Hard work to solve anything was a concept foreign to some of the drug boys.

He called Thomas after he had calmed slightly. "Robert here. Do you know where my car is being held? I'd like to check it for a few things."

"It's at the garage adjacent to the fleet lot north of West 1st."

"Good. I'm at Cafe Paulo. Think I'll walk down there now. I just had a visit from Donovan. Don't know why, but he seems very interested in what I'm up to. I didn't say anything. Seemed to irritate him."

"He may have a bad case of fear of missing out. It can be problematic if it's his supposed area of expertise and he perceives someone is way ahead of him."

"Maybe he could try working for a change."

"Do you believe in miracles, Robert?"

"Not really."

"There's your answer. Stay in touch."

Robert drained his remaining coffee and left to go find The Silver Bullet. He walked north up Cambie, past his last place of employment and towards the seawall where he would formerly go to ponder his cases, but turned right before reaching it, heading towards a nondescript metal warehouse sitting beside ranks of patrol cars waiting for their chance at the limelight.

A man-door on the side of the building accessed a small office where an officious-looking man sitting at a desk tried to give him the runaround. Robert showed him some identification but wasn't in the mood. "Call Thomas Harrow if you can't figure out how to let me see my car."

The officer blinked a couple of times, then relented. "Follow me. We are about to send it to Surrey, to the graveyard." Robert followed the man into the cavernous storage area. The infamous green pickup truck was right in front of him, being attended to by a technician clad in fetching white garments. He looked beyond the truck and spotted his car, what was left of it, against a wall, sitting on its wheel rims. There were hints of the colour it had been, with its sides mostly charred. Only one rear window had popped, so he remained hopeful about the glove compartment and what was in it.

"I'm going inside," Robert said. It wasn't a question. The minder started his objection, but Robert ignored him. He really had to yank on the passenger door to get it open. Reaching in, he managed to open the glove compartment, where no gloves had ever been. Success! A small pile of CDs and his insurance documents were sitting, waiting for him. They probably were unaware there had even been a fire. He looked over at the tech examining the truck, but he wasn't familiar. Declining to get into another argument with the minder, he grabbed his items, turned and walked out, leaving the garage official muttering to himself.

Robert headed south to his new car, in a happier frame of mind. He had his precious blood music. Once in, he started the engine and headed to Richmond. He was becoming very familiar with its flat and grid-like geography. He drove all the way south and again passed through Steveston to Garry Point Park where he parked, looking over at the slough. Seemed like more yellow tape had been added to the area. Perhaps he should buy shares in the tape company. Business seemed brisk, and he was certain it wouldn't slow any in the next few years.

He walked over to the entry at the storage building but no one was around, just the tape and a sign indicating entry was forbidden. He ignored it and, ducking under the tape, retraced his path of the day before. He came around the corner and realized that the tide was well out. The line of boats was several feet lower, and a relatively thin rivulet of water remained only in the centre of the channel, edged by ultra-smooth, sloping mud. No boat would be entering or leaving the slough while the tide was this low. He strolled to the top of the ramp and stared at the long dock stretching out before him.

None of the boats seemed to be resting on the slough bottom, but the wooden dock beside them definitely was. It rose and fell slightly over its length, except for one area near the far end. This section was sticking up a bit higher, out of alignment, as though it had come to rest on top of a beaver, or just maybe, something else.

Robert walked quickly out to the end of the dock, careful to avoid the warped wooden decking, ready to trip the unwary. At the raised area, he stooped down and leaned over the edge, holding on so as to not land in the muck. He was staring at a hardshell suitcase wedged under a wood beam. A fine sheen of silt covered its surface. The saltwater probably hadn't done any favours to its contents.

A clacking sound made him look up. He couldn't see anything, so he stood. Just north of the outer bank, a shimmering wooden canoe was wending its way through the reeds and bullrushes of the intertidal foreshore, which, considering the tide was out, should be impossible. A man with a cedar hat crowning long raven hair was paddling it slowly away from Robert. Then the head turned and looked directly at Robert. The man wasn't smiling. Was Robert trespassing somehow? He was astounded, then disturbed. What did this mean? This was the second time a spirit had acknowledged his presence recently. What if it tried to speak to him? What would he do in response?

He looked down as he picked out his cell and made a call. "Troy. It's Robert, back at the slough. Better get some people back out here. It's low tide, and a suitcase is preventing the dock here from settling gracefully into the mud." He looked up, but the native had vanished. Was it a Musqueam man? He had no idea.

"Wow. Good work, Robert. Why did you quit again?"

"Not certain. I'll wait here until someone arrives to make this all secure. Better make sure they bring a snack. It may be a while before the tide lifts the dock up." He looked over again for the canoe, but it was still gone.

"Someone is on the way. Also, we are having Alice come in today to identify her brother."

"Make sure she is escorted when she returns to her home to get her things, please."

"Of course. Thanks again, Robert." Robert stepped

back from the edge and sat down, waiting for the RCMP and thinking about the canoe and its occupant.

SIXTEEN

"We've been penetrated. I mean our system has."

"I don't think I have been, Candice, at least not recently. You, however … get a new pool boy? Enjoyable?"

"You can be such a dickhead. This is serious."

"How do you know?" Ross McDouguld asked, as he chuckled at his own humour.

"The guy who installed the system told me. He does occasional monitoring as part of his contract. He doesn't know who it was, though."

"Not much good then, is he? Installs a supposedly foolproof software system for our firm and now it has been entered. And he doesn't know who did it? I might as well have done it. Saved us all a ton of money. There's a dickhead involved here, but it's not me this time."

Candice had no answer for that. She and Ross were alone in a small conference room at their law firm, pondering the implications of this unwelcome bit of information.

"Why would someone be poking around inside our computers?"

Candice rolled her eyes. "Please tell me you didn't just ask that."

Ross changed tack. "What's the story on this Robert Lui?"

"He's an ex-detective. Used to be with the Vancouver Police Department. That's all I know so far. I don't know why he isn't with them anymore."

"Dangerous?"

"I don't know." Candice answered crossly.

"I'm taking care of him, so don't worry."

"What do you mean? You're not doing something stupid, are you?"

"*Moi*?"

"Emulating a pig. Very grown-up of you. Don't do anything we'll regret, please."

"I have my best people on it, don't worry."

"You don't have any 'best people'. You don't even know what 'best people' are. What have you done?"

"Some warnings, nothing serious. He should back off now. He also had a journalist working with him. I don't expect he will be a problem anymore either."

"Really? I hope you are right. A journalist? That doesn't sound good. Have you been able to find out who Robert is working for? And do you have a photo of him?"

"I don't know who hired him yet. I'm puzzling how to find out. Maybe I'll have him followed. I wouldn't be surprised to find him attached to one of the construction companies we have named in the lawsuits. And yes, I have a photo. I'll put it into a folder I created."

"For what it's worth, I think having him tailed is incredibly stupid." Candice said. "Maybe you should use your brain and try something else." But Ross had already tuned out, looking down at his notes. Candice shrugged, having delivered her warning.

Robert was home, lounging around and trying unsuccessfully to puzzle out motivations at work in his case. Sandra was at work, the kids at school. His cell rang.

"Robert?"

"Yup, this Troy?"

"Yes, you were correct. We opened the suitcase last evening. Inside were enough pills to supply a small town. Shrink-wrapped five times. Maybe four didn't work, I don't know. They are being analyzed as I speak, but definitely not aspirin."

"I wonder why Denton didn't just give up the case. That shit is not worth your life."

"Maybe he knew something about his brother's death? Or maybe he didn't think those guys would take it that far. I don't know, Robert. We may never know."

"Thanks for the call, Troy. Did Alice do the ID on her brother?"

"Yes, unfortunately. It was a terrible scene. She is not in great shape, Robert."

"Who would be? I think I'll try to see her before she leaves town. I assume she is still returning to Hong Kong?"

"Yes. She's still at the hotel you put her in, I believe."

"You have anyone watching out for her?"

"Manpower, Robert, so no. Think she's in danger?"

"I wouldn't ask otherwise. I'll definitely go down there this afternoon."

Over on King Edward Avenue at Mackenzie Secondary School, Sophie Lui and Rose Esmeraldo sauntered into their grade twelve social studies classroom together. It was the last course of the day for both of them.

Rose wasn't really looking forward to it. Her interest lay in the sciences, so this was just a course to tolerate. This didn't mean she did poorly in the class, far from it — she received excellent marks for her work in all the subjects she took. She was one of those 'wonder students' who seemingly sailed through the course load with no particular effort. This was far from the truth. She worked her tail off, her marks a reflection of this work ethic. Part of this attitude was drilled into her by her parents, but the other part was innate. She was driven to succeed, and her acceptance into a pharmacy program straight out of high school was the result. Rose's parents hadn't attended university, so they were thrilled about Rose's acceptance. And a pre-med program to boot. They told all their friends and relatives the good news. One or two mentioned something about what a leap it was to transition from high school to an institution where the faculty didn't care so much whether a student passed or failed, but these remarks were categorized as jealousy by Rose's mother.

Sophie wasn't quite as driven, her marks a couple of notches below Rose's. Once in high school, her interests became more varied and had slowly started coalescing around planning as a possible career, due in no small part to her late mother's job as a planner, first with Vancouver, then with the City of Surrey.

Despite the hour, a time when most students had tuned out, anticipating whatever was to come when the last bell rang, Sophie was looking forward to the class. Her teacher had promised a discussion on city planning and architecture. It was a topic receiving almost daily attention in the media due to pressing issues of the day but was rarely mentioned in any high school course, so this session was something to hang onto. After a semi-lively discussion in which about a third of the class participated, the teacher made an announcement.

"If you are interested, I have arranged for a few of you to attend a one-day seminar to be held in early July, so not exactly during the school year. It is being put on by the Urban Development Institute and will be delivered at a university building downtown. The topic is planning for the next century in Greater Vancouver. So, quite a general topic, but one I'm sure will be of interest to some of you here. In attendance will be a couple of developers, some planners, one or two lawyers and a couple of architects. There may be others, like local politicians, but it's uncertain at this time. Raise your hands if you're interested and I'll take names."

As Sophie raised her hand, she looked around the classroom. Only three other students had their hands up. The teacher noted their names and ended the class. "They were going to accommodate five from our school, so it looks like you are all in. It should be a lively day. Thanks, that's all for today. I'll confirm the date for you four in a week or two."

After school, Sophie and Rose walked east on King Edward towards home. "I can't believe I'm getting to attend that seminar," Sophie said, as she looked sideways at Rose.

"Lucky you. Where is the seminar on cadavers?"

"Yuck."

"Well, I guess it is a socials class after all. Can't expect too much from it, can you?"

"What are you saying?"

"Nothing. Hope you enjoy it. What are we doing tonight?" It was Friday and from there, the conversation drifted into the details of teenage girl's social lives.

Rose had evolved from a shy girl into a bit of a daredevil in their final year of high school. Sophie was both impressed and slightly taken aback by the change. Part of it probably stemmed from natural teenage rebellion against stern parents. The other part, when they had recently made their feelings about each other known. Sophie felt much more mature after their revealing conversation. And they had wasted no time exploring the physical side of their attachment to each other. For Sophie, it was electrifying.

Late that afternoon, Robert drove into the hotel parking lot in Richmond, parked, and went into the lobby. He had tried calling Alice before leaving home, but she wasn't answering. Robert walked up to the front desk, his nostrils tickled by the smell of mothballs. Perhaps they had just finished their daily cleaning. A young Chinese girl smiled at Robert from behind the plastic laminate countertop.

"Please call Alice Li. I don't know what room she's in."

The girl did as she was asked, then looked up at Robert. "No answer."

"Did she check out?"

She looked down at her computer screen. "No, still booked for two more nights."

"Her room been cleaned yet?"

"We don't clean every day, unless the guest requests it."

"But she's been here almost three days."

The girl shrugged.

He thought about asking to see the room, then remembered he wasn't police anymore. She'd likely tell him to buzz off. Well, not her, but someone more senior. He went over to the waiting area next to the entry and, sitting on a small uncomfortable sofa, he tried Alice's cell again. Still nothing. Undecided, he sat for a few moments scanning the room, realizing that this inn was at the low end of the quality range. Probably why the price was right. He went back to the desk and, after the girl gave him a small pad, he wrote a message for Alice and asked for it to be given to her on her return. The girl smiled again. Robert figured it was fifty-fifty as to whether Alice would receive it. He left.

CHAPTER
SEVENTEEN

Saturday morning, over coffee, Sandra raised a subject Robert had been expecting, and fearing just a little — a visit to Surrey to meet her parents.

"Sure. When do you want to do it?" Robert asked.

"How about this afternoon?"

"That's kind of sudden."

"You busy at something?"

Robert quickly racked his brain but came up empty. "Guess not," he said lamely.

"Scared?"

"Kind of."

"They're nice, like your parents, Robert."

This didn't give him any comfort. Hadn't he just had something to do with the death of two of their relatives? And that was putting it extremely nicely. He had killed both men as part of his VPD work, Sandra witnessing the most recent shooting. There wasn't any way this was going to turn out well.

He watched as Sandra called her home number. She

smiled across the table at Robert, waiting. He heard someone answer as he rose to get more coffee.

"Mom? It's Sandra. You and Dad both good?"

Robert returned with the pot, adding a tad more to Sandra's cup as she spoke with her mother. He turned to the paper sitting on the table, selecting the business section as he tried his best to not overhear what Sandra was saying when she wasn't speaking Punjabi. Which of course, didn't work in the least.

After about fifteen minutes, Sandra bade her mother goodbye and looked at Robert. "You heard?"

"Dinner out somewhere?"

"Restaurant on Scott Road, edge of Surrey, seven o'clock."

"We're going to talk about fun stuff, correct?"

"Absolutely, Robert."

"Cause, if it veers into gang things, I will not be a very happy man."

"We should be fine. Of course, they don't know I am living with you."

Robert managed to keep his jaw from dropping, but his eyes bulged slightly. "What did you say?"

"My parents are on the conservative side. They don't know about our living arrangement. They barely know about you, except for the marriage thing."

Robert was about to say something when it dawned on him that his parents hadn't known about Sandra either, so, fair was fair. Still, a daughter was different, and other than the gang action from his life as a detective, he had little knowledge of South Asian family customs, so he could only imagine what he was walking into.

"Have you told them I'm not from the Punjab?"

"Not really."

"Hopefully, they have open minds."

Sandra waggled her hand. "My mom? Sure. My father? Not really."

Robert winced. "Fantastic. How about the restaurant?"

"Don't know. I've been away for a while, remember? It's apparently fairly new and comes recommended."

"So, all in all, this could be quite the evening."

"Oh yes," as Sandra's head bobbed up and down.

With the evening plans set, Robert decided to spring something on Sandra. "Sandra, ever drive a standard transmission?"

"No. Is that the reason you bought that Volvo? So I couldn't drive it?"

"Good one. I hadn't thought of that. Maybe I won't teach you after all."

"Is it hard?"

"It's terribly difficult. That's why most cars have automatic transmissions." Sandra started to frown.

"Just joshing. I'll teach you. You'll be tearing around Vancouver in no time. I've heard that driving schools won't teach standard anymore. It's become a lost art. Well I, for one, intend to keep the art alive."

"Now?"

"Why not? Let's go."

Robert yelled to the kids that they were leaving and left through the front door.

Sandra got in the driver's seat, adjusted it, and was ready. Robert looked at her and grinned. "Gun the engine a bit and try to bring your foot off the clutch slowly. Let 'er rip, Sandra."

After a couple of springing lurches down Inverness, barely missing some parked cars, Robert had a better idea.

"We'll leave for dinner early and stop at a movie complex in Richmond sort of on the way. They have a huge parking lot where there's nothing to bump into. Decrease the anxiety slightly for you, okay?"

Sandra nodded, thus ending her first abbreviated lesson.

Once they were home, Robert tried Alice's number again. Nothing. He called Troy's cell, knowing it was Saturday and probably a day off.

"Troy, Robert here. Sorry to bother you, but could you get someone into Alice's room at the hotel? She hasn't answered any of my calls. I went down there yesterday, but the front desk didn't know squat and of course weren't going to let me in her room. I don't blame them. She may be checking out tomorrow. I booked it for four nights, but that was Wednesday."

"Okay, okay, Robert. Are you sure you quit the VPD?"

"Just humour a concerned citizen, Troy. I did find the suitcase after all."

"Fair point. Someone will let you know what we find."

Lesson number two was more successful. If Sandra wasn't exactly a smooth shifter yet, at least she was no longer stalling out. They called an end to it after half an hour and headed over to Scott Road.

Robert had received a cell call from the Richmond RCMP while they were at the cinema lot. An officer had gained entry to Alice's room, but she wasn't there. However, her cell phone was, which explained Robert's lack of success trying to reach her. It didn't explain why the phone wasn't with Alice. In Robert's view, most people would rather walk around stark naked than part with their phone. His concern grew.

He pulled into the parking area for the restaurant, feeling nervous. He looked over at Sandra., "Showtime." They walked into the entry. Sandra looked past the hostess, scanning the diners for her parents until she spied them at a table next to a window.

"There they are. Let's go."

Sandra's parents stood up as they approached. "Mom, Dad? This is Robert."

Robert detected surprise in Lal's eyes as they shook hands. Sandra's mother, Amrit, wasn't fazed in the least by Robert's appearance. She had a slight smile on her lips as they exchanged greetings. Amrit was an older version of Sandra, but equally beautiful. She was dressed in dark slacks and an olive top, decorated with a simple gold chain at the throat. Her eyes sparkled. Lal was more in line with what Robert expected — a severe face with bushy eyebrows under a mauve turban, almost as tall as Robert, with a thickening torso.

After sitting down, Robert across from Lal, and Sandra sitting near her mother, the questions started.

"So, you haven't told us where you are living, Sandra?"

"I'm staying with a friend in Vancouver, on Inverness Street."

"Good, but you know you are always welcome back home if you are trying to save money. You also mentioned working somewhere?"

"Yup, I'm at a caterer that is based on Main Street. It's going pretty well and sure gets me out all over. I'm also the one telling most of the rest what to do."

Amrit seemed good with her daughter's career move. Robert was impressed with Sandra's economical use of detail. It reminded him of his own spare use of facts when the situation called for it.

"And Robert, what do you do?" Amrit asked, Lal apparently playing backup for this grilling.

"I'm in the insurance industry, working with the claims department for BC Coastal Insurance." Even Robert was impressed with how bland his life seemed.

"Wow. You must be very busy when bad weather happens. There seems to be more and more of that every day." Amrit couldn't have said it any better.

"Yes, I don't have a dull time of it, despite appearances. Life is full of bad things happening." He tried to shift gears before he was asked to describe the bad things. "Sandra said this restaurant comes highly recommended."

"Indeed. We've been here a couple of times now. Do you like Indian food?" Lal came alive.

"Yes. I like all food. Sandra and I ...." Robert had to bite his tongue as he was about to hint at their living arrangement. "Sandra and I eat out at all kinds of places." Now he was flat out lying. He smiled thinly at Lal. Was he starting to perspire slightly?

Lal nodded. "Good, I'll do the ordering."

After the waitress left, the questioning resumed. "And how did you two meet, Sandra?"

Sandra told her parents an abbreviated version of what she had told Robert's parents about Bella Kind, omitting the police part. Robert couldn't discern if Amrit and Lal were buying the sanitized version of Sandra's life, but he doubted it.

"So, you are a fisherman, Robert?" Lal asked.

"Uh, yes. I like to go after the salmon when possible." He was fleshing out the lie started by Sandra.

"A long way to travel for salmon. Surely there are closer places to Vancouver where the fishing is just as good?" Lal seemed to be trying to trip Robert up.

"Undoubtedly, but a friend told me about the resort and that I just had to try it out." He was working his way deeper and deeper into trouble, he could feel it. It was the classic way most lying goes. He reached down under the table to adjust the ankle holster chafing his shin. He wasn't going anywhere these days without the Tomcat strapped to his leg.

Amrit came to the point. "So, a wedding. Have you decided when and chosen a venue yet? There is a large hall on King George Boulevard that we could get for a good rate. We would just need the date to reserve it, then get the invitations out."

"No, Mom. We haven't got to the details just yet. I'll let you know, okay? I think we'd like to keep it small."

Robert sensed discontent on the far side of the table at

this revelation. He saw Amrit looking over at Sandra's left hand, the hand where a huge rock should be if Robert was any kind of serious suitor. She didn't say anything but glanced at Robert. He got the message.

It wasn't until dessert was contemplated that the discussion veered into bad territory.

"Do you keep in touch with any of your cousins, Sandra?" Amrit asked.

"You know I don't. Nothing has changed there in my view."

"Yes, I know a couple of them passed away, but the others? They are okay, no?"

"I don't know, and I don't want to know. Two of them were incredibly bad people."

Amrit looked hurt, as though she hadn't kept up with the local gang news. Maybe she was just ignoring the bad stuff, like many people do.

"May I ask what your last name is, Robert?" Lal was fishing. Robert decided to let him hook something.

"Lui. My father is from Hong Kong, mother is from Vancouver." There was no point in telling anything but the truth. He suspected it wouldn't take long before Lal ferreted out the items Robert had glossed over, so he let loose with a few facts. "I used to be a detective with the Vancouver Police Department, but I've moved on to a new life, which I'll build with Sandra. I was previously married, but that came to an end when my late wife contracted cancer and passed away several years ago."

Amrit's eyes grew slightly larger as she digested these tidbits. Lal was looking sideways at Amrit. "I am so sorry to hear that, Robert," Amrit responded.

"Dessert, anyone?" Lal asked, evidently lacking the will to probe any further.

"Please, Dad," Sandra said.

The waitress came and Lal ordered some *gulabjamun* — dumplings served in syrup. Despite all the food already consumed, the dumplings had no problem disappearing quickly.

"That was excellent food, thank you," Robert said. His stomach was happy. He signalled the waitress, but Lal wasn't having it.

"Our treat."

"You sure? Thanks again. It has been a pleasure meeting you both. Sandra has told me so much about you." Veering into outright lies again. Time to get out while the getting was good.

"I've got to get Sandra back to her place. We should do this again, soon." They stood and, after Sandra kissed both parents, left.

Sandra looked sideways at Robert as they approached their car. "Someone was in a hurry to leave."

"I wanted to get out before they noticed the lies. I thought it was the prudent thing to do."

Sandra nodded. "I guess. My father didn't look too happy about us. I hope he doesn't do anything crazy."

"What do you mean?"

"He is pretty hardcore on the Sikh faith, that's all."

This revelation did not give Robert any comfort. Just another thing to worry about, he supposed.

As Lal waited for the bill, he looked sideways at Amrit, his head shaking from side to side. "They are living together, I know it. She will bring shame on our family. Also, did you notice how much older than Sandra he seems?"

Amrit shook her head in silence. But she couldn't remain that way. "Don't you dare do something you will regret. Our family already has enough shame to spare thanks to those nephews of ours. And don't forget, he used to be a police officer."

Lal responded, stone-faced, "The scriptures must be respected and honoured. I will do some checking up on this Robert Lui. That he is not Punjabi is a very bad omen."

CHAPTER
EIGHTEEN

Sunday morning, Robert was downstairs alone and feeling optimistic enough to turn on the television for the early local news. After a traffic report that, unsurprisingly, depicted no traffic at all, the anchor started in with a breaking story. A body had been discovered in Richmond on a riverbank beside one of the arms of the Fraser, a woman's body. Despite an on-site reporter attending, nothing further was known, except that a couple of rolls of yellow police tape were decorating the immediate vicinity between a hotel and a marina. The location didn't seem that far from the airport.

Robert was certain that the concept of 'news' had lost its meaning for the local television stations. The reporters were excellent at telling the audience what they didn't know or what they expected to know in a few minutes, but actual information? Not so much.

However, his concern grew again. He called the RCMP in Richmond. It took him a few minutes to finagle his way through the defences put up by the admin person.

He was getting tired of using Troy's name to get anywhere. She eventually relented and connected him to an officer.

"Any identification of the victim?"

"All I know is, Asian female, badly beaten. Don't know anything else at this time."

"Shit. Okay, thanks. I don't suppose you could let me know if you find out her identity?"

"I don't suppose. Who are you again?"

"Forget it." He ended the call. This was getting annoying. He needed a better modus operandi for his new role in life. Was the body Alice? Wasn't Richmond's population at least fifty percent of Chinese heritage? It could be anybody.

He left the television on and went to make coffee. His cell rang. He eyed it with trepidation. Richmond RCMP?

"Robert here."

All he heard was breathing, then finally, "It's Alice. I'm sorry, but I forgot my phone at the hotel, or I would have called you. I am back in my room now and finally got your message, but my mind has been a whirlwind. I'm leaving Vancouver tomorrow, for good."

"I've been worried for you, Alice. They found a woman's body by the river sometime last night. A Chinese woman."

"I am fine now, but I saw my brother Friday. It was horrible. Who are these people that kill?"

"I don't know yet. Can I come see you today, before you go?"

"Of course, I'd like to see you as well." The reply came too quickly, but Robert needed to talk with her. He felt that she might eventually help him to unwind this knot of a puzzle with killing at its centre. And there was the latent danger, seemingly inching closer to her.

"I'll come down around one today. I'll take you for late dim sum?"

"Yes, see you then, Robert."

"Don't let anyone in your room. Got that?"

"Okay."

He returned to his coffee operation. Sandra sauntered downstairs and into the kitchen. She hugged Robert from behind, still in her pyjamas. He quickly lost focus on what he was doing. Even coffee wasn't a match for Sandra's charms. Again, he realized how smitten he really was.

Perhaps he should contemplate a complete career change for the safety of those close to him. What else could he do, though? He felt that he'd only been adequate as a police detective, and the jury was still out on his private eye adventure. Something to consider, however.

"Breakfast?"

"Lovely, but maybe keep it light. I'm meeting that Alice girl for dim sum later."

"Should I be concerned?"

"Absolutely. But then, she is also flying back home to Hong Kong tomorrow. A body was discovered last night by the Fraser in Richmond, a Chinese female, so I was worried. Turns out it wasn't her obviously, so ...."

"Hmm, eggs of some sort? How about camp style?"

"What's that?"

"You know, Toad in the Hole, Egg in a Basket. That sort of thing."

Robert smiled. "Excellent, I'll finish the coffee

process." As he waited for the water to drip through, he glanced at the calendar on the wall. They had entered June several days earlier. "When is that winery party?"

"Less than two weeks. It's a Friday afternoon and evening. We are heading up there Wednesday to prepare. You're still coming, correct?"

"Wouldn't miss it. Have you fixed a place to stay?"

"I booked four nights in an Oliver hotel, which doesn't seem very large as far as towns go. They boast that it's the wine centre for the region, although I'm guessing other nearby towns are saying the same thing."

"While you're doing the prep work, maybe I'll do some recon work to address our depleted wine stock."

"I thought you were chasing this legal firm, no?"

"I believe I can do more than one thing at the same time."

"Successfully? Now you're bragging." With that comment, Sandra swung into action. It didn't take long for Sophie and Robin to make an entrance from upstairs once the cooking aromas started wafting around the townhouse.

As they sat and ate their breakfast, only a single question was raised, by Robin. "Pops, can we visit that contractor this week?"

Robert nodded. "I'll arrange a day." He still wasn't sold on Robin doing the labourer thing for the summer, but he'd gauge the builder first. The kids reluctantly cleaned up after some prompting while Sandra prepared to go to work, a Sunday community event in downtown's west end.

Robert went for a short stroll around his

neighbourhood instead of a run for a change. While he walked, he reviewed the events of the past several days, eyes on the ground, not noticing much. He was heading for home on Inverness when a youngster rode a small e-scooter on the sidewalk towards him, then whizzed past. He turned to watch the kid and immediately saw a small man a half block away turn sideways to study a house as though it was the most important thing in the world. Robert immediately knew he was being tailed, and by someone not very adept at it. He took out his cell and quickly snapped a photo while the man was engrossed in a rather sad-looking bungalow.

Why Robert was being followed, he wasn't sure, but he did know he didn't want anyone tagging along for a trip to visit Alice. He turned and started walking again, pretending ignorance. As he neared his home, he made a decision. He walked up to his car and quickly got in, gunned the engine and took off. He glanced in his mirror and watched as the man pulled out his cell. Robert turned at the next cross street, again at his lane, and idled into his carport, cutting the engine. He hadn't noticed any suspicious cars on the street in front of his townhouse, but that didn't mean much. Someone would probably be vainly looking to pick his vehicle up on the nearby streets, but it wouldn't take long for the small man to walk up the lane and find the Volvo, inept as he seemed. Robert entered through the back door.

"Sandra? Can I come with you downtown in the cab?"

"Sure, why? It'll be here in a minute or so."

"Gonna Skytrain it to Richmond instead of driving."

"Okay." The reply was slow and puzzled.

"I'll explain in the cab." He went up to his room and retrieved his larger gun with its shoulder holster, then added a windbreaker for cover to complete his ensemble.

As the two got into their taxi out front, Robert spied the little man farther down the street looking at the cab. Once again, he was talking to his cell. Arriving downtown, it was an easy thing to hop out of the cab at a stoplight, make for the nearest subway station and get on board a train heading south to Richmond. He doubted his trailers would be able to follow him but chose the airport train just in case. He'd switch where the line split at the Richmond casino to the train making for the centre of Richmond. It all felt very familiar, yet different somehow from the last time when he was shaking watchers from the VPD on the transit lines.

At the casino station, he waited until the last second before squeezing between the closing doors onto the platform. He looked down the short train as it started to speed away, but no one else had dashed through to follow him. There probably weren't any followers on the train, but better to not assume anything.

After arriving at the end of the line, he walked a couple of blocks to Alice's hotel and asked for her at the front desk.

Alice came out of the elevator, a thin smile breaking out as she spied Robert. She came over to greet him. Then she tried unsuccessfully to hug him. Robert wasn't having it.

"Hi Alice. You pick a restaurant. I assume you have cased a few out in your brief stay here."

"There is one a block away that is very good." She didn't appear put out.

"Okay. Lead on."

They had settled in at a small table near the kitchen doors when Robert's cell rang. He normally would ignore it when with a person but relented after the fourth ring.

"Robert? It is Troy. We have an ID on the woman found by the river hotel. Her name is Alice Li."

"I'm with Alice right now, my Alice. You think they got the wrong person?"

"Probably, not certain yet."

"Thanks, Troy. You guys should publicize the pill bust. Might make them stop looking for it and killing people in the process."

"Yes. We'll do it tomorrow, first thing."

He looked over at Alice as the first cart rolled by. She was concentrating on the food, as Robert had hoped. But now he was worried for her safety in Hong Kong. It wasn't a stretch to imagine someone finding her there and doing whatever they wished.

Alice picked out a couple of dishes off of the first cart. They started on some *siu mai*. "The restaurant food here in Richmond is surprisingly good compared with Hong Kong," she said.

"So I've heard, good choice, Alice." Robert's compliment was as much about her selection of a restaurant as it was about the food. "How large is your family back home?"

"I have only a younger sister now. My parents will be heartbroken, no sons left."

Robert nodded. "I understand completely. I was thinking about cousins, that sort of thing. It may be a good idea for you to disappear for a while when you get back there. Just in case. The woman discovered last night by the river had the same name as you." He left it for her to figure out the meaning of this.

It only took Alice a second for her face to grow pale. She stopped chewing and stared at him. She was holding her chopsticks so tightly Robert thought they might snap.

He came to a decision: "I believe someone should be watching out for you until you get on that plane tomorrow. I'll call the RCMP after we are done here."

The RCMP declined to provide bodyguard services, even after Robert graphically explained the situation to the person at the station. He wasn't surprised, and that left only one solution — Robert. As they walked away from the restaurant, Robert explained what he was going to do. Alice smiled for a change, contemplating the immediate future.

"I am not staying in your room, Alice. I'll be in the lobby, keeping an eye on things for you."

"Okay." She smiled her most fetching smile at him. He shook his head.

"Let's walk around. Maybe you can show me Richmond's highlights."

She started laughing at this fantasy. A couple of hours later, Robert realized she was correct. There were no highlights. It seemed to be mall after mall, with low residential towers behind them, separated by an overabundance of traffic. No building was higher than thirteen or fourteen stories due to the nearby airport, the entire city having a stunted appearance because of it. The fishing port in the southwestern corner of Richmond was starting to look better and better.

Eventually, they arrived back at Alice's hotel. Alice wanted to visit her room before dinner. Robert declined her invitation to follow along, remaining in the lobby. He called Sophie and then Sandra and left messages as to what he was up to.

There was a small cafe next to the lobby. They entered after Alice eventually reappeared and had a slow dinner, Robert realizing that a long night lay ahead. Alice described her life before her Vancouver adventure. Hard work, small pleasures, and love of family defined the Li's life in Hong Kong. She had been a cashier in a food store on the Kowloon side while taking a night course to work in the justice system as a courtroom aide. Vancouver was her first real venture abroad. Robert related a bit of his journey as a detective for the Vancouver Police. Alice's eyes widened as she listened, then relaxed slightly as she started to feel safer with this 'insurance agent' keeping watch over her.

After dinner, the two went back outside and took a stroll around the area. There weren't very many other pedestrians, but the breezes were languid and warm, the light softly bronze as the sun headed down between the residential towers to the west. It was a pleasant interlude and, Robert gauged it a nice last evening in Vancouver for Alice. Perhaps a bit dull, but after what she had been through, all she needed.

Back in the hotel, Robert said goodnight to Alice and had a word with the woman behind the front desk. "Are you here all night, or is there a shift change at some point?"

"Midnight is when Danny comes on, why do you ask?"

"I want to make sure no one gets up to Alice Li's room, that's why I am going to spend the night here in the lobby to monitor things."

The woman's eyes widened. "The elevator only works with a room card. Is she in danger?"

"Not as long as both of us do our jobs properly." There was no reply, so Robert pressed on. "I assume there are two exit stairs accessing her floor, correct?"

She nodded. "Who are you?"

"Ex-police officer. Any other way to get up to the third floor other than the elevators?"

"No."

"Good. I'm going to go look at the outside." The woman stared at Robert as he left the hotel. He knew that hotel staff were used to all sorts of weird things happening, mostly on account of their guests, but this seemed to be new territory for the girl. He ambled along through the parking lot to one end of the six-storey building. There was no basement, so he knew the stairs would end at grade somewhere. He walked up to a door sporting a handle. He tested it. Solid and locked. He'd have been happier with a blank door, no hardware at all, but firemen probably needed to be able to access the stairs in an emergency. He turned and walked to the other end of the building, finding a similar door. Satisfied, he returned to the lobby, went over to the seating area and selected a couch with its back to a wall. A television was on, showing a baseball game from the west coast, so he settled in.

Sometime after eleven, his cell rang.

"Robert? You okay?" It was Sandra.

"Fine, Sandra. I thought it prudent to keep a watch at the hotel here. The RCMP declined the job. Sitting on a bad sofa watching bad television in the lobby."

"Should I be concerned, Robert?"

"For sure, but I have both my guns, and staying clear of Alice, so concern for my safety is appreciated."

"Not exactly what I was thinking, but okay. See you tomorrow morning?"

"Yes, Sandra. Call anytime tonight, it'll help keep me alert." After he ended the call, he remembered to send the photo of his follower from Inverness to Vito with a text.

> Do you or anyone on the force know this
> guy? He's been tailing me. Thx.

Hopefully, he'd get an answer tomorrow. Robert made it for the shift change at midnight, had a short word with Danny as to his mission, then promptly passed out on the couch.

A hand grabbed his shoulder. Robert jerked awake, looking up as he reached inside his jacket for his gun, then relaxed as he realized it was only Danny, the gun partly drawn. Danny's eyes widened a bit at seeing the gun.

"Sir, I thought I should wake you. A man was in here asking for the Alice Li guest. I told him she was unavailable. He did not seem happy. A large and most disreputable looking fellow, I must say."

"Did he leave?"

"A few moments ago."

Robert stood, calling Alice's cell. It rang to voicemail. "Alice, if you get this, go to your bathroom, lock the door and keep all the lights off." He didn't know what else to tell her. He turned and ran out the lobby door, heading for the west exit stair. He looked around as he approached it. He was alone. He tested the door, but it was secure. He turned and ran for the other end of the building, cursing its length. He arrived and immediately saw the door handle on the concrete. He slowed, approaching the door carefully. It was slightly ajar. The immediate area was dim, and no light came from within the exit. Smoke tendrils were leaking out. Someone smoking inside the exit? Gitanes — he knew the strong smell, nothing matched it. A watcher?

He grabbed his gun, safety off, and pulled the door open. He couldn't see much, his eyes still adjusting to the darkness. He crouched down and entered slowly. He sensed something just as it swung at him. He started to rise as it connected with his neck. He hit the floor, and seeing a shadow close by, lashed out with his foot, hooking the guy's ankle, pulling and toppling him. The man hit the floor with a thud, accompanied by metallic sounds. Before Robert could react, he popped back up like a whack-a mole and bolted out the door.

Robert rose slowly, his neck aching, then looked down for his gun, but it was too dark to locate. He peered out the door, but the guy was long gone. It hadn't taken much to topple the guy, so he must have been on the small side. Not the fellow Danny had talked to. He touched his neck; his fingers came away sticky with blood.

The light fixture next to the exit door was smashed, but thin light filtered down from the floors above. His eyes were slowly adjusting, and he finally located his gun. He stooped to grab it, turned, and ran up the stairs to the third floor. He looked through the door's small pane of glass into the corridor.

Someone was in the hall halfway along, a large man at a door. Robert didn't waste any time. He opened the door and yelled. The man turned, studied him for a second, then raised his right hand and fired a gun at Robert. The bullet missed, and Robert hit the floor. Aiming carefully, he fired twice in return, the explosions loud. The light was low, and the distance wasn't conducive to hitting the mark.

The man evidently decided he'd had enough. He turned and fled to the far exit stair. Robert holstered his weapon, figuring his point had been made. By this time a couple of doors had opened, curious heads peering out, wondering what the ruckus was about. Robert ignored them, walking up to what he assumed was Alice's door. He knocked. "Alice? It's Robert here." He spoke loudly in case she had made it to her bathroom.

As he waited, he looked down. Was that a spot on the carpet? He stared at a sparse assembly on the floor leading to the other end of the corridor. Definitely not the remnants of room service, more like a thin blood trail. At the base of the door was a small sledgehammer, the tool of choice for lock picks the world over.

He pulled out his cell and called the RCMP. As he was

explaining things to the receptionist, a tentative voice came from inside the room. "Who is it?"

Robert answered in Cantonese. The door opened slowly, Alice's eyes wide open. He raised his finger, bidding her to wait as he finished the call.

"You okay?" Robert asked when he was done.

"Yes. I just got your message. What happened? You are bleeding." Her voice quavered. As he was about to respond, he heard a distant siren. Impressively quick. He'd need to compliment Troy when they next spoke.

Some guests were still in the hall staring at Robert and Alice. "Let's get out of the hall until the police get here." He touched his neck again; his fingers came away coated with his own blood. The bullet hadn't come close to him, so it must have been the midget in the stairwell taking a swing at him with something. He was lucky he hadn't been brained. The whole evening would be ending differently if he had, that was certain.

He entered her room and flipped on the light. Alice turned and hugged him tightly. "Oh, Robert." Her head nestled firmly on his shoulder, ignoring the blood.

How had he ended up in the exact situation he had been trying to avoid since first meeting Alice? He couldn't explain it. Perhaps the gods were laughing at him, testing him. Yes, that was it. They couldn't stand that he was happy for the first time in a long time, so they were trying their best to derail him. He wasn't having it.

He tried to detach himself. "You are getting blood on your hair, Alice."

"I don't care, Robert."

Well, that didn't work. Mercifully, there was a knock

on the door. Robert firmly put Alice to one side and opened the door. It was Danny.

"What happened here?"

"The short answer is that someone managed to get on the floor and was about to grab Alice when I showed up. You may need to get the renovators in; there are a few bullet holes in the corridor. Also, the east exit stair has some damage down at the bottom."

Danny's eyes expanded to about twice their normal size.

"Hear that siren? Police are on the way. You should get down to the desk to welcome them, don't you think?" Robert asked.

Danny nodded slowly, speechless. He turned and quickly headed to the elevators. Inside of two minutes, several officers were on the third floor. First, they shepherded the other guests back into their rooms, to be interviewed later, Robert supposed. He explained who he was and what he'd been doing, but in the absence of any 'bad guys' on the premises it didn't seem to impress any of them.

"We're going to take you and this girl in to verify your stories," the largest of the group said.

"At least please call Troy Geelham or someone at your station to verify who I am first," Robert proposed.

The sergeant peered at Robert. "You do look familiar. Check him out." This was directed at one of the constables. "I don't think I'm calling Troy this time of night. You said you shot at the guy?"

"Returned fire, yes."

"Gun please."

Robert reluctantly handed it over. They neglected to search him, however, failing to find his Tomcat. He found this extremely sloppy. He'd add it to the short list for Troy next time they spoke.

The constable nodded at his sergeant after he got off the call to the station.

"Your lucky day. Don't make a habit of this." The sergeant said.

Robert pointed out the trail on the carpet, finally giving them something tangible. Two of the officers went off like bloodhounds, leaving three to finish up with Robert and Alice.

"You should check the east exit stair. There might be a cigarette stub there with prints or DNA or something useful for you." Robert suggested. One officer nodded.

After the officers left, Robert dabbed his neck to get some blood off, then firmly said goodnight to Alice and resumed his post in the lobby. He texted Sandra.

> Bit of a ruckus here, but I'm generally ok.
> I'll make sure Alice gets to the airport in
> the morning, then I'm coming home.

CHAPTER
TWENTY

Monday morning and Robert was down a gun. After escorting Alice into the International Terminal at YVR, they parted, not before Alice unsuccessfully tried to kiss him. Nevertheless, she then gracefully thanked him for everything he had done for her. There was an invitation to come visit Hong Kong, which he acknowledged but didn't say yes. He waved goodbye as she was swallowed up at the security line.

Then he made his way back to the Skytrain and headed into Vancouver, completely worn out. He noticed people checking him out and then looking away quickly. He doubted he was looking very flash. He'd fix himself up when he got home. He wearily got off at the King Edward Station. Bus it east? No, there probably weren't any on this street, anyway. He dug out his cell.

"Sandra?"

"Thank goodness. You alright?"

"More or less. Could you drive over to pick me up? I'm at Cambie and King Edward."

"You think I should?"

"Sure. You are already driving better than fifty percent of the people out there. You won't improve if you don't get out and do it."

The reply was tentative. "Alright, see you soon, I hope."

He waited on the sidewalk across Cambie from the transit station, back from the foot traffic. He needn't have worried. People were giving him a wide berth after looking him over. His cell rang.

"Robert?"

"Yup."

"Vito here. The picture you sent? Guy is known as Jingles."

"You kidding?"

"Low level hood from Abbotsford. He got the name from carrying around a fair amount of change in his pockets. His gang is called the Chicken Coop."

"Sounds like a winner. Probably all birdbrains. Could we meet later today? At the Apollo this time?"

"After lunch, two or so?"

"See you then." He waited, shifting his weight from side to side. His neck ached. His back ached. Maybe he should really prioritize that career change before he ended up in some hospital ward on a permanent basis. Looking east, he spied a blue Volvo headed his way along King Edward. Sandra saw him as he signalled her to turn the corner. She complied and smoothly glided to a stop. He walked around the corner and got in.

"You alright to get home?" he asked.

"What happened to you?"

"Bit of a dust-up. I'm okay, really."

Sandra didn't seem to buy that explanation but put the car in gear and smoothly moved out into traffic heading north. She couldn't see the bad side of his neck.

"I'm impressed. Your driving is super smooth. You must have had a fantastic teacher."

"Teacher was barely adequate. Student was superb, however, a very quick learner."

Robert looked over, grinned, then put his head back. "I'm exhausted."

At home, Sandra saw to his neck after a moment of horror at what had befallen Robert. She cleaned the wound and needed to tape several bandages onto the area, their size inadequate to the task. "We need better first aid materials here," she said.

"You're pretty good at the doctor thing. Learn that up north?"

"As a matter of fact, yes, I did. Hospitals are few and far between once you leave the Lower Mainland. Why didn't you go to one last night?"

"I didn't feel as though I had a spare six hours when people were after Alice. Thanks, you are a godsend."

"Coffee?"

"Am I that transparent?"

"Yes, you are, Robert."

While he waited, he called Bernard. "Hey, it's your friend, Robert." There was silence.

"Giving me the cold shoulder? Very shortsighted, Bernard."

"Perhaps, but also prudent, I believe."

"You are a worrywart. How is your arm, by the way? News flash. Pills, Bernard. There was a bust in Steveston a couple of days ago. Huge cache. You can find out the rest from the Richmond RCMP. Take care." Then he added, "Maximum airtime, please and thanks." He ended the call, then looked in the fridge for something to accompany his coffee. Pickings were thin.

He ended up with some yogourt adorned with nuts. Sandra declined some but poured herself coffee after filling Robert's mug. They sat across from each other.

"What exactly do you hope to accomplish in Oliver, Robert?"

"Probably nothing substantial, but I'd hope to get an idea about these lawyers. I'll do some surreptitious listening as I refill their plates and glasses."

"Do you even know what they look like?"

"Good point. I'll get my secret agent to get that to me."

"Secret agent?"

"Yeah. He has entered their computer system, so it shouldn't be a problem."

Sandra shook her head as she sipped her coffee. "I hope you know what you're doing."

Robert smiled. "That's fifty-fifty, but I don't question you about catering, do I?"

"Good point. Here's to your spy mission in wine country!" She raised her cup, and they both drank, a caffeine addict's variation on a toast to success. Robert then made a quick call to Dan Prudence to fill him in on the latest developments.

Well before two, Robert left for the Apollo Cafe. He'd worry about Robin's contractor later. He was dog-tired. The weather was still pleasant, a bit warm and not uncomfortable. As he walked, he kept his eyes open the entire route, but couldn't discern anyone following him, even after trying a couple of tricks to see if anyone would reveal themselves. Perhaps his foes were licking their wounds literally and had taken a day off.

Robert had just sat down with his coffee at the rear of the Apollo, no sign of Vito, when his cell rang.

"Robert, Troy here. Heard you were keeping my officers busy last night."

"Doing my best. Any luck on the blood trail? I believe I winged one of them."

"Ended in a parking lot. Nothing at any of the local hospitals either. Drops were tiny, so not a mortal wound, I'd guess. We dug three bullets out of the walls and picked up a cigarette butt. Hopefully something has DNA attached, we'll see."

"I trust the hotel wasn't too put out by the commotion, but I didn't start the fireworks. I do have a couple of professional comments for you; response time was outstanding after I called it in, but procedure left something to be desired. They took my Sig Sauer away, which I wouldn't mind having back, but neglected to search me, leaving me still armed. It's a good thing I am an upstanding citizen." There was silence while Troy digested this.

"Gonna have a word with someone. You carry two guns?"

"Only when I'm feeling antsy, which happens after bombs go off in my carport."

"Understandable. And Alice is gone?" Troy asked.

"I saw her melt into the security lineup at YVR, so I believe so."

"Description of the men?"

"Only one, the large guy in the corridor, but he was a distance away. I think the staff at the front desk, Danny? He was face to face with him, so that'd be your best bet. The one in the exit stair, I never saw. Too dark and I was trying to avoid getting concussed. However, I heard some metallic sounds when I knocked him over. Ever hear of a hood called Jingles from Abbotsford?"

"No, sounds intriguing."

"I doubt it, but he was following me earlier in the day …."

"We are publicizing the pill bust today. But I happened to be tuned into CBC late this morning, and they were already talking about it. Don't suppose you know how that happened, do you, Robert?"

"They are bloodhounds, Troy. They can sniff out a story from twenty klicks away. Must be extremely well trained."

"Didn't think I'd get a straight answer. Stay in touch, Robert. And come by if you want your gun back." The call ended.

Still no sign of Vito, and his coffee was almost done. As he rose to order another, Vito finally walked through the door. Vito studied Robert's neck as they ordered, "What happened to you?"

"Cut myself shaving."

"No one shaves back that far." His eyebrows were raised.

"Okay, nearly got conked by that Jingles character inside a stairwell last night. I think it was him. Made that slot machine sound when I tripped him. The only reason he didn't get my skull was his stupidity. He had just lit a cigarette and, by doing that, screwed his night vision. He had smashed the light inside the stair, and he couldn't see any better than me when I entered. I got lucky, I suppose."

A moment later, the coffees were ready. Vito and Robert repaired to the rear of the cafe.

Robert started, "You heard about the lady found by the river yesterday in Richmond?"

"Yes."

"Her name was Alice Li, same name as my Alice. Beaten to death. I imagine a case of the wrong person in the wrong place. These people may be idiots, but they are also lethal. You heard about the pills I found?"

"Yes. Some kind of courier system at work?"

"Using our labourers hired from Hong Kong. It also seems they are dispensed with when they either become a liability or maybe refuse to do what they are told to do … I don't know."

"Quite bizarre. This is not how things normally work."

"I believe you should be treating all the recent construction deaths as possible homicides. I'd put money on it."

"In one sentence, you have just quadrupled our serious incidents caseload, thanks."

"Welcome. There is also an aspect of Keystone Cops to all of this. I don't know why. I am attending a party in the Okanagan next week hosted by the law firm that may be behind all this shit."

"They invited you?"

"Don't be daft, Vito. Sandra's company is catering the party. I'm going as one of the servers."

Vito studied Robert. "I know someone working out of the Oliver RCMP. His name is Jackie Chan. I'll let him know there'll possibly be trouble brewing."

"<u>The</u> Jackie Chan?"

"Don't be daft, yourself. He's a cop. Spent some time in Hong Kong, I think, but he speaks some Mandarin as well as Cantonese."

"English?"

"Better than you, anyway. Has a hint of a British accent."

"Let him know I am an honourable person, won't you?"

"You sure Jingles missed your skull entirely?"

"It's just that because I'm no longer with a police force, officers are not giving me due respect, in my humble opinion."

"You didn't think this quitting thing through, did you?"

"I thought I did, but I may have missed a couple of ramifications. I'll figure it out, don't worry. The party is a week this Friday at Possession Point Winery."

They sipped their drinks in silence, then Vito broke it. "The dates you gave me match up with extra street product, by the way. Looks like you were correct."

"Any luck with fingerprints yet?"

"Waiting for the Horsemen."

Robert studied Vito's face.

"Something you want to say, Robert?" A note of concern in his voice.

"Yes, Vito, I'm planning on marrying Sandra. I wonder, if we do it around here, would you stand up for me? I don't want a stag party. Just your company will be fine."

A smile broke out. "Of course, Robert. Congratulations!"

"Thanks. I finally met Sandra's parents Saturday evening."

"And?"

"I was thinking of eloping, but that's not happening. I get the feeling that her father is not impressed, for several obvious reasons. Then there is the gang thing. It's complicated. They don't know about my connection to Manny and Andy ... yet. But I wouldn't put it past Lal to ferret out something."

"Lal?"

"Sandra's father. Sandra says he is a bit rabid on the religion thing. It's not giving me any comfort. As if I don't have enough to worry about."

"It's the way of the world, Robert. Simple wouldn't be any fun, would it?"

"S'pose. Thanks for meeting with me. You'd better get

back to catching criminals. Say, have you ever heard of someone called 'The Mandarin'?"

"No, who is it?"

"A lawyer from Hong Kong. Just curious."

TWENTY-ONE

That same afternoon, the large conference room at Skyler, McDouguld, and Moon was almost full. Brock Kinross entered, looked around and noticed some of the same youngish legal people from both sides he had met at the previous pre-trial meeting he attended. He had no one with him. None were needed. Brock had been around the block a few times, first, eleven years with a private firm specializing in difficult defence cases, then signing on with BC Coastal Insurance when he decided a more civilized lifestyle might help him avoid a divorce. Enough with the nine PM home arrival act. He'd already mostly missed his two children's preteen years. He was determined to see them through their teen years. It was the kind of ass-backward thinking that had his wife start thinking she could do better, but she had to admit, at least he was trying to make up for lost time.

Brock nodded at a couple of the lawyers but before sitting he went over to a corner table and poured himself a cup of coffee, added some cream, then sat down between the contractor's team and a lawyer for the developer. He looked down at his off the rack dark blue suit. It was clean and not bad, but it paled in comparison to most of the suits adorning the lawyers around the table, especially the junior ones — certainly crafted by the youngest of the few bespoke tailors remaining in Vancouver. He rested his briefcase against the side of his chair, leaving its contents alone for now. His side of the table was facing a glass wall featuring a nondescript downtown office tower across the street. Perhaps SM & M thought the view might distract the teams doing battle against them, who knew?

"Is everyone here?" Wilson Yip asked, looking around the table. Ross McDouguld sat at the table head, nominally in charge, Wilson closest to him on the side not facing the view.

It was the kind of dim-witted question Brock had grown used to from this group. Besides, who gave a fuck whether everyone was present? Certainly not Brock. He looked over at the plaintiff's team, noting a hint of smugness on some of the faces as they assumed another pre-trial settlement might be in the offing — relatively easy money. Brock sipped his cup. It was disgusting enough for him to lay the cup back on the table, missing the coaster.

"To recap, we are meeting here to discuss a possible solution to the unfortunate Sherman Li case. We understand that you wish to avoid court time and will present an offer to us today?" Wilson's beady eyes peered from behind thick lenses as they travelled around the table.

To Brock's surprise, one of the contractor's lawyers spoke up. "Yes, we'd like to propose a settlement fee similar to the one agreed to in the previous case, Hong Li's." The reason for Brock's surprise was that he hadn't agreed to anything of the sort.

Wilson responded, "Well, we actually thought the Hong Li offer was very slim. We had recommended against accepting it, but our client had other ideas. I am afraid that this time we will want something much closer to our filed claim."

Brock leaned forward and looked down the line of people on his side of the table. Surprise and a hint of consternation were evident on most of the faces.

He smiled to himself as he finally decided to launch a pre-emptive strike in measured tones. "And this is a direction from your client?"

"Uh, no. It is what we feel would be fair in this instance."

"Do you often decide things in the absence of your client's wishes or advice?"

"We base our decisions on sound legal grounds."

"And do you then let your client know what you've decided for them?"

Wilson's eyes screwed up as he sensed something wasn't quite right. The remainder of the lawyers present were all staring at Brock.

Ross McDouguld came to Wilson's aid. "Of course we do. What is your problem today, Brock?"

"Just trying to establish whether you guys know what you're doing, is all. Do you know where your client is, Ross?"

"Richmond, Brock, as you well know."

Brock started shaking his head slowly. "No, she isn't. And she hasn't given you any instructions. You guys don't have a fucking clue what you're doing is what I think. You should really stick to construction law. Does Ben know you've wandered off the reservation?" He waited a tick and then added, "Based on what we've learned, we will be declining the opportunity to be part of any out of court settlements going forward. Best of luck with your cases, you're going to need it."

He stood up, clutching his briefcase, and looked down the line at the rest of the defence team. "Talk soon, I need to go get a decent coffee." Then, with a brief nod to Wilson and Ross, he turned and left the room. Mumbled conversation broke out among the defence team, while a concerned-looking Wilson stared at Ross, hoping for some clarification as to what had just happened.

After the meeting broke up several minutes later with nothing further accomplished, Ross and Wilson went looking for Candice, finally cornering her in the coffee room. Ross bent his head towards the corridor without talking. Candice took this to mean he wanted a meeting.

She worked slowly, first filling her cup, then adding two heaping spoons of sugar and a generous dose of powdered coffee whitener. It was the kind of daily regimen that would probably induce some sort of disease to happily take up residence in her stomach, confident in its future. She ambled back to her office and waited, not caring where Ross thought the meeting was to be. She wasn't a mind reader. After several moments, Wilson peered around the door jamb. "Ross wants to meet."

"I know. I'm waiting and getting tired doing it. I have things to do." Wilson looked confused, then he got it. He left. Candice shook her head. She wondered how they remained in business some days.

Ross entered her office followed closely by Wilson. "Being difficult?" he asked.

"What do you want?"

"We just had a pre-trial settlement conference for the Sherman Li case, trying to get a decent offer out of those jackasses. The lawyer for BC Coastal, Brock Kinross, up and walked out. Said they wouldn't be part of any further settlements out of court based on what he knew. It sounds to me like he knows something he shouldn't."

"You think?" Candice responded, the sarcasm thick.

He ignored the jibe. "He also seemed to know about Alice Li, like where she is, or isn't."

"And where is she, Ross?" She didn't want to say too much in front of Wilson.

"At the hotel in Richmond, where that Robert Lui put her — I think."

"But you aren't sure? Any other problems?"

Ross looked confused. "Well, the rest of the team stood up and left, no further offer on the table. Said they'd get back to us. I don't like it."

"Well, that's one thing we can agree on, Ross. What are you going to do about it?"

Ross's brow furrowed as he studied Wilson. Candice

knew he had no idea what to do about this sudden pothole in their plans.

"Let me know when you figure out something. I've got things to do." She looked down at her desk, grabbed a sheaf of papers and started looking through them. The two men slowly stood and exited her office, Ross talking to Wilson in a low monotone. When Ben Skyler had told her that Ross could be a bit slow at times, she didn't get it. She was now starting to understand, and the tiniest frisson of worry was seeping into her mind. She texted two people.

TWENTY-TWO

The next morning, Tuesday, Robert felt it was time to check in again with his paymaster. "Dan? Do you have time to meet?"

"I'll make time. This afternoon, three?"

"Yes."

"Our lawyer will attend. He'll report on a pre-trial conference he was at yesterday."

"See you then."

That set, he looked up the address for Fairweather Construction. Both Robin and Sophie were home, studying for finals, so he grabbed his son for a quick trip to assess the summer job. Fairweather's headquarters was located in a South Vancouver industrial belt between the Fraser River and Marine Drive. Robin aboard, they navigated south. Robert hadn't been to this area of Vancouver previously. Besides the expected sawmills, which drew their wood straight out of the water from massive log booms moored alongside, all manner of industrial and commercial activity was thriving. After a few wrong turns, Robert found the address.

"Do you have the name for the meeting?" Robert asked Robin, as they got out of their car. They were parked in front of a pale blue commercial building hosting a printing company, a furniture wholesaler, and several other diverse operations besides Fairweather. Robin pulled a mangled piece of paper from his jeans and straightened it.

"Marty Oswald."

"Okay, let's hope he's here." They asked for Marty at reception. After a moment and some explanation from Robert, they were asked to wait.

After a good twenty minutes, a short thin man wearing glasses, with a pink dress shirt and bright blue tie, came out of the rear. More like a bookkeeper than a construction manager, Robert supposed. After shaking hands, Marty led them to a small meeting room where they sat.

"I understand that, Robin, did I get the name correct?" He looked at Robin, who nodded. "That Robin wishes to work with us this summer?"

Robert answered. "Yes. His welding teacher at Mackenzie High School organized this. I'm here because of the recent deaths on construction sites. I'm the father."

"Understandable, surely." Marty continued to study Robin.

"Looking for some assurances. I know a labourer is the bottom of the pecking order. Will Robin be working on a particular site? Is there training involved? What's your safety record?" Robert paused. "You can understand my concerns."

Marty's attention turned to Robert. Did his eyes just roll ever so slightly?

Marty proceeded to answer in reverse order. "We've just exceeded four hundred days without a site accident, and we pride ourselves on that number. We don't let anyone on a site before going through extensive training and safety sessions. And yes, he won't move from place to place, he'll be on one project. We'll supply his safety gear." He sat back, waiting for more, but Robert couldn't come up with anything.

"Any questions, Robin?" Robert asked.

"What will I be doing?"

"Grunt work, I won't lie. Half the time you'll be doing site cleanup, keeping things orderly. Many of the subtrades operate like pigs, requiring others to clean after them. It's the way of the construction world. I blame it on Moses."

"Moses?" Robert asked.

"Yes. 'Clean up after yourself' should have been top five on his Commandment list in my view. The whole world might be a tad better off if it had been included, surely, and I'm not just talking about construction. But as far as Fairweather is concerned, we like our sites organized."

Robert responded with a laugh. "I'm not sure Moses had much choice in the matter, from what I've been led to believe."

"Give me a break." Marty peered over at Robert.

Robert had to admit, this was the first time he had

heard of construction being conflated with the Bible. Maybe this company would be just fine.

"Okay, this sounds good. Robin and you can organize details … I was just a mite apprehensive. I work in the insurance industry and have heard a few things." That was putting it mildly, but Robert declined to give out any more information. Meeting concluded, Marty thanked them and led them out.

"Got time for lunch, Robin, or do you need to study?" Knowing exactly what Robin would choose.

"Whatcha thinking, Pops?"

"I've heard about a small cafe close by that has some excellent reviews, top of a lumber yard. Let's see if I can find it. Chinese and Canadian cuisine, the classic Canadian prairie combo." After some more driving around, they discovered the lumberyard, parked by the roadside with difficulty, and went up the worst outside stairs Robert had ever set foot on. There didn't seem to be a straight line in the entire joint, ironic for a lumberyard.

When Robert and Robin entered the second-floor dining room, fully half of the clientele looked up from their meals to check out the interlopers. The place wasn't large, and the floor didn't seem level at all. One of the two chefs showed them to a table, explaining the daily special while doing it. Other staff seemed missing in action. After sitting down, no one gave them another glance. Robert decided on a house special noodle dish, while Robin went with the burger and fries. Neither were disappointed.

"Robin? I'd say the summer job is a go. But you need to pay attention to all the safety rules. If something doesn't feel right, don't do it. If they threaten you with being fired, ignore them. Another job is easy to come by. Another life? Not so much. And you should find out which project you'll be on and how you are going to get there. Those places usually start work kind of early. Don't know how you'll adjust to that."

Robin grinned silently, his mouth full of fries. Robert hoped he was making the correct decision. He pulled a creased photograph out of his pocket, unfolded it and put it in front of his son's eyes. "You see this guy, let me know right away, understand?"

"Who is he, Pops? He's kind of creepy looking."

"We think he killed a labourer recently. Pushed him off a tower to his death. So, if he shows up on your site, stay far away from him and let me know right away." His voice trailed off. Robin audibly gulped.

After finishing, and with a compliment to the chef, they headed back north to Inverness. Robert dropped Robin off and continued on to the downtown business core of Vancouver. He took a chance and tried the parkade under BC Coastal's offices. Unbelievably, they had a few guest stalls on offer. He slid into one and, returning to the main floor, took a walk as he was very early for his meeting.

He started sauntering around, witnessing none of the deviant behaviour displayed almost daily on local newscasts. The general downtown population seemed to be well behaved, at least today. Then he remembered something important. The ring. Maybe he should do some looking. It didn't take long to find a jewellery store on Granville. He pressed their door buzzer, waiting expectantly. The door popped open a few moments later after he had been appraised and found risk-worthy.

He recalled very little from the last time he had purchased a ring, only that the process seemed to be a more well-oiled version of buying a car. After the nicely dressed lady behind a counter showed him a few diamonds and some ready-made rings, he decided that Sandra better be part of this process. He knew what he liked, but really, who cared about that? This was Sandra's ring.

Robert looked at his watch, apologized to the lady and, after receiving her card, returned to Hastings Street.

He arrived on the twelfth floor of BC Coastal, aiming straight for the reception desk.

"Hi. I'm Robert Lui. Here for a meeting with Dan Prudence, but I also supposedly have an office here. You don't happen to know where do you?"

The receptionist frowned, catching a peek at the side of his neck. She then looked down at something on her desk and stood. "Follow me, please." After a few twists and turns, she stopped and silently pointed at a door. His name was on the glass sidelight beside the door handle. Very professional, he thought. "Thanks." He followed her back to the reception, admiring the rear of her tightly fitted black skirt as they walked. He had the distinct feeling that she knew what he was studying as they walked.

Dan arrived just as they returned. Robert followed him into a meeting room where Brock Kinross was sitting quietly, large hands resting on the table. "Brock? This is Robert Lui, the source of much of our information to date."

Brock nodded, not rising. "Pleased to meet you." No hand offered, which was fine with Robert. "And thanks for the intel. Puts us on quite a different level from the idiot crowd."

"I understand you were cavorting with the enemy yesterday?" Robert asked.

"Sort of. I believe I set the fox among the chickens over there. I didn't say much, but unless they are complete dolts, they'll likely figure out that we know a substantial amount that may put a big cramp in their plans. I've also had a few calls from the other defendants this morning. They don't seem happy and want to know what we know. I told them to be patient and that maybe they should do some of their own research. That didn't go over very well."

"What did you say yesterday, exactly?"

"I implied that Ross and that other pencil-neck didn't know where Alice Li was, while we did. I also might have insulted their intelligence, but it was difficult to assess if they understood that."

"Makes sense, I suppose." Robert answered. He proceeded to fill in the missing details about his Sunday evening adventure at the Richmond hotel. "I told Alice to lay low when she returned home. Not sure if the message got through, but she's pretty bright. Don't know if that'll be enough to save her, even with the latest pill bust out in the open. Hopefully, they are just after product and money, not revenge, but that's uncertain at the moment."

Dan spoke, "You mentioned that the recent tower death was probably a murder?"

"Most definitely, but the witness is a kid, ten years old. The VPD brought the pusher in for questioning, but he didn't crack. That he had been seen doing the pushing wasn't raised as yet."

"Well, we aren't involved with that project, so we'll be clear, but it'd be nice to bring pressure to bear and get the other suits dropped." Dan stared at Robert with raised eyebrows. Robert was tiring of his new role as designated saviour but realized it came with the new job. He wasn't getting paid to sit in an office and fill out forms.

"I believe the VPD will need to be the ones bringing up charges, or threatening the same, not me. I've given them my opinion, that it's likely murders on sites." He looked at Brock. "What do you know about fees for personal injury cases? How does seventy-five percent sound?"

"For a successful outcome — that's pretty good, I'd say."

"For the lawyers."

Silence, then, "Come again? Did you just say the seventy-five is for the lawyers?"

Robert nodded.

"Jeez, I'm working for the wrong company. Where'd you hear this?"

"Two different clients of Skyler, McDouguld and Moon, both from Hong Kong."

"In writing?"

"I am not presently in possession of said documentation, but I believe I may be able to produce something if it is of value to you. Both people are back in Hong Kong." Robert said.

"That would be good, thanks."

"On a different topic, I'm off to Oliver next Wednesday." Robert said.

"Vacation?" Dan asked, with evident concern.

"I wish. SM & M is hosting a party at their winery on the Friday, and I'll be hoping for some intelligence. My girlfriend's catering company is working the event. I'll be one of the servers."

"Great. What could go wrong?" Dan responded.

Robert could feel his cell jiggle in his jacket pocket. He pulled it out, looked down at the text. Rory wanted to meet. "Okay, gentlemen, I have to go meet one of my operatives. Nice to meet you, Brock, till next time." With that, he was off, heading to the Apollo.

Even at half past three, traffic was already thick in the downtown core, made worse by ever-present construction and the seeming absence of some traffic lanes — replaced by lines of planters and bike paths. How could people put up with this traffic every day? As he sat at a red light, he watched a cyclist fly through the intersection, ignoring the red light. His eyes followed what he assumed was a courier. A car turned right up ahead, ignoring and almost nailing the biker, who yelled and raised the one-finger salute. Ahh, urban life! The light changed and he carefully made his way east to Main Street in a stop and go fashion, then south to the Apollo.

Robert entered the cafe, immediately noticing one of his favourite baristas behind the counter. He smiled, "Adrianne, it's been a while, how are you?"

She returned the smile. "Excellent. Nice to see you back. What can I get you?"

"Couple of caffè macchiatos, please." He waited while the coffees were being constructed. As she was finishing, Rory came in with a nod of his head. Robert grabbed the cups and headed for the cafe rear.

"Hey Robert, what are those?"

"Macchiatos, never had one? It's time for something a bit different."

"No. What happened to your neck?"

"Bit of horseplay with some thugs. I'm lucky it didn't turn out worse than it did."

"I have a new friend, name is Sergio. I think he could help you," Rory said.

"Another computer guy?"

"Only if you need one thrown a great distance. He's more of a heavy lifter, for difficult situations if you get my meaning."

"Is his last name Bortolo?" Robert asked.

"Maybe, why?"

"Because I know him. He's a nephew of Tony, my friend who was killed last fall."

"Oh, well he's available."

"I'll keep that in mind. Enjoy your macchiato." They sat, and Robert looked at Rory with raised eyebrows. "Got anything computer-wise?"

"Some." He sipped at his cup. "This is good." Then he returned to the subject. "I went back into the company files, but somebody made a couple of very minor changes to the structure, as though they realized that someone had been inside their system."

"Oh jeez. I told you to be careful, Rory."

"It is impossible for them to figure out who was in, relax. However, they do know someone's been there. Item number two is a Robert Lui file. It has the barest of information about your time as a detective, but there is a photo of you."

Robert expected this, but still, not welcome news. "Just me, or any of my family included?"

"Only you so far. It's not a great picture — from a distance, a street shot."

"Send me a copy if you can? I'm serving at their summer party, and if they know what I look like — it'll be a waste of time. Also, can you get pictures of the partners?"

"On their website."

"I must have missed them when I checked. Case files?"

"They are there, but everything looks normal, except for the outlandish fees. I looked into their financials for fun. This is where it gets interesting. One of the partners, Candice Moon, has been making and receiving payments, some of which are quite large. They seem to be outside of the firm's daily business and don't show up on the company financial reports. They are located in a separate folder, not available to everyone in the firm, I believe."

"Can you get copies of the fee agreements?"

"I think so. USB okay?"

Robert sipped his coffee, staring at Rory. "Sounds fine, and if you could find out who is on the other end of Candice's payments, that'd help."

"One other thing. There was a reference to a Travis McDouguld in one of Candice's folders, so I checked it out. He's the father of Ross McDouguld and owner of a legal firm in Hong Kong. What do they say over in Britain? He's possibly skint."

"No money at all?"

"Not sure, but a couple of Candice's payments were to him. For what? I don't know yet." Rory paused.

Robert remained silent, staring at nothing as he moved his cup around, thinking about what little his father had told him.

"This whole thing may have started in Hong Kong. I know someone over there who might shed some light on this, maybe."

"There is more. I learned that the winery neighbour, Enchanting Grape, is Communist Party. Shou Deng is the sole owner."

"I'll check that with Hong Kong as well then."

"Do you need anything else from me?" Rory asked. "I'm still finding my way around the WorkSafeBC site. They have their own investigators. Haven't found anything useful as yet."

"Check on my file once in a while at the lawyers. It'd

be good to know before they start targeting my family. Other than that, nothing for now. Be careful, Rory."

Rory smiled as he stood up. "Yes, I've received that message loud and clear. See you around."

As Robert watched Rory leave, he started considering how he could change his appearance for the party. One thing was certain, he wouldn't be wearing his larger pistol, having nothing to hide it from prying eyes. He assumed he'd be wearing a fancy waistcoat vest of some description, but Sandra hadn't divulged that information as yet.

TWENTY-THREE

Wednesday, Sandra was attending a planning meeting on Main Street regarding the upcoming winery party. Both Sophie and Robin had exams, so Robert was alone. He called his father.

"Dad, I need something from you if you have it, a phone number for Winston over in Hong Kong. I lost it somehow."

There was silence for a full ten seconds. "I thought you had quit the police, Robert."

"Still true, but I think Winston might possibly fill in a few things for me. He probably won't be able to help, but I've got to try. It's about that legal firm we talked about."

"Be back, hang on." Robert could hear some rustling as Ethan leafed through his paper phone diary.

"Here it is. Better wait though. It's midnight over there now."

"Thanks, Dad. I'll say hi for you." He rubbed his chin, feeling the bristles. The alteration of Robert Lui was starting.

Over in North Surrey at the Kour residence, Amrit had gone out to shop for food. Lal sat in front of his old and sometimes useless computer in the den and started trawling through the internet looking for stories related to his two nephews, Manny and Andy. The few that he found focused on their deaths. He assumed that the police hadn't been able to pin much on the two, otherwise there'd have been more articles.

They weren't bad people really, despite what his daughter had said, they had just been caught up in an unfortunate lifestyle. Other gangsters must have led them down the wrong path. He read the articles about Manny's last stand carefully. Then he looked at the demise of Andy, who had passed away only last October. Police were involved in each case, but names weren't given out. In his estimation, it was definitely police officers who had killed his family members, but how to find out who was the question.

Lal sat at the phone in his kitchen considering options. After a few moments, he dialled the Vancouver Police headquarters and asked to speak with someone who had knowledge of Robert Lui's career. He identified himself as a representative of the Surrey Chamber of Commerce.

"I'm hoping to get some biography on a Robert Lui. We're doing a big spread in our monthly newsletter on officers who have had a positive effect on Surrey. I've been talking to a few other police forces in the Lower Mainland, and his name kept coming up." Lal was then bounced around through a few employees before finally ending up talking with someone named Ranit in media relations.

"What do you wish to know about Robert?" she asked, adding, "he doesn't work here anymore."

"Well, I've heard a few things, but really, I'd like to know if he had any dealings at all in Surrey. If he didn't, then I'll move on to other possible candidates for our article and thank you for your time and trouble."

"Oh yes, Robert definitely spent time on Surrey files," Ranit said.

"Doing what, may I ask?"

"He was on the anti-gang Taskforce. You may have heard that some gangs operate out of Surrey?"

Lal chuckled smoothly. "It would be hard for this to escape anyone's attention."

Ranit relaxed. She had just started working in the media relations department and found the position could be extremely challenging. This caller sounded sane to her, so her guard lowered enough for her to make a mistake.

"The person who would know Robert best here would be a Norma van Kleet. She is an administrator. Would you prefer to talk with her if she is available?"

"Yes. That would be very gracious of you."

"I'll talk to her, and she'll get back to you. Phone number?"

Lal froze for a moment, then realized he had no choice. He gave her a number. "It is my cell. I'll wait. Thank you very much." He fretted as he waited for the return call but could only hope it came before Amrit returned home.

Fifteen minutes later his cell buzzed. "Is this Lal Kour?"

"Certainly, thanks for your call. We are doing an article hoping to highlight contributions made by officers like Robert Lui to the safeguarding of Surrey."

"I am Norma van Kleet."

"You know about Robert?"

"You might say that."

"I understand he worked on gang things."

"Have you heard of the Two Tigers gang?"

"In passing. Were they based in Surrey?"

"Oh yes, very definitely. Robert was mainly responsible for their demise, making Surrey a much safer place today. And he led the investigation recently when a couple of Vancouver policemen were killed last fall. You probably saw the news clips, and Andy Dhillon was the culprit, I believe."

"Robert killed him?"

"I don't know, and I wouldn't tell you if I did know."

"May we return to the demise of the Two Tigers?"

"It was over a year ago. Again, Robert led that investigation. The gang wasn't really a factor after their leader died."

"Who was that?"

"A Manny Dhillon, I recall. It was all in the news."

"Thank you, Norma. You've been very helpful." He ended the call abruptly. His suspicions about Robert Lui were growing.

Norma looked down at her phone. Something didn't seem right at all. Wasn't he supposed to ask other questions for his article? Why was he only concerned with the gangsters? She had a sinking feeling as she called Ranit's number.

Sandra returned home just after three. The teenagers had also been home after their exams but promptly disappeared to spend time with their friends. She looked over at Robert, who was slumped on the couch, studying his laptop. "Guess who is joining Crazy Eats?"

"A sane cook?"

"Ha, no, definitely not. Deirdre is being hired. You remember her?"

"I remember the name, although I've been trying to blot out last fall's events. How come?"

"She got laid off a week ago from the hotel she worked at. We keep in contact, so she's coming on board. She'll be doing the Oliver trip."

"I assume you are happy to have someone on the team who knows what they are doing?"

"Extremely."

"Dinner ideas?"

"Well, I picked up a few things before coming home, including some pretzel buns."

"Pretzel buns?"

"For hot dogs, with all the fixins?"

"Excellent idea. I have a call to make first. I'll prep the grill, then the wine glasses."

From what Robert remembered, Winston was an early bird to work, so he called the number. It was well before eight am in Hong Kong.

"Hello? Who is this?"

"Robert Lui, Winston, over in Vancouver. How are you?" It was appropriate to ask this after the injuries Winston had suffered during his last foray to Vancouver on Robert's behalf.

"Recovered, thanks. I've been back to full time for almost a year now. How is your father?"

"He says a big hi. He and Mary are both fine. The reason for disturbing you is that I am looking for some information on a Travis McDouguld — a lawyer in your city. Not sure whether you might know of him?"

"Ah, Travis. He is well known to us through his work for the triads operating here. He is a regular, for the few times cases actually get in front of a judge. I've heard he sometimes shows up in court wearing a kilt — his family tartan naturally. He likes to lay it on thick when he can. I'm not sure how the judges view this, but …."

"Yes, my father gave me a few hints. How is he doing lately?"

"I understand that he has hit hard times. A couple of gangs are putting the pressure on him. He owes a lot of money to them. I'm not sure why, but it's not a good position to be in. We've heard that he may spend too much time at the racetrack, not to his benefit. Why do you ask?"

"It seems he may have rigged up a scheme to get himself out of trouble using poor people in Hong Kong. It is affecting us in Vancouver in a significant way. People are dying, drugs are moving here, and money is being made."

"What are the other officers making of this, Robert?"

"Not totally sure. I resigned from the VPD last month

and am conducting an investigation for an insurance company. I'm still in contact with a couple of local officers however, trying to guide them."

"I'm surprised, Robert. You seemed like an excellent detective. However, I bet your father is happy."

"Correct. Anything else you can tell me about Travis?"

"Only that he is probably desperate. What these triads do to people they're displeased with would be enough for him to try anything."

"One other name for you — Shou Deng. Heard of him? Seems to be CCP."

"Boy, you can pick the vipers, Robert. He is not only CCP, but he's also got his fingers in with the Wide Bay Boys. Remember them?"

"Unfortunately."

"These are not people to get mixed up with. I wouldn't doubt that if they keep lists, your name would be highlighted in neon all caps after what you did to their Vancouver operations."

"Yes, that was satisfying at the time. Message received. You don't happen to have a picture of Shou Deng? If not, I won't trouble you further. Thanks for taking my call."

"Anytime, Robert. I'll text that picture to you. Let me know if I can help further, and I'll call if we hear of anything useful."

Sandra looked over at Robert. "You okay?"

"I may have found the source of all the problems locally. It seems to have begun in Hong Kong. I'll call Vito in the morning. Maybe they can bring some pressure to bear here."

"So, we might be safe?"

"Not yet, Sandra. The more pressure is applied, the more desperate people usually get. We need to be very careful."

"Kids joining us for dinner?"

"No idea. Let's start. If they show, there is always the microwave and toaster."

Robert retrieved some shishito peppers from the fridge, skewered and slathered them with olive oil, then started the grill. They dined like gods, hot dog gods. After, as they sat at the dining table, finishing off the Chardonnay along with a bag of potato chips, Robin came in through the rear door with a mixed-up hungry look. The mixed-up part was quickly explained by the appearance of a girl following him inside. This was new.

"Hey Pops, Sandra, this is Rachael." Rachael wore her raven hair in a loose single long braid. Styled black eyebrows were atop serious eyes. As she offered her hand in greeting, her eyes twinkled. She had a rangy body, as tall as Robin.

"Pleased to meet you, Rachael. Would you two by any chance be hungry?" Robert winked at Robin as he waited for the expected answer.

"Did we miss hotdogs?" Robin asked.

"Yes, you did, and they were great!" Robert waited a couple of beats as Robin started to frown, then, "But we have more. Interested?"

Rachael and Robin both nodded enthusiastically. Ah, young love, thought Robert. It was inspiring to see.

"You two relax, and I'll get the grill going again."

TWENTY-FOUR

The next morning, Robert waited until he figured Vito was at work, then called his cell.

"Robert, good morning."

"Vito, I talked with Winston Chang over in Hong Kong last evening. The rat's nest here has its beginnings over there. As origin stories go, this one sucks severely. Triads are bringing pressure to bear on a Travis McDouguld, who is a lawyer and father of one of the partners at our favourite legal firm in Vancouver. And a Communist functionary named Shou Deng seems included in this drama — not in a good way. I'd say that Travis has cooked up this scheme to save his ass, dragging the local law firm into it."

"Winston is a senior HKPF superintendent, correct?"

"Yes. One other thing, this Shou Deng owns a winery called Enchanting Grape near Oliver. Maybe you could find out from your RCMP contact there if there has been any funny business going on?"

"I'll talk to Jackie and then confer with Thomas. On

another topic, Norma has a tale to tell. Remember her, Robert?" Vito knew he was poking at raw scars here but couldn't resist. "She was talking to a Lal Kour the other day. Isn't that Sandra's father?"

"Yes. Why was he talking to Norma?"

"Well, Lal said he was with the Surrey Chamber of Commerce and was doing an article on officers who had made a difference in Surrey. However, it seems he was mainly interested in the demise of two gangsters, Manny and Andy. She didn't understand what had happened until the guy ended the call rather abruptly. Your name came up. She says she is sorry."

Robert was silent for a moment. "I don't think 'sorry' will cut it when I'm dead. Sandra says her father has some religious mania going. Judging by what I've seen in the media about Indian family honour, etcetera, I think I'm in trouble."

"Until he tries something, our hands are tied, Robert."

"Yes. I get it. I'm on my own and getting used to the feeling. I need to go down to Richmond."

"Richmond?"

"To retrieve my Sig Sauer. Troy has it. I think I will need it."

"Take care, Robert. I'll let you know what Thomas and I come up with soonest." Somehow, Robert wasn't comforted in the least by this.

At the Kour residence, Lal had come to a conclusion and called a number he had retrieved with difficulty from

Manny's father. It had an American area code — Seattle. When he finished talking, he smiled to himself. It was going to be costly, but things needed to be rectified. His wife would be mortified, but she would get over it with time. Their daughter was headstrong but could not be allowed to do whatever she pleased as if there were no consequences for her actions or her desires. And more importantly, his nephews needed to be avenged, even at the significant fee quoted.

In Surrey later that same day, Bobbi Atwall finished up his report on the townhouse project he was in charge of. He worked at a smaller developer specializing in townhouse projects in the valley. So far, everything seemed to be on time and on budget for this project, virtually a miracle in the development business. Even though it was only a couple of modest buildings, he was feeling proud of what he had accomplished since extracting himself from the Two Tigers gang a year earlier. Only the company owner knew of his past and had been nervous for the best part of a year, expecting Bobbi to screw up somehow or, worse, bring gang pressure to bear on his company. But no, Bobbi managed to exceed expectations and the owner admitted to himself that his fears could now be laid to rest.

Bobbi's boss asked for an update on the project numbers, so they met in Bobbi's tiny office. Bobbi recited the anticipated costs to come, the timeline with the city for permits, and most importantly, the expected profit margin.

"Good work, Bobbi. You've turned a significant corner. Are you ready for something a little larger in a day or two? I've landed a new site in Fleetwood, and I'd like you to take it on. You game?"

"Of course. Thank you for sticking with me."

"One of my good deeds." As though Bobbi was some kind of charity case. Bobbi felt this to be patronizing but didn't say anything further. As his boss left the room, Bobbi's cell rang. He checked the number, but the area code was unfamiliar to him. He answered anyway.

"This Bobbi?"

"Yes, who is this?"

"Friend from Seattle. I have a job for you. Details will be delivered. Don't screw it up." As he stared down at the cell's screen, his neck prickled. Shit, it couldn't be. He didn't have any friends in Seattle. It could only be one guy — Manny's brother, Harjit, he of gun-running fame. What was he doing calling Bobbi? It meant that Harjit hadn't kept up with news of Bobbi's leaving gang life. This was not good. There was also nothing much to do until the 'details' arrived, telling him what he'd been tasked with.

He paced back and forth in his very small office. He considered calling Harjit back and telling him he was out of the gang business but decided to bide his time. Harjit probably wouldn't acknowledge what he was being told by Bobbi anyway, paranoid about being listened to. Bobbi then wondered if he was exclusive, or if this task had been given out openly for anyone to accomplish, as was sometimes the method for this type of work. The shine had definitely left his day.

Robert skipped down to Richmond's RCMP detachment, retrieved his gun with little difficulty and headed back home to do some planning. He sat on his couch in the otherwise empty townhouse, contemplating his appearance and how he might change it.

His beard was growing in, but he'd never be counted amongst the 'mountain men' in this respect. Whatever grew would be shaved into a respectable moustache and goatee for the trip east. Glasses? Hair dye? Whatever he came up with needed to be as boring and innocuous as possible. Most people should be concentrating on the booze or food being offered to them at the event, with no thought to the server, at least this is what he hoped. He was counting on the guests' eagerness to show off their intelligence or stupidity to each other while ignoring the help. If the firm's expertise really was construction law, then there'd be more than a few major developers and contractors in attendance. These people wouldn't shy away from a free wine-fest no matter how far away it was from their usual watering holes. It was the people he was most interested in who could be his problem — the firm's partners.

Robert walked west to Main Street, where a couple of optical outfits were located. He went right by one of them, having heard what they charged for their products and continued south. He turned in at the next store and started to examine the frames on offer.

"Can I help you?" A stylish young woman draped in black came up to Robert.

"Yes. I'm looking for some glasses that won't stand out." He was staring at rows of coloured frames, from the mildly tinted to ones with a psychedelic hue. He moved on to a section featuring more sedate options, finally picking a basic black offering. He tried them on.

"What do you think?"

She smiled. "Well, if an accountant look is what you are after, then I'd say those are fine."

Robert looked at the price tag. "Okay, I'll take them."

"Do you have your prescription with you?"

"I just need glass or plastic, no prescription. I can see fine." The sales agent blinked at this revelation. "How soon can I get these?"

"No prescription? They'll be ready Saturday. You know, you can get 'readers' at any drugstore if that's what you want."

"It's not, thanks. I'll return Saturday. Need a deposit?"

She wavered, taking his name and number, then deciding she liked what she saw. "No, we'll see you then, Robert."

Back home, Robert yelled a hello. No reply, so he sat down in the family area and did some research online about the Okanagan wine business. An annotated map indicated dozens of newish operations when compared with an older version. It seemed to be a very fast-growing industry. He had heard that one business model involved getting in and building up some credibility before trying to sell out to one of the multinationals hovering around. Prices for land were prohibitive, and starting an operation from scratch put some owners in extremely precarious financial positions.

Enchanting Grape didn't fall into this category, he was certain, but he didn't know how viable Possession Point was, even with legal money behind it. There seemed to be great emphasis put on wine tasting competitions and chasing medals. As far as he could discern from the number of categories available, a winery had to be offering kerosene-laced plonk in order not to win one.

As he studied his laptop intently, he heard a noise from the hallway. He stiffened, then relaxed as first Sophie, then Rose came down the stairs.

"Hi, girls. Didn't hear me when I got home?"

"We were playing video games, Dad," Sophie said.

Robert couldn't help observing a distinct flushness to both their faces. He was certain that what they were playing at didn't involve videos at all. Ah, young love — second time in two days.

"I am not sure if Sandra told you, but we are heading to Oliver next Wednesday for a work gig. Back on Sunday." He watched as the girls looked at each other, definitely contemplating more time alone. "Exams almost done yet?" He knew this was the last thing they were thinking about at the moment, but they answered anyway.

"I have two more." Sophie replied.

"Three for me," Rose added.

"Then, summer!" Robert said. Huge grins lit up both faces. "Any plans for summer jobs, either of you?"

Sophie answered for both of them, "We have applications in, waiting to hear. Local stores, a restaurant or two, stuff like that."

"You girls staying for dinner tonight?"

"We're heading to my place." Rose responded. About

time, Robert thought. He could count the number of times Sophie had eaten over at the Esmeraldos on one finger, as far as he knew, but maybe he was being harsh. There was no sign of Robin, so it was Sandra and him for dinner. He contemplated options.

CHAPTER
TWENTY-FIVE

Two days later, it was the weekend, and Bobbi Atwal was trying to relax in his Surrey condo but fretting about the Seattle phone call he'd received. His cell buzzed. A delivery guy was at the front door, asking for entry. Bobbi hadn't ordered anything lately but let him in anyway, after confirming that he carried a package. A minute later, the driver was at his suite door, leaving a thin cardboard envelope decorated with the bright yellow logo of an American delivery system in Bobbi's hands. He stared down at it, not really wanting to open it, but curious to see what he'd been asked to do at the same time.

He sat, tapping the edge of the envelope on the coffee table as he looked off to the west at the long view of Delta and beyond. He cursed, then ripped it open. A single folded sheet of paper fell out. He opened it and was staring at a crudely written message. A grade school child could have managed better.

Yor task is to kill a cop named Robert Lui. Soon is possible. $20k on completin the killin. This job is open so get to it. Harjit

Bobbi couldn't believe the guy actually signed the note. Twenty thousand dollars? To kill someone? He wondered who was behind this and how much Harjit was really being paid to set this up. A lot more than the quoted price, Bobbi figured. He also wondered if it was really open, or Harjit was merely trying to add some pressure to the matter.

He dropped the letter onto the table and sat back. There was no way he was killing anyone, let alone Robert after he had saved Bobbi's sister from possible death the previous fall. The question was whether Robert needed warning. Cops should be able to take care of themselves, right?

Robert had just returned home after picking up his new semi-useless glasses from the eye shop. His cell rang. "Yes?"

"This is Bobbi."

"Bobbi of Two Tigers fame?"

"The same. Thought I'd warn you. Someone wants you dead, but I don't know why. I was just offered twenty thousand to do the deed. Manny's idiot brother in Seattle signed the request. Thing is, it may be an open job, it's uncertain. This guy can barely write, so I don't know about the intelligence level here."

"Unsettling news, Bobbi." This was not good.

"Yes, I expect so. Do you want the note? I could send it on to you at the Vancouver Police, I suppose."

"I don't work there anymore, Bobbi, but I wouldn't mind getting the note. Maybe I'll come down to Surrey. Is there a place we can meet today? Preferably with coffee involved?"

"Lobby of the SFU campus? Know it? Off King George Boulevard."

"See you there. Ninety minutes or so? Oh, and don't handle the note more than needed — pop it in a plastic bag if you can."

"Okay."

Robert's mind started racing. Twenty thousand. Is this what his life was worth? It didn't take much to figure who was behind this. The tricky part was Sandra. Should he even tell her? How would she react? Not well, he guessed. Hearing that your dad wanted your fiancé dead would be unnerving at a minimum. Would she even believe it? He found it hard to fathom the mania at work here.

Perhaps he was being hasty. Manny's brother had reason enough to want Robert dead, forget Lal. It was just a little long in coming. The old adage 'revenge is best served cold' probably didn't apply to these gangsters. They traditionally had trouble waiting for anything. And actually, the trickier part would be staying alive, not Sandra's reaction.

Bobbi wouldn't be setting him up, would he? By telling him about the threat, Robert's guard would be lowered, figuring good old Bobbi wouldn't kill the saviour of his sister. The SFU lobby was as public as it gets, however. He was just feeling a bit of paranoia, yeah, that was it. He was alone in the townhouse, so he scribbled a quick note saying he'd gone to Surrey, returning soonest and left it on the kitchen counter. His upcoming trip out of town was looking better and better.

After a drive south into Surrey made painful by the usual Saturday traffic mess, he slowed, looking for a place to park near or inside the huge building. He circled the SFU campus block twice, finally spotting an entrance. There was a shopping mall and parkade included at the building base, which was where he left his Volvo.

He walked north, his eyes checking everything relentlessly. He had both his guns, ready for whatever was to come. He slowed as he entered the spacious lobby, searching for Bobbi. The obligatory coffee shop was there, with Bobbi Atwal sitting at a table, looking quite continental. It seemed busy, even on a Saturday. Robert scanned the area as he waved to Bobbi. Bobbi smiled back, and Robert's tension eased just a smidge. He walked past the table, ordered at the bar, then returned.

"Hi Bobbi, care to sit over there?" Robert gestured at a table by a wall.

Bobbi's brow crinkled. "Sure, I guess."

"Don't like sitting out in the open. Old habit."

Bobbi nodded, getting it.

Robert sat. "So, out of the gang business, are you?"

Bobbi nodded. "I'm in the development industry now."

"What's the difference?"

Bobbi smiled. "They are reputedly smarter."

"Which ones, Bobbi? You need to be more specific."

Bobbi's smile broadened. He sported an oversized mauve shirt, new black jeans and scuffed boots. Nothing to hide a weapon in, really. He reached into his shirt pocket and extracted a small plastic bag, laying it on the table in front of Robert. "As requested."

Robert's order was called out. He returned with his double long espresso and sat. It was a coffee chain; his expectations were low. "What do you know about Manny's brother?"

"Almost nothing. I don't think he's been back across the border in fifteen years. And I doubt if he is in the USA legally unless they are giving out criminal visas these days. Manny must have furnished him with a list of the old gang members, which is where he got my name, I assume."

Robert nodded. "The others around?"

"They must be, but I stay away from that life, Robert."

"Present circumstances excluded."

Bobbi shook his head wearily. "I *try* to stay away from them."

"How is your sister?"

"Good. So why the bounty on you? Revenge?"

"Remember the girl from last October with Safa? Sandra?"

"I remember."

"Getting married to her. It's the father's way of expressing his unhappiness, I think. On the other hand, you could be correct, just a man avenging his dead brother." He surveyed Bobbi's close-cropped hair, no turban in sight. "Are you a Sikh?"

"Kind of a personal question, don't you think? I don't ask you about your religion, do I?"

"Sandra's family is Sikh. Just trying to find out where in their scriptures it says I should be murdered for trying to marry a good Sikh girl."

Bobbi shook his head. "It's probably not in there, but I wouldn't know. Not a fervent believer, myself. Seems kind of extreme if you ask me. You're out of the Vancouver Police?"

"Yup. Work was too hazardous, but I must admit that my new life seems little different. Working for an insurance company looking into wonky claims, among other things. It's the other things that radiate the danger."

Bobbi sipped at his cup. "Isn't that always the way?"

"Any advice on how to dodge this?"

Bobbi tapped the table with his index finger, contemplating the seemingly impossible. "I suppose it might be possible to slow him down until you bring pressure to bear from your side."

"You mean the police. That'd be complicated with him being in Seattle and off the radar."

"Yes. But if this thing is truly open, then I don't like your chances. There'd likely be morons involved."

"Gang morons?"

"Endless possibilities, and once money is mentioned, they'll lose what little sanity they started with. Twenty is not much money, but for some, it'd be more than enough. You might remember an incident in this very place a couple of years back. One of our gang's brighter bulbs decided to be proactive and shoot a former member in quite a public fashion. And there wasn't even any money on the table. Didn't succeed but he got killed by a cop for his trouble, somewhere just over there." He gestured at the open space. "That's just one example."

"What if you were to do it?"

Bobbi's eyes widened.

"I don't mean actually to do it, but what if it appeared so? What would this guy need as evidence for you to get paid and close the matter?"

"Probably something in the Seattle news or BS in the media. Ex-cop gunned down, manhunt in progress but no suspect arrested, no leads. Definitely not an ex-gang member involved. Along those lines."

Robert had finished his coffee and was looking at the cup. "Another one?"

Bobbi nodded. "Small Americano'd be fine."

Robert returned with both cups after several moments. He sat, "Not sure how these guys remain in business. This is borderline coffee." He looked up at Bobbi. "I think this plan might be the best bet in the short term. I know someone at CBC in town. I just need to figure out how to organize my own death first."

"Not something you'd normally be thinking about." Bobbi took a sip of his new coffee. "Interesting problem."

"No kidding. Unfortunately, it's not a hypothetical." Robert paused. "Think you could find out if it's really open? Maybe stress how you could use the money."

Bobbi stared across the space, considering. "I really don't want to get mixed up with this ape, but for you, one time I'll try."

"I wouldn't ask for more, Bobbi."

"You going to stay dead? Cause if you pop back up, I'll probably be next on this guy's list for accepting money after not doing my job. Not sure how wealthy this guy is though … maybe he really is getting paid by your intended's father. I doubt he'd front this money himself for good old Manny's sake."

"Many possibilities. Thanks for meeting, and the note."

TWENTY-SIX

Dreams, recurring coffee dreams. He couldn't find the closest cafe. He was on foot and turned onto a familiar street, but it was miles from the coffee shop he needed. He was on the east side of Vancouver, yet lost. He couldn't solve his problem without the espresso. He knew the buildings but there was a strangeness to them. They weren't in the correct order. Streets folded and dipped where they shouldn't. The more he walked, the farther away the cafe seemed. He kept going, then Sandra came directly towards him, running on a sidewalk, alone. She was saying something, screaming, terrified. Robert shuddered as he opened his eyes. It was 5:10 AM, Sunday. The dreaming hours. His T-shirt was damp. He looked over at Sandra, but she was peacefully asleep, untroubled by his demons.

Robert sat on the sofa downstairs after finally rising, puzzling at how to die without dying. The problem wasn't really the dying part, it was all the officials who stuck their noses in to make sure you were really dead: the police, medics, coroner, journalists. The list went on and on, and this wasn't even counting friends and relatives. Sandra came down the stairs, looked over at Robert and noticed he had no coffee.

"You alright, Robert?"

"Sure, fine." He smiled back.

"I only ask as you have no cup in front of you."

"Damn. I knew I was missing something. That's why I can't solve my problem."

"I'll put water on for you." She moved into the kitchen. "What problem?"

He had decided early that morning to let Sandra in on most of the story. He couldn't not do it.

"After you bring the coffees over, I'll tell you. It's not a great tale, not even close."

After several moments, Sandra sat down beside Robert with their coffees. "I'm not sure I'm a fan of this beard thing you've got going. Very scraggly, I must say."

"It'll be trimmed up in Oliver. You'll be impressed, I promise. Crazy Eats will never see another server this good-looking. I expect a rather well-paying job offer after this gig."

"Right. So, what is this problem you can't solve?"

"I've found out there is a contract out on my life. Twenty K is all I'm worth dead, apparently."

"What?" Sandra shrieked, then calmed herself. "It was

all I could save up, Robert." She waited a beat. "And I thought you had life insurance."

"I'd like to laugh, but I can't. This is real, Sandra."

"How'd you find out?" She moved closer to him.

"You won't believe this, but the guy hired to do the job told me. We met yesterday at the SFU campus in Surrey. It is Bobbi, the ex-gang member and brother of Safa, who you met last October at the clubhouse."

Sandra looked puzzled. "Leaving aside the weirdness of you meeting with your supposed killer, did he say who hired him?"

"Manny's brother, in Seattle."

"Revenge?"

"Maybe. Hard to tell for sure. Long time coming, if it is. Thing is, it might be open." Robert left out Sandra's father for now. He wasn't one hundred percent certain about Lal's involvement, anyway.

"What's that mean?"

"Anyone invited can do the job, first one successful gets the money. That's the bad part. So, I've decided I need to be dead. It could hopefully stave off attacks. This is the problem I can't solve."

"Oh."

Robert tasted his coffee. "Excellent brew, Sandra. My mind is functioning better already. And yes, I have some insurance through my new job, in case you are concerned."

"I'm guessing they don't pay that out for a fake death, correct?"

"Probably not." He sipped some more coffee. "I

believe I have found the new barista for Inverness. This is outstanding."

"Same coffee, Robert, you just didn't put it together. Makes all the difference, I've found."

"However, I'm not coming up with anything. I may have to make it up using Vito at the VPD and Bernard at the CBC. I don't nearly have the energy or smarts to stage an elaborate death somehow." He stared at Sandra, perhaps looking for some encouragement for a half-baked idea. "Basically, I need to get a story into the Seattle media and hope for the best."

"I'll keep thinking, Robert, but this isn't really my area, you know." She wrapped her arms around Robert and kissed his ear. She whispered, "I do know no one is taking you from me."

Robert turned and kissed her. He felt a bit better but was still spooked by all this. "You guys ready for the expedition?"

"Getting there. Could we bring Deirdre along? Someone else will get her back to Vancouver."

"Sure. We're not hauling stuff up there, are we?"

"Just some outfits, one of which is yours. Hope you like bowties."

"Bowtie? Hmm … never met a guy with a bowtie who wasn't trouble. Now I'm going to be joining that group? This is unexpected news." He paused. "Think you could get the outfit here so I can see what I'll look like? I need to not look like Robert Lui."

"I'll bring the stuff back here tomorrow. There will be four other servers working with you."

"They know what they are doing?"

"Hopefully."

"Great. I'll watch and mimic."

After more coffee and no progress on his death plans, Robert made some toast for both of them. While slathering on marmalade, Robert looked at Sandra. "Like to do some ring shopping?"

Sandra grinned, "Sounds nice, Robert."

"I was downtown the other day at a jewellery store when I realized you should be along to do the choosing, no?"

"Good thought. Today?"

"We'll head into town after we're done here." He looked out to the lane, realizing heavy clouds were moving in, the entire townhouse darker as a result. Perhaps June was finally reverting to type, as in rainy and depressing like most years.

That evening, Robert reflected on his inability to save anything towards a down payment for a house, condo, or even a rabbit hutch. His newish car, jewellery for his intended, and upcoming university costs for Sophie were putting paid to that idea. A ring resided in his bureau top drawer, but it was Susan's. No one else would be getting that. It was sacred. That afternoon, they had settled on a diamond and a design, but the ring needed to be crafted, for which Robert left a hefty deposit. On reflection, he considered himself lucky to have a landlord who wasn't a shark. He shook his head. He had larger problems at present than trying to save money.

Rain that had started fitfully earlier in the day was now falling steadily, bouncing off the small patio outside the family area. His computer made its annoying sound. He looked over at the screen. An email from Bernard. It was the roster of directors for Taipan Construction. Finally, Bernard was coming through. He read the short list of names. One stood out, Shou Deng. Hmm. Taipan was the contractor on only one of the lawsuits BC Coastal was named in, but it seemed like the McDougulds were going after one of Travis's foes from Hong Kong indirectly. Robert wondered how smart that was.

He made a call. "Bernard, Robert here. Thanks for the list. I appreciate it. How is the arm doing?"

"Not too badly, Robert. Seems to be healing up. What do you want, Robert? Usually, when you call with concerns about my health, there is something else lurking."

"That's why I like you, Bernard, you're much smarter than the average citizen. I have a small problem with which I only hope you can help. I need to be dead."

"I could come over now if that's good. I think I have a crowbar I can use." Bernard paused, then, "Your kids are out and unavailable, I presume?"

Robert chuckled. "Good, Bernard. Your sense of humour is expanding. No, I have found that there is a contract out on me, and the only solution I can come up with is to be dead, so whoever is coming after me, stops trying."

There was silence while Bernard digested this. After a few moments he realized what this might mean. "This is the kind of thing that might get me fired, you realize this, right, Robert?"

"Maybe. I'm hoping Vito might help out here, so it wouldn't be so fraught for you. You'd just be reporting what someone at the VPD related to you. And the worst would be that you didn't check for a body. Not exactly what you are supposed to do. Hardly a firing offence." There was silence while Bernard considered this. "And don't you guys use retractions? This is made for that. You screw up and then issue a retraction. Could of used something like that in the police business — sorry I killed you, we'll issue a retraction, don't worry, you should recover any day now."

"That's harsh, Robert. Can I think about this? I mean, you have furnished me with some excellent stories, and with you gone, well I'd might have to start working harder. That would be extremely unfortunate. Let me know what Vito says, okay?"

"I'll talk with him tomorrow AM and get back to you. One other thing, it is the Seattle news that I would be aiming for. That is where the threat emanates from, not locally. You know, it's really a tiny bit of disinformation you need to get into the Seattle media. Isn't it all the rage these days? Disinformation? Maybe you just got confused when writing the story, Bernard."

"That may change things a bit, but it still sounds very hincky. Talk soon." Bernard ended the conversation.

TWENTY-SEVEN

Robert called Vito early the following morning after Sandra and the teens had vacated the townhouse. Sophie had an exam, and Robin was headed to his job site for a round of safety instruction prior to his actual job start, which was to happen on Monday, a week away.

"Vito, you well?"

"Of course, Robert."

Robert explained his problem, what he needed, and waited for a reaction.

"This is a big ask, Robert. I don't even know how to go about this."

"I have the same problem."

"What will your children say?"

"Yeah, I might need to let a few people in on the plan that doesn't exist as yet. And from there, leaks start to happen, I suppose."

"Should this be a public execution, downtown? Or out in a field somewhere in the dark?"

To Robert, it sounded like Vito was already halfway in

on this. "Maybe a car ending up in the drink, no body found? Trouble is, I just bought a newish car, and I don't want to sacrifice it just yet."

"Wants may not enter into this, Robert."

"Maybe I'll rent a boat and have an accident, that sounds better."

"Can you swim?"

"Might need a few refresher lengths for a tune-up."

"And you'd be going boating, why?"

"I don't know, maybe I heard there was salmon out there and I hadn't caught anything since Bella Kind … something like that."

"Sounds like a plan, a bad plan that needs some fine tuning."

"Suppose. I may need you to be a partial witness, then report it to Bernard Lily at the CBC. He'll take care of the rest."

"Robert, maybe you should get that head of yours checked out. Jingles may have damaged more than you thought. I'm still employed, in case you'd forgotten. I'd kind of like to keep it that way for a while longer, anyway. Reporting things that haven't really happened tends to be frowned upon."

"Okay, thanks for listening. But sometimes, if you think something has happened, then maybe it did. I'll try to firm things up."

"Is this an example of Robert Lui philosophy? I'll try to figure out what that means. In the meanwhile, good luck and call when you are ready with a sane plan."

"One more thing, Vito. I have the note from the guy in

Seattle asking for my demise. Think it'd cut any mustard with the Seattle constables?"

"Signed?"

"Unbelievably, yes. First name anyway. I'd guess there would be prints on it."

"Won't hurt to try. I'll send a patrol car over to pick it up."

"Thanks."

The call ended. Robert replayed it in his mind. Sounded like Vito might be game. Robert just needed to polish up a few points first, mostly to protect the innocent. Swimming, hmm. He didn't particularly like the sport, pastime, whatever people called it. But ditching someone else's boat sounded much better that driving his Volvo into the ocean.

The rain from yesterday had reappeared and it was decidedly cooler. Good weather to run in, but in light of the number of people apparently after him, he decided a day inside would be a healthier option. His thoughts drifted to his upcoming expedition. He texted Vito, asking for a contact number for his police buddy in Oliver. He then went upstairs to check the ammo supply for both of his guns. Finally, he cleaned his larger pistol due to its recent action in Richmond. As he went through the procedure surely and deftly in the family room, his mind wandered to food. He looked over at the cookbook collection.

With the cleaning complete, he selected the Italian book he had spied weeks earlier and sifted through the index, looking for an *Osso Buco* recipe. He found one and studied it. A trifle complicated, but nothing he couldn't pull off. After Oliver, he'd try it out.

A half-hour later, he was just finishing his coffee process when a knock sounded on his front door. He headed for the small front living room instead of the door, standing to the side as he peered out from behind the curtains. No point in getting ventilated before he even made it to Oliver. A patrol car sat in front of his place, so he figured it was safe to open the door.

"Roberto."

"Sergio! What a surprise. Great to see you, come in."

"Vito asked that I come over to pick something up."

"Coffee?"

He smiled, "A quick one. I'm on duty."

Robert understood the nervousness, so he tried to lighten things. "Don't worry, I won't add any grappa."

Sergio followed Robert into the rear of the townhouse.

"How are you making out so far, Sergio? The uniform looks good on you." He poured a cup and handed it to him. "Milk? Sugar?"

"Black is good. Things are coming along. Much to learn." He was smiling after the uniform compliment.

"Getting treated okay?"

"Depends on who I'm with on the day. Did you know there are some real bastards on the force?"

"Shocking to hear. I understand you've met up with Rory, of cybercrime fame."

"Yes, I have. How do you know that?"

Robert was impressed. The question spoke of some activity behind Sergio's eyes. Just maybe, he might make detective someday. "We keep in touch."

Robert could tell that Sergio considered his question not really answered but let it go.

"What have you got for me?"

Robert considered whether to tell Sergio, finally guessing it wouldn't hurt. "Don't tell anyone else, but it's a contract out on my life. Only Vito knows about this, and that's the way it needs to stay for a little while, okay?" He handed him the baggie with the note.

Sergio nodded. "A contract?"

"I'm to be made dead. For twenty K. I've narrowed the reason down to two possibilities, but that's all I can say for now."

Sergio remained standing, frowning as he sipped his coffee. "To do with work?"

"As a former VPD member, partly." Robert could see the tumblers rolling behind Sergio's eyes.

"Tony used to talk a lot about working with you. He liked it that you weren't a stickler for rules."

"Well, they're there for a reason, but after a while one gets a feeling for when they need to be bent or broken. There's no playbook on that."

"A while?"

Robert smiled. "A couple of years usually, Sergio. You need to get the lay of the land first."

Sergio nodded and finished his cup. "I should get moving. Nice to talk, Roberto. I'll get this to Vito."

In the early afternoon, Robin reappeared with some safety equipment, which he dumped on the floor, and then promptly disappeared. Heading for wherever Rachael was to be found, Robert guessed. A little later, Sandra came through the front door, dragging a mid-sized suitcase.

"Your outfit is in here, somewhere," she said, as she sat down. "Just one more day of prep, then we hit the open road. I can't wait to get there. Getting ready is exhausting."

"Deirdre is a help, I assume?"

"A godsend actually. She will cab it over here Wednesday morning, so we don't need to wander around Kits looking for her."

"Excellent. I hate backtracking."

Sandra smiled. "I assumed as much. What should we eat tonight?"

<hr>

Next morning, with Sandra gone to Main Street, Robert did a careful shave, then pulled on his server outfit. The bowtie was a clip-on version, mercifully. After adding the vest, he donned his new glasses and studied himself in the mirror. Who was that? Not Robert Lui, certainly. Mission somewhat accomplished, but really, the proof would be at the event, not here in his bedroom. He went downstairs for some breakfast and coffee. While he waited for his coffee to drip out, his son came into the room.

"Get a new job, Pops? You look different."

"Good. That is what I was after, a new look." Robert smiled.

"It's not a very good look, Pops."

Robert shrugged. "Trying to make people not

recognize me. Sounds like it might be working." Robin lost interest at this point and opened the fridge, peering in at the offerings.

After Robert changed back into his jeans and T-shirt, he again scrolled through the wineries on offer around Oliver, trying to get a feel for what he'd be encountering. His cell rang.

"Robert?"

"This Bobbi?"

"Yup. I made contact with Harjit. Turns out he only gave the job to two others, so not totally open. At least that's what he said. I know those idiots. Two Tigers members. One of them is Dev, who left the gang almost two years ago to go straight, so I kind of doubt whether he'd take on the offer. The other one is called Jonny, Jonny Singh. He is nuts. Framing lumber has more on the go than these two. Jonny also doesn't walk so straight anymore, so he should be easy to spot if he comes up on you. I think a Delta undercover kneecapped him a couple of years back — both legs. I have pics, which I'll send to you."

"Thanks for this, Bobbi."

"Good luck."

Sounded like Jonny could be a problem. Maybe he could get the Surrey Police to round him up.

TWENTY-EIGHT

Wednesday morning, the Volvo full, the trio began their journey to the Okanagan. Robert headed south to a highway below the Fraser River that'd link up with the Trans-Canada somewhere east in Surrey. Drizzle was intermittently falling, the sky leaden, making for a perfect travel day.

"Been to wine country before, Deirdre?" Robert asked, as they settled in for the ride.

"Sort of. I went to Kelowna a year ago, visited a few places. Good wine and good food."

"That's what we hear. First time for both of us."

"But you grew up here, didn't you?"

"Big province, Deirdre, can't see it all readily, especially when you do what I used to do."

"True enough. Way larger than Ireland, I think."

As Robert drove east, the traffic appeared far worse than the previous time he had headed up to the interior. The highway was in a state of construction for miles, and whatever they were doing looked to be ten years behind the need. It also appeared that all the people who didn't wish to live in Vancouver had chosen the valley to call home.

After over two hours, they hit Hope at the valley's eastern terminus and continued east on the southerly route towards Osoyoos. The scenery didn't change at all, trees on mountain sides everywhere, but the road was windy, single lane traffic for much of it, progress slower as a result. The sign for the local Park Lodge flew past. Robert slowed. After three hours a break was in order. They pulled into a long parking area surrounded by several buildings constructed of darkened Lincoln Logs. Very woodsy, Robert thought. They got out, stretching their legs, breathing in crisp but warming mountain air. Deirdre looked north at the surrounding peaks across the highway.

"You guys done any camping, ever?" Robert asked. Two noes were his answer.

"I looked this place up. There are several campgrounds around here. Might be worth trying someday. It looks serene. I feel better already."

"Same vibe as Bella Kind," Sandra answered. They investigated the small shop in the guest lodge. It was full of the usual tourist gifts as well as a selection of mostly unhealthy snacks. An attached cafe was half full. The whole affair lacked entrepreneurial sharpness, the result of being inside a Provincial Park, Robert assumed.

"Seen enough. Let's move. There must be fancier places closer to Osoyoos." Robert pointed to the door.

Half an hour later, they were making better time as the road widened to two lanes again. Trees were thinning and the hills were drier, more arid. Pines and aspens took over from the firs and cedars. Clouds were thinning too, with hints of bright blue drifting here and there.

"I believe we are hitting the high chaparral, girls."

Sandra turned her head. "What?"

"You know, cowboy country." The east gate to the park flashed by. They were back on Crown land, heading for Princeton.

"Where are the cowboys then?"

"Good question. Let me know if you see a cow. I used to watch some dusters when I was young. This land looks similar."

"Dusters?" Sandra asked.

"Old westerns. Classics. TVs used to be full of that stuff." He reached past Sandra, opened the glove compartment and slid out a jewel case. "Could you slide this in?"

A rich, cracked voice filled the car. "Who's this?" Deirdre asked from the back seat.

"John R. Cash, *The Man Comes Around*. His last album and one of his strangest, all covers, except the first song. I do believe someone was trying his best to resurrect Johnny's career. Very decent road music, nevertheless. As you can tell, he had a bit of religious belief going for him."

After transiting Princeton, the road linked up with the Similkameen River they had been following earlier, now more or less following its path through the Similkameen

Valley towards Keremeos and Cawston. The rain had frittered away, the road drying. They slowed as they came up to Keremeos. It seemed to be some kind of fruit centre, only without fruit due to the time of year. Rough roadside stalls, sheds, and shops were lifeless, waiting for the produce and customers that drove the local economy. Signs for wineries appeared; some fruit growers had evidently given up, turning to the latest trend for the region.

"We need to stop at a couple of places in Cawston, okay? One food store and a winery I've read about. Need to get some garnish material for the Friday offerings. Shouldn't take long," Sandra announced. The car headed southeast and entered a long, wide valley. Green fields stretched out on either side of the road, probably for hay production. A couple of signs flashed by — NO PARK — like a much-abbreviated haiku. What kind of people were against parks, Robert wondered. He'd ask at the next stop.

Robert slowed as they drove through Cawston, then took a left at Sandra's direction and parked in front of a newish market constructed of heavy timber. They sauntered in and looked at the produce on offer up and down generously wide aisles before picking out focaccia sandwiches from the selection on display. The place was not exactly crowded. It emanated a relaxed feeling.

They grabbed coffees as well and went outside to sit at the tables on offer. "I don't know if it's the air or what, but this is amazing food," said Deirdre. Sandra and Robert nodded, their mouths full. After finishing up, Sandra picked out her herbs and vegetables and, before leaving,

Robert bought some additional pastries for the next morning, just in case.

He asked the cashier, "What's with the 'No Park' signs on the road back aways?"

"Feds are trying to make a national park out of the area. It's unique land. Anyone with a business is dead set against it."

"Cause they'd have to close shop, correct?"

"Basically."

"Well, your food is excellent. We're impressed." They waved goodbye and piled back into the Volvo, driving a couple of blocks to one of the local wineries, following Sandra's directions. After a look through its retail area, they picked a four-flight tasting and were directed out the rear to a patio shaded by a group of elderly maple trees. It was a pleasant respite from the driving, and very good wine. Before leaving, Robert purchased a couple of whites. He liked to be prepared for any eventuality.

"Hope there's a fridge in our room," he noted, as they settled in for the run down into Osoyoos.

"If not, there are other ways to cool things down," Sandra said.

"That's good, because it seems to be getting warmer and warmer." Forty minutes later, they came down a long final cut into the Okanagan Valley to meet up with the route they'd be following north to Oliver. Osoyoos lay ahead of them, but Robert left that exploration for another day and turned left at the junction with Highway 97. This was Canada's only true desert and, today, it felt like it even if it was only June. Robert cranked up the AC another few notches as he headed north.

Another half-hour saw them entering Oliver, after passing sign after sign featuring wineries. It seemed like a one-street town, but Robert knew better, having studied a map of the area. He turned east off the highway, finding their hotel one street over. They pulled up to a four-storey building looking like a factory, or maybe a hard hotel. But Robert knew the new provincial prison was just up the road, so this couldn't be it. The banana-coloured sign said, 'STAY'N'SLEEP'.

"Maybe it's better inside." Robert commented. "I'm feeling dozy already."

Sandra pulled a face. "We're only here a few days."

"Yes, sorry."

They checked in, agreeing to meet up at seven with Deirdre to find a place for dinner.

Their room was on the top floor at the north end and indeed had a fridge, so Robert loaded the Chardonnay and Riesling in and relaxed on the bed.

"I assume you are busy tomorrow?" Robert asked.

"Yes. And you need to come by after lunch. There will be briefing for the servers."

"Briefing? Don't spill wine on the guests? Don't step on their toes? No looking down the women's tops? Directions like that?"

"I don't know. I'm running the food end. Just come, and don't say anything. The company owner will be giving the talk."

Robert's cell rang. "Yes?"

"Vito here. I talked with someone in the Seattle Police Department this afternoon. It didn't go well. They thought I was calling from Vancouver, Washington. Robert? They really couldn't give a shit about what we're doing up here and declined to be of any assistance. Sometimes, I don't think they even know where Canada is. They certainly don't care, that's for sure."

"Hmm. At least you tried. Thanks. I found that there may be two coming after me. One is named Dev, no last name. The other is Jonny Singh. He may be the one to worry about, but he doesn't move around well. Apparently, received an anatomy lesson from a Delta undercover a couple of years back. He got kneecapped."

"I heard about it. Amazed he can walk at all."

"It's all innuendo so far. I'll keep my eyes peeled. Thanks Vito. I'm up in Oliver now. Wish me luck."

"Take care, Robert."

The evening meal at a place on Oliver's main drag turned out to be half-hearted tourist fare, eatable but not worth the price charged, in Robert's opinion.

***

Next morning, after a hotel breakfast of sorts where you served yourself, Robert drove the women up to the winery. He had sampled the coffee at the hotel, always willing to give something a try, not expecting much. After sampling, he needed to find a cafe that knew what they were about pretty quickly.

A few kilometres north of Oliver, they turned west off the highway and negotiated a few switchbacks, driving higher and higher, then came upon a lane marked by a wooden sign close to the ground, 'Possession Point Winery'. Beside the sign was a pole about four metres high with a frayed Union Jack hanging limply. Was this some kind of breakaway principality? Were they leaving Canada by entering this lane? Robert entered and drove down the gravelled drive, rows of fruit trees on either side, possibly cherry, then turned a corner and into the parking lot. Not the grandest of entries. An older van sporting a Crazy Eats logo was sitting alongside two other small cars in front of a one-story building covered in weather-beaten horizontal siding. Three flagpoles sprouting at an angle from the wall featured Canadian and BC flags alongside a tartan flag. Maybe they were still in BC but on a clan reserve.

The entire affair didn't exactly scream cutting-edge winery design. More like rough and ready from the exterior. If buckets of money had been sunk into the place, it wasn't evident. They got out, looking at an entry door that stood out because it seemed brand new — indigo painted wood with bright stainless-steel trims and pulls. Fifty metres to the north sat a large barn-like structure topped by a sagging roofline, perhaps the wine-making centre. Between the buildings, they caught a glimpse of rows and rows of vines extending up to the base of a large rock outcrop perhaps three hundred metres distant. Robert walked up to the flag display and checked out the red tartan flag. It boasted the McDouguld name with an inscription around the crest. 'TOUCH NOT THE CAT BOT THE GLOVE'. It surrounded some kind of weird cat. He shrugged and they entered the winery.

The room's layout was lengthy but not very deep. An expensive-looking glass wall fronted a deck looking west over the vineyards beyond. A couple of distant farmhands were doing something to the vines, Robert didn't know what. Perhaps they were whispering sweet nothings to encourage growth. To their left, a small retail area offered wine accessories as well as some local foods and crafts, possibly to be paired with the wines on offer. Some decent artwork graced the walls, local by its look.

To their right, an obese older man rose from a group of people seated around a tasting table and turned to Sandra. Greying hair framed a wrinkled face featuring a merlot-tinged bulbous nose. "You made it. Good. We need to get started." He turned to Robert. "You the driver?"

"And server, come tomorrow."

The man scrutinized Robert. "Seen worse. Be back here by two for the briefing. That's when the others get here."

And hello to you too, Robert thought. Names didn't seem important. Sandra and Deirdre joined the owner, who returned to the table, leaving Robert by a cookbook display. He turned to the young woman behind the counter, blond hair gathered behind an open plain face, probably a student. "Hi. Do you know of any decent coffee places close by?"

"Best bet is Ricardo's. It's on Main Street in Oliver, just north of Co-op Avenue. I go there and like it."

"Can I go outside here, walk around?"

"Absolutely."

Robert leaned closer, talking lower. "The wines any good here?"

The girl blinked, seemingly taken aback. "They are outstanding."

"Thought you might say that, just checking." What else would an employee say? Any other response would get her turfed, he was certain. "How long you been here?"

"A month. I'm studying biology up at UBC Kelowna. Just working the summer season."

"Aah, good. Education is important." As he turned to go, he added, "Thanks for the coffee tip."

After leaving the way he had entered, he walked past the flag display and made for the gap between buildings. The north end of the tasting building he had just left was the business end. A couple of battered utility trucks sat close to a service door. He imagined a kitchen or servery lay just inside — the focus of the caterer's work.

He turned and walked over to the barn structure. A wide plywood deck edged its west side facing the vineyard. On the barn's siding hung dozens of rusty implements, some looking quite hazardous. Pickaxes, bandsaws, sledgehammers, scythes, tired wagon wheels, and hacksaws, along with strange, angled contraptions whose use eluded Robert's understanding, adorned the siding. Looked like a museum of sorts. Many of them were covered with a healthy dose of rust. Someone on a rampage could have their pick of lethal instruments to aid them if they so wanted.

He gave the barn the once-over. A surveillance camera was screwed up high on its west wall. He turned to check the tasting building and saw two more, one over the west deck and another above the service yard between the buildings. He estimated it didn't cover the area close to the wall. A barn door was ajar, so he checked inside. It was empty of people and didn't appear to be fully kitted out for wine-making either. A couple of large stainless-steel tanks stood to one side, but any other equipment was absent. It was dead silent. Cobwebs hung from beams and the tanks, dust motes caught by the lowering sun drifted to the concrete floor. No barrels of aging wine. The place seemed abandoned. The wine must be produced elsewhere. He backed out and headed for the vineyard, walking up the first alley between rows of vines. Everything was neat as a pin, almost industrial in appearance. This vineyard lacked the scruffy history Robert had seen evident at some of the famous French areas he had quickly studied as preparation.

The workers seen earlier wearing crinkled straw hats meandered towards him from about fifty metres away. As Robert drew close, he nodded at them. Their dark faces studied him, unsmiling.

"Hola," said the taller of the two. They kept going by Robert, obviously not interested in tourists. Maybe Mexican workers? He had heard that recruiting farmhands to work the orchards or vineyards was getting more and more difficult as the years passed. He kept walking. As the land rose and he neared the rock face, he noticed large hoof prints in the soil. He wondered what made them, satyrs on a midnight romp? Maybe deer? Would they eat the grapes? He was seriously short on wildlife knowledge. Too many years spent in the city.

He heard a faint sound to the side, then a sort of bark.

He started, then turned to face a coyote's snout, only several steps away. At least he thought it was a coyote. Its head was peeking through a gap between grape stalks. Unsure how to react, he stood still. Then the extraordinary happened. It spoke to him. '*You have come to a bad place.*' But the really shocking thing was the language — it was speaking Cantonese. Robert kept his eyes on the animal, if that's what it really was. He knew it would disappear if he glanced away. At least, this is what happened in the past. Then it spoke again, but he couldn't understand anything it said. Sounded like a native tongue to him.

He turned to see if the workers were still in sight, but they were gone. He looked back for the coyote, but it was gone as well, just as he expected, and hoped, if he was being honest. Was he having some kind of breakdown? He felt fine but the message was pretty clear. He wondered what it portended. Not good things if he was a guessing man, but then, this wasn't a holiday excursion. This was serious and maybe dangerous work. He'd had enough of this vineyard. After re-checking the hoof prints, he retraced his steps to the parking area, got into the Volvo, and headed back into town to get some decent coffee and do some considering about spirits.

CHAPTER
TWENTY-NINE

That evening, after a better dinner of salad and a mushroom pizza at another winery, Sandra and Robert discussed the day. Deirdre had met up with one of the other sous chefs for dinner, so they were alone. They returned to their hotel and, as the evening was cooling, took a walk south, discovering a small river with a trail hugging its bank. Eventually a sign told them it was the Okanagan River, not a large beast that was certain, more like a creek with ambitions.

As they headed south, things started looking industrial. Large warehouses sat just up from the trail, Co-op signs decorating some of them. Then they happened upon a sharp-looking group of townhomes, totally out of place. More like a modernist orphan abandoned by its parents. Robert guessed that cheap industrial land and an accommodating city council lay behind the development. It wasn't a large affair, maybe fifteen homes. They kept walking and weren't alone. The path looked to be a local stroll for those living in the town.

"You guys ready for tomorrow?" Robert asked.

"Yes. Just the final prep. Expecting a hundred and twenty roughly. What did you think of our owner?"

"Asshole is the best I can come up with. The serving lecture was moronic."

"The other servers aren't exactly MBA material, Robert."

"I guess."

"Today was the first time I've spent any amount of time with Marvin. He is a class A lech."

"What did he do?" Robert was mildly alarmed.

"Nothing physical, but it's the eyes, the innuendo, the really bad sexual jokes. I had no idea."

"So, he's not around usually?"

"No. Out drumming up business, I suppose, but really, who knows."

"I'm guessing this isn't a long-term job, then?"

"Probably not. We'll see what happens."

Robert's cell rang. "Yes?"

"It's Robin, hey Pops. Having a good time?"

"So far, so good. Something happen?"

"Those pictures you showed us? I think I saw one of them out on the street today. He was walking real funny, looking at our home for a while, then he got in a car and left. Fancy car, black Mercedes, I think. Smoky windows, low, you know, the whole gang look. Then I saw the same car out the back, cruising the lane, maybe checking for your car, I don't know."

"Be really careful, both of you. Don't get kidnapped again. This guy isn't very bright, so who knows what he'd try. I'm calling Vito, see if I can get some protection for you, okay? In the meantime, I think you should call your grandparents and head over there till we get back."

"I'll call them, but it'll be way too far to get to my job from there. We'll keep a good watch, Pops. Okay?"

"Talk it over with your sister, please."

He looked sideways at Sandra. "One of those gangsters is hanging around our home, looking for me, I'd guess. I'm texting Vito."

Inside of one minute, Vito rang Robert. "That was fast. I'll get someone over to your place first thing tomorrow and do a couple of drive-bys tonight. Didn't get a plate number, I'm guessing?"

"No, but it's a black Mercedes, tinted and chopped. Be hard to miss in our neighbourhood. I'm guessing a pretext might find him armed with no permit."

"I'll let you know how it turns out." Vito said. Robert fretted about his kids, finally calling his parents.

"Mom? Robert here. We are up in Oliver for a couple of days. Think you and Dad could go stay with the kids till we get back?"

"Why, Robert?"

"I'm feeling a bit of danger for them. Someone is after me. I've notified the police, but your presence would be a big help."

"Yes, we'll call them and head over tomorrow, okay?"

"That'd be great. Thanks. We'll be back Sunday."

"Seen enough of local industry. Let's go back to the room and drink some wine," Sandra suggested, so they aborted their stroll and returned to their room. Robert poured a couple of glasses of the Riesling, letting it warm a bit before trying a taste. They sat in the two worn chairs by the window.

"Much as I like wine, what would really go down well in this heat is a Heinie. I'll look for some beer tomorrow. I went over to Enchanting Grape for a look around after the lecture. Everything is brand spanking new. No expense spared. Landscaping, art pieces everywhere, someone's trying to make a statement. Even the paving looked like it had just rolled off an asphalt truck. Only thing missing is guest rooms, but maybe they were hiding out back. There was a decent crowd on hand, restaurant was half full at three pm, so they must be doing something right. Didn't try any wines though. There are plenty of other places we can visit on Saturday. Choices seem endless."

Sandra tasted her wine and nodded. "This is good. Hits the right notes, liquid and alcoholic."

"What time are you expected tomorrow?"

"Ten. Run me over? I'm calling it a night. Big day ahead." She left her glass almost half full and headed for the bathroom.

Friday morning, after dropping Sandra, Robert circled back for a second black at Ricardo's. The small parking lot held a Defender, a Mitsubishi, and an Audi hatchback, all newish. The worker's vehicles had left, second shift evidently in place. Kitsch artwork filled the cafe, like some sort of crafts gallery. Three well-dressed middle-aged women sat at a corner table talking with their hands, hair perfectly coiffed, not a grey strand visible. One was waving a phone around, the others bending their heads, trying to see either her offspring or the latest stupid pet video, Robert guessed.

The student at Possession Point was correct. The barista knew what he was doing, this despite having no visible tattoos. Somehow, Robert had developed a prejudice that a barista worth anything would be heavily adorned with ink work. This despite his two favourite baristas, Gilberto and Adrianne, not having any that were in public view, anyway. With the morning rush abated, Robert felt it'd be a good time to ask a few questions.

He stood at the bar, raised the demitasse and nodded, "Good brew."

"Not difficult to tell you're a fan. Second time in this morning." The young man was slim, arms clean, black hair cropped close, dark face.

"Any chance you'd know the native language name from around here?"

"*Nsyilxcen*, why?"

"Might have heard some yesterday, just curious."

"Local talk to you?"

"A coyote," Robert said, regretting saying it as soon as it had left his lips.

The barista laughed. "*Sin-ka-lip*, sounds about right. Be careful. They are real tricksters, always promoting trouble or getting into it themselves."

It didn't seem to bother this young man that Robert had been conversing with an animal. "You sound as though you know about this coyote."

"I know about coyotes generally. Maybe not yours. I'm native, name's Ray. Syilx Nation."

"Robert, pleased to meet you. May I ask you a question or two? I'm up from Vancouver for a few days."

"Sure."

"Possession Point Winery, know the place?"

Ray nodded. "Some lawyers from Vancouver own it. Not uncommon up here. They need to do something with all the money they make, I guess. And they seem to drink a lot."

"How's it doing?"

"The word is it's on the ropes, but again, not uncommon."

"Doesn't look like they make the wine up there."

"Farm it out. I heard they also got hit hard by the winter frost a year and a half ago. Need to do significant re-planting, which costs. I expect their prices will be going up."

"Enchanting Grape?"

"Have you been there?"

Robert nodded.

"Tells you all you need to know. Chinese guy with money spilling out of his pillowcase. Locals got rich constructing that winery."

"Pillowcase?"

"Briefcase, pillowcase, they gotta carry the cash in something, don't they?"

"Locals getting paid in cash?"

Ray nodded, suddenly wary, inspecting Robert's face. "What'd you say you did?"

"I didn't. But I work for a caterer today. Event at Possession Point tonight. I expect some drinking to be taking place. Wine reserves might be seriously depleted."

A couple more women entered and came up to the bar, one eyeing Robert. He excused himself. "Thanks, Ray. I'll be back tomorrow; let you know how it went."

He was due at the winery by four, so he had time to visit a few places south of Oliver off the main highway. By three o'clock, the Volvo's trunk carried a few half cases of various vintages. He made a stop in Oliver to pick up some beer. Robert was half cut from the tastings but made it carefully back to the hotel to complete his transformation into Robert, server to the stars.

As he was adjusting his ankle holster, his cell rang.

"Yes?"

"Vito here. You were correct on the Jonny thing. We had Sergio give his uniform a break today, and he was able to apprehend your man. Revolver in the car, no permit, no brains either."

"Did Sergio have a reason for the search?"

"Idiot parked on the wrong side of the street heading the wrong way. You can't make this up, Robert."

"Wow."

"Won't be able to hold him of course, but if his gun gets returned, which I doubt, the barrel might be slightly bent. Sometimes happens when you leave a gun in the sun for too long."

"Will someone do a drive-by or two tomorrow? We're not home until Sunday pm."

"Don't worry, we'll keep a watch posted. Have a pleasant party, Robert." The cell went silent. Robert texted his son.

THIRTY

Robert pulled up into the parking area at the winery just before four. A well-muscled and seemingly neckless attendant, dressed in a black tee and grey slacks, waved him around the corner to the service yard after he explained who he was. Shadows on the entry side were lengthening as the sun dropped to the northwest behind the tasting building, the whole facade dark because of it. The event started at five, but already a few high-end rides from Vancouver were in the lot — maybe the lawyer's cars. Winds were light and warm, a perfect setting for whatever was to unfold.

Robert got out of the Volvo, looked around and entered the kitchen/servery. Sandra looked up and gave him a wave from the other side of the room. A counter against the far wall was fronted with an island almost its equal in length, trays stacked on it alongside rows upon rows of glasses. There seemed to be one of every appliance, except for the fridges. Two extra-wide coolers stood at one end. Deirdre and three other sous chefs were busy beside Sandra, working on the food prep. He joined the other servers, two of whom were middle-aged women looking they'd done this once or twice before. The other two were younger, maybe mid-twenties, a guy and a girl, both not bad looking, probably hired as eye candy for the event. All wore similar outfits; black trousers, white shirts, and floral waistcoats, looking like a sad Motown R & B group.

Marvin came over to offer some vital last-minute instructions, "Serving only inside and on the deck outside. No one is to serve in the vineyard, got it?" He looked at the group like he was dealing with slow-witted monkeys. "And no eating the food."

Quite the pep talk, Robert thought. He was standing next to one of the older servers, so he said softly, "He seems well positioned for a second career as a motivational speaker." The woman started chuckling quietly. Marvin noticed, looked across at Robert, "What's your name?"

"Bob."

"Something you want to add, smart ass?" He then must have remembered that Robert had shown up with Sandra. He shifted to glare at her.

"Just wondering if the deck off the barn is a go-, or no-go serving area?" The woman beside him started making more noises, shaking as she tried to keep her laughter in.

Marvin's eyes narrowed as he turned back to Robert, obviously gauging whether he could get along with one less server. "That deck is off limits."

Robert was on the verge of cracking a reply but wisely held back. He didn't want to be fired before he got his chance — afterwards would be fine, however. The rest of the servers nodded; Robert merely eyed Marvin, who looked away after two seconds.

"Any other stupid questions? Good, first up will be the sparkling, some amuse-bouche, then a round of whites and reds, followed by the food, and more wine, dessert at the end." Marvin concluded. He was dressed in a slightly tattered grey suit, frayed at the edges, maybe the best he owned, who knew. His suit jacket was buttoned and definitely under stress. Then he added, "There is some whisky, but it's for the lawyers' special clients. They will do the pouring for that stuff." This caught Roberts's attention. He'd need to check out what was on offer, surreptitiously of course. Perhaps the McDougulds had their own distillery back in Scotland.

The door from the tasting room opened and Ross McDouguld entered, dressed in a freshly cleaned dark blue suit, no tie, cream shirt, hair combed fairly neatly. He waved Marvin over to him.

Robert froze, then slowly turned his back to them, pretending to check the counter. He did a quarter turn back, watching the pair out of the corner of his eye as they conferred. He saw Ross spot Sandra and try to get her attention. She ignored him.

Ross said something to Marvin, who went over to Sandra, taking her by her arm back to Ross. After introductions, Ross smiled and tried to say something charming. Robert couldn't hear what was being said, which was probably a good thing. He watched as Sandra smiled thinly in return, saying something that made Ross chuckle, then she turned back to her work. Robert watched as Ross said something to Marvin, making them both laugh as Ross continued to watch Sandra.

Great, thought Robert, the evening just got more complicated. Time for work, however. He joined the other servers, who were drawing the sparkling wines out of the fridges, replacing them with reds so they'd be the correct serving temperature when their time came. After the sparkling, there would be two whites on offer, a Riesling and a Sauvignon Blanc-Semillon affair. The reds were a Pinot Noir and a Syrah. They all started pouring the sparkling into flutes, carefully lining them up on the trays. Marvin went through the door to check on numbers, returned, and loosed the hounds. "Go, go, go," he said loudly.

Did Marvin think they were jumping out of air force planes? Robert gave his head a shake, grabbed a tray, and followed out last behind the other four.

Maybe fifty people were standing in the tasting room, several more outside. Most of the guests were clad in designer slacks or jeans with brightly coloured shirts or blouses, dressed for summer. Only a couple of men wore suits other than the lawyers. One stood out wildly from everyone else — an older man wearing a white shirt and a red kilt with a matching sash flung over his shoulder. A furry black sporran completed the outfit. Robert wondered if it contained, among other crap, a monkey's paw, or even some bear penises. He knew the British in Hong Kong were not immune to the superstitions of the local population. It could only be Travis McDouguld. Dark hair, obviously dyed, was neatly combed into place. Bushy eyebrows, not dyed, were atop widespread, intense eyes. He was standing very close to Candice Moon. Robert watched as Candice touched his arm. These two were more than mere friends or partners.

A young woman with stylish blond hair cut in a bob beckoned Robert with her eyes. He held the tray closer to her and was promptly two glasses lighter. He spotted Ben Skyler outside laughing it up with two young men, newish developers he suspected. As he returned to the servery, his tray empty, more guests were piling in through the entry. It was getting raucous as guests greeted each other. Many of them obviously knew each other and no doubt had attended events like this many times. After the sparkling wines were done, it was on to the first of the food. As Robert stood out on the deck, being mobbed by ravenous drinkers, he caught a whiff of smoke. Not just any smoke either, Gitanes smoke. He looked around the people present, but no one had lit up in the crowd. His eyes strayed over the barn's deck. Three men were sitting on camp chairs, drinking beers and talking, ignoring the party. Smoke was wafting upwards from them. The smallest of the three turned his head to look out at the vineyard. It was Jingles, he was certain. He assumed the other two were not exactly guests either. He turned around and went back inside to reload.

Next time out, Robert made a beeline to Candice and Travis. They were still close to each other, talking, not looking especially happy. He just caught the end of a sentence from Travis, "And they aren't waiting much longer."

Robert offered the amuse-bouches, a tiny smoked salmon brioche. They grabbed a couple each, not looking at him. Perfect, Robert thought, then he made an error. He didn't move away.

Candice looked up at him. "Something else?"

Robert shook his head. "Enjoy, please." He turned and went over to another couple. He didn't think she had recognized him, but her gaze had lingered. Shit. He could kick himself. He should have offered to get them some wine. This serving gig had some subtleties that he had yet to learn. Shows how much he knew. Hadn't he said that to someone recently?

He moved over to where Ross was holding court, offering what remained on his tray.

"And they ran away with their tails tucked up their ass." Three others made a show of laughing loudly. Ross was obviously recounting a victorious case for the guests. He moved away, nothing to be learned from this group. After re-loading with wine glasses, he aimed for Ben Skyler this time. By the time he got to him, only two glasses remained on his tray. It was like vultures descending upon dead game. Two of the group picked up those, and he was forced to retreat. As he suspected, this was turning into a mostly useless exercise. After several more sorties, Robert came back inside and sat down for a moment. Marvin noticed immediately and he swooped in. "I'm not paying you to sit around, Bob. Get up and back to it."

"Just taking a short break, then I'll get back to serving

the weasels." Marvin's eyes widened at the impertinence but didn't add anything. After Marvin shuffled off, Robert went over to Sandra, who was finally resting, her work done for the moment.

"How you doing?"

"Exhausted, you?"

"Okay. Not sure what I'm accomplishing, but it's interesting, that's certain. There's a group of hoods over at the barn. The guy who was trying to tail me several days ago, Jingles, is one of them. So, I'd say this law firm's prospects are looking even dimmer. Question is, what are they doing here, providing guided tours of the vineyard?" He stood up. "Time to get back out there, getting pressure from Marvin. And by the way, I've overheard several glowing reviews about the food!" Sandra looked happy hearing this.

The party was still going full bore three hours in. The sun finally dipped behind the stone escarpment at the far west of the property, the temperature dropping a couple of degrees, which was fine as far as the servers were concerned. They were all sweating from the work and the tension rising from the need to be perfect in their duties. Robert noticed more than a few revellers wandering in amongst the vines, despite being told not to. Very few people seemed to be sober. As he stared west, he could see something white flying up far off, then disappearing. Was it a bra? He shrugged and re-entered the tasting room.

Looked like Ross was moving things up a notch. The

deejay was playing something in the rap genre. Ross went over to him — the volume increased. Then he headed to a cabinet, opened it and moved several bottles onto an adjacent table. Robert's interest rose. He guessed the scotches had just appeared. Sure enough, several male guests gathered close, as though they had sniffed a blood scent, putting aside their wine glasses, their greedy eyes focused on the whisky. Robert sidled over, ostensibly to pick up empty glasses, but he really wanted to see where the bottles hailed from. Nothing less than fifteen years old, evenly split between Islay and Speyside. He took his time retrieving the stemware. It was an impressive collection.

Just as he turned to go back to the servery, the front door opened, and a tall Chinese gentleman dressed in shades of grey entered. Shou Deng had crashed the party. Robert was pretty sure the man matched the photo Winston had sent him from Hong Kong. Shou was alone, his eyes searching the room. His clothing wasn't anything you'd purchase at a modest retailer. He stood quietly for a moment, surveying the action, then he moved in the direction of the whisky group. Ross, who hadn't noticed him enter, was too caught up in showing off to his clients. Robert looked around to see what Travis was making of this, but it appeared he hadn't noticed Shou's entrance either. Robert should have been making his way back to the servery, but there wasn't any way he was going to miss what had the makings of a genuine brouhaha. Robert moved away, but still within earshot, which, given all the noise, wasn't far.

"Ross McDouguld?" The voice was raised but measured and calm.

Ross turned. No recognition registered on his face. Ross plainly didn't know what Shou Deng looked like. "Yesh?" Ross was already pickled, without the whisky.

"Nice party. I'm your neighbour. We are looking to expand, and I'd like to make you an offer for your winery."

Ross blinked. The men around him divided their attention between Shou and Ross, curious no doubt as to why someone would make a blatant business offer at a raucous party. Robert watched as Ross's face reddened, finally realizing what an ass he was being made of.

"How'd you get in? I'll get shecurity to deal with you."

Security? All Robert had seen was the bull-necked parking attendant and the three hoods over at the barn. This was going to be interesting. Then Shou dipped his head, smiled. "There is no need for such theatrics. I will leave. Please consider my offer." With that, he turned and left.

Ross started laughing, putting on a show for his clients, obviously feeling he had dealt very effectively with the challenge. He took a bottle and started pouring whisky into cut-crystal tumblers.

"And that's how you deal with assholes!" He raised a glass. "Cheers."

"*Slange Var* or up your kilt!" Travis had joined the group. He grabbed a glass, filled it and joined the toast.

"What was that about?" Travis asked.

"A neighbour. Wants to buy our place."

Travis was silent as he digested what his enemy was up to. Candice wandered over to the group. She picked up a glass and poured herself some Laphroaig, no ice or water added. She hadn't left Travis's side since the party started, as far as Robert could tell. As he was about to leave, Robert felt her eyes on him again. He looked up. She eyed him. Shit, he had a bad feeling as he turned away. Had he been marked? Probably. He grabbed his tray and retreated to the servery.

Sandra was addressing the other servers as he entered. "Dessert is up. A sorbet, a special Scottish shortbread, and a fruit cup. Let's go." Marvin was nowhere to be seen. The trays had been loaded. Robert picked up his and headed back into the fray. The music had been turned up, and it was actually music now. The whole place was thumping — men and women dancing in the middle of some shifted tables. At least it looked like dancing to Robert. He was never sure about what constituted dancing these days. The whisky group had grown in size and continued to listen to Ross's animated blathering.

As Robert moved around the room, he could feel Candice's eyes on him. She knew or was pretty certain as to his identity, he felt. Nothing to be done now. He kept working. Guests were asking for more wine. He wondered if the local RCMP were staking out the road. It'd be easy pickings; that was certain. His tray empty, he went back for more wine. This was starting to feel like work. An hour later, Ben Skyler appeared just inside the kitchen door, seemingly afraid to venture any further. He made a slashing motion across his throat to Marvin, who sat at a table doing his sums. The music was thudding throughout the building, some kind of techno-crap with a catchy beat. Looked like their work was done, except for the retrievals after the guests had departed.

Robert was talking softly to one of the older servers when the door opened and Ross McDouguld stumbled into the room, plainly sauced. He nodded at Marvin, then headed for Sandra, who had her back to the room, cleaning her knives. As Robert watched, Ross came up behind her and grabbed her ass, nothing subtle about it. Sandra shrieked and turned, wondering who'd try such a thing. She didn't waste any time, slapping Ross across the face so hard the entire room heard it. He grinned, shaking his head, cheek reddening.

Marvin had watched the ending unfold. "That's it, you're finished, Sandra. Get out now."

Robert moved over close to Ross, who seemed to be happy with the little scene. "Hey, Ross. Have a little word? Won't take long, then you can get back to it." His hand waved over the counter behind Sandra, grabbing a small paring knife, hiding it in his hand. "Let's do this out back, quickly."

Ross seemed confused that a server would know his name. Robert grabbed his arm and led him to the door.

Outside, the door closed, Robert took only one step, then turned, throwing Ross against the wall. He didn't want this to be seen by the camera. Ross's head thwacked the siding hard. Robert's forearm pinned Ross's neck to the wall. Ross made some gurgling sounds.

"Touch my fiancé again and I'll cut off your balls, or your pecker, your choice, and put it all in your shirt pocket for you. Understand?" He waved the knife in front of some very frightened eyes. Ross seemed to be trying to say something. Robert loosened the pressure slightly.

"Who are you?"

"Wrong question, asshole." He dropped the knife and with a short jab, drove his fist under Ross's sternum, not too savagely — he didn't want him dead exactly, well at least not too dead. Then he let his left arm relax and quickly got out of the way. Ross fell forward as an explosion of liquor-infused food flew onto the gravel. Robert bent down, picked up the knife calmly and went back inside, leaving Ross sprawled on the ground.

He walked up to Sandra, who wasn't crying, but instead was packing up her knives, furious.

Robert looked over at Marvin. "Better get out there to help your buddy. I think he tripped over a raccoon. Doesn't look too good." He turned to Sandra. "Got everything? Let's get out of here." He beckoned to Sandra's friend, who was munching on a leftover hors d'oeuvre. "Deirdre, want a ride?"

"Sure."

Marvin hadn't left the room yet, unfortunately. He spied Deirdre doing the forbidden. "You're fired as well. I told you not to eat the food!"

"Hey, I'm an honest gal." Despite what she said, Deirdre appeared only mildly concerned with this turn of events, probably happy at being lumped in with her friend. She grabbed her bag and joined the other two as they left through the service door. As they passed by Marvin, who had gone outside to help Ross to his feet, Robert couldn't resist, "Terrible way to treat good scotch. You should be ashamed."

They got into the Volvo and, as they drove past the two men, Robert could see hatred flashing in Ross's eyes. Robert waved, then they were gone.

THIRTY-ONE

The adrenaline rush was abating, Robert's chest starting its familiar ache. "Did I just punch out a lawyer at his own garden party? Jeez, I think I'm in trouble. I can't believe I did that." He glanced over at Sandra.

She said, "Well, I slapped a lawyer, but I'll sue that asshole for sexual harassment if he tries coming after you."

"Don't know if that'd be a good use of money. You had witnesses, but they all work for Mr. Marvin. I'm guessing they may not have super great memory by the time it came to a court case."

Sandra frowned.

They came to the tee at the public road. An RCMP cruiser was sitting, waiting. Robert rolled to a stop across from the car and slowly got out. He knew enough not to make any sudden movements. He sidled over to the driver's window, which rolled down. The driver was a young white officer. Beside him was a Chinese officer.

Robert bent down. "Jackie Chan? addressing the passenger, who nodded.

"Robert Lui. I believe Vito was talking with you?"

"Yes, hi. Good to meet you. What's happening in there?"

"The usual. Think you may need another cruiser or two. There are many very drunk people back there, and I don't see any taxis lined up to get them where they want to go. And oh yeah, there are three hoods as well, one named Jingles — small guy. They weren't part of the festivities but were hanging around, like hoods sometimes do."

Then Robert considered what he'd just done. "I needed to advise one of the hosts about proper manners after he groped my fiancée's rear. Just in case he complains to you. We all were working for the caterer."

"Otherwise okay?"

"Seemingly. We're around tomorrow before heading back to Vancouver Sunday. Take care."

Robert went back to the car, and they slowly made their way to the hotel, talking about the evening the entire way. "I'm hungry," said Sandra as they entered the parking lot.

"Me too. I think I saw a burger joint on the main drag — hope it's still open." Robert did a U-turn and two minutes later they pulled up in front. Lights were on, some teenage customers still visible. Fifteen minutes later, the three were wolfing down cheeseburgers and home-cut fries, just making it in under the wire, the kitchen about to close up.

"Guess we are all out of work." Robert said.

"We are. I hope you're still employed somewhere." Sandra responded. "Sorry, Deirdre. I had no idea Marvin was such a putz."

"Not the shortest job I ever had, but close to it," Deirdre mumbled, between bites of fries. "This is good stuff. At least I'm not getting fired for eating this. What a dork that guy was."

"I hate to say it, but you may both be victims of me being there," Robert said.

"I disagree. Ross was going to try something at some point. I've dealt with his type before," Sandra said.

Back at Possession Point Winery, Ross had calmed slightly but was still seething at being hit by one of the kitchen staff. After changing his shirt in an office and ditching his vomit-stained jacket, he re-joined the party and went over to Candice and his father. "That asshole server hit me. Sucker punched me, just outside the kitchen."

"Which one?" Candice asked.

"The tall one, with the glasses."

"Do you realize who that was?"

"Some servant. Marvin fired him."

She shook her head. "It was Robert Lui. He tried to disguise himself, but I figured it out. Why did he hit you? What did you do?"

"Nothing much. Do you know where they are staying? We should get Ilya's crew to give them a visit."

"Find out from Marvin, he should know."

"I need another drink."

Travis came to life. "I very much doubt that, but I'll join you."

"I'm going to sue that guy, make him wish he never came to Oliver. Tell our manager to get the security tape to me off the service yard camera."

Candice stared at Ross. "Tell him yourself. Do I look like staff to you?"

Ross looked confused. He lifted his glass and said, "Great party!" He emptied it. "Be right back. Where is Ilya?"

"Barn. Last I checked." Ross headed for the kitchen to find Marvin first.

At the hotel, Sandra said goodbye to Deirdre in the lobby as she was leaving Oliver first thing the next morning. Robert and Sandra headed up to their room, where Robert found a Chardonnay waiting in their fridge.

"Cheers, Sandra. Tomorrow, we relax." They both lay down on the bed, Sandra only sipping a bit of wine from one of the better-known local wineries, Robert drinking a green soldier. Sandra reached over, unbuttoning Robert's shirt so she could slip her hand in onto his chest.

"That feels nice. My ribs still bother me from time to time. Your hands are healing me, I just know it."

"That was some evening. I wonder if I should put it on my resume?" Sandra mused.

Robert was about to pour some more when the room phone rang. "Maybe it's Marvin, come to apologize." He picked up the phone. "Yes?"

"Someone was here for you. A large man. He just left. Didn't look pleased when we wouldn't give him access to the elevator. Thought I'd let you know."

He looked over at Sandra. "Get some shoes on, quick." He returned to the front desk clerk. "Did you give him our room number?"

"We're not allowed to do that."

"Not what I asked you."

He was reluctant. "Yes, I had to. He aimed a large gun at my face."

Robert ended the call. "Let's go, Sandra. Did you tell Marvin where we were staying?"

"Yes, why?"

"Those hoods are here. Candice must have figured it out." He grabbed his shoulder holster with the larger gun, strapped it on and added a windbreaker. "Let's get out of here."

He opened the door slowly and took a look down the corridor. It was empty. He grabbed Sandra's hand and took three steps to the near exit door. He opened it a fraction. He could smell smoke, Gitanes smoke. Jingles was somewhere on guard in the stairwell. He left the door, went back into his room looking for something to throw. The coffeemaker was too small. The microwave. He grabbed it, yanking the plug free, and returned to the stair door. He spoke quietly, "When I throw this, we're going down these stairs and outside, ready? That's if I hit what I'm aiming for."

Sandra nodded but was obviously frightened.

Robert opened the door. He looked down at the first landing. Nothing. He shifted the appliance and put his finger to his lips as they quietly moved down the stairs. If he followed patterns, Jingles'd be near the bottom, waiting. The pair moved down to the second floor. Robert spotted Jingles on the intermediate landing below, not really paying attention too much other than his cigarette.

"Hey, Jingles!" As Robert yelled, he threw the appliance. The man brought his right hand up as the microwave landed square on his head. Robert and Sandra ran down the stairs and passed him. He didn't seem to be dead, but he also wasn't conscious, splayed on the landing. Robert stooped to grab his gun, stepping on Jingle's gun hand as he went by, grinding his heel firmly on the hand. It sounded like someone eating peanuts.

"That's strong smoke. Interesting aroma." Sandra said as they reached the bottom.

"French. Not for learners."

They exited the stair at grade, hugging the building. Robert looked around the corner at the parking lot, figuring all three hoods would be coming for them. And maybe the large guy would be going up the other stair by now, hoping to surprise them in their room. He spotted a car with a driver studying the lit lobby. Robert kept Sandra with him, despite the danger. He didn't want Jingles waking up and taking her. All the remaining cars in the lot were empty. It wasn't difficult to sneak around to the rear of the car. He grabbed his weapon, safety off. He opened the rear door and slid in, pistol quickly to the back of the driver's head. Sandra got in the other side.

"We're going for a short drive, okay? Both hands on the wheel." The man tried to turn his head, so Robert smacked him hard with the flat of the pistol. His ear started bleeding. "Don't do that again. The gun might go off, get it?" The man nodded, mute.

"Okay, let's get going. Don't worry about your friends." A short drive later, they pulled into the lot at the local RCMP detachment. All the lights were on. One cruiser was leaving with another pulling in. Robert suspected that the Possession Point party was keeping the officers busy. He carefully got the driver out and walked him up into the station.

He addressed the sergeant at the front desk. "I'm delivering a hood to you, no charge. We're up at the Stay'n'Sleep hotel where these gentlemen were attempting to grab us — I think. His car is out front here. You will no doubt find some kind of prohibited firearm inside. And he had two partners. We noticed them at the Possession Point party. If you are quick, you might find one of the other two in the north stairwell, name is Jingles. I was trying to demonstrate how a microwave works, when it inexplicably slipped out of my hands. Sadly, it ended up on his head. The third guy was pointing a gun at the night clerk's head to get our room number, but he may have high-tailed it." He put a gun on the counter. "Jingles was waving this around. I'm leaving it in your capable hands."

"Who are you?"

"Robert Lui. Check with Jackie, he knows my story." At that moment, Jackie Chan walked into the detachment.

He was pushing a very inebriated customer over to the counter. He nodded at Robert.

"What are you doing here?" Jackie asked.

"Trying to be helpful."

"That party is keeping us busy."

"Well, I don't like to add to your work, but the Stay'n'Sleep might need a car sent over. Check both exit stairs. There'll likely be damage to the door hardware. And have a word with the night clerk."

Jackie studied Robert's face for a moment. "Okay, we'll see what's up."

"Thanks, we are heading back there now. We're staying there."

Robert turned to Sandra. "Guess we're walking back."

Jackie offered, "You can get a ride with the officer we're sending over."

Robert waved his hand. "That's okay. Rather not get in the back of a cruiser, if you know what I mean."

Jackie smiled. "Come by tomorrow then, please."

Robert nodded.

THIRTY-TWO

Back at their hotel, an officer was taking a statement from the front desk clerk in the waiting area. Ignoring them, Robert and Sandra went up to their room. The door was closed, but its handle was on the corridor floor. Robert pushed it open carefully, gun in his hand. The room appeared to be empty. He carefully checked the closet, then the bathroom. Nothing. And after a look through, their belongings seemed intact. "It's clear, Sandra." She entered cautiously. Robert put the safety chain on the door before opening the fridge, retrieving another bottle of wine. "Let's have a drink, Sandra, it's been a long day."

She nodded. "Robert? You have a very complicated life."

"And you, have been great through all this. Cool as a cucumber. How is it you aren't running around screaming?"

"I trust that you know what you're doing, that's why.

You were a detective, after all, and used to dealing with people like these. Seems to be working out so far."

Exactly what Robert was thinking as he slipped off his jacket, gun and waistcoat. "I'm cleaning up." He grabbed his wineglass and went into the bathroom. After stripping, he showered quickly, then shaved off his disguise, taking his time. Feeling more human, he returned to the room, naked. Sandra watched as he tossed his uniform into the garbage can.

"You look much better," Sandra said.

"I feel better. I'll try to get a haircut tomorrow. Maybe Marvin will change his mind about you after he's cooled off, but I am out." Robert said. "Guess I'll scratch serving off my career list. I need to do something different though. You shouldn't be losing your job because of my antics."

"Believe me, Deirdre's and my job loss wasn't due to you. It just moved up the inevitable result. I'm going to clean up myself. Don't pass out until I get back."

Robert changed his mind, grabbed a beer from the fridge and drained half of it in one long gulp, contemplating a life outside of what he was doing. This didn't lead him anywhere, but he knew he needed to somehow stop the harm that threatened those close to him. The beer was good. He drained the rest in a couple of seconds. He'd been thirsty.

Robert was rising to pour some wine when Sandra returned, naked, her hair damp, nipples standing at attention. He grew hard in seconds. He put his glass down. "Let's forget about this day, what do you say?"

"Your eagerness to forget is hard to miss, Robert."

He looked down as he moved to Sandra. "I guess." He ran his index finger lightly down her belly as he kissed her slowly. She shuddered, grabbing him.

The next morning, waking up was more than difficult, so they took their time. "Ricardo's?" Robert mumbled after they were dressed. "Time for some vacation, I think."

"Yes. Hope we don't run into any assholes there though."

On their way through the lobby, Robert went over to the desk. "Hi. Room 410 needs new hardware for its entry door. And I owe you for a microwave." The young woman looked confused, perhaps not fully up to date with the goings-on of the previous evening.

"Okay, let's go get caffeinated." He said to Sandra.

Today, the car display at Ricardo's was decidedly mixed. Some good, some bad, newer models, and very old ones, one or two with collector plates. The lot was almost full. Inside, a short line started at the machine. Most of the tables were taken. Ray was on duty, working his machine feverishly. He nodded at Robert when his eyes passed over the lineup.

Robert's turn came. "Double long, as strong as humanly possible, and a macchiato, please. How you doing?"

Ray smiled. "Busy, which is good. You look different today."

"Yes, back to my old self. Found out serving's not for me. It was an epic evening."

"Coming up." After Robert paid, he went back to retrieve the cups. He noticed a couple of people from the party, but not any of the hosts.

"Thanks for this. Any good barbers in town?"

"Welcome. Giordes is just north of us — pretty decent." Ray said.

"I'll give them a try." Robert gathered Sandra and they went out the back to a patio to sip their coffees in the sunshine. The weather was perfection. A couple of fat robins flitted around the trees. "Maybe we should move up here, what do you think? I get the feeling there are more than a few escapees from the Lower Mainland living here."

"I think Robin isn't finished school yet. And didn't he just meet that girl? I doubt he'd be onboard. Other than that, it does seem pretty nice here, definitely calmer, except when you are here."

"After I get my hair cut, let's head down to Osoyoos and slowly work our way back up."

"I'll get us something to eat for the road." Sandra disappeared back inside. While she waited for service, Marvin came in, followed by Ross McDouguld. She didn't see them enter. They came up behind her in the line.

"She does have a fine-looking ass," Ross said, taking a position behind her. She felt a chill on her neck as she realized who was behind her. She did her best to ignore them.

"Yeah, just kind'o a bad attitude." It was Marvin.

"Wonder what she'd be like in the sheets?" Ross said. It was a good thing she didn't have her knives with her.

Then Robert came back in. He sauntered over, standing behind the two men who didn't notice him.

"Maybe you could hire her back, get her to do a special catering job at our firm, after hours, of course." Ross speculated. It was the wrong thing to say.

"And maybe I could tag along, to help out of course." Robert said. "Apparently, you didn't understand my message last evening. My father told me Travis's son was a bit dim. My father is generally right about such things."

The two men turned around. Ross flinched and stepped back, right into Sandra. She pushed him back, into Robert. Fear was evident in Ross's eyes. His hands flew up in mock surrender. "I didn't mean …. "

"Of course you did. On another topic, Ben seems like a decent enough guy. Don't you think you should resign before you fuck up the entire firm?" He waited a beat then said, "But I realize thinking's not your strong suit." He touched Sandra's arm, pointing to the door.

As they left without their food, they could hear Ross yelling, "I'm going to sue your ass." Half the clientele turned their heads to look at Ross.

"Small town. Guess you can't help but run into people you want to see, and those you don't. I'll get that haircut, then let's head south."

"I don't ever want to see those people again," Sandra said.

A half-hour later, they were back on Highway 97, heading south, not before Robert called home to check that his parents had shown up. The day was warming nicely, no clouds. It'd probably be hot later. Traffic was light, at least compared to back home. One could almost drive around with their eyes closed, Robert felt. They started to relax again, the windows down, fresh air moving through the Volvo.

Downtown Osoyoos seemed to have a Mexican thing going on, perhaps befitting its desert locale. The adobe look was very big, with lots of multi-coloured clay tiled roofs and salmon stucco with crenellated wall tops. After walking up and down the main drag, the pair finally got some breakfast muffins the size of cakes at a cafe, then were pointed in the direction of the local First Nation winery across the lake and up a hill. The town seemed roughly the same size as Oliver, but it boasted the lake, making it a favoured summer destination for people from Vancouver and Calgary.

After an excellent tasting at the winery, they wandered over to the spa next door and out to the edge of its expansive deck overlooking the entire town. The lake was split in two by a causeway connecting the west to the east side of the town where they were. The distant arid hills were painted in shades of jade, olive, and bleached khaki. It certainly had little in common with the British Columbia they were familiar with. A hostess pointed them towards the adjacent Interpretive Centre, but before leaving Robert went back to the tasting room and purchased some more wine. After placing it in the trunk, they walked down a dusty path, coming upon a sign:

Beware of Rattlesnakes

Sandra immediately grabbed onto Robert, eyeing the immediate area closely. Scrub, thistle, and wild thyme plants didn't quite cover the dried soil.

"I don't like snakes," Sandra said.

"Don't blame you. They're not my favourite lizard either. I don't like reptiles or lizards, period. My interpretation of this is danger. Let's get back in the car. We'll be safe there. Let's leave the Centre for another day." Sandra agreed.

They drove in a leisurely fashion back north up a country road east of the Okanagan River from the 'Golden Mile' visiting winery after winery. Small groups of bicycles hogged the road, slowing things down, but then, no one was really in a hurry.

"This sure beats going all the way to Europe, doesn't it?" Robert said.

"Yes, we are pretty lucky."

"Can you smell something burning?"

Sandra nodded, "Faintly."

They looked around but couldn't discern any smoke over the hilltops or in the fields close by.

It was past two. "How about lunching at Enchanting Grape? At least none of those hosers will be there." Robert asked. The trunk of the Volvo was filling up. Robert had trouble saying no to anything he tasted.

"Sure."

"We should drop into the RCMP place first to check in."

<hr>

At the detachment's front desk, the duty sergeant was amiable enough to talk about the busy evening at the detachment after Robert reminded him who he was.

"Anybody still being held?" Robert asked.

"No. There was just the one drunk who seemed bent on driving and the man you brought in. He indeed had an unregistered weapon in the car, although he had no idea how it got there, or whose it was. The car wasn't registered to him. We kept the weapon and released him with conditions."

"Anything found at the hotel?"

"Like you said, some hardware on the floors, some blood in the north stair alongside a damaged microwave, no people. Got a description from the night clerk on the guy waving the gun."

"Check the local hospital?"

"Emerg was closed last night, as happens lately. No sign anyone showed up, so maybe a clinic in town? We'll look into it."

"Maybe check the vets as well. I understand they handle animals." Robert's eyes twinkled.

"Good idea."

"It's only the second time in the last week or two that this has happened to me courtesy of the same guy — stairwell with violence. The difference was that this time, I was ready. If there is a next time, maybe I'll just kill the guy, but you didn't hear that from me. Say hi to Jackie for me when you see him. We're heading back to Vancouver tomorrow."

"Ah, back to the rat race."

Robert nodded, then thought about it. The guy was absolutely correct; they were going back to a rat race. It was sobering when considered like that.

"Smoke outside, wasn't there yesterday."

"We just got word a small fire broke out north near Okanagan Falls. I hope they get on top of it quickly. It's been pretty dry here, and things can spread if they can't contain it. Don't need any more of what happened last year. Getting to be like biblical plagues around here."

Robert nodded. "Okay, Sandra. Let's go dine."

Meanwhile, back at Possession Point, Ross McDouguld received some bad news. He was sitting at a table with Candice and the winery manager in the tasting room. The catering crew had cleared out, leaving the owners and the few staff on site who were trying to clean up.

"What do you mean the security cameras aren't working, you asshole?"

"Only the barn unit is functioning. We can only do so many things here when the money is tight," the manager answered. He looked uncomfortable.

"That is fucking great. A guy sucker punches me, and we have no record of it, just supreme."

Candice spoke, "And you really didn't do anything to provoke him?"

Ross looked up at Candice and finally cracked. "I may have touched his girlfriend."

"Jeez, Ross. Why do you have to make things so difficult for us?"

"By us, you mean you and my father?"

Candice refused to answer. "I'm going to figure out how to deal with Robert Lui before any more damage is done to us. You stay clear, understand?"

Ross remained silent but nodded. Then, "How would Robert's father know about me?"

"What do you mean?"

"We ran into Robert at a cafe. He said this to me."

"I have no idea. Ask your father. Have we received anything from Shou Deng?"

"Not as yet."

"You realize how dangerous this guy is?"

"My father hasn't told me squat about him."

"Well, let me fill you in. He is a Communist Party member from the mainland, and a functioning member of the Wide Bay Boys in Hong Kong. They are the ones putting the squeeze on Travis, big time."

Ross's eyes widened.

"How do you suppose he got all that money to do up Enchanting Grape?"

"I assumed it was inherited."

Candice shook her head slowly and rose. "I'm going to get Travis and we're heading back to Vancouver. You should attend to your knot-headed muscle team. They are worse than hopeless."

Ross was silent, but he couldn't disagree with Candice. He stood up, sighed, and went outside to the barn.

He slid the door open wider. The three thugs were inside, lounging and drinking beer again. The little one had a huge bandage on his right hand and some smaller coverings on his face. He didn't look well.

"You guys are done. Clear out. Don't need your so-called services anymore this week." He threw an envelope onto the floor. "You're lucky to get this much." Then he left.

The largest of them picked up the envelope. "Six hundred dollars," he announced to the other two, after thumbing through the thin wad. "This won't even cover your missing guns. Teach you to be more careful with them." He took three hundred out and threw the envelope at the other two. "I'm leaving."

Sandra pulled into the parking area of Enchanting Grape, having taken over the driving. They slid out, stretched, and admired the sculptures placed among the line of cypress trees. It was as though Shou Deng had lifted his ideas after a grand tour of Italy. Heat was building. Robert and Sandra drifted along amongst at least a dozen other visitors, in no hurry. They came upon a tasting room off the main plaza, all glass and bright metal. They entered.

Beyond the guest waiting area, a tremendous view unfolded of the valley to the east. Un-prompted, the hostess told them it was a half-hour wait to do a tasting. They nodded and left, in no mood to wait. They headed in the direction of the restaurant, the focal point at the end of the plaza.

Inside, the hostess asked if they had a reservation. Robert looked at her as though she was crazy.

"No. We were just in the area, thought we'd get something to eat."

The hostess smiled. "No problem, follow me." They were seated at a table next to a window with the same fabulous view. The place was half empty, or half full, depending on your life view.

After a lunch that they couldn't have matched even with their combined skills, they finished their wine. "Well, this owner may be a Class A crim, but that was one good meal. The Flat Iron Steak was inspired."

Sandra nodded. "Agreed. My risotto was excellent as well. Wonder who the chef is?"

"Let's ask."

After paying, the hostess went to fetch the chef, who was not in the least troubled by coming out and talking to patrons. Given who the owner was, Robert wasn't surprised to find that the chef was Chinese, a young woman trained in Hong Kong. And she was chasing a Michelin star, which explained the high level of effort involved.

Back in their car, Robert texted his children asking for an update. He assumed that, not having heard anything, they were okay, but …. After a long moment with no answer, he called Sophie.

"Dad?"

"You guys both okay?"

"Yes. A cop car is on our street, and one of the cops checked in on us this afternoon. Nan and Gung have been here. No problems. Coming home tomorrow?"

"Yes, see you both soon."

They arrived back at the Stay'n'Sleep. A different young man was behind the desk. It seemed their reservation was still being honoured even after all the events of the last couple of days. They went for a short stroll, basically to see what else Oliver had to offer. Robert assumed the thugs who had come after them on Friday evening had moved on, but he took notice of everyone, nevertheless.

Real estate signs were numerous, but there wasn't much else, as it turned out, so they retired to their room and opened another bottle. This time, it was a Syrah. Sandra declined more wine, so Robert did his best. The door had been repaired. They made certain it was barred, then relaxed, contemplating a return to the rat race the next morning.

Sunday morning, with a trunk full of wine, Robert and Sandra departed Oliver. Robert convinced Sandra to do some driving for their first leg. He would take over at some point to do the harder part near Vancouver. Sophie texted Robert. Things were still quiet on Inverness.

Robert's cell rang. Sandra put the Volvo in high gear, foot to the floor. Robert watched the road nervously as he answered.

"Robert?" It was Vito.

"Who else?"

"Right, anyway, the upper floor has somehow learned about our activity around your home. We've been told to stand down, no assistance to be rendered whatsoever. On pain of excommunication."

Robert was silent, thinking.

"You there?" Vito asked.

"I'm still a paid-up citizen of Vancouver. Was it something I said?"

"Not sure. What happened at the party?"

"Some drinking, the usual. I may have punched out one of the hosts. Wonder if someone complained."

"Thought you were working there. Is this the way you were trained to deal with customers?"

"Directions were sketchy in the extreme. We all got fired in the end. No fault of our own though."

"Right, it never is your fault, is it?"

Robert ignored this jibe. "Any headway on those possible murder inquiries?"

"They've been given to Finn to deal with. I don't think he's making much headway."

"You don't have any spare vests, do you? I forgot to snag one on my way out the door."

"Did you miss what I just said? No help at all. But I'll see what I have in my trunk."

"Okay, thanks for the heads up, I guess."

That Jonny hadn't been spotted by his kids didn't give Robert any comfort. He still needed to deal with the implicit danger. Robert thought through the possibilities beside Sandra as she drove back along Highway 3, speed dropped a bit after a suggestion from Robert. Another idea had come to him, a much more dangerous idea. It was insane, frankly, but if Vito came up with a vest for him, he wasn't going to ditch it just yet.

"I think I'll see if my new company has work in the Okanagan. I can't imagine why they wouldn't. Perhaps not this year, but once Robin is done high school, we could think about a move up there if I'm still employed by them. Maybe we could even afford to buy something."

"Wow, you dream big."

"Unfortunately, I have a few problems to solve first." He watched the green fields speed by, no rolls of hay stacked and waiting as yet. He didn't know what he was looking at. Clover, alfalfa? The land sported short, new growth. To the west, cloud heads were forming over the low mountain range, miles away but looking vaguely ominous. Snow still graced the tops of some peaks. "Think you'll look for another job?"

"I'm going to give it a rest for a bit, consider options. I feel bad for Deirdre, though." Sandra answered. She was concentrating on the road, conversation not top of mind.

A couple of hours in, they stopped at the same tourist place inside Manning Park they had hit on the way out, changed places and Robert took the wheel for the slog into Vancouver. The day had darkened considerably. They joined the Trans-Canada at Hope, traffic thickening, and stopped to pick up some gas. Shouldn't these people be in church, or at home on a Sunday playing dominoes? After Hope, speed slowed. Farther west, as the trees parted, the sky bloomed with blackened clouds, as though they'd been hiding in a coal mine. Large drops splattered the windshield, mixing with the dust, first a couple, then a barrage. A jagged yellow sliver flashed ahead. They waited. Ten seconds later the boom arrived, then a second flash. What was happening? Thunderstorms rarely hit Vancouver. Was this another omen? He didn't really need anymore signs, but it felt personal.

Clouds roiled, rain being driven into the Vancouver-bound traffic. Heading towards Chilliwack, progress grew slower and slower until they finally came to a complete stop. Shit, it had to be an accident up ahead, and there was no way off the highway. Robert's shoulder muscles were bunching up, the pleasanter parts of the interlude in the Okanagan quickly fading. Rain was pelting down now, bouncing off the windshield. The cars finally moved again, first slowly, then with speed. After a few kilometres, he realized there had been no accident, just too many cars for a road to handle.

Arriving home mid-afternoon, the townhouse was empty of teens, and Robert's parents were more than ready to return to their place. Robert thanked them profusely, knowing his father wouldn't be at all impressed that Robert was still causing danger for his family.

It was raining steadily, the thunder abated for now. Sandra took in their suitcases while Robert hauled in the boxes. Hmm, maybe he overdid it on the wine, then he shook his head. Impossible. In another few weeks he'd be kicking himself for not buying more, he was certain.

After texting his kids, asking as to their whereabouts, he fired up his laptop and checked the security footage from the last couple of days. It was painful, even at high speed. He stopped and made some coffee while Sandra searched the freezer for something edible. When he started again, he spotted the infamous black car. He slowed the replay and watched as the Mercedes drifted past the front of the house. This was yesterday. He checked the rear camera and eventually found the same car, actually stopping for a moment by the carport. The tinted windows made it impossible to see who was driving.

Perhaps he should park his car elsewhere for the next few days.

"I found a couple of containers of Italian Wedding soup in the freezer. Good enough?" Sandra asked.

"Outstanding. I'll do up some toast as well. Fancy a wine?"

"Red Bridge Red? From the Cawston winery. I'll try a taste."

First Robin, then Sophie came through the front door. "Hi, Pops. You look much better." Robin grinned.

"I feel better. That server look wasn't meant for me. And my serving career is over. I was fired. Not a natural fit for me."

"Too bad. I'm starting work tomorrow. Good thing someone will be bringing in a paycheque in this house."

"That's a bit lippy. What's the start time?"

"Too early. But the site isn't very far away. South Fraser."

"Exams done then?"

"Yup. Aced them, I think … or maybe not, hard to tell."

"Rachael?"

"She's great, Pops." He was beaming.

Over dinner, Robert laid out the danger everyone was in, especially him, just so everyone knew what was what. Both Sophie and Robin started fidgeting, obviously perturbed by the news. He had previously neglected to fill them in on the bounty placed on him.

"I don't expect this Jonny guy to give up. I'll park the car over a street or two after dinner. Maybe he'll look elsewhere for me. And oh yeah, Sandra has decided to take a break from the catering business for a bit."

"Why?" Sophie asked.

"Got fired this weekend. I had to slap a lawyer groping me. My boss noticed," Sandra answered.

"Oh."

"Yes, oh. It's a tough world out there. You need to stand up for yourself, especially if there are creeps involved. And believe me, there's no shortage of those."

Robert tried to calm things. "Any luck on the job front, Sophie?"

"An interview this Tuesday. And I have a school thing next Monday — it's a day on development in the city. At one of the universities right downtown on Hastings."

"Through your high school?" Robert asked.

"Yes."

"Food for your planning career. The soup was excellent, Sandra. Nothing like home cooking, is there? I'll clean up, then move my car."

Sandra gave up a small smile. She looked happy to be back on Inverness, especially after the travails of Oliver.

Late afternoon, two days later, Robin came home from his site, exhausted.

"Hey, Pops. That guy you showed me the picture of? He arrived on our job today. He is uglier in person than the photo shows."

"That was quick."

"What do you mean?"

"I'd bet money that he's there because you are. That's it. I'll take care of this. Stay away from him, understand?"

Robin nodded uncertainly.

Robert called Bernard. This was not a texting kind of thing.

"Yes?"

"Robert here. I had an eventful time in Oliver. I'll do you lunch soon and tell you all about it. On another matter, you better let what's his face know that his son, Rex/Sam, whatever, is going to be interviewed for the tower diving death, okay?"

"What? Why?"

"The Cro-Magnon guy has turned up on another building site. It's time he was off the streets. I'm going to let the VPD know in the morning. Your tech can expect a call."

"Okay, I guess. And I'll look forward to that lunch."

Robert knew he should have told Bernard that his son was involved. He suddenly felt smaller for not doing it. On the other hand, it really shouldn't matter who was in danger, this guy needed to be off the streets. He shouldn't have waited this long. It was obvious what needed doing. Then he kicked himself. Sending a warning through Bernard was worse than stupid. What if the tech decided to scamper with his son? It was a distinct possibility after what he had told the guy at the CBC about his son perhaps not being protected enough by the authorities. Not that he'd likely get very far. He couldn't stop thinking like a detective.

He picked up his cell and placed a call. "Vito?"

"Who else would it be?"

"Right. The diving incident on 41st Avenue? I'm sending you the child's name and address. You need to use kid gloves, yes? You know what those are?"

"The ultimate in professionalism as usual, Robert. Why now?"

"The Cro-Magnon showed up on my son's construction site today. Robin is working the summer as a labourer, Fairweather Construction. I'll send you the site address in case you can't pick him up where he lives with Mrs. Cro-Magnon. I'm going out on a limb here and saying he showed up because Robin is there."

"I'll get someone over there tonight. His name is Ollie Standpipe, by the way. I trust he'll be at home watching television or working on his crafts."

"Tell your squad to watch out for a club. Has Finn checked on whether this Ollie was on any of the sites where labourers died?"

"I'll ask. Seems like an obvious thing to do, but …."

"Also, I had an interesting weekend in Oliver. If you have time this week, I could come in and tell a tale."

"Bit jammed here, I'll call when it works for me."

A day later, Vito let Robert know that little Samuel Brown had been interviewed at his home and his credibility was sufficient to keep Mr. Standpipe in custody pending charges.

"The kid was great. Liked the cops and robbers thing, even if it's not robbers. The father was less than enthusiastic. Bit of a pill, really."

"Well, I may have been responsible for some of that. Gave him a little speech a while back about security or the lack of it around witnesses, things like that," Robert responded. "Got anywhere with questioning Ollie?"

"Not yet, but he's not nearly so confident anymore. A murder charge can do that to a person. After we indicated charges would be laid, he decided a lawyer might be useful. We'll see who shows up for the next conversation."

Ollie had been picked up at his apartment on South Knight Street the night Robert had called it in. Robert rested a little easier after this news but warned Robin to be sharp about anyone new coming onto his work site.

Dinner was just over, Robin having eaten everything on his plate, as well as anything that would normally resemble a leftover.

"Maybe I should have purchased a pickup instead of the Volvo to haul vittles home. We are going through food here at a supercharged rate." Robert said.

Robin grinned. "Yeah, I'm kind of hungry most of the time."

"No injuries so far?"

"Nope."

"Keep it that way, please."

"I think I'll start doubling our recipes," Sandra added.

Robert remembered *Osso Buco*. He was going to make it for the family. He got up and headed to the bookshelf. Halfway there, something shattered. He felt a bee's sting on his back. Had someone dropped something? No, it was the large window. His shoulder blade felt hot, searing hot. He looked down at his shirt. Another shattering sound. The window fell to pieces, glass mostly inside the family room, but no more bee stings. Everything was in slow motion. Robert slumped to the floor. "Get down, all of you." He turned and looked over at Sandra on her knees beside the island, eyes wide as she stared back at him. His kids were beside her, looking at him, eyes equally round, motionless.

"Phone? Someone call 9-1-1." Was that his voice? It didn't come out as loud as he expected. He felt dizzy. Was he losing blood? He could hear tires screeching from the lane. Shit, how could he be so careless? Wasn't he a trained officer in a recent life?

Sandra crawled over to him while finishing the call.

"Towel! Throw me a dish towel."

Robin squidged over to the oven, grabbed a towel off its door, and made his way over to Robert and Sandra.

"I think he's gone, whoever it was. I feel tired," Robert murmured.

"No, Robert, don't fall asleep on me." Sandra pressed the towel on the wound, trying to staunch the flow. It reddened quickly. A faint sound could be heard, a siren.

"They're coming, Robert." She ran her fingers through his hair over and over. She pressed the towel. The dark stain grew.

The ambulance pulled up on the street, followed closely by a patrol car. Sophie crawled to the front door, stood to let them in, pointing to the rear of the main floor. Two techs came in with bags. The patrol car came to a stop. Neighbours were coming out of their front doors. Then another VPD car stopped with a squeal. It was Sergio. He was on patrol and immediately figured out what had happened when he heard the alert but ran up to the townhouse door for confirmation. He returned to his car, telling all and sundry to be looking for a black Mercedes on the routes south, adding the licence number. Then a firetruck, siren blaring, pulled up, completing the traffic fiasco, flashing lights everywhere.

The medics were better than good. They stopped the blood loss, got Robert stabilized and onto a stretcher, ready for transport. He looked over at Sandra. "Call Bernard? Tell him I'm dead. Shot."

"No, buddy, you'll live. We got you in time." The tech expressed optimism.

"Call, please." He tried to smile, but it came out as a grimace. His back was aching something fierce.

"Okay, then we'll head to VGH. See you there, Robert."

After Robert had been rolled out to the ambulance, the firetruck left, leaving the patrol cars. Three officers were in the townhouse. Two more cars rolled up. Neighbours in clumps were gawking at the action, talking amongst themselves. A tech team was called in to document the scene.

"I'm heading over to the hospital. You two stay here to watch the house. I'll let you know if anything changes, okay?" Sandra said to the kids. They nodded.

Sergio called Vito after some hesitation, unsure if he should do it, but he knew the pair were connected.

"Sergio here. Attempt on Robert at his home. He's on his way to VGH. I notified units to watch for the black Merc."

"Craps. So he wasn't bullshitting."

"Guess not. I'm going to stay a while. Only his kids are here. Shots came from the lane."

A day and a half later, at the CBC, Bernard was asked to a meeting. He sighed and went down the corridor swinging his ungainly left arm, sick of the cast and all it represented. He entered the room. This didn't look good. The local news editor, his associate editor, and an older reporter who hated Bernard's guts were sitting at the long table. The reporter had a smirk on his face.

"Bernard, have a seat. You know Dawn?" His head nodded in the general direction of his associate.

"I know who she is, that's it." Bernard then gave the barest of nods to Dawn before shifting to face Dimitri. "What's up?"

"I'll read a short article, so everyone knows what we're discussing.

> **Yesterday evening a man was gunned down inside his home on the east side of Vancouver. He was identified as Robert Lui, formerly a senior detective in the Vancouver Police Department. He left two teenagers in the home, Sophie Lui and Robin Lui. Robin was the subject of a kidnapping by a local gang two years ago. The police have no leads yet, but request anyone with information to come forward or call the TIP line if they prefer to remain anonymous.**

That's it. The byline is Bernard Lilley."

"You are so screwed, college boy." Scott came to life. His hatred of anyone with a degree behind their name competing with him for stories was visceral.

"Why is that, Scott? And why is he in this meeting?" Bernard turned his head back to Dimitri.

"In case we need some re-writing."

Scott jumped in. "Cause the guy isn't dead. Due diligence, journalistic standards, etc. You are a halfwit. I checked the hospital today."

"Calm down, Scott." The editor turned to look at Bernard. "He does have a point, though."

"Retraction, you're going to have to do a retraction!" Scott couldn't help himself.

"Retraction? What for? Everything I wrote is true. There is nothing to retract, surely." Bernard turned to the editor. "Yes?"

"Well …."

Bernard boldly decided to stick a knife in, jiggle it a little. "The story is pretty clear to me. Maybe Scott has a problem reading, or maybe he doesn't understand what he has read, which is probably worse."

Scott rose, a look of fury, "You little shit. I was writing stories before you knew what ABCs were!"

Bernard didn't bother looking at him. "Could I have a word, Dimitri? Just the two of us?"

Now Dawn looked pissed off. Bernard wasn't bridge-building this day, that was certain.

"Okay. I'll catch up with you later, Dawn." He waited until they both exited, Scott reluctantly last out, closing the door with a bang. "This better be good," Dimitri said.

"Sources, Dimitri. As I understand it, in this business we are lost without our sources. Might as well collect stamps or mow lawns. Robert Lui is a source for much of my crime work the last couple of years. A little while ago, he let me know that there was a contract out on his life. He needed to be dead, so that the danger would go away. With me?"

Dimitri nodded.

"But he couldn't figure out how to do this, at least as far as I know. When this happened Wednesday evening, he had Sandra, his fiancé, call me to let me know he was dead. So, I wrote the short story as carefully as I could, journalistic standards and all that."

Dimitri had just the barest hint of crinkles at the corners of his eyes. "I understand now."

"Perhaps I could issue a clarification in a day or two?"

"That would be best. And I don't believe Scott is very happy with you."

"Just me?"

"Probably not."

"Well, I'd have to say it's mutual. Thanks, Dimitri."

———

At Ben Skyler's law firm in Vancouver, Ross McDouguld knocked on Candice's office door.

"Please enter." The door opened. "Oh, it's you. What do you want?" She looked back down at the brief she was studying.

"I can't believe it. I just found out that Robert Lui is dead. You had him killed?"

"Keep your voice down, you moron. What are you talking about?"

Ross closed the door. "I found out someone shot Lui the other night. I assumed it was thanks to you. You mentioned you would handle things up at the Point. Remember?"

"Yes, I remember, but I assure you, I had nothing to do with whatever happened to him."

"Hmm, well I guess we got lucky."

"Seems so. Anything else?"

"Nope."

"Then I've got work to do." She looked back down at her desk. Ross got the message and left. Candice started humming. Finally, things were looking up. She texted Travis.

THIRTY-FIVE

S aturday morning, Robert was kicked out of the hospital. The bullet, which was not a large calibre, had thoroughly nailed his left scapula and made a bit of a mess. But after surgery removed the bullet and cleaned things up, nothing a few weeks' rest wouldn't cure. It was just another ache added to the pantheon of issues Robert's body faced. He was happy to be back home, principally to get some decent food. As far as he was concerned, the nurses were all saints and should be hailed as such. He'd be writing to the Pope shortly with his recommendations. The hospital catering would not be included in the praises.

He came in the back door with Sandra. Sophie rushed over and tried to hug him. She started crying.

"Easy, Sophie. Still injured, okay?"

"I'm just glad you're home." She finally relented, taking her hands off his shoulders.

"As am I, believe me. You know what I could use?"

"Real coffee?" Sandra asked.

"I am so transparent."

"You are, Robert." She moved to put some water on. "Have you heard anything from Vito?"

"I'll text him, don't want to disturb his weekend."

"Did they give you any drugs, Robert?"

"Yes, I'll put them with the others upstairs. I don't generally like drugs. They usually have side effects, which I really don't need. I have whisky, thankfully, it seems to work fine. But I could open a small neighbourhood pharmacy soon, I think with the things I have upstairs."

"Shouldn't you take them back to the pharmacy?"

"I do that for the older ones. I hang on to the recent stuff in case of the big one. You never know when real painkillers might be needed, and availability might be severely limited after a quake."

"Have you heard the news about your supposed death? Your father called last evening, and I had to calm him down. Told him you were fine, sort of. Not dead at any rate, and that he should keep it quiet for now. Did I do right?" Sandra asked. "Maybe you should let your work know as well?"

"Good idea. They probably didn't want to text a dead man's cell. On the other hand, many people would have no qualms about doing such a thing." He sat down and typed a short message to Dan Prudence. When he was done, he walked over and poked at the plastic-covered hole that used to be a window. Thankfully, it was summer, so keeping things warm inside wasn't an issue.

"Sophie, could you call our landlord and ask nicely for new glass to be installed asap? Tell him we had an incident. That's all he needs to know right now. Hopefully, he doesn't pay close attention to the news."

Sophie nodded and went to the kitchen cupboard end, where some phone numbers were posted.

"We have any noodles around, Sandra? I have an overwhelming urge for some."

"Yes. Add some dumplings as well?"

"Recovery food. I'll be back on the horse in no time."

After a filling lunch, Sophie and Robin disappeared, saying they'd be back late afternoon.

"I think I'll go upstairs and have a lie down. Thanks for making lunch. It was delicious."

"Hospital gives one a certain perspective, doesn't it?" Sandra asked.

"Indeed."

<hr>

A few hours later, Robert woke. Where was he? He looked around. He'd been sleeping on his stomach, home thankfully. What woke him, beside the pain? Voices from below, not teenage. Was it Sandra and the kids? No, it sounded like adults, a deep voice rising. He slowly rose and gingerly headed down the stairs.

"What do you mean, he's not dead? We saw the story in the news." It couldn't be, but it sounded like Lal. He entered the room. Sandra was talking with her mother and father, standing next to the kitchen. Lal stared at him, a look of astonishment, his mouth wide open.

"Hi, Lal, Amrit. Surprised?"

Nothing came out of Lal's mouth. He shook his head, nonplussed. "But ...."

"I know. It's a miracle, I grant you." He waited, pretty

sure he shouldn't say anything further, but he couldn't help himself, couldn't just let it drift by. Someone had taken a shot at him, tried to kill him.

"I trust you aren't out too much money, Lal."

There was silence while everyone calculated what this meant.

"What do you mean, Robert?" Sandra spoke first. Her eyes darted between Lal and Robert.

"I know what you've been up to." Robert stared at Lal, his eyebrow raised.

"What have you done, you bastards?" Sandra was spitting as she yelled at the men. Robert had never seen her like this.

"The cousins needed avenging. There was no other way," Lal conceded.

"What?" It was Amrit's turn. "What did you do?" It came out as a scream.

"How did you know?" Lal turned to Robert.

"I didn't, until you just admitted it. But I heard all about your short conversation with the Police Department. And one of the designated killers contacted me. It wasn't hard to figure that it was possible."

"And you didn't think to tell me?" Sandra's eyes were blazing. "I'm done. I'm leaving." She went up the stairs.

"But …." Robert stopped. He realized it'd be hopeless saying anything right now. The damage was done and she looked furious.

"Lal, drive us home. We came to comfort our daughter, now this? I am disgusted." Amrit collected her jacket and walked out the door, not waiting. Lal looked at Robert, utter hatred lurking in his dark eyes. His hands were clenching and un-clenching at his side, as though he was contemplating strangling Robert on the spot. He shook his head and followed Amrit, not bothering to close the door. A minute later, Sandra came down the stairs with a small bag and a purse.

"Don't try to call me," she said loudly and avoided looking at Robert as she brushed past him, then opened the front door and was gone. Once again, a taxi would take away someone he cared about, but this time, it was serious — he intended to marry her.

Robert sat down. How could a day go from joy to utter shit in a few hours? He stood up again, went to the cupboard, got his whisky glass and poured a few fingers of a Japanese single malt. He took a healthy gulp, then added a bit of ice, sitting back down. He felt the familiar warmth radiate as it took the edge off the stress of watching Sandra walk out, not to mention the ache from the hole in his back.

He felt her judgment to be on the harsh side. What was he supposed to do? Tell Sandra he suspected her dad wanted him dead? That'd go over well. One thing was certain, he'd never be joining that family. Sandra? Fine, but even that now seemed in grave doubt. And what would she now think of her father? Actually, Robert wasn't so concerned about that. He knew the bond was between mother and daughter. She was probably now angry with all males of the species and with fairly good reason, Robert supposed. And she had left town once before because of family issues.

He made a call. "Bernard?"

"Robert?"

"Thanks for the story, very well written. You should be a journalist."

"You are welcome. Got a little grief over it, but because of my extensive training, it's all good. Tomorrow I'll be issuing a tiny clarification, that you aren't dead as such. At least my editor gave me a few days."

"And they are much appreciated, Bernard. They took that labourer into custody, charges pending I understand, thanks to Rex."

"Maybe we could meet for coffee — the wounded club cafe?"

"Yes, I'll let you know soonest. I have a few things on at present." He ended the call.

He sat back, trying to spare his left side, and grabbed his glass, rolling it in his hands. Thank God for whisky, he thought.

Once Robin and Sophie returned, he spilled the news about Sandra's absence.

"I fear it's my fault, but I really had no clear path. Life is like that some days." He really sucked at explaining the chain of events.

"Well, I don't blame her, really. Her dad really did that?" Sophie said.

"Afraid so. He admitted as much."

"What kind of father is that? She can't be very happy. I hope she comes back here soon."

"As do I, Sophie." He slowly shook his head.

Sunday morning, after a partial shower, trying not to get his dressing wet, Robert tried Sandra's cell, not expecting her to answer. He wasn't disappointed. Then he punched in Deirdre's number. She was the only person Sandra may have gone to that he knew about. She hadn't mentioned any other Vancouver friends. He doubted she would have gone south to Surrey, having made a point of escaping it once before.

"Deirdre?"

"Yes?"

"It's Robert. Is Sandra there?"

A pause, then he heard Sandra's voice in the background. "I'm not here."

"She's not here, Robert."

"Give me a break. I can hear her."

"Hey, I'm an honest gal, or I try to be." The connection was broken. Robert laughed to himself. He liked Deirdre. At least Sandra'd be safe with her.

He texted Vito.

> Find time for a coffee tomorrow and a
> sharing of news?

Nothing in return. Maybe Vito was actually doing weekend things. Good for him if so. There were more than a few things Robert was out of the loop on: fingerprint matches, how interrogations were going, whether Jonny had been apprehended. Was he missing the detective life? Impossible. He was just missing the information, being in the know.

He made coffee and sat, savouring it.
His cell binged, Vito replying.

> Find time for a coffee tomorrow and a
> sharing of news?

> Tomorrow, 1:00 at Apollo.

Well good, he wasn't totally outcast yet. Just shunned by Sandra. But he hoped she'd relent after cooling down. He'd try calling Deirdre again tomorrow. Maybe she'd be a mediator. He could only hope. In the interim, he texted her, trying to find out the lay of the land, see if she'd be up for it.

A knock on his front door signalled the arrival of a glazier. Robert showed him what needed doing. He took a few measurements, then said he'd return Monday with a replacement.

"Mid-afternoon if possible. I'll be out early afternoon."

"Fine."

THIRTY-SIX

It was Monday, the start of a better week, Robert prayed. Sophie had left for her downtown planning session, Robin was at his site, leaving Robert alone to contemplate life. He had watched an early newscast, which included a short clarification indicating Robert hadn't really been killed a few days earlier, just wounded. The CBC was terribly sorry for any misunderstandings that may have occurred. As far as Robert was concerned, they seemed to be apologizing for the fact that the public couldn't read or understand what they read. The story had seemed pretty clear to his way of thinking. The search was on for the shooter, no stone unturned, and also no leads to report. The segment didn't give Robert any comfort, knowing the bounty was likely still up for collection, but he also knew the entire story was not likely to be uncovered by the media. He needed the meeting with Vito.

Then the news took a turn. A fire that had erupted a few days earlier near Okanagan Falls had ballooned overnight into something now out of control. Evacuation orders and alerts were being issued for the communities south, including Oliver and Osoyoos. A few smoky shots from a helicopter circling south of the flames were added to demonstrate that the reporters weren't just making this up. Winds from the north weren't helping. It seemed that the rain barrage on the Lower Mainland's valley the previous Sunday had never made it farther east. Maybe living in Vancouver wasn't so bad after all, Robert considered. He sipped his coffee.

His cell pinged. Dan expressed hope that Robert was on the mend, and could he possibly pencil in a meeting downtown when he was feeling up to it. A question about lawyers' fees was appended. Robert responded in the affirmative, sipping his brew. He needed to find out where Rory had ended up with his search for incriminating contracts. Then he considered how he'd get to his meeting at the Apollo; car or walk over? The car might be smarter, even with his wound aching from whatever he sat against.

A short text arrived from Deirdre.

> Sandra is weakening fast but don't call
> just yet.

Finally, something positive for Robert's world. He knew Sandra would be working through her confusion from the events of the weekend, not that there was much to be confused about. Her father had hired a hitman to kill her fiancé, and her fiancé hadn't told her about this, even though he suspected as much. On the other hand, Deirdre was probably tiring of hosting Sandra at her place. He didn't imagine Deirdre was living in large digs, and an extra person probably'd make it unbearable after a few days.

He scrounged the fridge for items to fashion an early lunch, finding a few leftover dumplings from his post-hospital meal. He made a quick dipping sauce, then, as he ate, he went through the list of questions he'd ask of Vito. He felt tired afterwards, so he lay down on the couch, again on his chest, which he was fine with, promptly passing out. A half-hour later he reluctantly roused himself. He checked his watch — damn, it was almost one. He needed to hustle. He left the shoulder holster for now but strapped on the small gun to his ankle and headed for his car.

Robert entered the Apollo, searching the clientele as he headed for the counter. Vito was sitting at the back. He nodded. Robert approached after ordering.

"Sorry, I've been resting, fell asleep. How are you?"

Vito responded, "Fine, better than you, apparently." He grabbed his coffee and sipped while waiting for Robert to relate his Oliver escapades.

"Any progress on the crime-fighting front?"

"Lots, Robert. These people are not very bright. But you already know this, correct?"

Robert nodded.

"The evening you were shot, for which I apologize for on behalf of the entire VPD, by the way, Jonny in his Merc did not get picked up. I figure he got confused and headed east rather than south. Anyway, we got him yesterday and he's being held on Cambie, charges pending. No gun, of course, but we got your camera views thanks to Robin. It was his car in the lane, as you may have guessed. Of course, he said he lent it to a friend, was nowhere near Vancouver on the day in question. Problem was, there were no other prints on his steering wheel, so his story seems highly suspect. And that his window was wide open as he was shooting at you didn't help his case. He is on camera. Didn't those guys used to steal cars and burn them after a shooting?"

"Not sure Jonny is totally cognizant with the latest in gangster operations. Or maybe he is too lazy to steal a car. How about Mr. Cro-Magnon?"

"Interviewed again, by me. A lawyer showed this time — from your favourite firm, go figure. The lawyer didn't have a clue what he was doing, that much was evident. Don't think defence cases are his specialty. Mr. Standpipe's prints were found at your friend's place in Richmond by the way, so he was probably one of the boat killers. The prosecutors have dreamed up a deal for Ollie on the construction death, but it hasn't been presented as yet. Charges will be laid today. No link to your favourite legal firm either, but we can always hope with enough pressure applied Ollie may cough something up. I'd doubt he'd say anything with a lawyer present from the firm in question, but again, anything is possible where the truly ignorant are involved." Vito waited, then, "Your name came up."

"How?"

"The lawyer mentioned your name in passing, seemingly unconnected to any of the conversation. It was strange."

"Well, I am definitely not the flavour of the week with that firm." Robert wondered what was at play.

"Suppose."

"Sounds like you are on top of things, Vito. Has Jonny been interviewed?"

"Later this afternoon."

"Think I could get a minute or two with him afterwards?"

Vito appeared to think this one over, maybe suspecting what Robert had in mind. "I suppose. We'll need to be careful about it. Don't come in the front lobby. I'll let you in at the rear. And if a lawyer shows, it may not happen."

Robert nodded. "Thanks, just want to have a quiet word with Jonny. More of a philosophical discussion than anything."

Vito nodded. "I understand."

"How is Finn doing with his cases?" Robert asked.

"Getting nowhere fast. The Ollie thing might break a few things open, but until then, it's all uphill."

"Let me tell you about Oliver." Robert related the key events of the trip. He needed to stand at one point during the monologue to settle his chest and back. He looked down at his empty cup, then over at the bar to signal Adrienne. Sitting back down, he finished his tale.

"Any idea about the other two hoods, apart from Jingles?" Vito asked.

"No, maybe ask your buddy in Oliver. The RCMP did the on-site interviews at the hotel. I assume the men after us are all from the Lower Mainland. I doubt there is a dial-a-hood company up in the Okanagan for those in need of quick services, but who knows. I've heard Vernon has some issues. Then there was that shooting at the Kelowna casino several years back."

"And this neighbour, Shou Deng, anything more on him?"

"No, but again, let Jackie know about him if he doesn't already." Robert rose gingerly to retrieve his second cup, then sat and asked, "What time is the Jonny interview?"

"Four. I'll leave him in the room after and come up to get you. I doubt it'll last very long."

"It'd be handy if the recording equipment was entirely off."

Vito nodded slowly. "I need to get back. See you in a while." With that, he stood and left Robert to finish his coffee and contemplate what he needed to do.

Downtown, the Monday morning session at the university conference centre had been an animated affair. The name given to the day by the organizers said it all:

Planning for a Brighter Vancouver Future in the Modern Age

Three local residential developers had given up part of their day to espouse views on how to house Vancouver's ever-growing population while dealing with the myriad issues trying to derail their best intentions. No one above assistant vice-president deigned to attend, however, so the city staff present were left to wonder how serious all the talk was. Most of the students didn't grasp this subtle nuance. The PM session was to be given over to a couple of city representatives from each of Vancouver, Burnaby, and Coquitlam and would be bound to highlight all the problems they were required to solve, or not solve, depending on their city's financial capabilities.

It was the lunch break, served in the same large room where the presentations were made. The students got a chance to mingle with presenters and discuss the issues of the day. Sophie found this part to be more exciting than the talks as they got to talk with the professionals. She felt that her intended career was somehow closer to reality. She looked at all the people in the room, finally feeling as though her future was being firmly etched out before her eyes.

A middle-aged woman dressed in a jade green pantsuit came over to Sophie as she was about to grab a sandwich off the long serving table. The woman peered at her name tag, which was lacking a last name. "Sophie?" The woman's name tag was absent.

"Yes, hello. Pleased to meet you."

"I was checking through the registrant's list, are you Sophie Lui?"

"Yes, I am," she replied confidently.

"I believe I know that name."

Sophie was ecstatic that someone speaking actually knew who she was but didn't reply. She smiled.

"May I ask what your father does, if you don't mind?"

"He used to be a detective with the Vancouver Police, but what he does now doesn't seem much different."

"Well, I am very sorry for your loss, Sophie. I heard

there was an incident at your home last week." The woman's eyebrows furrowed in condolence.

Sophie looked puzzled. "What loss? My dad is fine, mostly anyway."

Now the woman looked equally at a loss. "But I heard he had been killed."

"Don't think so. I was there. I should know."

"Oh dear. I must sound so foolish to you. I apologize and hope you enjoy the rest of the afternoon." As she moved away, she pulled out her phone before Sophie could ask any questions of her. Sophie shrugged and went over to the salad section of the buffet where a couple of her classmates were loading up their bowls, chatting animatedly.

Robert had headed home after the meeting with Vito to grab a hat and change his clothes, donning some things he rarely wore. The glazier showed up and had the replacement sealed unit installed inside half an hour, then Robert was off to Cambie Street.

The mandatory camera positioned over the back door of the station required consideration. Just before four, he parked on Yukon Street and slowly made his way down to the lane behind the headquarters where he had spent several years of his life. He loitered beside the adjacent building, watching the door, waiting, not nervous for a change. He was alone in the alley.

Around twenty after four, the door finally opened. Vito's head peeked out, checking both directions. Robert lowered his head and strolled nonchalantly, close alongside the building wall, then darted inside. The door closed quietly. He followed Vito to the stairs and down to the interview rooms.

"Cameras are off. Don't be long." Vito said. Then he handed Robert a bag. "As requested."

Robert nodded, looked in the bag, then entered the room. On the other side of the table sat Jonny Singh. He looked up at Robert, seemingly at a loss as to who this was, or why he was being interviewed a second time.

Robert sat, staring across at Jonny. He waited, heightening the tension. Was he to be an avenger? Avenging for who? Himself? Sandra, after what had transpired Saturday afternoon? What he really wanted was to throw Jonny around the room a few times, concentrating on his near useless knees. But that would be bound to come back on Vito in a very unpleasant way. He also inexplicably felt sorry for this miserable sod. Why? He couldn't say at the moment. Sandra would not countenance a beating of his nemesis, particularly a one-sided affair, he was sure of this one thing.

"Know who I am, Jonny?"

He shook his head slowly.

"I guess they weren't wrong, were they?"

Jonny's eyebrows scrunched up until it appeared that Robert had asked him to explain Einstein's Theory of General Relativity. "They said you were a few bricks short of a full load. I'm Robert Lui, your target of late."

Jonny's face did a sudden U-turn. It went from puzzlement to understanding to fear in a second. It was a wonder to behold.

"Stand up, Jonny."

"Why?"

"Just humour me."

Jonny slowly stood, gripping the table edge.

"Walk around, please."

Jonny uncertainly started shuffling slowly behind the table.

"You are a mess, aren't you, Jonny?"

Hate entered Jonny's eyes. "Thanks to some cops in Delta. How did you get here?"

"I drove here, Jonny. Yes, I'm not dead, despite your best efforts. I heard about your knee problems. I was going to add to them, because I don't really need someone trying to kill me." He waited a second. "Did you get paid yet?"

Before Jonny could properly process this, he answered, "No." A look of regret instantly entered his eyes.

Too bad for Vito that the recording equipment was off. Jonny had basically confessed, not that it would be needed.

"Here's what I'll do for you. If you don't kill me, I'll give you the twenty K you were going to get. The other option is that I beat the crap out of your knees so you can't get around without a chair for the remainder of your fucked-up life. Your choice."

Jonny's head dropped as he considered this. Twenty grand instead of a beating. It seemed to be a very good bargain. "Can I sit down?"

"Why not?"

"I agree."

"Good choice, see you around, Jonny." With that,

Robert grabbed his bag, opened the door to leave the room and almost bumped directly into Marcus, one of the officers who kept things in order on the lower level. Marcus looked startled.

"Good to see you, Marcus."

"Robert? What are you doing here?"

"Checking my locker for anything I may have left behind — turned out I did," he said, nodding at the bag. "Can you let Vito know I'm done? Thanks."

Marcus saw the interview room door closing, then looked back at Robert. His blank face didn't give Robert a clue as to what he thought about this rather lame excuse for being in a place he had no business being anymore. Robert wasn't about to wait around to learn what Marcus was thinking. He headed for the stairs, went up a level and let himself out the same door he had entered a few moments before, mercifully not encountering anyone else.

Vito received a short text from Marcus. He reluctantly returned to the basement and gingerly opened the interview room, expecting blood and mayhem at the minimum. Jonny looked up at him, his puzzled look firmly re-attached. Vito was surprised, but he backed up, signalling Marcus to take Jonny back to his cell. Marcus rose from his hallway table.

"Robert was here."

Vito didn't say anything, but nodded, then left.

Robert arrived back on Inverness around half past five. He wondered how long it would take before Jonny had realized he'd been hornswoggled. Robin was sitting in the family area snacking on something while studying his phone.

"Any ideas for dinner?" Robert asked.

Robin shrugged.

"Where is your sister? Can you raise her, so we can find out if it's just the two of us?"

"Sure, Pops."

A few moments passed. "Try calling her then, please."

Robin fiddled with his phone. "Rang out."

"Try Rose."

A moment later, Robin hadn't anything more to offer. "Rose hasn't heard from her since noon today. She hasn't returned any texts or calls, and from what I know, those girls keep in constant contact."

Something unpleasant began to creep into Robert's mind.

Robert called Vito.

"Robert? I appreciate your relative neatness this afternoon, thanks."

"Not why I'm calling, Vito. By the way, he confessed. Shouldn't have had those cameras turned off. Thanks for the vest. Could you get my daughter's phone pinged? She hasn't returned from her downtown course today. No one knows where she is. It's definitely not like her."

"You sure about this?"

"No, but given recent history …."

"I'll get back to you soonest. Text me her number."

Robert paced around the kitchen island, his newest wound forgotten for the moment.

"You worried, Pops?"

"Yes. Craps, craps, craps. If something has happened to her …." He turned to his 'medicine cabinet', pulling out an Irish offering. He poured three fingers and added a small chunk of ice. He hated the waiting game. He didn't know what else to do.

Twenty minutes later, Vito called back. "Located her phone near Hastings, a unit found it behind a dumpster in a lane. No sign of Sophie, I'm afraid, Robert."

There was silence while Robert's mind sifted the possibilities. "It's those fucking lawyers, Vito. Who else would it be?"

"Possibly. But let's not jump to conclusions just yet."

"It's hard not to." He took a long pull of his whisky. Robin watched him anxiously.

"I've put the word out to all units. I'll let you know what we find, okay?"

"I guess. Thanks, Vito."

He hesitated, knowing the blowback he'd receive, but called his parents. They had nothing to tell him but expressed extreme alarm at what might have happened. They hadn't heard anything from Sophie either. He hung up, staring at Robin.

"Can you let Rose know what's going on?"

He no longer felt like eating, but he suspected Robin might need something. He'd call the high school if he could, but it was summer vacation and after hours. Who would be there to help him? No one was the definitive answer. Where had she been? SFU or UBC? He wasn't even sure who had hosted the event.

"Do you know where she was, Robin?"

"SFU, I think. Downtown campus."

Robert scrolled through his laptop, finally finding the event. He called a number listed, but there was no answer. He wondered if they were giving out medals for really terrible parenting, because he'd certainly be first on the list. Not an honourable mention, no. Hands-down, he'd win the award as worst father in British Columbia. A thought came to him. He texted Sandra.

Have you heard from Sophie at all?

"I'm going to make a sandwich, Pops, I'm hungry." Robin said.

"I'll put some pasta together for you. I don't know if I'll have any, though." He rummaged through the fridge, then the freezer, finding some bacon and a roll of pepper butter. "Can you dice up these snap peas, and then I'll put it all together for you."

His cell dinged. An answer.

Have you heard from Sophie at all?

No, she hasn't contacted me. What's wrong?'

She has disappeared. The police are looking but I'm at wit's end.

He waited, but nothing further lit up his phone. He shrugged and took another long pull of his whisky. He grabbed a knife and sliced the bacon, finding a modicum of comfort in the familiar actions of meal preparation. "Put the water on, Robin."

After the meal was done, Robert eating a small portion of the dish, there was nothing left in the pot. Robin had demolished whatever remained. His appetite was unaffected by Sophie's absence. They were putting things into the dishwasher when the doorbell rang. Robert looked at Robin apprehensively. Who could it be? Someone selling painting or lawn services, no doubt. As he came to the door, a hope sprang from nowhere. Could it be? He opened the door.

"Hi, Mr. Lui."

"Hi, Rose. Come on in. I assume you weren't at the session today, were you?"

"No. Not my thing. Maybe I should have been though. Any word yet?"

"Unfortunately not." They walked to the rear, where Robin sat fidgeting. He looked up at Rose, giving her a wan smile. Robert couldn't sit down. He kept pacing. "I'm going downtown to check out the area. I can't wait for the VPD." Not mentioned was his lack of trust in the basic services offered by Vancouver's finest.

The doorbell rang again. Robert went to the front and opened the door. Sandra stood there uncertainly, bag in hand. "I'm sorry, Robert."

"Well, I'm the one who needs to apologize, for not telling you what I suspected, but I really didn't know how to voice what were only suspicions. I didn't think you'd take it well."

"You're correct." She moved closer, dropping her bag, grabbing Robert with an embrace that made him yelp. "Sorry, forgot you are the walking wounded."

"I'm just heading downtown to do my own search. Think you could stay here and be with the kids? Rose came over."

"I want to come, Robert."

"It's not the best part of town, Sandra. Stay here,

please. I won't be long." As he told the lie, he went to the rear, announcing, "Sandra is here. I'm leaving, see you soon." He'd be down there until he found Sophie. As Robin got up to hug Sandra, Robert made sure both of his guns were ready, then left out the rear.

Twenty minutes later, Robert was parking on Richards Street near the conference centre. He started with the alley behind the building. An anorexic couple sampling something slumped over against a rusted steel dumpster amongst some coffee cups and other garbage, heads lowered, ignoring everything else. A VPD car appeared at the end of the lane, slowed, but continued on. Robert didn't see any officers doing what he was doing, seemingly unable to locate the door handles inside their cruisers.

He widened his search but it was fruitless. All he ran across were more lane rangers in among the obvious tourists wandering aimlessly, probably curious as to why there were so many damaged people in what was supposed to be one of the pre-eminent tourist destinations on this earth.

Someone had grabbed his daughter, he was certain. What was he doing down here? He wasn't going to find anyone like this. After an hour of walking the streets, he reluctantly headed back to his car. He sat in the seat, murmuring a small prayer to Sophie. Then, starting the car, he headed back to Inverness.

He parked in the carport and sat, not getting out. He could see Sandra and the kids in the family area, talking.

After a moment, Sandra rose and came over to the window, looking out at Robert. A look of concern. He shook his head and then finally got out.

"No luck," he said, as he came through the door. "Police call at all?"

"No."

"Those lawyers took her, I know it, or their thugs."

"Lawyers, Pops? Why would they do that? Isn't it against the law, especially for lawyers?" Robin asked.

"Yeah, it is. But people under pressure do stupid things if they are desperate enough. Doesn't matter what they do for a living."

"I don't like it." Rose was succinct. The sun had lowered enough that shadows lengthened across the room.

"I'll drive you home, Rose. I don't think there is anything we can do until we or the police hear from whomever took her. I'll let you know when we do."

When Robert arrived back home, Robin had headed up for bed, his work definitely re-adjusting his habits. Sandra sat alone in the family room, staring at nothing. Robert figured she was probably wondering how she had ended up with such a loser.

"Anything to drink, Sandra?"

"Ginger ale will be fine, thanks." Knowing full well that boxes of wine lay somewhere in the townhome.

"You sure? There is still plenty of what we bought available. I haven't drunk it all as yet."

Sandra smiled thinly, but nodded. "How is your back?"

"Aches, like the rest of my body, but seems to be healing. Hard to tell as I can't see it. Probably need to get the dressing changed."

He returned from the fridge with a glass of wine and a soda. He sat next to Sandra.

"I'm really sorry for the last couple of days, Sandra. Thought maybe you were done with men and might take up with Deirdre."

"That's a thought. She is nice, but her place is too small. And after thinking, I really couldn't let you weasel out of the marriage thing so easily."

Robert raised his glass. "Thanks for giving me a second chance."

They clinked glasses. Robert's cell rang.

The number displayed didn't mean anything, but he stood up as he answered, "Yes?"

"Robert Lui?"

"Speaking."

"We are in possession of something valuable to you, we assume. Present yourself if you want her back." The line cut out. Robert stared at his phone, unable to do anything.

Sandra looked up at him, awaiting illumination.

"Kidnappers, I think. They have Sophie. I have to go to them to get her. They neglected to say where they were, however. I'm calling Vito."

Vito answered mercifully, although Robert wouldn't have attached any blame if he hadn't. It was past nine, and Robert was probably keeping him busier than the rest of the VPD combined.

"Robert?"

"Just got a call from the kidnappers. Could you trace the last call to my cell?"

"Yes. What did they say?"

"Not much, just that I should go to them to get Sophie. Where wasn't specified."

"Get back to you, Robert."

Robert sat down, replaying the demand in his head. "They said they were in possession of something valuable. Weird word to use unless she is at that winery in Oliver. Could they have made it there already?"

"Four-hour trip? Yes, it's possible," Sandra answered.

"Not likely though," Robert countered. "Jeez, what's taking Vito so long?"

"You just talked to him, Robert. Try to calm yourself." She grabbed his arm, stroking it in an effort to ease his worries.

"Did you eat, Sandra?"

"Not really."

"I'll find something for you." He knew full well they didn't have much left after the Robin tornado had been devastating the Inverness supplies. He studied the inside of the fridge. "Omelette?" He asked lamely. Sandra nodded, knowing he should keep himself busy. Otherwise, she would have made it.

Robert went outside to cut chives. Then he pulled out the eggs, cheese, and found some bread in the freezer.

His phone rang while he was chopping the chives. Robert eyed Sandra as he picked it up and answered.

"Call was made from an old payphone, Robert. The Eagle Resort, in Osoyoos. It's one of the old motels along the main strip just on the east side of the lake, which is maybe why it still has such a phone. Nothing much else to tell except that there are no pay phones left in Oliver. I'm alerting the guys in Osoyoos and Oliver."

"She's at that winery. They used the word 'possession' in their call. Has to be. I'm heading there."

Vito knew better than to try talking Robert out of it. "Please link up with Jackie when you get there, okay? And we'll get the winery checked out."

"Sure. Thanks, Vito. Wish me luck." He broke the connection. The last thing he'd be doing was any 'linking up' with the locals. They'd just screw things up ten ways to hell.

"I'm heading to Oliver." In Robert's mind, it wasn't a discussion.

"Not now, Robert. You've been drinking, and you need to let Robin know. And I'm coming with you. We can leave first thing tomorrow."

Robert was ready to argue all these points, but Sandra's face was brooking no dispute. He emptied his glass and finished preparing Sandra's meal. Then he started to assemble all the things he'd take along, starting with his weapons.

CHAPTER
THIRTY-EIGHT

Tuesday morning, Robert and Sandra rose roughly the same time as Robin, told him their plan, and hit the road just after six. Even at this hour, the steady stream of vehicles heading the opposite direction on the No. 1 Highway into Vancouver was mind-boggling to Robert. Is this what people did every day, this early?

Sandra flipped the radio on once they had cleared Surrey. The seven o'clock news started. The first item related to the growing and un-contained wildfire south of Okanagan Falls. Mildly concerning given their destination. Second item was the apparent kidnapping of a certain former detective's daughter off the streets of Vancouver. Despite no leads, or any possible motive as yet, a full search was being mounted. Well, now everyone knew about Sophie. Robert's expression hardened, and their speed increased.

After a few moments of this, Sandra felt the need to comment, "Robert, maybe we don't want to get pulled over for speeding, do we?"

Robert glanced at Sandra, his appearance softening slightly. "A good point." The car slowed a bit, but they were still moving quickly. No one was passing them.

"We're going to need a plan. Ever fired a gun, Sandra?"

"As a matter of fact, I have. Up at Raven Island, one of the sous chefs hunted. He had a rifle that he showed me how to use. We did some target practice, but other than that, I've never aimed at a person if that's what you want to know. And I don't think I've got a hunting licence in my purse, or a gun licence for that matter."

"I am loving you more and more. This is just for an 'in case' emergency situation, if it comes to it." He reflected. "I'm guessing that the local boys won't be finding Sophie at the winery. That would be too damn easy. We may need to split up, deceive and decoy."

They hit Hope and sped east, Robert still trying to work out some kind of a plan but wasn't getting anywhere. "Guess we'll try to book into that same place we stayed last time, okay? Hoping they don't recognize us."

Sandra nodded. "You hungry?"

"Not really." They flew by the Manning resort, not stopping this time.

"I'm eating one of those nut bars then," Sandra responded.

Ninety minutes later, they made the turn at Osoyoos and headed north to Oliver. They had seen the clouds billowing up beyond the hills lining the Similkameen

Valley. Then they were in it. Everything was bleached out by wildfire smoke, a pillowy grey, the temperature rising. Car windows were closed, the air conditioning on, but it couldn't filter everything. There was more traffic headed south than in the direction they were going — an ominous sign. Robert worried about an evacuation order being announced, which would make things ten times more difficult as roads heading north-south were minimal. So far, they hadn't encountered a traffic stop or road barrier, so an order wasn't on just yet. He assumed an alert was in place, which meant everyone needed to be ready to leave pending the fire status.

As they neared Oliver, a tent village appeared off the west side of the highway. A firefighter's camp, by the look of it. There had to be at least fifty tents along with a couple of RVs. Robert wondered if they got free wine rations at least, as they put their lives on the line for the local community.

They pulled into the hotel. The parking lot was fuller than it had been last time they had visited, perhaps people fleeing the flames from farther north. They opened their doors, the acrid smell inducing a cough or two. Sandra's eyes started watering.

Robert made for the lobby, asking Sandra to remain in the car. Last time, the room was in Sandra's name, and Robert hoped to avoid a 'no rooms available' situation just because someone might have taken exception to the inadvertent damage that had occurred on their last visit. He didn't recognize the welcoming clerk, thankfully, and was able to bag the second to last room available using his credit card.

"Folks fleeing from up north?" Robert asked.

"Yes. But we are under alert here, so your stay may be short. If you hear a siren, then the evacuation is being ordered, things have become dire, and you must leave. Also, your room will not be ready for two more hours," she added.

Robert nodded. "Restaurants in town still open?"

"As far as I know."

"How about the hospital?"

"Yes. Are you planning on being ill, sir?"

"Never know what may happen in the next day or two. Thanks." He grabbed the room cards and went back outside. Even though he had only been inside for all of ten minutes, it seemed clearer outside, less smoke. Perhaps the wind had shifted. He could hear the thudding of a heavy-lift helicopter from the north, probably bucketing from one of the small lakes.

"We're in, but they aren't ready for us just yet. Let's walk over to the RCMP, then maybe Ricardo's."

Robert and Sandra entered a crowded station, seemingly even busier than the wine evening that was their last opportunity to witness the smooth running of a small-town detachment.

Robert didn't recognize anyone. He asked the woman at reception for an update on Possession Point.

She looked puzzled. "Ernie, has anyone been up to the winery to check for that girl?"

A moustached officer wearing his official hat, sitting at

a desk, answered, "Yup, didn't find her there." He didn't even bother to look up.

"May I talk to Ernie?" Robert asked.

"I don't think so. You heard what he said, didn't you?"

"I'm the father."

"Oh."

"If you have a problem, check with Jackie Chan."

"Jackie is up north, close to the front line of the fire. We've lost contact with him for the moment."

"I used to be a detective with the VPD." The lady's expression didn't change one bit, seeming unimpressed with his nugget of information. "Ernie?" Robert wasn't giving up. She turned and beckoned to Ernie, who reluctantly rose and slowly came to the front and around the counter, pointing to the rather public lobby chairs. Robert wasn't in the mood to make an issue of it.

They all sat. Robert turned his chair so he faced Ernie. "You look pretty sharp with that hat." Robert smiled. "When were you up there?"

Ernie took the compliment as he thought it was given, with a hint of a smile. "This morning, first thing. Checked the barn as well. Nothing." His eyebrows raised, as though he figured he was done.

"Who was there?"

Now Ernie looked irritated. "Don't know their names."

It took all Robert's power to refrain from swearing. "How many? What did they look like? Women? Men? Basic information is what I want, or is this too difficult?" He immediately regretted adding that last bit.

Ernie stood up. "We are done. You can leave now. If

you refuse, you'll be escorted out. These people are upright citizens and taxpayers. We don't need you bad-mouthing them."

Robert looked up at Ernie as he held in his rage. "This your best police work, Ernie? Cause if it is, you'd better stick with the small towns, you'd never make the grade in a larger city." He stood, waved to Sandra that they were leaving. Ernie's face was turning a pleasant shade of beet.

As he passed by the counter, he leaned over to the receptionist. "Think you could let Jackie know that Robert Lui was here when he checks in? Thanks." He turned before she could respond and, with Sandra, left.

"That went well. Assholes."

"Don't we need their help, Robert?"

"Not really, only at the end if some of those winery people survive what's to come. We'll do our own recon. I really wouldn't trust what Ernie told me, anyway. They seem a tad clueless. I guess I was hoping for better." They headed back to Main Street and a date with coffee.

"I'm worried for Sophie," Sandra said.

"Yes, but it's really me they are after. They don't want to be holding onto a girl any longer than necessary. This seems to be a spur-of-the-moment thing, and they'll probably not be set up for it. I just hope Sophie doesn't do anything crazy. She took those self-defence courses. Seemed like a good idea at the time, but maybe it wasn't."

As they approached Ricardo's, Robert finally felt a pang of hunger. "Something to eat as well?"

Sandra answered, "That'd be a good idea. I'm getting thin."

They walked in. It was after two, and there were a few

leftovers from the lunch crowd, but Ray was behind his machine, looking calm and unhurried. He smiled at Robert after spotting him.

"Ray, how are you? We could use a couple of strong Americanos."

"Sure. Back so soon. Missed us, is what I'm thinking." He started the coffee prep.

"Yeah, something like that." Robert leaned in closer and asked softly, "Are the Possession Point owners around?"

"Not sure who all the owners are actually, but the younger dork came in with what I think is his father first thing this morning — Scottish-sounding guy. Didn't understand a thing he said."

"Thanks, Ray, useful to know. Think we'll both have one of your sandwiches as well. The tuna ones."

After the coffee and food were ready, Robert and Sandra proceeded to the farthest corner, and Robert started plotting. He eagerly sipped from his cup.

"Good coffee. I needed that. If Ernie the muppet is correct, then perhaps Sophie is being kept in an outbuilding on the property. My computer's map program is good enough to spot those. Problem is, I don't know how thorough Ernie was. I'm guessing, not very. I'll do some planning at the hotel, then we'll do a little nighttime recon work before knocking on their front door." He paused. "Maybe we'll go in from the neighbour's side — Enchanting Grape."

"But we are sticking together tonight, correct?" Sandra asked, as she bit into her tuna melt.

"Yes. I'll give you the smaller gun, in case. It'd be

better if you could fire it once or twice to get the feel for it, but … and I have a protective vest. Maybe I'll give that to you to wear if it's not too large."

Sandra's eyes grew a trifle larger. "So that is why you insisted we bring some hiking gear."

"We'll be in unknown country, in the dark, so yes."

Sandra checked her phone, looking at it intently. "Waning moon tonight, but it may not matter with all the smoke drifting around. Visibility should be extra shitty."

"Good report. You could be a weather person on the television, succinct and to the point."

Finishing their food, they gave Ray a wave as they left to head back to the Stay'n'Sleep to start planning their nighttime manoeuvres.

CHAPTER
THIRTY-NINE

After a nap attempt that accomplished nothing, Robert and Sandra rose to prepare for the night ahead. Robert checked his phone for message and calls, but there was nothing about Sophie. "Make sure your phone is on silent," he told Sandra. He strapped a knife to his ankle, and removed his shirt.

Sandra studied his back.

"Your wound has been bleeding, Robert. Let's get this changed."

Once fixed up, he strapped a second knife to his chest, and dressed. He hoped his old training would kick in if he was desperate, but he also knew how out of shape he was for this kind of action.

"Your turn." He strapped a holster to Sandra's ankle. Then he gave her the Tomcat along with some extra ammo after demonstrating how to reload the gun and how the safety worked. Did he miss anything? Probably. Bringing Sandra along was a bad idea. He was tired, pretty sure that Sandra felt the same way, the pressure of the whole situation having its effect.

He studied his laptop, and found two outbuildings along what he assumed was the north side of Possession Point's property. There was a third one not far away that might be on Enchanting Grape's property, there was no telling for sure. He planned to park the car near the entry to that winery. He assumed they had some mechanism for closing things off at night, but maybe he was being pessimistic. The vest was too large for Sandra, but he made her don it, anyway. Hiking boots on, Robert applied shoe polish to their faces.

"We'll go down the stairs, don't need staff in the lobby seeing us like we are." Robert stated the obvious. It was half past nine, and the sun had disappeared. They reached the parking lot, and the smoke, which had returned with a vengeance, made everything much darker. A car pulled into the stall next to them. The driver looked over at Sandra. His eyes widened as he presumably registered her appearance. Robert hoped he'd assume they were refugees from the fire. They pulled out, heading north towards the unknown.

Fifteen minutes later, they were rolling silently down the inclined road towards the entry to Enchanting Grape, engine off. There was no gate, so they cruised in and slid to a stop. Except for them, the lot was empty. They got out and adjusted their clothing.

"Here is the other key for the car. If something happens in there, just get the hell out of here, okay?" Robert stared at Sandra, waiting for her answer.

"I guess." Robert didn't believe her but didn't press the issue. They moved out, flashlights in hand, eyes smarting from the smoke.

Robert had the layout of the property firmly etched in his mind, at least what the map had shown him, but it wasn't long before he was disoriented. It would have been tough in the bright daylight to navigate unknown terrain, but in the smoky darkness, it was madness. They weren't walking through a vineyard, that would have been too easy. They were in brush, getting denser by the metre. At least they were heading downhill.

By his reckoning, the first shed was maybe two hundred metres southwest of where they had started from. They entered a copse of trees where the undergrowth lessened. Robert stopped and listened for sounds at periodic intervals. Nothing, no animals or birds. He was certain all the animal life had high-tailed it for safer grounds south. Only humans would be stupid or desperate enough to hang around in this mess.

About fifty metres beyond the copse, the land dipped. A brook lay at the bottom, not a strong current, but something needing a good jump to cross. After navigating this little intrusion without getting wet, they headed uphill for aways. Robert swung his light around as they trod the uneven ground. North of them, he thought he spotted a structure, maybe the Enchanting Grape outbuilding.

They pressed on, finally spotting the fuzzy outline of the first building, to their left on the edge of a vineyard. They came up to a wire fence, not barbed, thankfully. Robert pulled out a pair of snips and created a hole for them. They slowly came up to the shed, no light or any noise emanating from it. Leaving Sandra, Robert checked the door. A padlock was in place. No one around, seemingly. He went to one window, shone his light in. Just sacks of something and shelves against a wall, no Sophie, no nothing.

"You doing okay?" Robert asked.

"Little hot, but sure, I'm fine." She was breathing heavily.

They pressed on. The next building was a hundred metres due west. They were walking in the vineyard now, so it was easy by comparison. As they finally neared the second building, they tried to hold in their coughing. They slowed. A window glowed. Robert held up his arm. They stopped.

Robert quietly spoke. "You stay out here. Get your gun ready. I'll go in." That was it for a tactical plan. Robert wasn't one to stand around second-guessing himself. He went to the door and opened it quickly, gun ready.

Three men were sitting at a table, playing cards. Two of them looked like the Mexicans Robert had briefly met the last time he was at the winery. The third one was Jingles. His left hand dropped and came up firing at Robert. It was a deafening explosion in the confined space.

Unfortunately for Jingles, he was right-handed, but that hand was still out of action. He missed Robert. Robert returned fire and didn't miss, hitting Jingles in the gut and tipping him backwards to crash onto the floor. The other two raised their hands, not afraid seemingly, but extra cautious.

Robert waved his pistol at the two to get to the rear of the room. It was obvious that Sophie wasn't here. He went over to Jingles, who was on his back, moaning and holding his belly.

"Where is Sophie?"

Jingles was mute, but his eyes were darting everywhere. Robert looked at the labourers.

"Hands on your head, *muchachos*." They obeyed.

"I'm waiting, Jingles. Remember what I said last time?"

"You didn't say anything, you just crushed my hand."

"Maybe I said it to someone else. I said next time I meet Jingles, I'll just kill him." He bent down and pulled his knife from his leg sheath. "Which is what I'll do if you don't tell me where my daughter is."

Jingles's eyes went to the Mexicans, but they weren't going to assist a gringo, a small obnoxious gringo at that.

Robert drove his knife into Jingles's thigh. He screamed. Robert wiggled it. The screams grew louder.

"Shit." He moaned. "She's in the other building. The one at the winery next door."

Robert took his knife out, wiped it on Jingles's pants and put it back in its sheath. Blood was flowing freely now. "Who is with her?"

The moaning was increasing. "My gut, you bastard."

He pulled his knife out again. "Who?"

"The other two." This came out in a gasp. Robert didn't like his prospects.

He nodded at the labourers. "*Via con dios.*" He walked out the door. Where was Sandra?

"Sandra?" He heard a small moan, looked over. Sandra was lying on the ground.

He knelt at her side. "What happened?"

"Think I got shot. Bullet came from inside the building. Lucky you made me wear the vest."

Robert looked down. There was a pockmark on the vest at her abdomen. A few inches lower, and it would have been a different story. He helped her up. "We have to move. I think Sophie's at the other building we spotted on our way here. You okay to walk?"

"I think so," she said. Robert looked behind him, but the labourers weren't peeking outside. Maybe they had resumed their card game, minus a player. Robert and Sandra moved off, back the way they had come. Sandra was ahead of him, and he could immediately tell that she was having trouble, even on relatively flat ground.

"I'm taking you back to the car, Sandra, then I'll check out that other building. Sophie may be there."

Sandra grunted in reply.

"Do you need me to carry you?"

"No, don't think so, just don't feel too good," she responded.

Robert's mind flashed back to when he had been targeted by a sniper. The bullet hadn't penetrated the vest, but he had a couple of cracked ribs out of the deal. He could only hope that the wall of the shed had absorbed enough of the energy of the round that had hit her.

They reached as far as they could go in the vineyard. Robert snipped another hole in the fence, and they headed up through the dense brush. Sandra's cough was worse. Her light was wandering; the flashlight no longer being held straight. After another fifty metres of slow going, they came upon the creek. There was no jumping this time. Robert hoisted Sandra onto his back, and he gingerly stepped into the water to get across, thankfully not snagging anything. He grunted as he set her down, his back probably bleeding again.

"Can you keep going?"

"I have to, Robert. Nobody is coming to get us." It almost felt like an accusation after what had unfolded at the RCMP station.

"Okay, let's move. I'll carry you if you can't make it."

It took the better part of an hour to get back to the car. Sandra bent over at one point and threw up. This was when Robert changed his plan. He'd take Sandra to the hospital before doing anything else.

It was almost four by the time they pulled up at the hospital. Robert took away Sandra's vest and the Tomcat before helping her into the emergency area. Naturally, it was busy even at this hour. Info was taken, then they were forced to wait. But Robert couldn't do that. He told Sandra to text him when she had been checked out. He kissed her, then left, heading back to Enchanting Grape. He was exhausted, but fear for his daughter kept him moving.

After scans were done, Sandra endured more waiting. She was finally taken in to be seen by a doctor around five.

The doctor studied Sandra. "You on manoeuvres or something? The boot black on your face? I thought it was soot at first. There is no damage from whatever hit you, but you need to rest. The baby is fine, if you were worried."

"I was, actually. That's a relief."

CHAPTER
FORTY

A small meeting took place at first light, Wednesday morning, at Possession Point. Three people sat at a table in the tasting room, evaluating things.

"How come we haven't heard bupkis from that cop?" Ross whined. "You'd think he'd be eager to rescue his kid." He paused. "Maybe he doesn't like her."

Candice looked at Ross but remained silent for a moment. "That was a good idea, Travis, stowing her in that shack on Shou Deng's property. Blame gets attached to him if she's found."

Travis nodded. "Yes, but I agree with Ross. Why hasn't he made contact? I could use some coffee. Candice, do you want some?"

"Sure, I'll make it." As she was leaving the room, the front door opened and two of their labourers walked in, hair pointing in several directions. She stopped.

They stood, evidently uncertain, then one finally spoke. "We are leaving, going back to Mexico. This is not what we signed on for."

Candice spoke. "Well, you'll have to. Your contract was with us. You can't work anywhere else. Where is Jingles?"

"At the shack, not looking so good. A gringo came to our place last night and killed him. He didn't die right away, but he is sure dead now." They waited for a reaction.

"Did Jingles tell the man anything?" Candice asked.

"Si. He told the gringo where that girl is." They shrugged, turned and walked out the door.

"Jesus, he's here!" Ross's eyes were practically popping out of his head. His head snapped around with jerky bird movements. "We need to get them back here before Robert discovers them, if he already hasn't."

Travis and Candice stared at Ross, waiting.

"You want me to go up there? Are you crazy?"

"We aren't going, Ross. Get moving, and you better take a gun," Travis said.

"Jesus, Jesus." Ross stood, went over to a cabinet and, opening a drawer, pulled out a firearm. He checked the clip with shaking hands and stuck it in the waistband of his trousers.

"Wish me luck." With that, he left. His father shook his head. "Good luck," he said softly.

Thirty minutes later, Ross made it to the large shed on Shou Deng's property. He opened the door, shocked at the scene in front of him. Sophie was lying on the floor, her pants missing. She was bleeding from the side of her face, a black eye swelling up, a look of loathing in her eyes. One of the men tasked to watch over her was holding his crotch, groaning. The larger one, Ilya, was in the process of taking his pants off.

Ross pulled out his pistol. "What's going on?" It was a rather stupid thing to ask, given the evidence in front of his eyes.

Ilya spoke. "Just about to have some fun. This girl nailed Fred right in the gonads. Gotta be careful with these hussies, right Fred?" Fred's response was a groan.

Ross shook his head. "Get her pants on. We have to leave. The dad is around here somewhere. He killed Jingles last night and knows about this place. Quick, let's get moving."

Sophie's heart soared at this news. "You guys are dead meat walking if my dad is near."

Ilya swore, then dragged Sophie upright. He cut the rope binding her hands. "Get your pants on. We'll continue this later at the barn." He smiled at Sophie as he buttoned his jeans. "You're going to be in for quite a treat."

"Come on, let's move already," Ross said, a hint of panic entering his voice. He opened the door, looked around, but couldn't see much for the smoke. They left, heads on swivels as they aimed south.

***

The smoke was worse, if that was possible. Robert retraced his path from a few hours earlier, except now aiming for the closer shack once he was in the bush, eyes smarting from the smoke, his breathing as shallow as he could make it. At least it was easier going in the hazy daylight. He stumbled a few times, catching his foot in the undergrowth, his fatigue catching up. Then he fell, smacking his head on a stump, narrowly missing putting an eye out. A sharp piece of the stump opened up his cheek, blood running freely. Coughing, he picked himself up, trying to be more careful, came around a large bush and the shack was right in front of him. To its right sat a vineyard, Enchanting Grapes', he assumed, its extent hidden by the smoke.

Then he heard a sound from his left, an animal sound. He turned his head and was looking at a coyote. It stared back at him. "She is not here. Go to the barn. The fire is coming."

This time it was speaking English. Robert's eyes darted towards the shack, but silence reigned. When he looked back for the coyote, it had vanished. He grabbed his Sig Sauer and went up to the sole window and carefully looked in. Empty. Shit. He went to the door, opened it to survey an abandoned space. Rope lay on the floor beside an overturned chair. He went over to it. It had been cut. And what looked like blood drops were beside it. He bent down and wiped a finger through one of the drops. It was fresh. It had to be Sophie's. So, she had been here, and not long ago either. Anger rose. He felt sickened as he wiped the blood from his chin.

He left the building and immediately headed south to Possession Point. They had to have taken her there. Where else would they go? And they probably had heard about

Jingles, who had likely clanged his last nickel. He moved as quickly as he could without making noise.

Just over thirty minutes later, he spotted the barn through the trees. He slowed. No one was around. The rusty tools on the barn's siding were all in place. He crept across the deck and, without waiting, opened the barn door. Nothing in front of him. To his left, a man was advancing on his daughter, who was tied to a column. She saw Robert but wisely held her tongue. Her eyes moved back to Fred, who was in the process of unbuttoning his pants.

"Hey, asshole."

Fred jerked. His head turned, fear entering his eyes. He didn't say anything, but turned and stood right in front of Sophie, cutting off her eyesight for a brief moment. Robert had his gun levelled at Fred, ready to fire if he so much as twitched. Sophie screamed just as something cold jammed into his neck. "Drop the gun, dickhead." A voice from behind him.

He did as he was told. Careless again. He was making a bad habit of this.

"Search him, Fred," Ilya said.

Fred came up to Robert, poked him in his belly, grinning, a couple of front teeth missing. "Who's the asshole now?" He flipped open Robert's windbreaker. An empty holster was all he found. He patted Robert's legs, finding first the Tomcat, then the knife strapped to his other leg. "This guy's a walking armoury. Clean now, Ilya."

Fred stood, then stepped back and drove his fist into Robert's gut, doubling him over. It wasn't a very powerful blow, but Robert could have hugged Fred. It was perfect cover for what came next. As Robert grabbed his stomach, he extracted his other knife from its chest sheath, the double-edged one honed to razor sharpness. He slashed as he whirled. It was a blind move but very effective. The blade sliced deeply through Ilya's cheek and nose to the bone, opening up his face. Blood spewed everywhere. Ilya's gun crashed to the floor before he could think about firing it. Robert turned back and drove the knife into Fred's shoulder, causing him to scream before dropping to the floor. More blood.

Sophie was grinning, a bit lop-sided from her injury but happy that her dad had triumphed in the moment. Robert stooped, picked up his gun, grabbed Ilya's gun, then went over to cut Sophie loose from the wood post. Sophie tried to hug her father, but Robert was still all business. "Rope?"

"Over there," Sophie responded. He tied up Ilya first, then Fred, and he wasn't very kind with the bindings. Half of Ilya's nose was resting on his upper lip.

"Hey. I can hardly feel my hands," Ilya complained, through the blood from his face.

"That's a shame."

A siren sounded in the distance. The evacuation order. "Don't worry too much guys, you'll be fine once the fire burns off the rope, then you'll be able to feel your hands, just before you meet your maker." He finished the job by securely binding them to the same wood column that Sophie had been roped to just moments ago.

"Are you okay, Sophie? What did they do to you?"

"Nothing. I nailed one of them right in the balls. I

think they were going to rape me. They bounced me around after that, but I'm good, Dad, really. Thanks for saving me!" She was beaming.

"We aren't out of the woods yet. I assume there are more people around?"

"Another one came up to the place where they kept me. Younger. That's it, I guess."

"Let's visit the winery building, maybe have a little discussion with whoever's there."

Sophie turned as they left the barn, pointing northwest. "Aren't those flames over there?"

"Jeez, let's get out of here, we'll leave the discussion for another time." He looked at her feet. "Can you run in those?" She was wearing the same dress shoes she had worn to the conference.

"I think so."

"Then let's go. We'll stick to the roads this time." They headed for the entry lane at a trot, coughing as they ran. Robert hurled Ilya's gun far into the bush as they ran down the entry lane. At the road, they headed north. Sophie was slowing badly, so Robert made her walk, then, when he could see the blurred entry to Enchanting Grape, he asked her to run again. He looked over at her. Her facial wound had opened up, blood running down her cheek. He knew she was in poor shape, but she was gamely running for all she was worth.

They could see flames above the tree line, getting closer. Then they spotted the outlines of a helicopter dumping water, the thudding close by. No one else was around; everyone had probably lit out, heading south. They were both dripping from the heat. Thankfully, the last stretch was downhill. Firebrands were floating around them, starting new fires wherever they landed.

They reached the car, got in and Robert started it along with the AC. "There is water on the back seat for you. We have to scoot." He watched in the rearview as the fire reached the winery buildings. It looked as though the restaurant would be the first to go up.

Once reaching the highway, it was but a few minutes before they came up to an RCMP roadblock. Robert stopped and lowered his window. Jackie Chan came over. "Robert, you're back! You look like a mess." He looked over at Sophie. "This your daughter, I assume? Find her north of here?"

Robert nodded. "Possession Point people had her. I left a couple of them tied up. Don't know what the owners are doing, but I thought we'd leave while the leaving is good."

"One of us will need to go up there then. You'll have to get down to Osoyoos pronto along with everyone else in town."

"Thanks, Jackie. Enchanting Grape is burning. Talk later." Before he went any further, he called Sandra. He hadn't received a text.

"Sandra? Where are you?"

"Still at the hospital. Can you come? Where is Sophie?"

"I've got her, she's safe now. It was a near thing though. We'll come get you, then we need to get out of Oliver."

Robert walked into the emergency area, leaving Sophie in the car. Sandra waved at him.

"You okay?"

"Yes."

They walked out of the hospital.

"The baby is fine as well."

Robert stopped, mute for several seconds. "Excuse me, could you repeat what you just said?"

"The baby is fine. I forgot to tell you something. I'm pregnant, Robert. Maybe I should have told you sooner."

"That's what I thought you said. Bit of a surprise, is all." His mouth was open and he was squinting at Sandra. He bent over to hug her and whispered in her ear, "If I knew, I wouldn't be dragging you along on nighttime raids. Good gravy. That's fantastic."

"You're happy then?"

"Of course. The other night? Ginger ale? I thought it a bit strange at the time."

After getting Sandra into the car and a boisterous reunion with Sophie, Robert made his way back to the hotel as quickly as he could, but the streets were filling up with the last cars scrambling to leave town. At least Sophie and Robert's bleeding had stopped. They cleaned up a little, grabbed their bags from the room, then checked out. Robert desperately needed some coffee. He reluctantly realized Ricardo's would be shuttered, so instead he sent a text to his mom, Robin, and Vito.

> Got Sophie, we are safe but heading to
> Osoyoos. Fire is coming. I'll call soon as
> I can.

They then joined the long, slow line of vehicles heading south, Sandra sitting in the back with Sophie, listening to her story of the last couple of days. Sophie borrowed Sandra's phone for a call back to Rose. When they arrived in Osoyoos, it was busy, but the town was no stranger to being 'busy'. Luckily, the full summer tourist-fest hadn't gotten into high gear as yet, so lodgings would likely be found for everyone fleeing the fire.

Robert found a cafe on Main Street that had decent coffee. And he got the addresses of two clinics in town, the nearest hospital being back in Oliver. They grabbed their drinks to go and walked over to the closest clinic where, naturally, they needed to wait. But this time, Robert was more than happy to sit with his daughter and fiancé by his side, patience in abundance now that the danger had passed, until he thought of something.

"Can you guys wait here without me? I need to find us a room for tonight." They both nodded. He retrieved his car and headed east across the causeway dividing the lake. The first 'budget-friendly' motel he tried was full up. Rather than try the neighbouring hotels, he headed up to the native winery and resort where he had no problem getting a room, probably due to the higher price. And he liked being in a loftier place — one could see things coming at you from a ways off. Before heading back, he called Vito, who picked up immediately.

"Guess who?"

"Robert. Good grief, you all okay?"

"Yes. It was the lawyers behind it all. I didn't treat their help very well, but it was deserved. Fire is heading for Oliver. I sure hope they contain it. We're in Osoyoos for now. We'll head back home tomorrow, I think."

"I've got news. Ollie rolled over. He's named Ross McDouguld and Candice Moon as the people hiring him and getting him to do things he would never do on his own. I get the feeling that Ben Skyler didn't clue in to what they were doing. It is a good thing stupidity isn't a crime, otherwise, we'd need to hire way more officers."

"Right. And here I was thinking Ollie was prime minister material. It's always someone else's fault, isn't it?" Robert said.

"Yeah. Did the Horsemen arrest all the people who were in on the kidnapping?"

"Don't think so. I think this one's going to be a little blurry. Sophie said a couple of apes took her. She was kept on the property but only saw that Ross guy once, so I'm guessing the hoods will get all the blame. And the fire was coming down fast on Possession Point when we left, so I don't know what may be left there." He paused. "Jackie could help you, but I think he's kind of busy right now, heading up the evacuation of Oliver."

"Call when you're back and come down to Cambie."

"Yup. Thanks, Vito."

Next, he called his employer. "Dan? Robert here, up in the Okanagan again. Your problems are a thing of the past. The source of your troubles will soon be facing charges, I believe."

"Excellent news, Robert. Thanks are in order, as well as a bonus."

"I'll come around to visit once I'm back in Vancouver, take care."

He then called his mother, who had received his text, expressing relief that Sophie was safe.

"I also have some other good news for a change, which I'll tell you and Dad when we get back."

"Okay, give our love to Sandra and Sophie, please."

He had only one call left to make but needed to wait until Robin had clocked off work. He returned to the clinic.

That evening, the three ate a celebratory dinner at the winery restaurant. Sophie had been bandaged up and was animated as she ate.

"Sophie, Sandra has something she'd like to tell you." Robert grinned at Sandra.

"Hmm, well it is a bit early to be spreading the news, but it seems as though I am pregnant."

Sophie exploded, a rib flying off her plate. "Fantastic! I get another brother or sister." She grinned at Sandra. "I wondered why you weren't drinking wine."

"Bad timing, I guess, after all that good wine made it back home from our last visit up here."

Robert contentedly watched as his two favourite women talked back and forth, ignoring him.

Robert had called Robin. He was elated that Sophie had been recovered in one piece but was running low on food. Robert told him to hang tight; they'd be home tomorrow. He presumed that, like most teenagers, Robin knew how to order in.

Two days later, back in Vancouver, Robert called Vito to arrange a meeting at Cafe Paulo. He then called Bernard at the CBC and arranged an afternoon coffee date at the Apollo. He'd address his caffeine deficiency all in one day.

Robert walked into Gilberto's domain. A huge smile broke out on his face. "Roberto!" came the booming greeting. "Your family is okay?"

"Yes, thanks, Gilberto."

"And you? Not that I really care," as he smiled.

Robert responded in kind. "I'm fine. Any chance you know how to do espresso here?"

Gilberto's eyes rolled. "Very funny. How many?"

"Double long, extra strong, please. I have a deficit I must overcome."

As Gilberto shook his head, Vito came into the cafe. He grinned at Robert. "Back, and in one piece!"

Robert turned and grabbed Vito in a bear hug.

After coffees were laid on the marble counter, the two men retreated to the rear.

They sat. Robert searched Vito's face. "Any word from Jackie?"

"Yes. He went up to the winery and came upon three lawyers trying to cut two thugs loose from a post in their barn. They all made it out in the nick of time. I think the whole place went up. The five were taken into custody and transported to Osoyoos. Naturally, the lawyers were protesting their innocence, saying that Robert Lui should be arrested for aggravated assault on their winery help." He paused as he sipped his coffee. "The 'help' had a few medical problems which couldn't be put down to the fire."

"They find anything else?"

"Too early. The fire got stalled just to north of Oliver,

but I assume you saw the news. Everything is too hot to examine just yet."

"I had to chuck my gun into a river on the way home. I need to contact Roy about a replacement."

"I won't ask, but I assume you fired it at someone?"

"Maybe."

That afternoon, Robert made his way over to the Apollo, walking this time, fairly sure that people wanting him dead for whatever reason were all securely locked up. He entered the cafe and waved at Bernard, who had beaten him in. He sat after ordering a latte with two shots.

"Hey, Bernard. The 'no cast' thing is a good look on you. There shouldn't be any further danger to you." Robert then related most of what had taken place in the last week. Bernard seemed happy as he realized the scope of the story he could write.

"I don't think they have everyone involved in the construction accidents yet, but I've no doubt Vito and Finn will sort it out. The people directing things will be charged shortly, to my understanding."

Bernard studied Robert's face. "It must have been slightly hairy up there, going on nighttime manoeuvres with a raging fire closing in."

"Yes. You know the saying: Quickly get in, get out — nobody gets hurt? In this case, someone got hurt, and I'm thankful it wasn't those close to me." He paused. "You know something else, Bernard?"

"What's that?"

"I think I made a big mistake a couple of months ago. I should have taken that offer of a desk job at the VPD."

Bernard looked down at his arms. "Well, Robert, we all make mistakes, don't we?"

ABOUT THE AUTHOR

Glenn Burwell was a registered architect who practised in Vancouver, British Columbia, for almost forty years. He's seen all sides of the local development industry and how it affects the lives of people living in the region. Now retired, Burwell is working on more stories of detective Robert Lui, manages a small tomato and herb garden, and continues to keep an eye on the never-ending saga of housing problems in Vancouver.

This is Burwell's fifth novel. Robert Lui was introduced in *The Chapel of Retribution*, defended his family against gangsters in *A Sin Offering*, investigated government corruption in *Greenside*, and made professional and personal mistakes while looking for a cop killer in *The Girl From Raven Island*. All titles can be ordered from any bookstore.

You can contact Glenn and learn about his other books at the Somewhat Grumpy Press web site: SomewhatGrumpyPress.com

Help independent authors and small presses by leaving a review at your favourite online retailer or review site, or sharing on social media.